Praise for The Serpent's Game

"A solid espionage novel that respectfully employs a real-world tragedy to great effect."
—KIRKUS REVIEWS

"An intelligent and intriguing spy thriller that chases secrets across the globe."
—CRIMESPREE MAGAZINE

"Frieden keeps the suspense high...in this gritty, complex and satisfying thriller."
—JAMIE FREVELETTI, #1 AMAZON BESTSELLING AUTHOR OF *DEAD ASLEEP* AND ROBERT LUDLUM'S *THE JANUS REPRISAL*

"Some of the best writing about the early hours of Katrina."
—M.K. TURNER, *BOOKREVIEW.COM*

"A myriad of twists and turns... as potent as snake's venom."
—MARC PAOLETTI, AUTHOR OF *SCORCH*

"Full of suspense, realistic action."
—DITTER KELLEN, AUTHOR OF *EMBER BURNS*

The Serpent's Game

A.C. FRIEDEN

For other titles and author news,
visit A.C. Frieden's official website:

www.acfrieden.com

Avendia Publishing ®
Chicago, Illinois

This novel and other books in the Jonathan Brooks series are
works of fiction. Any names, characters, organizations, locations
and events are the product of the author's imagination and must
not be construed as real. Any resemblance to real events, entities
or to actual persons, living or dead, is entirely coincidental.

The Serpent's Game
© 2013, 2018 by A.C. Frieden and Avendia Publishing

eBook versions of The Serpent's Game are published
exclusively by Down & Out Books

ISBN-10: 0974793442
ISBN-13: 9780974793443

Editor: Julia Borcherts
Poetry editor: Nicholas Marco

Cover design by Adell Medovoy, Angelo Giaquinto and Elaine Davis
(based on a photograph taken by A.C. Frieden in the Panama Canal)

Author photo by Efe Babacan Photography, Istanbul, Turkey
© 2011 A.C. Frieden

Printed in the United States of America
P-IVMM/1811

A.C. FRIEDEN

The Jonathan Brooks Series

TRANQUILITY DENIED

THE SERPENT'S GAME

THE PYONGYANG OPTION

LETTER FROM ISTANBUL

DIE BY NOON

AVENDIA PUBLISHING

DOWN & OUT BOOKS

www.acfrieden.com

New Orleans, Louisiana

Lake Pontchartrain Causeway

Lake Pontchartrain

Lakefront Airport

R.E. Lee Blvd.

City Park

Wisner Blvd.

Interstate 10

Interstate 610

Metairie

New Orleans

Interstate 10

Lower Ninth Ward

Tulane Ave.

Broad Ave.

Carrollton Ave.

Interstate 10

French Quarter

Mississippi River

Superdome

C.B.D.

Algiers

Clairborne Ave.

Crescent City Bridge

Audobon Park

Uptown

St. Charles Ave.

Garden District

Gen. de Gaulle Ave.

Magazine St.

Tchoupitoulas St.

Mississippi River

Highway 90

Gretna

West Bank Expr.

Harvey

2 miles

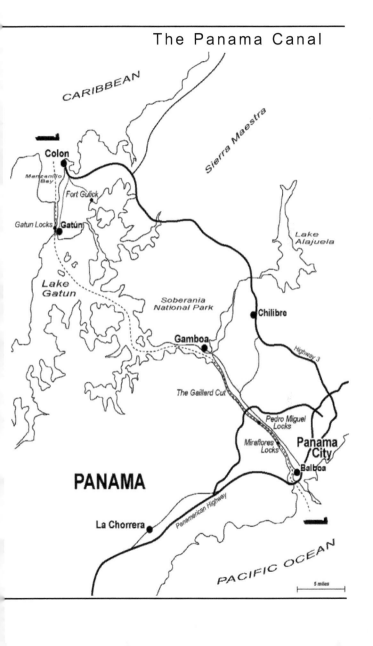

The Panama Canal

For my parents

For former NOPD Officer Chad Perez, a true hero in the turmoil of Hurricane Katrina, and for his kind assistance in this literary project.

For my former law school classmates at Loyola University New Orleans who worked tirelessly to rebuild their lives and community after the devastation of Hurricane Katrina.

The answers come like splashes of boiling water
from fretful questions that only simmer the wounds;
the reasons stray like ashes of that unlasting winter.
Since we met, my darling, pitter-patter maker,
it's you who imprison a helpless me.
Don't you grasp the idle chances passing, breathtaker,
and the prying eyes I cast on your beauty, pointlessly?
My love, given...

1

New Orleans, Louisiana – August 2005

SILENCE IS A LETHAL TUNE—SATAN'S ANTHEM FOR THOSE souls so bruised by this ruthless world that its stealthy carriage of melancholy and anger sends the mind into near-paralysis. Jonathan Brooks understood this too well. To him, silence was a ruse, oversold as peace. Hyped as longed-for solace. This morbid tune brought only maddening echoes of failed love, his soul bled dry by Linda's caustic slurs lobbed from afar.

Silence. Dreadful silence.

If he'd turn on the radio it would quell its assault. He'd survive a little longer. He gazed at the worn surface of his oak desk, one palm down on it, the other still gripping the phone's handset that he'd just slammed down to hang up. Linda's venomous tirade still festered unpleasantly. Her voice had stirred up only anger and despair.

"I'm not answering again," Jonathan whispered alone, the scorching heat in his office now even more stifling than earlier. "I won't," he again told himself.

But he would. She'd call again. Pumped-up on God knows what meds, she'd dialed his office twice already that morning, for no good reason—just to open old wounds and salt them with her spitefulness. And he'd hang up on her again.

Then his cell phone rang. He'd had it. Jonathan pressed Ignore, scrolled through the contacts list, opened his ex-wife's profile, went to her first name and changed it to "Bitch," then to her last name: "DontAnswer." He didn't have the stomach for more fights. Not today, at least, and this day had barely begun.

The noiselessness. The corrosive stillness.

Jonathan stood up and walked out his office to extinguish this dead air with the cacophony of the secretarial cubicle just outside, where Amber would surely have her radio turned on, or be typing loudly on her keyboard, or talking on the phone. Or his law partner Dino might be there, babbling useless drivel into Amber's ear while undressing her with his eyes, his amplified masculinity tiptoeing the fledgling firm ever closer to a sexual harassment lawsuit. Noise. The comfort of chatter and random sounds. Even that annoying thud of drops from a leaky ceiling hitting the bucket next to Amber's chair. Any noise would suffice.

Amber looked up at him nonchalantly, a bag of dried banana strips in her hand. She did it so well: pretending not to notice that Jonathan had just ended another yelling match with his ex. It felt odd, as she never muffled her opinions when it came to clients or the other lawyers.

Jonathan, still hearing Linda's voice bounce around his skull, looked up at the ceiling above her.

"When are they fixing this?"

"Today, supposedly," Amber replied with a long sigh, brushing back her wavy auburn hair over her bony shoulders.

"If they don't, we'll find someone else who will."

"Well, if the building weren't a hundred years old."

"I know, I know." And he did. She'd reminded him enough. This squalor was the only space he and Dino had agreed on, and that's with Dino's insistence that they'd sublet the crappiest of the three offices to yet another lawyer, one who hardly ever showed his face, preferring instead to spend most days hunting for clients at funeral homes and hospitals. Jonathan had accepted the conditions ever since they'd haphazardly joined forces a long four years ago. Because good-paying clients give you choices. Because they were harder to come by these days. Because billable work is what ultimately pays the rent. He stared down the hall at Dino's closed door.

"Soon," Amber said quietly. "Very soon."

"Yes, I'm counting the months," he uttered, again eyeing her, "and I'm taking you away from this, too."

She returned a tepid smile. She hadn't yet said yes. Perhaps she understood Jonathan's difficult decision. Two months earlier, he'd given Dino notice that he would be out by mid-spring. Out of the partnership that had only fomented frustration. Out on his own, and with whatever clients he'd manage to take. How Jonathan would afford Amber was still a huge question mark, but he'd promised himself to find a way, somehow.

Amber again gazed up at the ceiling. "If Katrina hits

us, that leak could get a whole lot worse," she said, her gaze turning snooty. "My computer isn't waterproof, you know."

Jonathan sighed. "We'll get it done."

Amber sometimes acted like a princess. She certainly dressed like one; she walked like one; but it annoyed him when she spoke like one—though her resume gave no hint of anything more than a modest upbringing in Baton Rouge and a few stints as a receptionist at law firms no bigger than Jonathan's. But she was also damn good at what she did, and with the meager salary they'd settled on, she surprised everyone to become the firm's miracle worker.

"Oh, I forgot," Amber said, jumping to her feet and stretching her lean build, veiled by an orange sundress, over the edge of the cubicle. "This came in for you a little while ago." It was a small, gift-wrapped package decorated with a lavender ribbon. "I bet it's chocolate," she added, barely disguising her smirk as she shook the box near her ear. "Can't possibly be from a client."

"Probably not a client," Jonathan surmised. He didn't have many left. His largest client—a subsidiary of a national shipbuilder—had moved offices to Norfolk in June and hired East Coast admiralty lawyers for their future legal needs. And his next largest had given him only a trickle of litigation work over the last year. And none of the remaining clients—all much smaller— would be so kind as to send him anything more than an occasional past due payment. He took the gift and turned toward his office.

"It's gonna melt in that oven of yours."

Jonathan's office hadn't had a working A/C in two weeks. He'd thought of taking the window unit near Amber's cube, or even Dino's. But that would mean war. He half-smiled, chuckled and shut the door.

He plopped down into his creaky chair and lobbed his feet up on the credenza. The ribbon came off easily, as did the neatly wrapped ivory paper. She was right. A box of candy, black, with a label that read "Golden Globes" in both English and what he assumed was Russian. Though he had never mastered Cyrillic, he still remembered enough to mumble the syllables.

"*Zolo...Zolotye Kupola*," he whispered, deciphering the characters printed above an image of ornate domes of an orthodox church that covered the front packaging.

A chill suddenly crawled through his veins. Who would send him anything Russian? It had been nine years since his painful experience took him to that country. A client's banal trial over a collision at sea had mushroomed into a perilous race to save his brother's life, as well as his own. Now, this box of chocolates scared the bejesus out of him.

His hands began to perspire. Jonathan got back up, tossing the box onto his desk. He paused at the window and gazed out the grimy glass onto a quiet, sun-drenched Julia Street. *It can't be.*

A flood of disturbing memories suddenly ransacked his thoughts: his brother lying in a hospital bed gasping for air in a run-down clinic in central Russia; his hand clenching his brother's until his last glance; his final hard breath. But it wasn't just what had happened there; it was everything else in his life that had collapsed since then, and as a consequence. He turned and gazed at the box, motionless, tempted to open it but fearing what more it would resurrect.

The eerie silence had returned, this time dragging with it more unbearable wounds from the past. He vented a long sigh as he flipped open the lid. A handwritten note slightly larger than a drink coaster rested on top of four rows of individual candies wrapped in gold-colored foil. He returned to the window with the note in hand and unfolded it slowly.

Need to see you. Urgent.

It was signed simply "M". His heart began to pound hard at his chest. There was no phone number, no email address, nothing else—only a faint watermark at the center resembling a logo or coat of arms of sorts. The note's brevity surprised him, but the sender didn't. It was her, Mariya, just as he'd feared. That Russian hellion who'd murdered a man in cold blood right in front of him. A psychopath extraordinaire who'd both helped and tormented Jonathan nine years ago.

Jonathan rushed back to Amber. "Let me see the original package."

His question triggered only her raised brow.

"The package!"

Amber shrugged. "It wasn't mailed."

Jonathan caught his breath. "But it's from...Russia."

"Russia?" she asked with an embellished frown. "What are you talking about? I told you, it wasn't mailed. Some kid dropped it off."

Jonathan opened Mariya's note once more and gazed at the watermark. "Shit..." It suddenly hit him. "The Monteleon," he mumbled, recognizing the coat of arms of the landmark hotel in the French Quarter. "Isn't it?" He held the note a few inches from Amber's face.

She turned to her computer and typed a search for the hotel's website. An instant later, the screen confirmed his suspicion.

"Dammit, she's here," he said, gripping the walls of her cubicle till his fingers hurt.

"Who?"

"Nothing, nothing."

He stepped back into his office, grabbed his jacket and brushed by Amber on his way to the stairs.

"Wait, wait—listen to this," she said turning up the radio by her computer monitor. "It may really be headed this way, they're saying. I'm worried now."

Jonathan stopped and turned. "What will?"

"Katrina."

The radio announcer spoke fast. "Folks, the National Hurricane Center is now advising that Katrina is turning northward over the Gulf and will probably make landfall in seventy-two hours or so..."

"That's right," a second announcer butted in. "Experts we talked to are saying it could become a Category Four——or even Five—real soon, and it could slam anywhere between New Orleans and Mobile, Alabama. We'll have a better idea by tonight."

"God..." Amber put her hands to her cheeks and stared vacantly at her boss.

Jonathan knew what this meant. Hell, there wasn't a

maritime lawyer who didn't know what a hurricane that size could do. "That means landfall on Monday."

"Guess I'll take the day off, huh," Amber said, her hands still over her jaw.

"Don't trust weathermen." Jonathan didn't want her to bail without more certainty about the storm. A key deposition was scheduled for Tuesday, with her playing wingman—at least for appearances—and they needed all of Monday to prepare. Most importantly, it was for Cramer, the owner and president of his largest client, an engineering and logistics company with a handful of lucrative contracts with the Port of New Orleans and the State of Louisiana. Cramer was volatile but a fairly reliable, good-paying client that Jonathan wanted to keep happy—but a client who'd take a sudden schedule change with indignation, regardless of the storm.

Amber lowered the volume. "What if they're right?"

"They've been wrong before; they'll be wrong again." Jonathan turned to leave and headed through the cramped guest sitting area between her cubicle and the front door.

"But you have a meeting."

"Cancel it."

"But it's—"

"I'm leaving, so make up something."

"Are you upset?" Amber asked, her voice tapering.

"No."

"I mean, it's not my business or anything..." Her words sputtered. "You don't have kids and you've been divorced three years now—why d'you guys even talk? She's in Idaho, for heaven's sake."

Jonathan froze. "Iowa."

"And you haven't even seen her in over a year."

"Ten months."

He stared at the frosted glass door with his name etched on the other side in between those of his two co-tenants—an order that still jabbed him with insult, as it did each time he walked in and out of this space.

"I don't get it, but that's just my two cents."

Like being hit by a baseball bat, but without the pain. That's how Jonathan took the assault. Amber—with her faux blue-blood demeanor, and her bad timing—had come out with all guns blazing, finally breaking her silence about all the crap she'd overheard since he'd hired her almost two years ago. He tilted his head to one side and stabbed Amber with scorn.

"I'm leaving for other reasons, if you must know."

Jonathan wasn't sure if he was more embarrassed than angry. Perhaps Amber was right. Yes, Linda and he hadn't completely severed their ties, despite the long, drawn out divorce—an astoundingly lengthy fifteen-month legal battle to unwind a childless marriage with little property to divide. There was no logic to it then, nor now. Jonathan had confessed this to himself many times, even more so on the nights he'd staggered to bed with a full bottle of wine in his stomach. How could Amber not see this as odd? Especially given the strain she'd seen on his face time and time again. For a brief moment he pondered how ludicrous his tolerance seemed, but he couldn't fathom changing anything, not yet anyway.

"Please, *never* bring up Linda again."

Amber blushed, her eyes widening, and disappeared behind her cubicle wall without uttering another word.

He inhaled the musty air of the decrepit office space before heading to the stairs. Closing the door behind him, he paused, recycling Amber's shot across the bow, and realized he'd been harsh. He reopened the door and poked his head in.

"I'm sorry...I didn't mean to react like that," he said, shaking his head. "Please don't quit," he added.

"No worries," Amber voiced, still sheltered in her cube. Her head emerged timidly. "I know things have been difficult here, but I'm sure it will get better, especially since you're...you're going to have your own place, you'll be done with them."

Jonathan paused and nodded.

"You're an amazing lawyer. Just the way to speak with clients; manage their crises; remember their children's names; make them feel strong; and your near-magical sense of predicting every move from opposing counsel. Do you hear what other lawyers say about you? You're what every attorney in town wants to become. And you know I'm not exaggerating. But even the best lawyer's sometimes fall on tough times. What makes them great is that they can get back on their feet faster than anyone."

"You're too kind, Amber," he replied, taking a deep breath, but then worried about Mariya, realizing he didn't want her to show up here and involve Amber in any way. "If Dino's out, why don't you close up early?"

Amber looked surprised. "It's ten in the morning."

"Yes, I know, but I'm serious, lock up early and take care of things in case Katrina's headed this way."

He sighed and left, his head now bursting from the anxiety of Mariya's message and Linda's earlier tirade. This was not the morning he'd wanted, nor the Friday he'd longed for after a grueling week with difficult clients and a judge's ruling that severely weakened his most promising lawsuit. Then he remembered the radio announcers' warning. Hurricane Katrina was the last thing he needed, but by the time he'd descended to the darkened lobby, he sensed it would pale in comparison to the storm Mariya was likely to cause if he allowed her to find him.

He stopped at the glass doors that also served as the entrance to a run-down salon full of Vietnamese girls who Jonathan was sure, judging from the demeanor of their male clientele, gave cures to more appendages than simply toes and fingers. Two of the beauticians turned, waving and smiling.

Jonathan now had only Mariya on his mind. He imagined she was back to cause trouble. He could think of no good reasons. He peered through the glass and scanned the street for any sign of her. Looking further down, west and east, he eyed a few pedestrians—none of whom looked like her.

Two blocks, he thought. That's where he'd parked his car, in an open lot. The shortest path was through an alley across the street, but he'd avoided it since a jewelry store owner got stabbed in broad daylight two months back. He leaned on the door but stopped short of opening it. He had a bad feeling, but he couldn't let Mariya set the rules. She'd tried long ago, and now, on his turf, he would not allow her to taunt him without paying a price. He'd find her at the Monteleon, he thought. He'd confront her there. She'd likely not do anything stupid in public.

2

Moscow, Russia – Three weeks earlier

"NOT ON THE SEVENTH," THE MAN WHISPERED HIS RULE alone, unmoved that it was mere superstition. There was no mistaking it. The date leapt from the dial of his watch. But fallacy had so many rules: wear black—anything black—before each hunt; sleep facing east; touch the fallen's blood after the crimson madness has been splattered—often with strangely chaotic beauty—and calmed; the Bible placed face down under the bed, a virgin bullet resting across Proverbs 6:16. *Rules*. For justice, for pardon, for survival—all concocted over two decades at the friendly end of a barrel.

Huddled in the driver's seat, eyeing the nearly empty street, Sal continued to deliberate over the date. Seven had cursed its way into his trade like no other omen. A dagger had gone through his bicep on the seventh of January, the night he'd cleansed the world of a Colombian "horticulturist," if you will; he'd been trapped in a rat infested tunnel under the Berlin Wall for an agonizing seven hours; his father passed away on the night of his seventh birthday. He sighed and glanced at the wires that dangled from the steering column, searching for anything to dispel the wicked prophecy. He'd started on the sixth, he told himself, but it wasn't convincing. Now was nevertheless the seventh, and blood would spill today. *This can't be good.*

The cell phone began to vibrate loudly, trembling its way across the dash toward his side. The man's gaze panned to the device as it continued its unanswered path along the molded plastic surface, past the center vents, behind the wheel, which he gripped firmly, his hands perspiring in their motionless state. An assassin's hand is quick and steady only when things are crystal clear, but they hadn't been since his botched hit in the seedy Cairo slum of Manshiet Nasser. Then again, things hadn't gone well for some time, he thought. Not in Damascus, not in Yerevan, not in Tashkent. The phone's subdued rattle competed with the sounds of Tchaikovsky's *Symphony No. 4* that filled the stuffy, cloistered space of the Volga sedan he'd hot-wired the night before. He didn't answer. The device rumbled a little further, butted the windshield and went quiet.

Cold sweat oozed down his chest. He scrounged his blazer pocket for pills. He unwrapped the wadded tissue, picked his potion, tossing three tablets down his dry tongue, and swallowed. But they did nothing to stop him from plunging right back into his pool of thoughts, a grim mosaic of diffuse images: the cryptic instructions from CONTROL crumpled up and aflame over the logs of his furnace; a fresh cigarette burn on the armrest of his leather chair, the one by the windows, the one he'd sit in for hours before and after each kill; the flag-draped coffin being wheeled out of the back of a plane; the stone-faced doorman slouched over the front desk of his apartment bloc as he departed, weighed down by lead, gun metal and bewilderment. He knew the flickering from reality had long become resistant to the downers, no matter the dose, the frequency, or his sporadic delusions of a cure. He understood without believing.

He gazed ahead at the sooty pavement of the bleak street that bordered an area of shoddy brick warehouses and dilapidated Soviet-era tool shops. Dark smoke spewed from a distant power plant, its funnels piercing the gray morning sky above the nearby rooftop of Clinic Number 14, a pricey medical facility strangely thrown into this unglamorous corner of Moscow.

Another call came in. He shook his head, dispersing the haphazard mental footage that had clouded his vision. His palm greased the steering wheel as he checked his watch. He shook his head again and stared intently at the rattling phone. He didn't expect any calls, and there was no caller ID, but this time he answered.

"Sal." The woman's voice was as cold as this place in January.

"Jesus," he muttered and then lined up forceful words in her native Russian, his American accent nearly hidden. "I told you never to call this number."

"I have no choice. I left you many messages, and you haven't replied. Not a sign. Nothing! What am I supposed to do?"

"Isn't *that* a sign?" he mumbled.

He felt a rage accompany Irina's exaggerated sigh.

"I'm no fool," she spat out. "You promised me...just last week. You swore you'd tell her. And I'm sure you didn't."

Sal instantly replayed his own words that audaciously clumsy night when he'd pledged to her the world as their bodies frolicked in miasmic eroticism, the escape soothed by barbiturates and inebriation, with the one woman who could—and who did—take him to Shangri-la as often as his unrepentant soul meandered her way.

He swallowed hard. "You're right, I didn't..."

He anticipated her next rant. She'd warned him enough. And he cursed himself for having made the promise in the first place, not because it wasn't what he wanted. God, no. He'd long craved to catapult his wife out of his life, and to set her on fire doing so. But he preferred to fuel his grotesque lies over surrendering any admission or giving up the charade. A divorce was the last thing he'd wanted to get dragged through. A man in his position couldn't risk a scorned, vengeful wife. Lying was easier, then and now, no matter the price— easier because his wife was across the pond, a figure of distance, rather than a demanding, pestilent creature at his side, though now it all mattered less.

"I've given you everything," he said. "Look at your damn wrist. What do you think that cost me? And look in your living room. What's there that I haven't paid for?" He reached into his shirt pocket and pulled out his pack of Marlboro Reds, plucked a cigarette out and brought it to his dry, chapped lips. "And your mother... her car, her new teeth?" The scent of bourbon rose from his wrinkled shirt. "What more do you want?" He flicked the lighter, his hands shaking slightly, enough to alarm him.

"Your devotion, your honesty."

Sal snorted. "Fidelity is for the dim and the dead." He then siphoned a long drag of his tobacco. "And honesty, my dear, is something you've never known yourself." He replayed one of the first things she'd told him some eight months earlier—that she twirled from a brass pole to raise money for her sister's surgery and for no other reason, only to discover that for years she'd tramped the tables of nearly every gentleman's club in Minsk. *There is no honesty among whores*, he thought.

"You don't need me," Irina said, her words crawling to a mere whimper. "It's clear. I...I give up." The line went dead.

A glimpse of himself in the rearview mirror hit hard. His eyes were swollen, red and glassy, a raggedness worse than he'd ever put himself through. A killer in repose shouldn't look like a corpse, he thought, the remnants of the pride he'd once carried with his gun withering each second he met his reflection in glass and in spirit. But he knew it wasn't fatigue alone. His demise, as the doctor had said, would surface in many forms: pain, disorientation, weakness, gauntness. That's what being terminal meant, no matter his effort to block this reality from his mind.

He counted the hours he'd been awake: thirty, thirty-two, maybe, nearly the same number of years he'd been scouring the planet for someone else's filth, without question, without remorse.

The cell phone vibrated again.

He'd always despised Irina's feistiness, her condemnations, her relentless, futile search for concreteness, for certainty well beyond what he was capable of delivering. But it was not like him to back down. He'd allow her to be right, but she could never win. He reached for the phone and let it pulsate in his palm for a moment, his hesitation nearly accidental, until he flipped the cover and answered, his mind prepped to resume the duel.

"What?"

"Dad, it's me."

His jaw dropped. "How the hell...?"

"Please, hear me out. I need help."

Sal had heard those words before, and it stirred him up with disgust to witness another plea, and especially now when all that mattered was one important trophy—Yuri Chermayeff—about to roam the halls of Clinic Number 14 bearing the future resting place of his 9mm hollow point bullets. He thought of hanging up.

"Dad?"

"I can't talk now."

"Please, they arrested me."

Sal's heart sank. His son had failed him once more. "This isn't the time."

"I'm at the Sheriff's. I can't get ahold of Mom."

"Stop!" Sal fought his instinct to want to hear more. It seemed easier to hang up. He clenched his fist.

"They're saying I stole a 'Lex.'"

"A what?"

Paul sighed. "A Rolex. At the mall."

"What do you mean *they're saying*? You stole it,

I'm sure, right? Didn't you?" Sal slammed his fist on the door and kicked the brake pedal. He kicked it again. But the shock suddenly felt oddly artificial, morphing quickly into the same wrath he'd felt so often before. His voice hardened. "Why? Why the hell are you destroying yourself, your future? It's wrong. You steal, you cheat, you lie...I didn't raise you this way." But Sal knew it wasn't so clear. He was like so many neglectful fathers playing the blame game. He hadn't been there much for Paul, not for many birthdays, even fewer Christmases. So many lost opportunities.

"Help me; I'm begging you."

"No."

Sal's heart raced as he suddenly remembered the countless unfriendly stares: the neighbors, the principal, the school bus drivers, the old woman at the convenience store, the whole pack of them armed with some tale of his son's mischief, and he'd appeased them all as a father must. There was no more innocence left in Paul's youth, not a thread of it for Sal to cling to. And it made him angrier to recall the past. But it also tore him apart to speak to Paul so harshly. A disarmed, disjointed part of him wanted to leap through the phone lines and embrace his son. It had been months since they'd been face-to-face, back in tranquil Pensacola, but even then they'd simmered over another disconnect. "Find your own way out of this mess," Sal added. "You're paving a horrible path for your life."

"Don't preach to me, Dad. I know all about you now, what you do, what you're hiding. I've known for longer than you think."

That's impossible. He'd prided himself on his shroud, the elusiveness worthy of acclaim and infamy in the darkest corridors of power. His son was no smarter than any of the governments and syndicates he'd deceived. Sal didn't answer. He didn't believe.

"I also know about your woman," Paul uttered in a shaky voice.

Sal cringed. "I'm warning you." He rubbed his bristly cheeks.

"How d'you think I got this number, huh?"

He abruptly suspected a conspiracy. Was Irina capable of unleashing such malice? Or was his son toying with Sal's failings? Nothing made sense. "Shut up!"

Sal closed his eyes and rested his head on the glass, the coolness crawling across his scalp as he heard faint sounds of a bicycle, pedals cranking, training wheels wobbling, the chain rattling. The metallic noises blended into reality accompanied by sounds of giggling—a child. His own. "You can do it," Sal had exclaimed proudly, pushing Paul's back as he ran alongside. "Go for it, go, you're almost there." Laughter reigned. It echoed enchantingly until Sal opened his weary eyes.

"I need bail money," said his son, now sounding on the verge of tears. "And a better lawyer than that slacker you used last year."

Sal's hands began to tremble, his teeth grinding. He threw the cigarette out the window. "You're doing this deliberately, aren't you? You've always wanted to be the opposite of Joel. The bad versus the good. The rebel in the shadows of my little prince. And you know why he was a prince? Because he didn't screw up his life like you've done ever since you could walk. But why now, why continue your streak of uselessness? He's dead. Joel's DEAD! Taken away for God and country, just as I'd feared when I fought so hard to stop him from going off to war. You don't have to compete with him any-more. You win. You're the winning loser. Why can't—" He was abruptly overcome by his vile cocktail of wrath and shame, choking his diatribe into a feeble gasp, all the while wanting to hold his son ever tighter in his fold, ever closer to the vague notions of forgiveness that Sal briefly contemplated.

"This is the last call they're letting me make."

"I can't help you now."

"Please!"

"No!" Sal slapped the phone shut on his thigh and slumped back into this seat. He wasn't going to cry. *Damn it.* He fought not to. "I love you, you fool," he whispered alone, now feeling awful that he'd again let his anger go unchecked. And now he also worried over Paul's words—that he somehow knew his father's trade. This was the last thing Sal ever wanted his son to know, as it was unfathomable, unforgivable. Early on Sal had not been the father he ought to have been, and now, as a seasoned spy and occasional deliverer of death, there'd be no explanation good enough, and no hope at all, for repairing the broken past. *I am a failure*, Sal admitted, his fist still clenched.

He closed his eyes and let himself get dragged into a remembrance minefield, reeling in from the past the very moment he crossed that line, when he'd given up on his younger son. He'd never forget. There was no overt act, but rather an omission, an absence, a message so scarring it now gripped him with such strength that he began to breathe erratically. Paul had purposely chosen to miss Joel's funeral, his own brother, his own flesh and blood of twenty-four years. He'd disappeared for days, not out of sorrow, but rather to flaunt his spite on those closest to him, using a weapon even Sal couldn't counter: apathy.

3

"This is nuts," Jonathan told himself, holding the glass door halfway open. The door pane was warmed by the morning sun that every day this time of year made the sidewalks sizzle and turned parked cars into kettles.

He eyed the shadow under the mauve-colored awnings of Mrs. Lorraine's flower shop across the wide one-way street. *No one there.* The shaded, recessed entranceway of Jason's Pizza also appeared unoccupied. There were few places anyone could hide along this block, unless Mariya had crouched inside or behind a parked car. There was no sign of her, but he couldn't shake the tension running through him. He couldn't imagine her wanting to make contact after all the years, but she had. And the absence of any good reason made him only think of the obvious. She was a killer. A woman with no soul to speak of, and a decade's passing would do little to change her, he told himself.

Ten years, he thought further, meeting his reflection in the glass. He chuckled. The man Mariya had met so long ago had indeed aged. He looked tired. He'd put on a few pounds. The expensive clothes were no more. The old days of legal stardom were long gone. He scratched his bristly jaw. Even if his curiosity could outweigh the apprehension running through his blood this very moment, he wouldn't want her to see him, not like this, even if she had some farfetched justification. The hell he'd gone through in Russia, and the utter emotional and physical destruction of it all—the charred remains of his home, Linda's horrific injuries, the subsequent divorce, the colossal debt, his firm's collapse. Unspeakable agony. Nothing had gone right, and for so long. Whatever pride he had left made him want to hide.

But the longer he stared at the street, the more he knew hiding was pointless. Suddenly, he spotted a woman walking with a man on the sidewalk. But judging from the cameras they carried and the way they dressed, they were harmless tourists. He sighed again, feeling relieved, and then scanned both directions once more.

Jonathan knew Mariya. She was no fool. She was as resourceful as she was devious. Jonathan recalled her disguised appearance in New Orleans nine years ago: a blonde wig, large sunglasses, and a wicked grin, as she stood behind the wheel of a rental car about to track her prey—a rogue official, a murderer himself. Two days later, the papers announced the man's mysterious death. There was no mystery for Jonathan, but he'd said nothing and let it go. Justice had somehow messily prevailed, and punishment had been duly dispensed, albeit by a woman with no respect or patience for judicial processes, or for rules in general. If indeed Mariya was back in town now, she'd know how to find Jonathan better than he'd know how to evade her. After all, he'd seen firsthand her skills, perfected over decades in the name of the Soviet and then Russian intelligence *apparatchik*. A master spy. And a killer, he reminded himself. A woman with no qualms about terminating her enemies in cold blood. *Could she still be like that now?* She was in her late forties or early fifties back then. Nearly ten years had passed. Perhaps she'd mellowed out. He further entertained the thought. Retired. Wrote her memoir. Maybe she'd gotten married and spent her days growing vegetables and flowers at a remote dacha. He thought about this some more.

No, not her.

His mind was again captive with scenes he couldn't erase. A cold, wet Moscow alleyway where he'd laid face-down, half-conscious for God knows how long until he'd finally mustered the strength to get up. A bullet ricocheting off the walls of a dark tunnel and piercing his shoulder. Running with all his strength through a snowy forest to escape armed men with dogs. Mariya shooting a man's head off at near point blank range and then, seconds later, lighting a cigarette, as if she'd just finished having sex. Mariya. *The* Mariya. A sparkplug like that simply can't retire.

His eyes scanned the street. There were no good options. Chasing her down at her hotel felt rash. Going home would be foolish. He thought of driving to Mandeville, across Lake Pontchartrain, to lay low for a while at one of his favorite restaurants. For a second he even thought of heading back upstairs. *I'm not scared*, he told himself. *I'm not.*

The sidewalks were empty. He left his building, weaved past the few parked cars and crossed the street toward the alley on the other side. He heard only his own footsteps on the rough pavement and the distant whispered sounds of traffic on Magazine Street. He kept a steady pace into the alley. His old, green Camry came into sight some forty yards away. Just as he reached for his keys, an accompanying sound came from behind him. Heels. At a woman's pace. He fought his urge to turn and quickened his walk, gripped the car key tightly, straight out, ready to unlock the door.

The stranger's pace hastened.

Jonathan suddenly heard his name. Softly the first time. Louder the second. The woman's voice—stern and with a subtle accent—was unmistakable. The crazy, death-smitten Russian spy had crawled out of the bowels of hell and found him. He stopped, holding his breath. Running the remaining yards to his car would be senseless. Besides, he wasn't about to show her any fear.

Her pace slowed.

"What do you want, Mariya?" He didn't turn, quickly trying to picture her, factoring in what ten years would do to her pale Slavic features.

"I need your help." She sounded only five yards behind him.

Jonathan slowly turned.

Mariya hadn't changed much—still petite, fit, with a slightly muscular figure. There was no disguise this time. Her hair was longer, but the same hazelnut brown.

The same deep dark eyes that shamelessly withheld countless secrets. The same woman he should now run from with Godspeed.

She stood there, poker-faced, wearing linen trousers and a blouse too thick for New Orleans in August—though it exposed her deep cleavage in plain view. No surprise. She'd always been at the borderline of high fashion and gaudiness, he remembered. But that was to be expected if you were the devil. All that was missing was the smell of sulfur.

She cracked a smile, then brought her small, black leather purse up to her chest and hugged it as one would a teddy bear.

"Nice to see you," she said, tilting her head and added, "You have a few gray hairs, and you gained a bit of weight, but you still look okay."

"You're too kind," he said.

She shrugged.

Her gaze was different somehow than he'd expected. Her eyes quixotically hinted that there was something warm-blooded behind them, though he struggled to imagine a selfless side of her.

"You didn't come all this way just to say hello."

Mariya took a step closer in her four-inch heels.

"You're right. But I'm happy to see your face."

Though she'd always spoken near-fluent English, her accent had thickened slightly since he'd last seen her nearly a decade ago. Perhaps she was spending more time in her native Russia. Maybe. *But why is she here?* In New Orleans, of all places, where she faced being charged with a long-forgotten murder.

"You can help me."

He shook his head.

"Did you read what I wrote you?"

"Yeah, so what? You want my help."

"You really read every word?"

"What? Yes." Jonathan recalled only the four hand-written words on the note.

She looked down. "That's all you have to say?"

"I'm going to tell you this just once," Jonathan said, crossing his arms and meeting her gaze. "I'm not help-ing you because you are crazy. Yes, I've never said this so bluntly before, but you are certifiably insane, and mean, and violent, and cold-blooded, and egocentric and sexually demented. And that's aside from the fact that people around you die prematurely. Have you noticed that about you? Have you?"

"I didn't expect this greeting." Her smile withered. She raised her chin and loosened her grip on the purse.

Jonathan shook his head. *How could she not?* They weren't friends. Even though she'd helped him, he'd also witnessed her madness firsthand.

"I'm leaving, Mariya. I'm sorry you came all this way, but I want nothing to do with you."

He turned and briskly walked the short distance to his car, got in and shut the door. He fiddled with his keys for a second, fighting the urge to roll down the window and ask what help she'd needed. His curiosity tempted him. He glanced at her. The fact that she stood ten feet away comforted him that his car probably wouldn't explode upon turning the ignition. It didn't, and he chuckled. *Crazy broad.*

Jonathan pulled away from the parking spot, turned toward the Constance Street exit, but suddenly the pedal fell flat. The engine died and the car coasted silently for a few yards until he pressed on the brakes. He threw it into Park and quickly tried to restart it. He looked over his shoulder and spotted Mariya through the back wind-shield. She'd walked out from behind the row of cars into his lane and threw her hands in the air.

He turned the ignition key again, and again. The engine whined but failed to start.

"Jerk!" He punched the dash with his fist. After kick-ing open his door, he jumped out, pointing the finger at her. "What did you do to my car?"

"I'm sorry," Mariya shouted from twenty yards out. "You have to help. You owe me that."

With every step he took on his angry march toward her came a different insult for this Russian hazard. Towering over her petite figure that innocently and deceptively veiled her viciousness—and with excruciating restraint in his voice—he asked, "What on earth do you want from me?"

She looked up at him calmly. "My nephew is dead. He's in the morgue, and you're the only person I can turn to."

He felt his face turn red—but he told himself it might be from mild embarrassment, perhaps, but certainly not sympathy. For all he knew she was a pathological liar spitting out another ruse.

"Your nephew?"

"Yes."

"I don't believe you."

"I swear." She raised her right hand as if the gesture would sway him.

Jonathan's next thought was that he should be doing other, more important things—like preparing for Cramer's deposition—rather than waste time bickering with this can of gasoline from the past.

"Do you understand the risk I've taken to come into this country? He's my nephew, and he apparently drowned a week ago."

Jonathan didn't want to be outright rude, but everything coming from her was suspect.

"How do you know it's him?"

"I just do—it will take too long to explain. His body is here for certain." Her voice shook, and her gaze turned frosty. "You have to trust me, if only this once."

"Trust you?" The thought of that unsettled him. It reminded him of Dino, who'd used the same phrase each time he'd roped in a new client. Yes, the *best* client, he'd often brag. This case will bring in millions. It'll let us have offices with real views of the city. We'd each have our own secretary. Believe me. *Trust me*. Jonathan had counted the losing cases by the number of times he'd heard Dino profess those words. The mental echo pulsated like a brightly illuminated porn shop sign. It was a clear indication Dino didn't trust himself. And an equally clear clue Mariya was also full of it.

She grabbed the sides of her head and growled. "I helped you find your brother, didn't I? And I protected you, and got rid of the man responsible for his death. You could at least do something for me in return."

Jonathan had expected her to use that card. How

could she not? She'd rescued him from a debacle in the cold, dreary Russian capital. The cerebral images once again scrambled his thoughts. Studying her face, he sank deeper into the memories of the ordeal. The unbearable pain returned. The pain of finding Matt—a dying Matt. He'd hoped to forget the details forever. But Mariya's voice—and the way she'd said the word *brother*—made him all of a sudden nauseated. He clenched his jaw.

"Please."

She looked into his eyes intensely, waiting, perhaps wishing, pleading, and feigning a gentler look than the one she'd usually carried. Her eyes began to water. And then a tear streaked down her cheek. He'd never thought she was capable of it. She was cunning enough to act this out, he cautioned himself. But he wasn't sure. He met her gaze—and calculated as lucidly as possible—seeing perhaps for the first time this Russian troublemaker finally reveal a sliver of compassion.

She dug into her purse and retrieved a tissue. She delicately dabbed the corner of her eyes with it, careful to leave her makeup intact.

"I want to be left alone."

Mariya squinted, squeezed her purse with both hands, and butted Jonathan's shoulder with it. For a small purse, it sure felt heavy—and he guessed why.

"I came a long way!" Her voice cracked. "I want to tell his wife, his mother, his children, what happened, to give them closure—the same closure you found ten years ago. You should understand this. And they're poor, from a small town in Siberia, so they can't come here. I don't know anyone else here who could help."

Jonathan scanned the parking lot, unsure if she was really alone. A half-empty lot in broad daylight was hardly a scary place except to someone already afraid. To someone who'd been tracked down. And nothing she'd said so far had attenuated his fear. "Go to the morgue yourself. It's at Tulane and Broad."

She grabbed Jonathan's wrist and jolted him toward her. "I'm here illegally. The last thing I'm going to do is walk into a government office. The FBI is still looking for me. If it's money you want, I'll pay you—"

"Stop!" The thought of taking anything from her, be it money or praise or affection or chocolates or anything else, riled him up.

"I beg you." Mariya stepped closer. Closer yet. She threw the purse strap over her shoulder and raised her hands to his collar.

Jonathan looked up at the blue sky blotched by small, charcoal-colored clouds. A refreshing, long breath laced with the scent of her sweet perfume vented his lungs. He didn't repel her embrace, but the awkwardness crept through her grasp, the timid squeeze strengthening with each passing second. She pressed her head into his chest, her solid grapefruit-sized breasts planting into his ribs. Surely now she'd feel his racing heartbeat, he thought, anxious that she'd sense his fear.

"I'm not the same woman. And now, I'm sad and need to know what happened to my nephew."

"What's his name?" Jonathan didn't look down.

"Igor."

Jonathan imagined an enormous, toothless beast from Siberia with biceps the size of a bear's thighs.

"Igor what?"

"Yakin. He was a good, kind, honest man. A father. A dedicated worker, with a hard life." Mariya squeezed Jonathan even more tightly into her hold, her palms pressed flat on this back.

He stood motionless. He pondered reciprocating her hug, if anything out of pure human impulse, out of kindness or empathy, but her gesture contrasted sharply with every vibe he'd ever gotten from her. It mattered little that no woman had held Jonathan with such closeness in over a year. It mattered even less that she'd momentarily effaced her hardened warlord persona. Her act, whether genuine or fabricated, would not pierce his armor. He couldn't allow himself to trust her. At least he recycled the warning to himself again and again as he lingered motionless in her embrace.

"One day," Mariya said softly, "I'll tell you things that will surprise you. But now, I need this favor from you."

His back was drenched with sweat, as much from the heat and muggy air as from her uncomfortable clasp. An entire minute passed, silently, her arms still wrapped around him. His hands drooped to his side. He began to feel a weirdly soothing aura. Something comforting. He quizzed himself. It was obvious. She was part of his past—intertwined in a momentous and tumultuous piece of history, albeit brief. She embodied that reality in her very existence. A history he both abhorred and secretly valued that very instant in her proximity. He felt his resistance fade, as if witnessing it from outside his body. What harm could she really do? She was not in Russia, after all, but rather on his turf.

He closed his eyes. He reached his arms around her shoulders, his hands over her back. She wore no bra. Her hair smelled of lilac, not sulfur. Her heart was also racing. It brought back the images of the night he'd first met her. He'd tracked her down at a Moscow hotel. And he remembered how attractive she was the moment he laid eyes on her. But that was long ago.

"Only on one condition." He moved back, gently peeling her hands off him.

Peering up at his face, she asked softly, "What?"

"You don't lie to me."

Her poker face returned. She didn't answer right away. Her lips stayed as straight as a hyphen, until she said, "*Horosho*."

Identifying a corpse at the coroner's office might be simple enough, he thought. But what gave him pause was going on behalf of Mariya, a woman associated with an unsolved murder, among other unpleasant liabilities. He weighed the risks some more. "Fine, I'll find out what I can."

Mariya's face lit up.

"What does he look like?"

"Dark hair, dark eyes, not tall...and you will recognize him by a tattoo—a snake wrapped around an anchor. It should be on his right arm."

Jonathan sighed.

"*Spasibo*, my old friend." Mariya pulled out a receipt, jotted something on it and handed it to him. "My mobile number. Please ask them all the right questions, as quickly as possible. I must go, now."

Jonathan felt strangely relieved that he'd agreed to

help but wasn't sure why. Perhaps the guilt of having said no would have been too unpleasant, even knowing who this woman was.

"Please undo what you did." He handed her the keys.

It didn't take long for her to again amaze Jonathan with her resourcefulness. She popped open the hood and quickly dug into a space behind the battery. She grimaced, appearing to struggle with something, pulling hard at whatever was buried in there. A few more tugs revealed a black tube the size of an empty paper towel roll, with a coiled wire dangling from one end.

"Done." She slammed the hood shut, rubbed the dirt off her hands, and got behind the wheel. The engine started instantly. She stepped out and grinned.

"Don't do it again, or I'll kill you," Jonathan said with a seriousness meant to confuse or amuse her.

She raised her brow and chuckled.

He took out his cell phone and scrolled through some names until he found the one he could count on for help.

4

Moscow, Russia

At 5:45 a.m. a large black Mercedes pierced the thick haze that lingered over the street alongside Clinic Number 14. Sal rubbed his face with both hands, his eyes never leaving the approaching sedan, its windows tinted, its body weighed down so much it nearly scraped bottom as it sped over the rutted pavement.

The vehicle stopped at the side entrance. A white-haired man in a trench coat wearing dark Ray-Ban shades stepped out under the shadow cast by the over-hanging ledge of the clinic's second floor. But he wasn't alone. The driver and three refrigerator-size men got out, one of them scouting a path to the doors ahead of the target.

"You've got to be kidding me," whispered Sal.

He had planned everything in infinite detail, except for one error. Chermayeff was supposed to be accompanied only by his fat-bellied chauffeur, Vladimir, who was no more lethal than a penguin.

"It *is* the seventh," Sal mumbled, recalling he'd

only brought three loaded magazines—forty-five rounds in all. His odds now seemed poorer than a blind man winning a hand at Blackjack.

Sal removed his SIG-Sauer from his underarm holster, pulled the silencer from his duffel bag, twisted it onto the tip of the barrel and then concealed the weapon into a deep, specially sewn pocket of his trench coat. He was outgunned and outnumbered, although, he thought, this had seldom barred him from collecting his human trophies over his long, violent career. But he was no spring chicken. Seasoned, yes. Invincible, no longer. He slipped the spare magazines into his other pockets and removed the scarf he'd found in the trunk that had kept him warm through the long night in the front seat. But now he'd broken out in a sweat, his heart battering his chest. He removed a stethoscope from his bag and threw it around his neck, and then grabbed a white overcoat from the back seat.

After one of the bodyguards returned from inside the clinic, Sal watched Chermayeff scan the parking lot and then enter alone. His goons—their jackets and trench coats bloated from whatever artillery they were carrying—lumbered about the entranceway, their eyes too far away to judge their demeanor, their skill, their thirst to protect. Eyeballs had always forewarned Sal. Perhaps, he considered, beneath their intimidating builds they were nothing but drunk and maladroit. He gazed at them and calculated. But what if they weren't like the countless thugs he'd wasted across the Shitistans in search of Chermayeff's plutonium-peddling associates? After all, they were guarding the deity himself, his veil lifted serendipitously for this rare, clandestine outing. Surely, they were the best the Russian could buy.

Using his other cell phone, Sal dialed the number he'd only intended to call from his leather chair long after he'd riddled his prey with lead.

"CONTROL here," a man answered in a deep monotone voice.

"It's me."

"You're early," CONTROL said, his tone disparaging rather than humorous.

"Don't screw with me. I've got the target in sight, but there are three *heavies* with him."

"Are you sure they're all protection?"

"They look like linebackers, and they're all packing for sure."

"What's a linebacker?"

"Never mind," Sal hissed.

"One vehicle?"

Sal was getting angry. "Yes."

"Well, I didn't expect this."

"Wonderful," Sal said, hearing the sounds of flipping pages, a checklist, perhaps.

"Your instructions are to proceed," CONTROL said coolly as if Sal's warning had meant nothing.

"Proceed? How about abort?"

"Negative. This is the moment we've been waiting for."

Sal tightened his grip on the phone. "Where are you, you jerk? Tel Aviv? London? Do you know the risks I'm taking, doing this job for you? Imagine what the Americans would do to me if they knew."

"You should calm down," said CONTROL, his voice demonically sedate. "It won't help you to insult me."

"*Lekh tiz'da'yen.*" The only Hebrew Sal knew was fighting words. His frustration brewed. CONTROL had been the puppeteer of his failed mission in Yerevan just four months ago, having given him outdated floor plans of a prison. It had nearly cost Sal his life. "You think it's easy? What do you know about this? When have you ever left your desk to do anything remotely dangerous? The only risks you run are paper cuts and a bruised ego, you useless..." Sal's right hand patted his pistol, idling snugly under his left arm. "Get me someone else."

"You know the drill. I am CONTROL. No one else."

"Listen, I'm going to save my bullets to blast that cockiness out of your mouth."

"You have less than fifteen minutes to do the job."

"Get me CORAL," Sal said, though he wasn't sure what he would ask for. Aborting the mission would likely be the last straw. CORAL had long threatened to cut Sal out if there were any more failures. Then again, he'd heard CORAL was itching for new, younger, fresher, subservient blood to take over. The old school of prudence and finesse was on its way out. And it wasn't just CORAL, but also Sal's other master—the one to whom he owed his prime allegiance. *Perhaps I deserve this shit—to be taken out for good. I'm nothing but a loser, a killer, a burden to humanity, a pathetic father to Paul. Of what use am I in this world?* But Sal knew that if CORAL cut him loose, he would still have leverage elsewhere. Dangerous leverage that he could use, but only once and only as a last resort. But now was not the time to use this wild card, no matter how angry he felt.

"No," insisted CONTROL. "We're following the rules on this one. Call me when the job's done." He hung up.

*   *   *

6:16 A.M. Sal stared at the time on his other cell phone, his face still warm. A chill slithered down his spine. He felt lightheaded and queasy. The meds were kicking in, but too fast. He stepped out of the decrepit car, a ragged physician's gown draped over his arm.

Strangely, he couldn't hear a sound from anything he saw moving. An ambulance whipped out of a garage next to the clinic, but he heard nothing—not its siren, nor its engine, nor its squealing tires. Everything seemed muffled, if it was even real. He ran his fingers through his oily hair, his nails scraping his scalp. An urge to laugh—at what, he didn't know—sprang out of nowhere, his abdomen knotting to do so just as he sensed uncertainty, confusion. Profound sadness, with no forewarning nor origin, gripped him before the first grunt of laughter could exit his mouth.

Suddenly only voices—loud, cluttered chatter with cylindrical echoes—hemorrhaged from the inner depths of his head. Sal nearly stopped. He searched to comprehend the logic of the acoustic chaos. He shook his head, but the cacophony intensified with voices that now became recognizable. With each step over the weather-worn lane, words hammered their way uncontrollably. Irina's words. Her tantrum. Sal shook his head again. Irina's voice faded, interrupted by his wife's annoying humming of a Janet Jackson tune on their anniversary, drowning out his mistress's bellowing. His own cries echoed dispersedly, almost as if they were again incarnate, until the lowering of Joel's coffin appeared in front of him, overshadowing the clinic, the street, a piles of old bricks, the cars in the lot. His only sight was a million miles away in time and space from where he walked, from the battle that lay ahead. The dark oak casket descended further, until all he saw was the freshly cut grass around a hollow pit. A gun-firing salute shattered the disharmonious chorus of irate voices, leaving an eerie quiet. The street reappeared, the faint noise of the ambulance's siren returning but vanishing with the whooshing of the breeze. His hands trembled.

He stopped and looked up at the monotone heavens and breathed hard, harder still, his eyes squinting. He reached under his collar and caressed Joel's pendant, the coarse pewter dog tags he'd carried for six months and sixteen days, not because he believed, not because divine powers would condone, not for redemption, not even for luck. Only because it stood for all that was pure. And all that was now gone.

He made his way into the clinic's parking lot as tears ran down his cheeks.

The dusty, dense air filtered through his nostrils. He wiped the tears on his face with his sleeve. Paul's faint voice murmured in the back of his mind, the words incoherent, the tone sedate, surprisingly so.

The bulkiest of Chermayeff's bodyguards noticed Sal and turned to face him, the man's eyes now closer, surrendering a tale of hardened mercenary know-how able to bash any threat into digestible powder. Indeed, Sal superimposed the man's face onto the dozens of photos that had slipped under his nose over the prior months. "Molotok," Russian for hammer, was the beast's *nom de guerre*, Sal remembered from a file folder he'd been given and instantly realized he'd just entered the ring with an equal. Hammer's companion in arms, whom Sal did not recognize, had a similar square-chiseled, Aryan face, his glare deconstructing Sal's approach. The gangsters' bodies formed a corporal barricade of the clinic's narrow side entrance, but as Sal neared with his white lab coat in hand, they lazily stepped aside.

Sal nodded courteously, his heart pounding, his hands clammy and tingly, all the while hoping the men would take him for a doctor and overlook the scruffiness that resembled that of a patient or clinic laborer. A confrontation at that moment would mean the end. He needed at least five seconds to take down all four—the two giants in front of him, the unknown driver strolling back to the car and the one behind the glass doors, all of them close, surely armed for Armageddon. Five seconds. *Too long*. He'd be dead in two if he tried.

Sal opened, walked in and closed the door smoothly. From his periphery, he again spotted the fourth henchman, whom he recognized as the thug of a Moscow casino mogul. Sal was surprised to see he was now on Chermayeff's payroll. But then again, the Russian had the cash and wherewithal to shield himself from the prying tentacles of Western intelligence agencies. The guard's wide frame rested against the wall of the dimly lit corridor, his leather jacket bloated from the weapons concealed under it.

Sal avoided the man's eyes and walked ahead purposefully. He was surprised that for whatever reason, all four bodyguards were standing nearby, meaning none of them had gone to protect Chermayeff inside the clinic. *Are there others I haven't seen?* Sal feared.

He pictured Chermayeff's face, which he'd never seen in person, only in black and white photographs, most of them grainy, which was indicative of the challenge to spot this venerable scientist, especially after he'd gone into deep hiding a year ago.

Chermayeff was a number high on a list of shadows, where only a few knew to look. But Sal had let his curiosity run amok upon learning Chermayeff too had lost a son in the military. His only other child, Pieter, was here, in this clinic, clinging to a comatose existence after a car accident. The rule of distance had been severed for this target. Do not know more than you must, Sal had always demanded of himself...until the hunter and the hunted mourned equally; until their surviving offspring lingered in the same moroseness, the same defeat, a mere heartbeat away from hopelessness; until the parallels frayed and Sal's chagrin demanded justification—perhaps for the first time.

Sal's strides shortened. The corridor of the nearly vacant medical ward seemed to stretch, its walls bowing, the ceiling twisting and darkening. He wiped his eyes with his sweaty hand, but it barely restored reality.

He knew where the hallway turned, his mind flashing the same path he'd scouted days earlier, that time doing so by memory of the facility's floor plan. This part of the clinic appeared desolate. He heard the sounds of his shoes hitting the vinyl tile floor.

Room twelve was dead ahead. There were no bodyguards. No nurses. No one in sight. Sal approached. He swallowed hard, his eyes fixated on the small viewing window of the room's door. Daylight radiated from the glass. He raised his chin and moved closer. Chermayeff, his back to the door, sat motionless on a stool, clenching his son's hand. Pieter's eyes were closed as he lay idle in bed. They had been closed for over a year. Shut to all judgment, and as impervious as they were helpless. A tube taped to his mouth and the ventilator by the bed were all that connected the boy to this world. *What would he think of his dad?* Sal wondered, the sadness that had gripped him minutes earlier now weighing him down with a vengeance. *What would he say? What would he plead for?* Paul's phone call returned. "Children of death," Sal whispered.

Sal glanced at both ends of the corridor. There was still not a soul in sight. Only faint voices disturbed the stillness, and they seemed to come from somewhere at the other end of the floor.

He again carefully peeked through the glass. Chermayeff appeared to speak, the attention to his silent heir unyielding. Sal already knew the words, the questions with no answers, the logic twisted into an infinite knot. "My Paul," Sal mumbled alone, his hand caressing the wooden lip of the little window, his other hand reaching into his open coat for his weapon. But he stopped, disturbed by the continued trembling of his fingers. He stared at the Russian huddled at his son's side.

Abruptly, the scratchy snippets of Chermayeff's last intercepted phone call months ago burst through Sal's head. The static vibrated intensely as if it were emitting from the base of his spine.

"We are not doing this," Chermayeff's words twisted through his reincarnated memory. "Let's not stain our comrades' honor." Sal had heard the words firsthand, from a transmitter he'd rigged in a flower pot at the home of an Armenian arms trader, a man who'd courted Chermayeff at the behest of a secretive source. It was on that rainy morning stakeout that Sal had understood his adversary for the first time, independent of what he'd been fed by CONTROL and his other faceless masterminds. Chermayeff had suddenly morphed into a man of conscience. When all was within his power to give the go-ahead to a horrifying deal that would have put fissile material in the hands of an al-Qaeda sympathizer, he'd said no. Not just any "no", but a massive, hit-the-brakes kind of no that halted a plan set in motion by the most sinister, disenfranchised warriors of the Arab-Israeli conflict and a decision that instantly put his name on yet another hit list. He'd said no, and Sal secretly admired the man for it. Sal had gathered every scrap of information about his target, more so than any he'd tracked or eliminated before. CONTROL had once called him obsessed with this curiosity, and he'd been admonished by CORAL, too. But Sal longed to know more about this man whose depravity had waned the deeper he'd dug into this man's life—even to a point where Sal's own existence seemed more evil.

Sal felt an urge to pull up a chair and observe this father and son more closely. Perhaps it was the way the man held young Pieter's hand, or simply the innocence gleaming from the boy's face.

Sal pulled his out pistol, his grip tight and warm and still shaky. An assassin's hand never hesitates, he thought—not on the seventh, not when the odds are stacked, not when concubines betray, not when you discard your flesh and blood, not on unfriendly ground, not for any damn reason. But he froze, completely, with only his rapid heartbeats telling him he was still alive, though he felt more undead than alive. He felt the meds ooze through his veins. His joints tingled. The skin on his face numbed, as did his pain. He forced himself to move.

Sal pushed on the door and in a harsh whisper said, "*Chto vy delayete!*" He aimed his weapon at Chermayeff, who jumped to his feet.

The Russian stumbled backward, his hand holding the wall behind him. He opened his mouth, his eyes wide open.

"*Zatkni yebalo!*" Sal demanded in a louder whisper. He shut the door behind him with his foot and again told Chermayeff not say a word.

Chermayeff stepped back until his head butted the wall, his eyes shifting and his hands half-raised.

Sal glanced at the man's son. The room wheezed with the sounds of the ventilator.

"Don't hurt him," Chermayeff said with the air of an order, not a plea.

Sal stared at the young patient, whose face resembled a younger Paul. The longer he gazed, the more the resemblance deepened, so much that suddenly Sal was frightened. He lowered his weapon, his eyes never leaving the boy, who had the same hair and eyebrows, the identical chin and rounded cheekbones, the same, all the same. Sal's eyes blurred with tears.

Chermayeff said something, but it didn't register.

Sal stood back and cried. He wiped the tears with his sleeve but he couldn't stop crying.

"No, no, I won't," he mumbled, suddenly re-immersed into the night that he'd been at his own son's bedside, the night hope came crashing down, the night the army doctors said it was over. The night Joel passed away. Sal reached under his collar and yanked his son's dog tags, the necklace breaking, its tiny pieces pinging across the floor. He moved away from the bed, toward Chermayeff and quickly thrust the silencer into the man's jaw.

The Russian was pinned to the wall. His eyes seemed to acknowledge that no bodyguard would come rescue him in time.

"Always remember," Sal said in Chermayeff's native tongue, "that today I could have killed you. I could have obeyed those whose orders I am not allowed to question. Never, never forget this moment."

"Don't kill me," Chermayeff said, his eyes turning to Pieter. "My son is all I have left, and he needs me."

"Shut up." Sal again wiped his face, blinking away the tears and trying to regain his senses. "This is the deal: I spare your life and his in return for you taking care of my son. His name is Paul, and he is my future."

Sal glanced at Chermayeff's own child. "He needs guidance, hope, faith, love, money, everything I've been unable to give him unconditionally."

"He has no mother?"

"Only a cunt who deserves to die."

Chermayeff uttered, "I don't understand?"

"Find my son and give him a good life. Promise me. Promise me! I know your word to be honorable."

Chermayeff said nothing for a long half-minute, his nervous, intense stare stabbing Sal with doubt.

"Promise me!"

The Russian let down his arms, his eyes narrowing.

"*Da.*"

"Good answer. And I've made sure someone will check on you."

Sal stood motionless, his gaze losing itself in the haute couture threads of Chermayeff's sport jacket. He raised the weapon again, flicked the release lever and let the magazine drop to the floor. He pulled the door open, his hands no longer shaking, and his heart slowing. He met the Russian's gaze one last time before exiting.

Sal held his unloaded gun down at his thigh as he passed a nurse scurrying through the hallway, the fear leaping from her eyes until she turned the corner. Then two of Chermayeff's guards by the side entrance locked onto him. A sense of peacefulness doused Sal's mind like a tropical downpour, his tormented soul searching quickly for atonement. The men drew their weapons and shouted. Their motions didn't faze him. Their words melted in the air. Atonement he knew could only come from death, and death only from overwhelming force by a well-armed adversary—a sure thing if he disarmed, if he let go. Chermayeff gave him his word, and it sufficed.

The Russian's promise lingered as a mental echo. Paul would be fine. Sal was sure. The guards charged toward him, yelling, their guns aimed at his face, but they hadn't fired yet. Sal tightened his grip on his empty pistol and slowly raised it, filling his lungs, closing his eyes, and holding his breath. "Paul," he whispered, consoled, cleansed, atoned. "You're now in better hands."

5

Sergeant Claude Boudreaux was a busy man, over-seeing a nine-strong contingent of homicide detectives in New Orleans' 6th Police District precinct, a modern two-story brick building at the corner of Martin Luther King Boulevard and Rampart Street that served as the base of operations for the Central City, Garden District and the Irish Channel neighborhoods. But the sergeant's duties were one step removed from the day-to-day crime-scene trawling he used to endure as a detective. His was now a more managerial role—at least that's what he'd told Jonathan the last time they'd commiser-ated over drinks in the Quarter some months ago.

In the station's atrium, where the tall windows at the entrance let the sunlight warm the chairs in the waiting area, Jonathan sat impatiently gazing at Boudreaux's name on his cell phone. He recalled some of the insanely depressing accounts his law enforcement pal had shared with him over the years. Boudreaux had seen it all—serial murders, murder-rapes, murder-suicides, home-invasion homicides, fatal robberies, gang related deaths, child-killings, the works—but having failed three marriages, lost his only daughter to an overdose, and devoured his way past the two-hundred-eighty pound mark, it was no wonder Boudreaux had lost his craving for the ugly and the morbid. The scars had left the cop a bitter man. A long way from the cheerier days of high school when he and Jonathan had competed over women and football, and life was simple. When they were close friends. *Yeah, much simpler times.*

Today, they had virtually nothing left in common, Jonathan thought, his finger hovering over the call button he'd already dialed minutes earlier. But in this town it was nearly a requirement for a lawyer to astutely befriend at least one cop. Especially a rather senior, resourceful one, and even better, one who—for all Jonathan knew—wasn't a crook. It mattered most now since Jonathan had burned his bridges with Linda's family and could no longer turn to her brother, an NOPD lieutenant with the 8th District. Boudreaux was Jonathan's last remaining go-to guy for favors requiring the strength of a badge and the familiarity with the oft-weird ins and outs of this city. Surely Boudreaux would give him a hassle-free, fast track to someone at the morgue.

"Hey, one call is enough, you know," Boudreaux said, appearing at the far end of the nearly empty lobby, his body taking up most of the doorway that led to the work stations and offices.

Jonathan shrugged his shoulders and got up. "You've made me wait too long here many times before, so just making sure."

The sergeant waved at Jonathan to follow him, his uniform so stretched over his belly that his shirt buttons could become ballistic weapons.

The floor was a compact space with beige-colored walls and a mix of shoddy cubicles, cluttered desks and tables, and a few windowed offices at the far end.

"Did I catch you having lunch?" Jonathan eyed a food stain the size of a silver dollar on Boudreaux's chest, which prompted the officer to smudge it further with his hand.

"What brings you here, Johnny boy?"

Jonathan despised that diminutive. It reminded him of the way Boudreaux teased him in front of girls when they were in school. *Johnny boy...become his honey, and he'll be your toy...*so it went. He only still tolerated it because they went way back.

"A dead guy."

"Another corpse...so what?"

"I need to see the body today."

"Call the funeral home."

"He's at your morgue."

Boudreaux turned, and as if suddenly Jonathan had said something that piqued his interest, he asked, "A homicide?"

"Hardly," Jonathan replied, realizing, however, that he hadn't asked Mariya that question. He'd assumed from her words and tone that this was not the case. "Just a drowning, I'm told."

Boudreaux squeezed into his office. Jonathan followed, and his lungs quickly filled with the pungent odor of a half-eaten plate of Taco Bell nachos swimming in sour cream and cheese sauce, next to an unopened can of Diet Coke at the center of the sergeant's desk.

Jonathan gazed at the dozen awards that adorned one wall of the office. One plaque had a picture of Boudreaux with the former mayor. Another with the former chief of police. But there were none more recent than 1999, when the 6th District was located on Felicity Street. Perhaps he'd become too large to be photo-graphed with others.

Boudreaux dropped into his chair and wasted no time digging back into his artery-clogging meal.

Jonathan stayed standing. "They found the body in the river."

"A client of yours?"

"A relative of one, and she's asked me to see the body, today if possible."

Boudreaux's mouth smacked. "You know where to go, right?"

"Claude, it's not like going to Winn-Dixie. Help me get in there today." Jonathan didn't know the process, but he assumed it wasn't so simple, particularly since he himself wasn't a relative of the victim.

"Have they done an autopsy yet?"

Jonathan threw his hands in the air. "I don't know anything more than the guy's name and that he drowned last weekend."

Boudreaux stopped chewing long enough to wheeze out a sigh. He checked his watch, leaned forward and planted his elbows on his desk. "It's almost two. These guys love their weekends just like the rest of us. I think you're out of luck until Monday."

"C'mon, Claude, help me out here."

Boudreaux swallowed loudly and popped open his soda can. "Typically the Harbor Police picks up the body, and with the NOPD, they assess the scene, and then later the coroner IDs the body and does an autopsy. If there's evidence of foul play, a detective gets assigned and the investigation begins. That's what happens, so I can't short-circuit the process, if that's what you mean."

"I told you, it's no homicide—I just want to look at the body on my client's behalf and get a few details on how the guy drowned. Nothing more!"

"Well, if it ain't a homicide, I really have no say. Besides, even if it's an accidental fatality, it may take longer than you think. After you ID the guy, there's paperwork; they'll have to review the case file while you're there; and there may be other procedures."

"It's not really to ID him in a formal sense—I just want to see, and hear what they have to say."

"I don't see the difference."

Jonathan had prepared for Boudreaux's slipperiness. He reached into his back pocket and pulled out two tickets. "For your kind assistance, you'll get great seats at the upcoming Saints-Giants game." He laid them face up on the edge of the desk, his hand partly covering them.

"Bribes, bribes, bribes," Boudreaux replied, shaking his head as he scraped a wad of cheese off the side of the plate with a large nacho as if not fazed by the offer. "You lawyers..."

They weren't really bribes. Just convenience fees. Besides, they hadn't cost Jonathan a penny. They were a gift from his client, Cramer, but the game fell on a day Jonathan had scheduled a deposition. He looked at Boudreaux's face hovering above the junk food. For a football fanatic like Boudreaux, Jonathan was surprised he'd not instantly taken the offer. But that was the strangeness of his police pal—often unpredictable and always striving to make things difficult, but a good man in all other respects.

Jonathan picked up the tickets and held them out over Boudreaux's plate. "Section 116, third row, VIP access, free parking. Need I say more?"

Boudreaux's chewing stopped. "Got a third ticket?"

Jonathan tilted his head. "No."

The sergeant now seemed in deep thought.

"Take it or leave it. Just make a quick call to the morgue and tell them I'm a friend and need to see the body. Nothing complicated. Please, buddy."

The veteran cop leaned back, wiped the food off his hands and shook his head. "I'm telling you, it's Friday, it's not a homicide and they're worried about Katrina. I'm gonna piss them off asking them to do this. Can't you wait till next week?"

Jonathan didn't answer and fixed his eyes again on the framed pictures and awards, hoping to hear something better from his buddy.

"Jesus," Boudreaux uttered in between bites. "Is this really so damn important?"

"Uh-uh."

"Alright, I'll call." He reached for the tickets.

"Not so fast," Jonathan said, pulling them back. "Promise me I'll get in there today."

Boudreaux frowned and rubbed his puffy face, his eyes shifting between Jonathan and the tickets.

"C'mon, just one quick call to the morgue."

The sergeant raised his chin. "Okay."

*   *   *

Judging by how few people were in the aisles of Winn-Dixie, Jonathan felt more reassured that Katrina wouldn't head this way, even with all the hype from the weathermen. Jonathan had loaded his car with water bottles, duct tape, vinyl tarps and an assortment of canned soup, tuna and sardines, though he was sure it was all for naught. New Orleans wouldn't get more than a long shower.

The drive up St. Charles Avenue was always soothing, come storm or drought, bad times or good ones. Soothing. Warm. What calmed him was the placid elegance of the massive oak trees, their gigantic, lush-green, moss-tipped branches that stretched over the road from both sides like an embrace. This part of town was his very own memory lane. An archive of a million flashbacks. His childhood, his brother, his mom's endless comforting smile—a woman who never raised her voice, her eloquent Southerness still vibrant in his mind. And dad, the gentlemen-lawyer who wore pocket squares and never left the house without the longest of umbrellas, his seriousness offset by the constant contentment and warmth that made everyone feel so safe, so loved. This very road had it all. His old home. The sidewalks where he'd played. The biking. Running. The playful shrieks of rambunctious children. It was embedded in Jonathan's DNA. The mental footage of good years spun by, the nostalgia warming him from inside while the A/C vents blew the crisp, cool air with the force of a hairdryer, drowning out the radio weatherman's chatter about the height of the levees and the dire condition of the pumps that help New Orleans stay dry despite being below sea level. He turned off the radio just as the announcer aired news of Katrina's latest wind speed: 105 miles per hour.

As Jonathan passed the Touro Synagogue, near Napoleon Street, his cell phone rang. He clutched it from the drink holder and glanced at the screen—the caller ID flashed "Bitch DontAnswer." It was Linda. He eyed the traffic ahead, and looked down again, fighting the urge to answer. Amber's earlier outburst rang out as if she were in the car that very second, her hand yanking the phone from his hand and scolding him for even considering listening to one more rant from Linda. He deserved her chiding. How could anyone understand why he still gave his ex a say in this life? He eyed the caller ID again. The longer he held out, the more senseless his feeble thread to her seemed. But the urge persisted. A shadowy desire to hear her voice, whether angry or confused or insulting or corrosive, or whatever it would be on this call, and it began to win him over. If only he could listen to it without being fazed by the caustic words that were sure to be thrown his way, from the former woman of his dreams. The woman he'd so proudly married long ago. If only her words didn't matter. He stared at the screen as the ring tone continued, hoping it was the final ring. His breath shortened. *I can't answer*. But he did.

"What are you doing?" Linda asked, mildly slurring, as soon as he picked up. Her questions were never innocent or passive. Every word was a Trojan horse.

Her voice betrayed far more than she realized—that was the key upper hand Jonathan had gotten from the routine cross-country telephone battles. He'd gotten quite good at deciphering which potion greased her words of spite: downers, uppers, booze, pot or just her bitter self. Now, if he were next to her at this very moment, he thought, he'd asphyxiate from her alcohol breath.

"I'm driving," Jonathan said.

"Yeah, well, I'm not."

"That's probably good for everyone else on the road."

"Screw you."

"That's more like it."

"Stop telling me what to do, how to feel, how to talk..."

"When are you going back to work?" He'd gotten tired of asking, but it was filler—so much of their talks were fillers, in between the yelling, the insults. Idle questions to fill the void. Rhetorical at best.

"I don't know...if I'm up to it." A loud sneeze interrupted her slurred words. "Fuck!"

He heard a glass shatter and what sounded like ice cubes tumbling over a hard surface. "Don't tell me... orange juice."

She cursed some more as she shifted and wallowed in self-commotion. The sound of a chair screeching across the floor came through the phone, followed by the tearing of paper towels, her straining as she wiped the spill, her hard breaths.

Suddenly he heard a faint whimper. Then, seconds later, loud weeping.

"I can't take this—I can't." Her voice trembled.

"You need more money?"

She didn't answer. The sobbing echoed in his ear.

He'd sent her a few hundred dollars two weeks earlier. She hadn't asked, nor thanked him, but he was sure she needed it and had already spent it.

"I'll send you more soon, I promise." Jonathan knew she needed it. How else would she get by? But he quickly came to terms with reality: he had no idea where he'd get the money if she needed a lot more.

The *Fairfield Daily Ledger* was not at the leading edge of news gathering, and with a circulation of just under three thousand central Iowans, even the visually impaired would not confuse it for the *New York Times*. But like most papers, Jonathan thought, it was not unreasonable in expecting its reporters to be sober during work hours and not bark at editors as a matter of course. The tolerance they'd exercised with Linda was, frankly, outlandish. And that they'd put her on medical leave, and not fired her, told Jonathan she'd either had something good on the chief editor or her reporting in complete sentences with good punctuation and a lexicon of more than thirty words was so unusual that they'd latched on to her talents at all costs. Regardless, he was sure she was barely making a living now.

Her sobbing drowned the phone lines for a long minute, until she simply hung up. Jonathan didn't dial back. No need. There'd be other calls, sadly. He drove on, lamenting the pain she'd suffered, and the scars that reminded her every day of the fire. Those disfiguring scars that ultimately took her TV career from under her. Scars only she and the world saw. Not Jonathan.

I understand, and I miss you.

*   *   *

The Orleans Parish morgue was located in a large, concrete building complex that also housed many of the city's judicial services, including the main courthouse, as well as the NOPD headquarters. Jonathan eased into a parking spot kitty corner from the edifice. Minutes earlier, he'd gotten the call he'd hoped for from Sergeant Boudreaux: the coroner's office had agreed to meet him, extraordinarily, on this Friday afternoon before the weatherman-hyped end of the world. Boudreaux had told Jonathan that the head pathologist would side-step the normal protocol so long as Jonathan was either the attorney of the deceased's or of the deceased's family or estate, and, as expected, Boudreaux made it abundantly clear that he'd pulled the toughest strings to make this happen and had saved Jonathan several days of red tape.

Mariya had better be grateful, he thought, all the while shaking his head in disbelief that he'd let her coerce this favor out of him.

Jonathan sprinted up the steps past the tall Roman columns that gave this drab-gray, art-nouveau building a façade as bland as a crypt.

The coroner's office was in the back of the building,

a half-floor up. Reaching the cramped waiting area, which made Jonathan's own office look palatial, he knocked on the reception window that appeared to be bullet-proof. A large, well-endowed African-American woman in a sundress raised her chin momentarily from five yards away, silently studied Jonathan, and then looked down at her stack of folders as if nothing had happened.

"I'm here for Raymond Garceau," Jonathan said through the small hole in the glass.

This time she raised a stop sign with her hand without even looking at him. She slowly stood up, lifted a pile of folders, and plopped it onto an adjacent one as if working faster might break her concentration, or worse yet, her long hot-pink fingernails. He was already late and was not about to let Boudreaux's good deed be unraveled by this lethargic paper-shuffler.

"Ma'am?"

"You mean Doctor Garceau, is that right?"

Jonathan couldn't tell if she was shouting because he was far away or because she was annoyed. Before his next words left his lips, he felt a light tap on his shoulder.

"Looking for me, I assume? I'm the Chief Forensic Pathologist."

Jonathan was relieved. "Glad I'm not too late." He shook hands with Dr. Garceau, a tall, thin, bony-cheeked black man with a touch of graying hair, dressed in a knee-length lab coat with what appeared to be a small blood stain near the second button. He'd expected someone with that title to be older, not a man in his mid-thirties.

"Is the relative with you?"

"No, she doesn't have the stomach for this." Jonathan almost laughed as he said this. Mariya's blasé proclivity to kill in cold blood jumped to mind. A morgue would be a place she'd choose for a picnic.

Dr. Garceau merely asked for a business card and driver's license—just as Boudreaux had said—to which Jonathan obliged with the relief that this seemed the only formality for getting to the body.

"Your client is related to this individual, right?"

"Yes, the deceased is her nephew."

"And the name of the individual?"

"Igor...Igor Yakin."

"I see." The pathologist frowned a bit, turned and signaled for Jonathan to follow him. They headed into a dimly-lighted hallway, up a few steps and turned into another corridor, the air now stuffy. He opened a door and ushered Jonathan in. The room was at least ten degrees cooler.

As Dr. Garceau passed by a refrigerator, he reached up at a stack of folders on top of it, pulled a file folder and tucked it under his arm. "This way, please."

The two headed into an adjacent room, this one even cooler and with a stench of disinfectant. On each side were metal bunks, with one filled body bag on the right. Jonathan only glanced at it.

"From earlier this morning," Garceau said casually, as if he'd just pointed to a book on a shelf.

Jonathan kept pace with the pathologist into yet another chilly room, its tile floor cracked and worn.

"Your guy's over here," Garceau said, closing the door behind Jonathan.

The wall facing them had six large, refrigerated body drawers, in two rows, each one numbered and with a protruding metal grip. The pathologist grabbed the one labeled "3" on the top row, which was just above waist high, and gave it a strong tug.

"Hope you're not squeamish."

Jonathan held his breath. Since a young age, he'd felt terribly uncomfortable about dead bodies.

The drawer slid open towards them, the body appearing face first—a bluish-olive face of an Asian man, his skin dry and wrinkled. Flaky, withered flesh around his ears and eye sockets appeared to be signs of decomposition. But one thing was crystal clear: the man was one-hundred percent Asian, and not mixed-race. A plastic sheet covered the body from the neck down.

"And this is..." Jonathan said, concealing his surprise as best he could.

Garceau raised a brow. "Well, yes, the only drowning this month."

Jonathan was stumped. The guy was as much Mariya's nephew as Jonathan was Bruce Lee's brother. He certainly could not be her blood relative. It had to be a mistake—or a ruse.

"This is your client's relative, right?"

"Yes...that's him." Jonathan went along, if anything not to look like a complete idiot.

"And you're sure his name is Igor? I mean he doesn't—"

"Yeah." Jonathan nodded, but he was instantly thrown into deep anger. He'd not imagined a man named Igor looking like this. Mariya had to be mistaken, as farfetched as it seemed for the venerable spy to make such an error.

"When did this man drown?"

Dr. Garceau pulled the manila file folder from under his arm and flipped a few of the pages stapled to the top of the folder. "Another pathologist is assigned to this body, so I don't know all the facts. Looks like the 19th... last Friday. Exactly a week ago."

That was what Mariya had said, and apparently it couldn't be confused with any other drowning. Clearly, she'd nailed the right date, but this couldn't possibly be her relative, unless there was a mind-boggling mutation in her family tree. *The bitch is lying to me again.* Jonathan's annoyance simmered as he stared at the cadaver's closed eyes.

"Well, if you're certain, then we're done," Garceau said. "You'll simply need to sign the paperwork upstairs confirming the identity, and then your client can make arrangements to retrieve the body some time next week, after the autopsy."

The idea of making a legal identification based on Mariya's claim troubled him, and Jonathan wasn't about to risk his law license if it was a fraudulent act. But he now remembered something else she'd said.

"Just to be certain, doctor, he should have a tattoo on his arm," Jonathan said.

Garceau checked his watch and sighed. "Fine, let's see." He reached for a box of latex gloves on the counter behind him, donned a pair and rolled down the plastic sheet to the man's knees. The naked body seemed to have no injuries. Jonathan glanced at the brown paper bags that covered both the man's hands and were secured by a rubber band.

"What's with the 7-11 bags?"

"After being in warm water for so long, the skin of the hands tends to loosen and slip off, like a glove. The paper helps keep it in place and reduce moisture accumulation, and more importantly preserve the fingers for identification." He reached for the victim's closest hand and added, "I'll show you."

"No, no, you don't have to."

Garceau went no further. "They were still good for prints, which we ran the same day we got the body." Garceau returned to the notes in the folder. "Yep, there's no match, we're told. Nothing in Louisiana. Nothing from the Feds either."

Jonathan glanced down at the tattoo on the man's right arm, two or three inches below the shoulder. It had an anchor design—just like Mariya had described. The arm's flesh was wrinkly, dry and appeared loose, with the same bluish-gray tint as the man's face and chest. Jonathan felt his anger rise. She may have been right about the body, but it was no relative. Something was clearly awry, and Jonathan began to feel like a fool. Used. Manipulated. Insulted. And now his mind jumped to the possibility that Mariya was setting him up for something. Something devious, no doubt. Sweat began to roll down his back, even in the cool confines of the morgue's coldest room. He reveled in the brief pleasantness of imagining Mariya stretched out in an adjacent drawer, next to Igor, if that was his name.

"You okay?" Garceau asked.

Jonathan nodded. All he desired now was to make a clean exit and give back to that Russian con-artist a potent dose of his anger, if not an outright ass-kicking.

Garceau moved around Jonathan to one side of the body. With one hand he lifted the man's right arm so Jonathan could take a better look at the tattoo; with his other, he spread the skin to flatten the wrinkled surface, but Jonathan was fixated on the back of the shoulders, which had a dry, blackened quality, as if it had been roasted.

"That's normal," Garceau said. "The arms, thorax, abdomen and legs typically dangle in the water, while the back of the head, the upper back and shoulders may stay above the waterline. So, the sun and heat make the air-exposed skin look like this."

"Nasty."

"The reality of human physiology, Mr. Brooks."

Despite the discoloration of the skin, the tattoo was clearly distinguishable. Mariya had described it correctly: a snake tightly coiled around an anchor with a black circle—about half the size of a dime—right above the anchor.

"Is he a sailor?" Garceau asked.

Jonathan wanted to say what he thought: no fucking clue, but a 100 percent Caucasian psycho-spy-bitch sent me here to find her drowned nephew who by some phenomenal genetic feat is apparently Asian. But he held his tongue. "My client didn't tell me much. She's come a long way and is quite distraught, as you can imagine."

Garceau lowered the victim's arm. "Maybe he had something to do with medicine?"

Jonathan leaned over the tattoo. "You mean because it resembles the caduceus?"

"The real caduceus has two snakes entwined around the staff and wings at the top, but in this country it's often confused with the Rod of Asclepius, which is the correct traditional sign for medicine. It has only one snake and no wings, like here."

Jonathan crossed his arms and mumbled to himself, "Maybe my little Russia troublemaker had it right after all."

"Russian?"

"My client's Russian."

"I see. This man doesn't look Russian."

"There are several million Russians who live in Asia."

"I guess you're right." Garceau chewed his bottom lip and wiped his forehead with the back of his gloved hand. "As you can see, this man's Asian, he's got a naval-type tattoo, and we found him in the river. We first thought he was a crewman from a passing ship. I mean, we have ships coming to New Orleans from all over the world."

"I'm well aware of that."

"You sure he's not a crewman?"

Jonathan shrugged. "I'll ask my client, but I don't think so."

"I'm simply asking. Neither the Harbor Police nor NOPD reported a missing sailor, so far at least."

That didn't mean he wasn't. Jonathan had practiced maritime law enough years to know the mindset of many unscrupulous foreign-flagged vessel captains and owners. They tended to despise rules. That's why so many had Liberian or other nation flags, so they could benefit from lax or nonexistent regulations in operating their ships. They hated trouble, particularly when it came to injuries or deaths from the poorly paid—and poorly treated—Filipino, Chinese, Indian, Ukrainian and Russian labor pool, the nationalities that accounted for most of the crews in foreign-flagged ships. So, to Jonathan, nothing surprised him about a boat captain not reporting a man overboard.

"The more I think about this," Garceau added, stepping back from the body, "the more I'm bothered that this guy ended up drowning. Look at him. He's probably thirty-five. In great shape. Not an ounce of fat on him. And there were no storms that night. Nothing."

Jonathan gazed at the man's upper body, which seemed disproportionately wide. "He's got the chest of a swimmer or diver, don't you agree?"

"He sure does. That's what puzzles me."

"The Mississippi is a dangerous place, with currents that can kill the best of them." Jonathan thought this should be obvious to a seasoned pathologist.

"I know, Mr. Brooks. Even our rescue divers don't go in. That's why I find it hard to believe he'd gone in the river knowing that."

"Maybe he didn't know or perhaps he accidentally fell in."

Garceau tilted his head to one side and frowned in thought. "Or was thrown in."

Jonathan began to line up the questions he'd toss at Mariya. Yelling at her about her lack of resemblance with the body was not enough. There was far more to this, and she'd better cough up answers as soon as he could confront her. His reputation was on the line.

"It's just odd," Garceau mumbled.

Jonathan was now distracted by the questions assembling in his head. "I'll ask my client."

"We were originally planning to do an autopsy yesterday," Garceau said, removing his gloves and tossing them in a biohazard receptacle behind Jonathan. "But we're short on staff and now that Katrina might come our way, I'm not sure we'll get around to it till Tuesday. Depends how busy we get with the storm, you know?"

"I understand," Jonathan said, continuing to simmer at what Mariya had done: poisoning their re-encounter after nearly a decade with another blatant half-truth.

Garceau pushed the drawer, and the body returned to the depths of the refrigerated unit. "Frankly, now that you've ID'd him, and my colleague's initial assessment doesn't indicate foul play, I'm not thrilled to use time and resources to do a pointless autopsy. But it's standard procedure."

Jonathan didn't give a damn about an autopsy, unless it was Mariya's. "My client suspected this was a simple drowning."

Garceau escorted Jonathan back to the waiting area and asked his receptionist to pass him a form, which he then quickly filled out the top portion and handed it to Jonathan. "Please print your name here and sign and date below."

Jonathan scanned the form but wasn't sure what to do. He was apprehensive about the body's appearance, which had no physical resemblance to Mariya. But he hadn't asked her the right questions. Perhaps her nephew was not a blood relative. She had not proven herself trustworthy, but she was right about the tattoo, and the drowning in general.

"Is there a problem?" Garceau asked, tapping his index finger on the signature line.

"No." Jonathan quickly inked his signature. They shook hands, and he left.

Before he'd even hit the sidewalk his anxiety had returned, the mental images of the body reigniting his irritation. Though he wanted to believe otherwise, the likelihood that the corpse was Mariya's nephew again seemed remote, if not absurd.

6

"You're a fucking liar!" After restraining himself to a simple text message asking her to meet, Jonathan had carefully lined up umpteen questions by the time he'd pulled up to her car, but those words were the opening salvo that came out instinctively.

Mariya was silent, her arms crossed, leaning against her silver rental car parked at the gravelly end of Front Street, a short road that tapered off into the scruffy weeds by the levee at the river's edge, a few blocks from Audubon Park. A large container ship eased along the calm waters behind her. The chirping of seagulls echoed above.

"Are you listening?" Jonathan wanted to smack her.

"Yes." Mariya seemed to hide behind her large Chanel sunglasses that made her resemble an oversized insect.

"D'you recall what I said about telling the truth?" He marched toward her, to within a foot of her face, his fists clenched.

She didn't flinch, her coolness as provocative as it was suspicious.

"I will not accept you lying to me." Jonathan said.

She grabbed his elbow, her nails digging into his skin. "You're rushing to judgment."

He swiped her hand off him as one would a critter. "There isn't an honest bone in you."

She scowled, but now any face she made would seem nothing more than mere stage performance. "Tell me what happened."

"What happened?" Jonathan's entire body had stiffened. "I wasted almost a full day with your bold-faced lie. And worse yet, I signed a document confirming your nephew's ID, which clearly is false, and as an attorney my signature perpetuates the fraud that you're involved in, whatever it is." He sighed and looked away briefly, and added, "I just can't believe I signed it. If this is some sort of bizarre Russian joke, it ain't funny. Right now I should be making sure the leaky ceiling in my office is fixed so that if Katrina heads this way, it won't flood my secretary's cubicle. Or maybe—if the idiots on the radio are right about how dangerous this storm is—I should pack my shit, board up my windows and get the hell out of Dodge. But *no!* Instead, I'm wandering the halls of a morgue in search of a short, long-dead Asian man you claim is your nephew but who couldn't possibly be related to your sorry Russian ass, and—"

Mariya lunged forward and covered Jonathan's mouth with her palm. "I'm sorry!"

"You're not," he barked, slapping her hand away and jerking his body two steps back. "That's just who you are. You and the rest of your kind." He scrambled for the right label to affix: spies, slime, liars, murderers, con-artists, but none was harsh enough. "Your kind disgusts me."

"Isn't that what they say about lawyers?"

If he'd had a drop of alcohol in his blood, and she'd been a man, he'd have knocked her accent out of her mouth, along with her front teeth.

Mariya checked her watch and looked down at her shoes, at the gravel, at anything but Jonathan.

"I want answers. My license may be on the line."

"You're right, he's not my nephew." She locked her fingers together, as if she'd just noticed how fidgety they were. "It was the *only* way I could make you go. If I simply told you that a stranger had drowned, you would have given me the finger."

"You should try being honest for a change. It might actually get you somewhere."

"You don't understand. I need to know what happened to him. He was just passing through here and... well...I need details."

"Not unless you tell me more."

"I am on to something very important, Jonathan. I need to know this. It has no value to you. Tell me what you found out. Please."

"No."

"Did he have the tattoo I described?"

Jonathan said nothing.

"Was he wounded in any way? What did they find on him?"

He shook his head, stabbing her with his irate gaze.

She lightly slapped his chest. "Don't be like this."

"Don't mess with me."

"I'm at a dead end without your help."

"Tell me why a cadaver half-way around the planet from your beloved Russia is so important to you." Jonathan wasn't about to drop this one bit. "Who is he?"

"I'm not ready to share that with you." Mariya's eyes remained glued to the ground. "Not yet, at least. But I had to try. Besides, what's the harm?" She sighed and looked up at him with a resigned pout.

"The harm? How about lack of respect. Dishonesty. The fact that you didn't give me the courtesy to decide based on truthful facts. I've never done anything to be undependable or untrustworthy to you. I was grateful to you—and always will be—for allowing me to find Matt and for helping me avenge his death. Yet this is how you treat me? Is respect a foreign concept where you're from?"

"I'm sorry." She ran her fingers through the ends of her wavy, brown hair, her eyes revealing an inner conflict of sorts.

"You're not sorry, so stop using words that aren't in your vocabulary. If you don't spill the truth right now— this very second—I'm going straight back to the morgue and telling them my client made a mistake. Period. Or maybe I'll call the cops and tell them someone interesting has returned to New Orleans."

"You wouldn't..."

"You better spill what you know."

Mariya shook her head but didn't utter a sound. She

turned her back to him and faced the river, her hands planted on the hood of her car.

"Well?" Jonathan asked, taking a glimpse of the inside of her car through the side windows.

"I can't."

"Then *das vidanya*."

She only glanced his way after he was again seated behind the wheel of his Camry. He gazed at her once more, secretly wishing she'd stop him from leaving. She'll do it, he thought, taking his time to put the keys in the ignition. She'll run to him with apologies, with answers, with a smile that will undo her insults. But nothing of the sort happened. She didn't budge—her stubbornness stayed intact.

He stepped on the gas, slowly, glancing into the side mirror for a sign of surrender, then in the rearview mirror as he was about to lose sight of her. Nothing.

"Goodbye, Mariya," he whispered alone, unsure if he should be angry, annoyed or relieved.

Mariya's opaqueness was no surprise, just like a decade ago, but this time she blatantly disregarded his questions—all of them legitimate, given what he'd seen at the morgue.

He tried to think of other things, to put it behind him, and this seemed easier now, as he drove down Riverbend. It held a treasure trove of memories, transposing a cocktail of joy and sadness onto the quiet open road that bordered the levee, with the mighty Mississippi on the other side. For Jonathan, the levee was more than the sum of its parts. More than its modest raised soil, or the weathered grass that covered its rising and descending slopes, or the paved path that enchanted bikers and joggers along its apex. The levee was history, his history. A library of laughs and childhood hubris. Snapshots of better times. He could hear the giggles, the barking of ecstatic dogs. The tune of an uncomplicated life, long before joining his first firm. Long before beginning law school. Long before the struggles of life shredded the delicate idealism and sheltered innocence he'd grown up with in the Crescent City. Goosebumps trickled along the skin of his back and his arms as he gazed ahead, at this green stretch of land.

He smiled—a heavily burdened smile—until the road merged into another and it had passed, but again Mariya was back on his mind. "I will find out," he told himself.

7

Langley, Virginia

"ARE THEY HERE YET?" DIRECTOR GLEN SANDERS ASKED gruffly from behind his desk, his finger pressed hard on the intercom button.

"Mr. Felder just walked in," his assistant replied.

"And Porter?"

"Not yet."

Ron Felder quietly entered Glen's large office, holding a red file folder. He squinted as he crossed the bright light of the setting sun coming through the floor-to-ceiling windows.

"We're waiting for Porter," Glen said, noticing Ron's disheveled black hair and wrinkled shirt. "Have a seat."

Ron nodded coolly and pulled back the chair facing Glen's desk but stayed standing.

"Sit, sit."

Ron didn't budge. His eyes narrowed. "Director, with all due respect, I just don't get it."

"Get what?"

"My promotion," Ron said curtly as if Glen should have known.

Oh God, Glen thought. He had no time to deal with this now. Besides, the decision was final and had gone out to Ron by email only this morning. "This has nothing to do with why Porter called this meeting, right?"

"Right." Ron shrugged. "But I—"

"Then save it for another time, if you don't mind."

"I worked so damn hard for it," Ron added and shook his head, his mouth now closing and his jaw pulled to one side.

Glen raised his brow.

"I'm more than qualified." Ron seemed to tighten his grip, enough to bend the folder in his hand.

Glen looked into the man's glassy, blood-shot eyes, unable to tell what Ron was holding back most: anger, bitterness or sorrow. "There's a process, and a result. Sometimes it's what you want; sometimes it's not. That happens every day at the CIA, just like any other agency——and the corporate world, quite frankly."

"But I deserved that post."

"You've managed the North Korea desk for over four years? D'you know how many dream of having that."

"I feel shafted." Ron briskly ran his hand through his thick hair and returned a frosty gaze. "Really shafted."

Glen sighed. He despised administrative matters of this kind, be it promotions, demotions, firings, disciplinary action. And now that the global war on terror had consumed his every synapse, with the CIA's Directorate of Operations—under his watch—stretched thin across the globe, he had little tolerance to deal with squabbling among his minions, especially now that Congress, the White House, the Pentagon and countless other political and military torrents sucked more than two-thirds of his time and attention.

He turned, again jabbed the button on his desk phone, and said in a strained voice, "Susan, get Porter."

Ron finally took a seat, his hands fidgety. "Give me London. Let me show how well I can run things there. I'm perfect for it, and you know that."

To Glen, the man's words began to give off the odor of entitlement. He knew Ron had kissed all the asses that needed the puckering—and there were many. Ron had surely calculated each move to increase his odds at the CIA's coveted open position in the English capital—the agency's prestigious hub of counter-proliferation ops stretching from Scandinavia to North Africa and as far east as Kazakhstan. Perhaps it was for the pay hike or the expat perks, too, Glen mused, or simply a chance at a new beginning far from Langley.

Ron's venomous stare made Glen uncomfortable.

"Drop it, please." Glen's voice hardened, and then he remembered how their last meeting had ended. "Have you located Sal?"

Ron didn't appear keen to shift gears. "Porter's making a fuss over something rather small."

"Tell me...I only have a few minutes before I head to the Hill for a meeting, and I won't be late on account of you or Porter. So, have you found Sal or not?"

The door opened. George Porter's bulky six-foot-three frame lumbered into the room. He closed the door

behind him and gestured an apologetic wave as he casually strolled to the windows instead of taking the chair
next to Ron. He then leaned on the glass, as if posing,
wearing a beige cardigan and his obnoxiously large gold
watch. The sun seemed to set onto his left shoulder,
casting a long shadow over Ron.

"George wanted me to tell you that we've lost an
asset," Ron said, glancing at Porter, who stood expres-
sionless, his hands deep in his pockets.

"Another one?" Glen threw his hands in the air.
"Who this time?"

"A special asset."

"Just like Sal," Porter added.

"What do you mean lost?"

"Dead." Porter said at the same time as Ron.

Glen rolled his eyes. "I'm afraid to hear more."

"George thinks you should," Ron said, as if to clean
his hands of the matter.

"Damn right," Porter said. "Tell him, or I will."

Ron's shoulders drooped as he looked down at his file.

"Well?" Glen imagined Ron didn't want to be here,
only hours after learning of his failed promotion. Glen
also anticipated the fireworks the moment Ron would
eventually find out the London gig had gone to Porter,
though no one other than Glen and his boss, the CIA
Director, yet knew this. He checked his watch. "I'm in a
hurry, so let's have it."

Ron flipped open the file folder's reddish Top Secret
cover page and took out an eight-by-ten black and white
photograph and placed it on the desk.

Glen slid it under his nose and instantly cringed.

"Our asset was found dangling on a meat hook at a butcher stand for everyone to see," Ron said.

"When?"

"Early this morning in the souks of Marrakesh."

"Who is he?" Glen slid the photo back to the edge of his desk.

"Hasan Okyar," Ron replied, peering down at his folder. "You might remember his work in Baqubah last year. He joined the manhunt for Iraqi and Iranian traffickers who were peddling depleted uranium rounds and IEDs. He took out all four suspects in less than two weeks."

"Uh-huh." Glen again checked his watch.

"Overall, a reliable, sharp asset. Meticulous. Tech savvy. And plausible deniability always maintained."

"Was it random?" Glen asked. "I mean, those shitholes in Africa aren't the safest places, right?"

"No worse than Detroit or New Orleans," Porter countered.

Glen was surprised at the ostensibly racist remark coming from Porter, himself African-American.

"What was Hasan doing for us recently?"

"He lived mostly in Morocco. We were prepping him for a job in Armenia. Small fish."

"What exactly?" Glen prodded.

"Pyongyang-funded counterfeiters—nothing major at all."

Glen was disappointed.

"But no one knew where Hasan lived," Porter added. "He was too careful."

Ron again glanced at Porter, frowning deeply. "Let our team handle it. It's no big deal—a non-issue."

"A dead asset of this kind is never a non-issue. And you know that." Glen sat back in his creaky chair. He sensed Ron was anxious to drop the topic and crawl into a hole to brood about his lost promotion. "What do you fellas need from me?"

"More resources," Porter said deliberately. "I want to know why he was killed. It's not random. That kind of death is meant as a message. We need a handful of good field operatives for starters."

Glen shrugged and eyed Ron. "Do you have enough folks working this?"

"Yes, a local team on site and others here. We're combing through everything. I don't need George's guys making things more complicated."

"You better clean up that mess. I don't want anything coming back to us."

"We're already on it," Ron said, rubbing his jaw.

"Good." Glen stood up and began stuffing papers into his briefcase.

"There's something else Ron hasn't told you," Porter then said, stepping away from the windows. "Hasan's last assignment was in Moscow, and that—"

"Don't start that crap again," Ron interrupted. "Let's not—"

"Let me finish, dammit," Porter pressed, almost shouting. "I think the Director of Operations is entitled to know that Sal's disappearance may be linked to our slab of meat in Morocco."

"Linked? Glen asked. How so?" He dropped his

briefcase on his chair and watched Ron stab Porter with a fierce gaze.

Porter raised his chin at Ron before answering. "Just like Hasan, Salvatore Brusca has been assigned to track Chermayeff."

"The physicist?" Glen asked, beginning to feel angry that Ron was keeping this from him.

"Yes, Yuri Chermayeff."

"The same Chermayeff that the Israelis have been pestering me about recently?"

"Yeah," Porter said, "Same motherfucker, and the Mossad want him dead, I've heard."

Glen tilted his head, recalling that the search for Chermayeff had begun under Porter's watch, since he ran the Russia desk. "Isn't Sal your asset, too?"

Porter frowned. "Ron's team and mine have been sharing him. Sal's been tracking Chermayeff for the last few months, and Hasan did the same for the three prior months. We haven't heard squat from Sal in two weeks."

"And Hasan's dead," Glen added, glancing at the meat-hook photo on his desk before setting his eyes back on Ron.

Ron shook his head. "The Russians keep refusing to do anything about this prick, no matter the evidence we've shown them."

"Regardless, your team hasn't shut him down," Porter said.

Ron's eyes oozed with hate. "Obviously someone in the Kremlin has his back, and that's your turf, George."

Glen leaned over his desk toward Ron. "Remind me where Sal was last seen?"

"Moscow," Ron said.

"And where's Chermayeff now?" Glen already knew, but he wanted to make a point.

"Not sure."

"Isn't it your job to know?"

Ron didn't answer.

"I shouldn't be the first to learn about his where-abouts, right?" Glen pulled a one-page printed cable from under a small pile of folders. "Here," he said, hand-ing it to Ron. "Chermayeff was seen leaving the North Korean ambassador's residence in Damascus three days ago."

Ron looked at Porter with contempt. "Did you know?"

Porter shrugged. "Nope."

Ron appeared to speed-read the eight-sentence cable and handed it back to Glen. "Who told you this?"

"MI-6 reported it to our Beirut chief of station."

"Maybe your team isn't quite up to the task," Porter said, seeming to relish the jab.

Glen knew the two were like water and oil. Though they now headed different groups, with different geo-graphic responsibilities, they crossed paths when people like Chermayeff seemed to meddle both in North Korea and the former Soviet republics. George Porter had once been Ron Felder's boss and they hadn't made a great team. Their egos and animosities made them vulnerable to mistakes, which worried Glen. "This better not be the beginnings of a major screw-up."

"Look, Sal's got personal problems—we've known that for some time—but he's good," Ron said, his tone less confident than earlier. "He'll resurface. He's always done so in the past. Maybe he's in Damascus as we speak, keeping a low profile as he's tracking Chermayeff."

"Bullshit. He's gone cold," Porter said tersely. "Not a peep from him in two weeks, and now apparently Chermayeff is roaming freely."

Ron's eyes betrayed enough disquiet to make Glen unsure that either man had a good handle on this, or that their mutual enmity wouldn't hinder the way forward.

Porter pressed his hands on the edge of the desk. "Glen, I'm telling you, something's not right. Sal was reporting back regularly on Chermayeff, who's one of the hardest guys to find. All was fine, as far as I know. And then nothing. His cell phones don't work. He hasn't been seen at his apartment."

"You searched his place?" Ron asked in a raised voice.

"Yes, of course."

"Without telling me?" Ron stood up, pushing his chair back hard.

"He's disappeared. And now Hasan, previously assigned the same target, goes down, albeit in Morocco. Are you waiting for other bad news before you connect the dots?"

"You're creating dots that aren't there."

Glen again checked his watch. "Guys, cool it. Is Sal dead or just unreliable?"

Ron opened his mouth but said nothing.

"What if Sal and Hasan collaborated?" Glen asked.

"Doubtful," Ron replied.

Porter crossed his arms. "But there was a brief overlap in their Moscow posting."

"They work alone," Ron snapped.

"You can't be entirely sure," Porter said.

Glen thought for a few seconds. "Are you saying Hasan, one of our best operatives, would tell a colleague where he lives?"

Porter shrugged. "Maybe. And what if Chermayeff caught Sal and made him talk?"

"Farfetched." Ron's voice rose in anger. "You know damn well this is my team's responsibility. Let us handle this." He turned to Glen and raised his hands. "Am I right?"

"Chermayeff—and Sal, for that matter—are as much mine as they are yours," Porter barked. "Just because he's set foot in Pyongyang doesn't break his Russian ties that I've spent two years piecing together."

Glen had had enough of the pissing contest. "I don't care whose shit this is to clean up, I'm going to look to both of you for answers."

An uneasy silence engulfed the air as Glen grabbed his briefcase, crossed the room and opened the door wide. "I hate bad news, gentlemen. Come back when you can make me smile again."

Ron quickly left, but Porter stopped at the door and eased it half-closed. "Got a second?"

"For what?"

Porter leaned into the door until it was all the way closed. "There's something wrong with Ron. He's constantly trying to screw me."

Glen met Porter's gaze. "You sometimes take things

too personally. And you seem to forget that you're not his boss anymore."

"No, I don't care about that. I just don't trust him anymore. It's a gut feeling, Glen. Can't prove it. He's become a lone ranger. He doesn't mix well with others, even in his group. For starters, look how many times he's gone abroad?"

"Everyone's entitled to vacations."

"I wouldn't be too sure. He's taken more trips this year than I have in the last five."

"You're making pretty serious allegations about a colleague, and someone who's playing a crucial role here. You should either substantiate it, or keep it to yourself."

"I'm telling you, ever since his fucked up divorce, he's really changed. He's hiding stuff, he's sneaky..."

"Well, he's a spy, like you," Glen said, smiling. "I've seen no surprises so far. And he's passed all the yearly checks."

Porter scoffed. "Anyone with solid training can do that."

Glen chuckled. "By the way, last week he asked to be taken off the Stockholm operation. He's trying to pawn it over to a local team. You okay with that?"

"What?" Porter's mouth opened wide and his eyebrows rose. He seemed dumbfounded. "No way. Ron's bitched about the operation for a long time, but he's been knee deep in making sure it happens."

"You want it?"

"No, it's his masterpiece."

"Might be quite impressive if it works."

"Perhaps, but I'm not lusting for glory. I just want the job done right, and at this late hour Ron's our only logical choice. I wouldn't let him off the hook."

Glen sighed. "Tell me the truth: you want him to fuck it up, don't you?"

"No, that's not true."

"You don't have to say it."

"Don't let Ron off the hook."

Glen nodded. "Fine, but he's going to be pissed."

"So be it. I just don't trust the guy."

8

FOR THE LAST SIX HOURS SINCE BREAKING THE NEWS TO Director Sanders, Ron hadn't left the confines of his office overlooking the woods lining the Potomac. Surprisingly, Porter—as irritated as he seemed when they'd ended the meeting—hadn't stopped by. Ron had feared further hostility from his former boss for having resisted divulging Sal's disappearance. But Ron knew Porter was the type who'd likely choose to get even rather than losing his cool, and that worried him.

Ron had spent most of the time emailing his web of contacts in Morocco and Russia, and more importantly, he'd asked an old colleague, Walid, at the embassy in Rabat, to get to Marrakesh as quickly as possible. Walid was one of Ron's old contacts, many of whom hadn't heard from him since he'd transferred from the Russia desk to head the North Korean portfolio of intelligence work. That was simply the way things went at the CIA.

It was almost nine. Ron gazed at the jaundiced night sky over Langley and the faint lights further away over

D.C. He was anxious. He'd given Walid the address of Hasan's apartment in the Guéliz neighborhood of Marrakesh. That was six hours ago.

At about ten the secure line broke the silence. Ron picked up the handset on the first ring.

"I'm here at his place," Walid said hastily, his British English peppered by a mild Arabic accent.

"And the cops?"

"No sign."

Ron stood up, feeling too edgy to keep his ass seated. "You know what to do, right?"

"Tss..." Walid knew it well. He'd done cleanup work for Ron before, most recently two years ago in Cairo when a Russian call girl had harassed the CIA chief of station for allegedly getting her pregnant. Walid was tasked with the dreadful job of removing all traces of the woman and her Ukrainian pimp-boyfriend from the diplomat's home after they'd broken in and gotten their heads blown off by the well-armed chief himself. Today, Ron needed Walid's clean-up skills, though there were no human remains—only documents and other possessions that could potentially tie Hasan to U.S. intelligence.

"I got numbers for Hasan's last calls, cell and home," Walid said with the sound of paper shuffling in the background.

"And?"

"He wasn't a popular guy," Walid said, chuckling. "Only eight calls in the last five days, it seems."

"If he didn't erase other calls. I've already asked NSA to run the numbers."

Ron fixed his eyes on Hasan's file photos, three of them, sprawled over the surface of his desk. He'd never met Hasan. Except for Sal, Ron had stuck to the rules: no senior agency officer based in Langley was ever to meet a "special asset" unless cleared by Jesus Christ himself. They were contract cleaners, mostly non-citizens based overseas. Ron quickly thought of Sal and the others under his tutelage—four names in his former portfolio of non-existent assassins he'd relied on now and then to terminate the vile thugs who'd made the privileged list of targets that few below Glen Sanders' rank ever really knew about in any detail. Given Sal's disappearance and Hasan's death, he'd called the other two assets to make sure they were still in the land of the living, which, to his relief they were.

Walid's breaths shortened. "I've never met a man with fewer possessions. Did he really live here?"

Ron heard the sounds of drawers open and close, and items being tossed about. "Just collect the sensitive shit and get out. I don't want you there when the cops show up."

"I'll dig some more and call you back in ten."

*   *   *

The ten minutes felt like thirty. Ron was relieved when Walid redialed.

"Aside from the two cell phones here, it appears he was carrying a third when he died—I tried calling it but it goes straight to voicemail. The last call I see here came from a number I traced to a phone booth at the airport."

"When?"

"Eleven fifteen, about five hours before his body was found. I'll email you the number."

"Find out the flights that arrived and departed around that time," Ron said as he paced about his office, holding the phone cord up high to avoid knocking things off his desk. "Anything else?"

"Yes," Walid said, pausing for a moment. "Did he usually carry his piece around town?"

"I don't know."

"Well, there's a pistol under his mattress and loaded magazines under the couch. And I heard no weapon was found at the scene."

It was interesting, but Ron couldn't make the leap stick. Maybe Hasan had been in the souks unarmed. Maybe because he was meeting someone familiar. But Walid's information didn't paint a full enough picture to make this certain.

More random noises filtered through the phone. Walid sounded more hurried, his breaths stronger, the echoes of cupboard doors and drawers coming in louder.

"Hurry," Ron said. He heard furniture screech across the floor and things being thrown into what sounded like a garbage bag.

"Okay, I'm nearly done," Walid said. "Do I torch it?"

"God no!" As good an idea as it seemed, Ron didn't want a repeat of the Cairo cleanup. In uniquely serious cases, the Agency often considered setting fire to the place. In Egypt he'd told Walid to burn it down since the forensic evidence was too dispersed to properly clean up. The chief of station had fired seven times at the intruders, their flesh littering every surface, floor to ceiling, of two rooms. Fire was the only option. But things went awfully wrong. The flames quickly spread to the neighbor's house—which happened to be owned by the country's Deputy Finance Minister—and severely wounded his beloved chauffeur. The bodies of the Eastern European accomplices were never found, but it had caused a few ulcers at State and the CIA. To make matters worse now, Hasan lived in a five-story apartment block. The bonfire option was most certainly unappealing.

"Just leave." Ron continued to pace as he heard Walid unlock the front door.

"I've got everything in two bags."

Ron sighed and sat in his chair.

"What about Hasan's body?" Walid asked, his voice trembling as he sprinted down the stairs.

"It's at the coroner's, right?"

"Yes."

Ron hesitated. Knowing the cause of death might help him determine whether Hasan died at the hands of a professional or by a random act of violence. But claiming the body would pose risks, among them that the authorities would somehow give the man an American connection, which was out of the question. "Leave it unclaimed, but get your hands on the death certificate, the police report, or any autopsy results as soon as you can."

Walid's voice was now accompanied by street noises. "They may not do an autopsy."

"Then anonymously leak something to make them do it. Figure it out. I need to know how he died."

"Wasn't he carved up like prime rib?"

Ron wasn't amused. "Send me all you've got."

*   *   *

The south parking lot was close to empty, with the tall lamps casting a bright glow over the concrete. The night air was slightly cooler than usual for August. Ron strolled to his Volvo, his briefcase in hand, his mind carrying the load of his failed promotion and the angst of dealing with a mess he hadn't created. As he got closer he spotted a car parked behind his, a charcoal Cadillac that he quickly recognized as Porter's. His former boss was in the driver's seat, his window down, a lighted cigarette in his hand that rested near the side mirror.

"What a coincidence," Ron said curtly.

"You just had to be a jerk." Porter threw out the cigarette and stepped out of the car.

Ron stopped and set his briefcase down. It had been a long, difficult day, and the last thing he wanted was another confrontation with Porter.

"You didn't have to mention Sal to Sanders."

Porter shook his head. "I disagree. And why d'you still have an axe to grind with me? You don't work for me anymore. You're in your own little world and are free to piss all over others below you and suck up to plenty of asses above you. So why all this animosity, Ron? Why? Is it that promotion of yours? Maybe you just didn't earn it."

"Look who's talking," Ron said but without the confidence he had mustered in Sanders' office.

"Whatever." Porter's eyes narrowed, his jaw clenched tight.

Ron grabbed his briefcase and unlocked his car. "I'm not having this here."

"If you wish," Porter said, walking along side. "But I got some news for you: Sanders is making sure that you run the show in Stockholm."

"That's not his call."

"It is now. Blessed from high above. Your ass is going there Monday. So, good luck."

Ron felt his gut twist. It was Porter's doing, for sure. That snake. Ron understood what this meant. It was hard enough to swallow the lost promotion, but now he faced managing an operation he never wanted in the first place, and whose failure could cost him his job. For months he'd done his damndest to distance himself from what might unfold in Stockholm. Only weeks ago, Ron had managed to hand off part of his role to a motley crew of Cold War cling-ons reporting to Porter's Russia desk, all of whom had been itching for the mother of all defections—a North Korean vice-admiral, supposedly with plenty of information to spill.

Porter smirked all the way to his car and drove off, squealing his tires as he turned onto the street.

If Sanders had indeed made the decision, Ron would have no choice. He'd never get an ounce of sleep if he went home. Not even with his nightly scotch whiskey. His job was in peril. There'd been enough fuck-ups—in Langley, and all the other intelligence agencies, since the invasion of Iraq—to make superiors keen to get rid of the bad apples. And the meager prospects for a good paying job in the real world seemed no less daunting than the Stockholm operation, especially since all he really knew was the world of espionage—a world he was so addicted to it had cost him his wife, a family, a life beyond his mere self.

He leaned on his car for a moment. Everything had suddenly turned upside down. And this compounded his primary fear: that Sal and Ron shared secrets that could destroy Ron's career in no time. *This is the beginning of the end.*

He headed back to his office. Angry. Scared.

9

New Orleans, Louisiana

THERE IS A CERTAIN ODDITY ABOUT THE MOST TRIVIAL events of the past, how sometimes they crawl back into the present, their haunting strength sometimes reinforced by the passage of time and by weaknesses we have in stopping their resurgence, no matter how poorly their details are remembered, no matter how forgotten are the exact words uttered, the sequence of events, or the granular specifics of those bygone moments. Even for something as trifling as a meal.

Jonathan closed his eyes, fleetingly dragging himself back to the not-so-distant past, holding the coffee mug close to his lips, the steam rising over his face, and the heat tingling his cheeks. Since Linda had left him, breakfasts were never the same: a simple croissant with a hurriedly splashed blob of jam, and perhaps a yogurt or a bowl of cereal. The pageantry of carefully arranged brie and smoked salmon slices had vanished. The aroma of craftily cooked omelets no longer caressed the morning air. The occasional flowered vase at the center of the kitchen table and the butter in its own silver container, these too were gone, replaced by a purely utilitarian function, with an uncomfortable accompaniment of solitude that forced Jonathan to hurry through his breakfast and guzzle his dose of caffeine before the looming depressive cloud would settle in his just-awakened mind. These were his mornings. A daily chore down remembrance lane.

For whatever reason, today was harder. Jonathan couldn't shake off his foray into the past. Everything seemed to propel him that way. He glanced up at the brightly dressed musicians in the abstract painting that still hung above the breakfast table. A festive acrylic work of cubism by a local artist, René Nagi, whom Linda had befriended soon after she and Jonathan had tied the knot. They'd been sauntering one evening along the south side of Jackson Square when Linda had caught sight of the painting. Nagi had displayed several of his works along the park's fence, some tied side by side on the wrought iron itself, and others lined up on the pavement below. There were similar paintings hung around it, but something drew Linda to this one. Bright orange and blue, with streaks and splashes of purple, red and white, it created its own motion, the jazz sounds leaping from the canvas. Strangely, she'd said it was the sadness in the pianist's expression that had attracted her to Nagi's artwork, and how it contrasted with the faces of the other three musicians, all of them with exaggerated smiles, their bodies jostling with their instruments. She was that way. She was drawn to the oddity, the misplacement, the runt, the odd one out. Linda was a perpetual apologist for the lost and downtrodden. Where there was joy, she could find the sadness. Not because she was depressive, but rather her nature was to dig past the veneer. To understand. That's what had led her to become one of New Orleans' top television anchor-women. And it was this voice and strength that Jonathan longed for, now, over a breakfast of the abandoned and departed. A time to eat and mourn over the unfinished slaughter at the hands of solitude. He ate the last morsel of croissant and the misery ended, temporarily, until tomorrow's repast would greet him to a new day. He sighed, placed the empty mug in the sink and turned the light off.

"Why can't I go beyond this?" he lobbed the question into the emptiness of the kitchen, gazing out the window at the darkening sky. "Oh, Linda."

Jonathan looked out over his small front yard and the pile of plywood he'd had delivered from the hardware store. If the storm's path looked more ominous this morning, he'd planned to board up most of the larger windows of his one-story shotgun-style house, and if there were any spare panels, he'd also cover the kitchen windows and those facing the back porch. But the ache that came with Linda's absence continued to weigh down any strength he had to start this day. He returned to the bedroom and sank his head into the pillow, and soon the sad thoughts drained him into a restless, exhausted sleep.

*   *   *

Jonathan glanced at the clock on his way to the end table to answer the phone. It was a bit after ten. He answered and slumped onto the couch as he heard the man's voice on the other end of the line.

Dr. Garceau, the pathologist who'd shown him the body the prior day, asked for him in a quiet voice.

"How did you get this number?" Jonathan had always kept his home number unlisted, and he hadn't shared it with Garceau. He got back up and walked to the windows.

"Sorry to bother you, Counselor," Garceau said with background noise that told Jonathan the man was probably driving.

"I'm serious, who gave you my number?"

"That's not important."

"There's no—"

"Listen to me, Mr. Brooks," Garceau interrupted. "After you left, I was quite curious and took a closer look at the victim. It's just that, well..."

"Go on."

Garceau had now put Jonathan on speaker. "That tattoo, you know—not sure if it means anything—but it's actually two tattoos."

"Two? I only saw one."

"It appears that one is superimposed on an older one."

Jonathan struggled to find the relevance of what Garceau had just said. "I don't see how that matters."

"I don't either," Garceau said, "but it just seems bizarre. You may recall, the top of the tattoo has a black circle, but under strong lighting I can see beneath it what appears to be a red star. It's barely visible, easier to see by stretching the skin. It looks like the dark circle was added to hide the star—just my guess, but—" Garceau interrupted himself. "Did you ask your client if her relative worked on a ship?"

"No, not yet."

"Another thing, Mr. Brooks," Garceau said, sounding distracted by his driving. "I found a minor but unusual injury on the deceased's back, and I'd like the opportunity to ask your client a few questions."

"What kind of injury?"

"Minor stuff, but I can't quite make sense of it."

Garceau's words triggered an uncomfortable chill in Jonathan's chest. He immediately thought of the form he'd signed. Penning his signature had been foolish for sure. And he hoped Garceau hadn't found something else that would expose his misrepresentation. Tempting as it was to think of the form as a trivial administrative nuisance, Jonathan understood how grave things could get if it appeared that he, as an attorney, had signed it fraudulently. His anger again turned to Mariya. Her lie is what made him sign it. She was to blame, but that might not be enough to undo his error if things heated up. He wanted to end the call before Garceau could lob further questions or raise any more disconcerting issues.

"Let's discuss this during the week if you wish," Jonathan said, his forehead now starting to perspire.

"Bear with me for a moment," Garceau insisted. He'd apparently stopped his car and turned the engine off. "It's just that these things all point to this man coming from a ship."

"Let's discuss this when—"

"Just one more thing, if I may."

Jonathan sighed. "Sure."

"I'm assuming you—I mean, your client—is telling the truth about the deceased, but I suggest you have a long chat with your client and get some background on this individual with whom she claims a relationship. You know, when you're in my profession, you see a lot of things, and you learn to trust your gut. Something's not right here."

His heart now pounding hard, Jonathan said, "Dr. Garceau, I'll follow-up with her as soon as I can." A near-panicked fear collided with the fury he felt at Mariya. She knew much more than she'd shared with him. Jonathan then thought of something else he'd missed earlier: How on earth did Mariya know there was a man with that tattoo in the morgue when Garceau's team never identified the victim? How could she possibly know? And to do so within a few days of the man's drowning? She was resourceful and smart, but not clairvoyant. Suddenly, the more ominous question came back to mind: What if Mariya was somehow responsible for the man's drowning, or knew who was?

"We are scheduling an autopsy for early next week, depending of course on what happens with the hurricane this weekend. I've already prepared additional samples for toxicology, though these may take two or three weeks for results. Again, I don't think there's anything nefarious with the cause of death—at least from what I can gather now—but there are more questions than answers, and I urge your client to come in to sort this out."

Despite the pathologist's assurance that there didn't appear to be foul play in this case, the fact that he'd called an unlisted number on a Saturday rattled Jonathan. He thanked the coroner and hung up.

He'd barely walked into the living room when the voice on the TV caught his attention, but he wasn't sure he'd heard the words correctly. He turned the volume up. The stone-faced anchor announced the mandatory evacuation of low-lying areas in various parishes, including St. Charles, St. Tammany, and Jefferson, and a voluntary evacuation for St. Bernard Parish.

Jonathan chuckled. The forecasters he'd poked fun at earlier in the week weren't wrong after all. The storm was headed this way for certain and he'd better evacuate or hunker down.

*   *   *

The CNN correspondent echoed through the opened front door as Jonathan toiled on the porch, nailing one more plywood board over the third large window facing the yard. But his attention was drawn elsewhere. Having unsuccessfully tried to reach Mariya by phone, he instead fished through the tidbits of information that he'd witnessed and gathered in the last twenty-four hours. Probing. Calculating.

He was sifting through the bottom of the toolbox for nails when all of a sudden he recalled a fragment of Mariya's statement that now jumped out like fireworks. He deliberated a moment more, replaying the words he thought he'd heard her say. Her voice echoed in his head, and the words became more precise as the sequence of events looped back into memory. Mariya indeed had said something telling. When she admitted the man wasn't her nephew, she'd also said he was just passing through. As a sailor would, Jonathan realized.

Jonathan again pondered whether Mariya had misspoken, or if he'd misheard her, or if she'd simply gotten her English wrong. Continuing to deconstruct their conversation, he remembered catching a glimpse of a book. A large green manual, in fact, that resembled the Port of New Orleans directory. He had spotted it, partly covered by a large purse, on the front passenger-side seat of her rental car during their encounter by the river. He closed his eyes momentarily, trying to picture it again as best he could recall.

He ran back into the house and headed to a bookcase in his bedroom. The second shelf held the answer. Last year's Port directory. Though it was a different color, the front cover layout and aerial image of a docked ship appeared the same. The lawyer in him said it wasn't enough, but his gut was amply satisfied. Mariya had clearly already made the connection that Jonathan was only now piecing together and had held back from sharing it with him.

Why hold back that the man was a crewman on a passing ship? he wondered.

Mariya's secrecy was to be expected, but he'd hoped she'd changed. She'd promised not to lie, yet she did. The broken pledge disturbed him more than anything.

By about three o'clock, Jonathan put his tools down and stepped outside, inspecting the work he'd completed. The house looked terrible, with plywood covering what used to be large windows and doors, but it was in better shape to survive the pounding that Katrina might unleash.

He then checked his phone and was surprised to hear Linda's voice. She'd left a message. Her tone was sedate, her words surprisingly empathetic. She'd heard of Louisiana Governor Blanco's order to evacuate all Southeastern parishes and asked if Jonathan was planning to leave. He clung momentarily to the idea that she'd called him out of genuine concern. He replayed her message three times, letting the rare softness of her voice ease into his soul. For a few minutes he fended off the pessimism, the anger. It seemed real, if only for a moment.

*   *   *

The bedroom ceiling didn't have the answers, but Jonathan stared at it as if miraculously one would pop out of its pale surface, barely illuminated by the two candles next to an empty vase on the dresser. The light cast a wobbling shadow, the flame disturbed by the blowing air-conditioning unit below the boarded window. Jonathan pondered the problem: a strangely-tattooed Asian sailor, washed up on a riverbank, with some sort of injury that the coroner can't figure out but no sign of foul play, and no one reporting him missing—except a pathological liar who's arrived from Russia just for this body.

The odd assortment of disjointed facts, Mariya's resistance to his questions, and his fear that Garceau's suspicions could lead to trouble, had wired him up more than any caffeinated drink could do. He eyed the clock: 11:50 P.M.

A ship. His mind imagined the multitude of vessels moored at any given time along the docks near downtown. He thought of the current and pictured the body drifting with it. *Yes, the current.* His eyes still aimed at the plaster, he pictured the wide body of brownish water easing past the riverbank, carrying branches, plastic bottles, other trash, and, of course, Igor's body.

Suddenly he slapped his forehead. *Yes!* The abrupt excitement propelled him out of bed. He quickly pulled sweat pants from the drawer and threw them on, hopping clumsily to get the second leg in without falling over.

Two years earlier, or maybe three, a drunken tourist had drowned off the rocky incline just east of the French Quarter. The incident had made the *Times Picayune*, and the story now cried out to Jonathan, his synapses crackling, impatiently hungering for the details that could shed more light on his evidentiary conundrum.

Jonathan turned on his desktop computer, tightly squeezed on a narrow wooden desk not much wider than a dinner tray in the corner of the bedroom. He then brushed aside the inch-thick stack of unopened mail over the keyboard which had accumulated over the past week or so. *It's always easier to open bills when you have money to pay them,* he thought while the computer fired up.

Pushed by curiosity, duty and fear, he quashed his need for sleep and embarked on an all-nighter—an ordinary course of action for any trial attorney worth anything. Loyalty to a client had often forced such nearly instinctive nocturnal perseverance, most often in the days leading to a trial or on the cusp of an appellate brief deadline. But Mariya was no client. Her only payments for his troubles were lies, and there was little chance of glamour or applause awaiting the results of his efforts. But that didn't stop him.

He perused countless websites on the Internet, clicking through the vast electronic wasteland in search of the few kilobytes of value. He'd pulled down scores of maps of the river, navigation charts, water temperature tables, dockyard addresses, and anything remotely associated with the few clues Mariya and Garceau had shared with him.

Persisting further, well past 4 A.M., he finally stumbled on the newspaper article that had kick-started this night-time venture. The tourist had fallen in 78-degree water, substantially cooler than the 88-plus Mississippi this time of year. The story explained how the temperature affected the amount of time the body stays submerged. The warmer the water, the faster the bacteria will create gases that then increase buoyancy. Jonathan thought about it some more. The drunken woman's body was found four days later three miles down river, almost two and a half miles further downstream from where Mariya's false nephew was recovered. While it was impossible to extrapolate distances and surfacing times based solely on the article, Jonathan now understood that to get anywhere further he'd have to nail down three essential facts: the speed of the current, the relative buoyancy created by the higher water temperature, and

the time of death. If he could estimate these with sufficient confidence, he'd probably be able to tell a general
geographic boundary from where the body fell into the
water. With that, and a bit more luck, he might tie the
location to a particular vessel moored along the river or
sailing through the area. For that, there was only one
source from whom he could get this information, and
he'd call a little later in the morning. In the meantime,
he forced himself to get a couple hours of sleep.

10

THERE WAS NO MISTAKING THE ELECTRIC YELLOW AND drab green exterior of Kelsey's as the morning sun radiated off its façade. The cozy, unassuming Uptown eatery on a quiet stretch of Magazine Street at the corner of Austerlitz was a favorite of Jonathan's, and a short drive south from his house.

He stepped into the restaurant on the ground floor of the two-story building, waving at the chef-owner leaning against the opened kitchen door before being taken aback by the empty tables—bizarre for lunchtime on Saturdays, when visitors usually lined up on the narrow sidewalk waiting for tables to free up. Today, apparently, the fear of Katrina had cleared the place but for a handful of patrons, including a stocky man in his mid-fifties occupying a seat at a table near the farthest window, his back turned to the entrance.

Jonathan walked toward the man. Cramer Banks sat alone, a baseball cap covering his curly grayish hair as he brusquely dredged the last of his turtle soup.

He looked up at Jonathan, who'd just pulled up a chair, and said, "Sorry, couldn't wait. I was hungrier than an African baby."

"*Bon appétit.*"

"What, you fuckin' speak French now?" Cramer's weighty Louisiana drawl always sounded as if he had stones lodged in his throat.

"No, but what's wrong with French?"

"You not turnin' gay on me, are ya?" Cramer brought the bowl to his mouth, slurped it clean and set it down on the worn vinyl table cloth.

Jonathan shook his head. He was immune to Cramer's abrasiveness and his foul mouth—at times filthier than a seasoned prostitute. But what amused Jonathan most was how this devout Evangelical Christian had somehow adapted quite comfortably with the evils of capitalism to build himself a local empire of sorts—the eleventh largest Louisiana-based business, he'd often bragged to Jonathan, though it seemed only Cramer was keeping count. But Southern Seas Logistics was Jonathan's last large client, and Cramer, as its chairman and CEO, was a man to keep happy.

Cramer wiped his face with the paper napkin. "You make me nervous when you do this."

"Do what?"

"Ask to meet me on short notice...like that morning when that fucking loser filed his injunction."

"That loser happened to be the Assistant Attorney General, and we got rid of the injunction, right?"

"Not soon enough." Cramer sat back, sipped his beer and wiped the foam off his lips with another napkin.

"Beer for breakfast?" Jonathan said, sitting down.

"I'm fighting a hangover." Cramer straightened in the seat. "So, why are we here?"

"Don't worry, this has nothing to do with our current case or anything else of yours."

"Then shouldn't you be busting your ass on my case instead? Especially after you canceled our meeting yesterday out of the blue. And aren't they deposing me next week?"

"Yes, I'm sorry...something came up. But are you sticking around for Katrina?"

"Not sure. You?"

"I boarded up my house. Just weighing if I should go."

"So what the fuck are we here for?"

"The gumbo," Jonathan said, glancing over Cramer's shoulder.

"What?"

The waiter had walked up behind Cramer.

"A bowl, and a soda water," Jonathan added and then eyed Cramer, a discomfort creeping into his skin as he mulled over how best to convey his request. "I need a favor but I don't have time now to explain."

His client tilted his head and seemed disappointed.

Jonathan had never dared ask Cramer for favors, not even the minutest of wishes that wasn't strictly connected to any legal matter he'd been hired by Cramer to handle. Never. He'd always treaded lightly, treating the man with the deference and craftiness a lawyer senses is necessary for any large client, and particularly Cramer's company, which lately accounted for over half of Jonathan's monthly billables. On top of that, Jonathan knew of two other local lawyers doing work for Cramer's company and its subsidiaries. One screw-up, and they'd yank the work from Jonathan in a heartbeat.

Cramer finished his beer and eyeballed his watch. "I got things to do, so spit it out."

"I need the names of the ships that were in or near the port on August 19."

"Which port?"

"Here—New Orleans."

"Why?" Cramer grimaced as if his attorney had lost his mind.

"Can I tell you another time?" Jonathan sensed a modest irony. He had just asked his client for a favor—a hugely important one—while withholding most of the critical details, just as Mariya had done with him, it seemed.

"We tap into many databases, but the main one—the official one for the Port of New Orleans—is only for authorized users, and you ain't one."

"I really need this, Cramer. And didn't you develop your own software to track vessels?"

"You better give me a damned good reason."

Jonathan explained what he could without volunteering details that would alarm Cramer into saying no. He described Mariya as an innocent, former client from out of state. He left out Dr. Garceau's concerns and a whole host of other doubts that rumbled in his head. Fortunately for Jonathan, Cramer listened, attentively, with a patience Jonathan had seldom seen in his habitually volatile client.

"Alright, alright," Cramer blurted loudly, interrupting Jonathan's explanation, and then let out a protracted sigh.

"How about now?" Jonathan leaned forward.

"I can't access it or use it myself."

"Got someone who can?"

"Hold on." Cramer picked up his cell phone and scrolled through the numbers. "I want to make sure my guy is there."

There was no telling if or when Cramer would change his mind, and this precariousness gave Jonathan no choice but to press for access now rather than later. He waited impatiently for Cramer to wrap up his call and give him the final answer.

*   *   *

For the first time that morning, Jonathan felt a mild sense of relief. Cramer had relented, and in doing so Jonathan imagined the possibility of tying a named ship to the stiff Asian in the morgue.

Jonathan sat in the passenger side of Cramer's giant Ford pickup as they headed south over the river toward Algiers. A minute after crossing the Crescent City Bridge, they turned onto Charles de Gaulle Drive, a wide avenue with a narrow canal in the median, between the opposing lanes now devoid of traffic. They then turned left onto Rue Parc Fontaine, a short distance from the grounds of Lakewood Golf Club, where Cramer had recently built a grotesquely opulent, six-bedroom home facing the seventh hole.

Cramer pulled into the lot facing a square, three-story, mostly windowless building with an unassuming sign partly covered by shrubbery at the entrance that read "Southern Seas Logistics, Inc."

"You been here before?"

"Once," Jonathan replied, but he'd come only to drop off a document and had not gone beyond the lobby.

"The brains of my business is here."

Cramer unlocked the front doors and led the way into the darkened atrium. When he'd switched the lights on, Jonathan recognized the spacious lobby with high-tech lighting and an L-shaped leather sofa in the waiting area. They reached the second floor by elevator.

"This way," Cramer uttered, walking briskly in between two rows of tall cubicles. When he reached the large, double-wide metal doors at the far end of the windowless floor, he turned back to Jonathan. "This, buddy, is true state-of-the-art." He placed his thumb on the adjacent reader attached to the wall, then keyed in a four-number code, which triggered a buzzing noise.

Both doors opened automatically, exposing a large brightly-lighted room with high ceilings that resembled a Star Wars command center. Eight large flat screen monitors—each displaying annotated maps—covered most of the far wall on two rows. A lanky, Southeast Asian-looking man, wearing jeans and a bright green polo shirt, seated at one of the ten consoles in the center of the room, turned and acknowledged Cramer with a subdued wave of the hand.

"Morning, Prasanth. Come meet one of our lawyers."

The man stood up and approached them.

Cramer patted Jonathan's shoulder. "From here we can monitor our transatlantic, transpacific and gulf freight operations down to the smallest detail," he said proudly.

Jonathan shook hands with Prasanth.

"He's our weekend-shift IT guru," Cramer continued. "This center never sleeps, and it's thanks to him and a couple other brainiacs that our systems are reliable and our customers love us."

Jonathan scanned the rows of computer terminals.

"The servers take up the entire basement of this building and we have servers co-located in two places in the U.S. and one in Canada."

"Redundancies, huh?"

"That's why I'm not too worried about Katrina."

"You're the first person I've talked to this weekend who feels that way."

Cramer turned and pointed at the monitors on the wall. "You see those green and blue blips up there? Each one represents a ship in transit or docked, loading or unloading, all updated every four to eight minutes. It's all secure, managed by our own proprietary software applications. Top of the line stuff—the best in the world, I think. We know the location, heading, cargo and crew for fifty percent of the freighters passing to or from the industrialized world. Our data management services are used by twenty-two of the top fifty shipping companies. My goal is to have them all as customers, but for that to happen, we need to beat three competitors, all of them bigger, just not better."

Jonathan nodded. "Sounds like a lot of legal work."

Cramer chuckled. "You'll get your fair share." He

again pointed at the screens on the wall. "That top screen on the far right covers the lower Mississippi—that is, from Cairo, Illinois all the way down to the Gulf."

Jonathan gazed in amazement at the sophistication of the system. Though he'd seen data centers before at former clients' companies, he'd never witnessed such an extensive one.

"Prasanth, put up the Port of New Orleans traffic on screen seven."

Cramer's employee leaned over a workstation and clicked the mouse a few times. Seconds later the screen showed dozens of blips—presumably ships—on the river from Hahnville to Belle Chasse.

Cramer pulled a chair out, sat down and threw his feet on the console. "That view gives you about a 20-mile stretch of the Mississippi both upstream and downstream from New Orleans."

"I see. That's exactly what I'm looking for," Jonathan said. "Do you have data in real-time only, or can you also pull up records from the past week?"

"We got it all." Cramer grinned and turned to Prasanth. "Show 'im."

*   *   *

Jonathan was back in the passenger seat of Cramer's truck, this time clenching a file folder thickened by over a hundred pages of printouts that Prasanth had put together in the two hours it took to sift through the data and get background information for various freighters that had passed through the port in the relevant timeframe. Jonathan hoped that somewhere in those pages was the answer to the burning question: Which vessel did the mysterious dead Asian likely come from?

Cramer, driving at a high rate of speed with only his palm loosely pawing the steering wheel, glanced at the folder on Jonathan's lap. "What do I get in return?"

It didn't feel like an innocent question.

"I mean, I probably saved you several thousand dollars in research fees." Cramer said.

"My deep gratitude," Jonathan smiled, shrugged.

"How about a deep discount on your hourly rate?"

"What? Any more and I'll have to eat grass."

"Tell you what," Cramer said, slowing the truck and pulling over to the curb. "I got a business venture taking root in Europe, and I could use your help."

"What sort of help?"

"Transactional work. Could be a huge move forward for my business, though it's somewhat complicated."

"And where exactly?" Jonathan said slowly.

"Ukraine."

"Tell me more."

Cramer eyed Jonathan as if he was letting him in on a juicy secret. "For starters, you would be my scout—I'll pay your travel and living expenses, of course. I want you to foster some interest in negotiations. Things are still a bit murky, and they're hard to gauge, but there's money to be made for sure. If we get a green light, you'll help negotiate the deal and charge your regular fees. But if there's no deal, you charge me nothing."

"How long are we talking?"

"A week or two, maybe more."

Jonathan frowned. "Essentially for free, right?" Talking fees with Cramer meant only one thing for Jonathan: losing. Inevitably he often wrote off a large chunk of his billable work to keep Cramer happy. It was one thing to take contingency fees for plaintiff's work in civil litigation, but engaging in speculative work for free that may or may not lead to transactions seemed like a waste of time.

"Look at it this way: if you manage to bring us to the table, then you can charge to your heart's content going forward."

"Why would I be any more successful than you?"

"You have skills I don't have, Jonathan. You have the patience to convince them that doing business with one of the savviest entrepreneurs in the global sea freight business is in their interest. I just want it done."

Jonathan tilted his head. "Would you say yes if you were in my shoes?"

"Depends how much other work you've got cooking. Money don't fall from trees, bud."

Jonathan sure wished it did so he could flatly reject Cramer's offer.

"I'll think about it," the prudent side of him replied, now wanting to get back to the hot topic: the vessel data.

Cramer shrugged. "Saying yes would be a fair way of thanking me for that folder."

Neither men uttered another word about the offer the rest of the way back to Jonathan's car, which was parked near Kelsey's, and the only thing Jonathan had on his mind was parsing through the printouts to narrow down the cargo vessels.

He'd barely walked into his house when he darted for the couch, opened up the folder and started separating the pages by key data points—type of ship, assigned dock, transit points, country of origin, among others. He also spread over the hardwood floor a large map of the city and the river along with screenshots Prasanth had printed of the Port of New Orleans area in three-hour increments, from Wednesday on back to the prior week, showing the position and heading of each vessel, identified by a unique alpha-numeric code. Jonathan sat back into the couch and gazed at the papers scattered across the coffee table and floor and cushions on each side of him, confident that his answer was there, somewhere, buried in the data in front of him.

The critical timeframe was the thirty-six hours before the body was found, given that the estimated time of death was about eighteen hours prior to the body being discovered. Jonathan began jotting down the names of the ships that Prasanth had identified on the printed charts that covered a fifteen-mile stretch of the Mississippi going upstream from the location where the body was found. In addition to the ship traffic data, he'd also gotten from Prasanth the river current information, with estimated variations along different parts of the same stretch of water. He began with the first of the thirty-odd ships on the list, checking each aspect of its course, destination, time in transit, manifest summaries, relative positions to the body at various estimated time intervals. The time passed with ease, his attention focused and a strange excitement pushing him on.

11

"Do you ever answer your damn phone?" Jonathan snapped after Mariya finally picked up. He'd been trying for over an hour, at times dialing back-to-back.

"I didn't feel like talking," she said.

"Meet me now, at the gas station on the corner of Claiborne and Eagle Street."

"But I'm leaving town."

"You're still here, aren't you?"

"Yes, so?"

"You'll want to hear what I have to say."

There was only silence on the other end.

"Shit, Mariya, I've gone to a lot of trouble for you. And now I have the name of the ship that I'm certain the dead guy came from."

"Tell me the name."

"Only when we meet."

"Why do you want to see me?"

Jonathan sighed. "I'm not sure, frankly."

"Do you ever think about me in a nice way?"

"I'll be there in ten minutes. You'd better be there too." Jonathan hung up and shook his head. *Why does she have to be so difficult all the time?*

During the short drive to the gas station, Jonathan recycled everything he'd searched the prior day. From dozens of freighter names and images to location data, dates of arrival and departure, to cargo manifests and maps. His eyes felt tired. He gazed at the sky, but found it hard to believe that a hurricane was barreling down this way. He'd expected a couple days of showers as a prelude, and not the intense blue skies with only scattered dark gray clouds, and with the blazing sun turning this Sunday afternoon into an oven. He pulled into the station's lot and turned the car off, unsure if Mariya would show up.

The Russian troublemaker finally pulled up.

He smiled. She didn't.

Jonathan got out of his car.

She stepped out of hers more hesitantly. She wore a beige sundress with high-heeled sandals, her makeup flawlessly reducing her age by a good ten years.

"Look," Jonathan said as he unfolded a large chart of the Mississippi and spread it over the trunk of his Camry.

Mariya moved gently next to him, placing her keys and cell phone on the far edge of the map.

"Your precious slim-eyed nephew was found here, at the edge of Orleans Parish, at the border with St. Bernard Parish, on the river's left descending bank." He tapped the spot with his pen and marked it with an X.

Mariya briefly checked her cell phone and then turned back to Jonathan.

"The coroner estimated the time of death to be about eleven at night the Thursday before last. The river current was not bad—about three to four knots at that time, although there are dangerous sporadic, localized currents throughout the area. At around that time there were five ships located in the Mississippi between the turn at the tip of Algiers to the spot downstream where the body was found.

"Only five ships?"

"Yeah, in that limited area. There were many more farther upstream, but I don't think they are relevant. If the dead guy was indeed a crewman who fell overboard, it would most likely be from one of the five."

Mariya looked up at Jonathan and said nothing.

"Now, before I tell you any more, I want to know the real reason you came all this way to check on a dead guy? What's so important that you would risk getting caught here?"

"I'm only doing as I'm told. I don't always know the reason, and I don't choose all my assignments, and that's the honest truth."

"Whatever, Mariya." Jonathan said curtly, realizing that he wouldn't get an honest answer out of her. "Anyway, of those, two cargo ships were berthed at the Alabo Street wharf and another not far upstream from there, at the Poland Avenue wharf. Given the current, the relative positions of the wharfs, and the slight southeasterly curve of the river, I think it's unlikely a body falling from any of those berthed vessels would end up where it did. It would have been caught on the banks sooner. There were no major abrasions to the body that would be expected from hitting or scraping along the shoreline, as one would if falling overboard close to a wharf."

Mariya leaned her hips on the trunk of her car, puckered her lips and focused intensely on the map.

"That leaves two ships. One had passed upstream at around ten-forty that night on its way to the Napoleon Street wharf. The vessel is strictly container cargo, operated by a Norwegian-Panamanian company that I'm familiar with, and they simply don't have Asian crewmen. So, again, in my opinion, this ship probably is not the one."

"That leaves one," Jonathan said, tilting his head.

"My theory—and I may be wrong, of course—is that the ship is the *Nixos-Dakar*, which from 6 P.M. on that Thursday to 8:30 A.M. the following day was located in the Quarantine Anchorage, a half-mile stretch off the Algiers riverbank where the Coast Guard requires certain vessels that haven't been pre-cleared for docking to undergo a safety inspection."

Crossing her arms and taking in a long breath, Mariya paced away from the car and gazed at the pavement. "How sure are you that it's the right vessel?"

"Pretty certain. Does the name ring a bell?"

"I've seen that name before, I think...maybe...but I can't recall exactly."

"I've got photographs and other details about the vessel. It appears to have been built in the late 80s or early 90s. It's Liberia-flagged but there's not much information about the owners. Perhaps you can dig up more details with the help of your *special* resources."

Mariya was absorbed in thought, seemingly ignoring Jonathan's presence.

"I think I know." She grabbed her keys off the trunk and darted back to her car.

Jonathan whirled, but she'd already locked her doors. "Where are you going?"

She shook her head as she started the engine.

He pounded on her window. "You can't just leave like this."

She rolled down the glass about an inch and said, "I have to go to Houston for a few days. I don't want to be in Katrina's path anyway. Are you staying?"

"I don't know yet."

"We can talk later."

"Wait." He tried to open her door, but she waved him away, signaled a gesture for a phone call and drove off. He immediately dialed her cell, but she refused to answer.

*   *   *

The weather had turned for sure. Gusts of wind picked up as the sky darkened to an ominous charcoal hue. The branches of the two trees that cast much welcomed shade over the backyard in the steamy summer months now shook violently, a stream of leaves swirling about in the wind, with rain drops the size of marbles battering Jonathan's head as he dashed across the backyard. The bird cage that Linda had nailed on the tree closest to the house had been ripped away, and the plastic patio chairs were flung like toys toward the wooden fence.

To make matters worse, he had more than his home to contend with. Dino had texted him to say he was packed up and heading to Shreveport. His other law partner had been incommunicado since Thursday. This left Jonathan with the burden of dealing with the office. He tried reaching Amber several times but had no luck. He headed indoors to finish securing the house, unfolding a tarp to cover his prized antique chest, the only remaining heirloom—every other family item had been lost in the fire that had engulfed his home and nearly killed his wife almost a decade ago.

He paused, lost in thought, until the beeping of the car horn from the front of the house jolted him back to reality. He left through the kitchen door, the only door he'd not boarded up, and walked through the narrow path alongside the fence to the front yard, where he spotted Amber stepping out of her car.

She waved excitedly.

"You okay?" Jonathan asked, not at all expecting her.

"Fine, I guess."

"You should leave town," he said as he approached her and glanced into her car. She'd tightly crammed bags, hangered clothing and shoes almost to the roof of her car. "Oh, I guess you are."

"Going to Baton Rouge," Amber said, taking out from the passenger side a plastic shopping bag that appeared heavy. "I was worried about you. Didn't you get my voicemail?"

"No." Jonathan felt odd that he'd missed it. "I'd invite you in if..." He turned to his house and pointed at the boarded up windows. "If it were more presentable."

"No worries. I have to run anyway." Amber handed the bag to him. "Things I didn't think you wanted to keep at the office, just in case."

Jonathan peeked inside. She'd put in an old framed picture of him and Linda in the Ozarks and a smaller framed photo of him with his brother when they'd gone kayaking twenty years ago. There were some papers and mail, too.

"Thank you." He was taken aback at her thoughtfulness.

"You know, no one showed up to fix the ceiling, so I packed things away as best I could in case the leak gets worse with the storm."

"I really appreciate it, Amber."

"Sure, but when I was putting away some of your files in the safe, I saw something mortifying." She grimaced and leaned on her car with one hand.

"What happened?"

"A rotten sandwich—I'm guessing a week old! Right there, next to our stack of backup CDs."

Jonathan immediately thought of Dino. He'd done it once before.

"I cleaned it out, but the safe and room still reek."

Jonathan shook his head. "I'm sorry you had to see that." Dino was not only a scoundrel and a cheapskate, but also a slob who often ate food on the run, with bits and pieces falling all over the office space and the stairs. Jonathan felt relieved as he reminded himself that he was leaving the firm in a few months.

"We both know him all too well," Amber said. She then explained a few more things she'd done, like emptying their small fridge and unplugging all the electronic equipment.

Jonathan smiled for the first time that day. Because of her assistance, he wouldn't have to go to the office.

Amber's smile grew. "Admit it, your practice wouldn't survive without me."

Jonathan snorted. "Yes, you're indispensable." He wouldn't further inflate her ego, though it was so true. Amber was the glue that held his dysfunctional firm together.

"Oh, I almost forgot," Amber said, smacking her head with her palm. "A guy came by looking for you. Said he worked for the parish."

Jonathan had no more reason so smile. "Was his name Garceau?"

She scratched her temple. "He didn't say his name.

"What did he look like?"

"Black, late thirties, well dressed. Said he'd call you."

"When did he come by?"

"As I was leaving."

Jonathan was sure it was Garceau, but asked, "Did he say he's with the coroner's office?"

"I don't remember. I was rushing out, and he crossed me at the front door, and he spoke fast."

"Was he alone?"

"Yes." Amber tilted her head and frowned. "What's this about?"

"Nothing, nothing, but what exactly did he want?"

"I'm not sure...something about you providing him additional information or something like that. I was in a hurry, so I barely listened."

Jonathan again began to worry that Garceau may have stumbled onto something else that could further stain Jonathan's credibility. He couldn't think of any other reason Garceau would go out of his way to see him personally at his office, especially on Sunday—and a day when tens of thousands of people were leaving the city.

Amber crossed her arms and seemed to scrutinize Jonathan's expression. "Is there something I should know?"

"No." Jonathan didn't want his office manager to know he was possibly in hot water with the authorities over a false statement. The predicament Mariya had put him in was his alone to solve.

"Are you leaving, too?"

"I'm staying, I think." He really didn't know, but her question had all of a sudden thrown him into seriously contemplating getting the hell out—the first time since Katrina started making headlines. This was his town. His turf. His home. He hadn't seriously thought of bailing before. Not until that moment.

Amber got back into her car.

"Be safe, but don't disappear on me," he said, helping close her door.

She drove off, but her question brewed in his head long after her car had turned the corner two blocks away. Why would he stay? What if it really was the big one—the storm of the century? Besides, home meant something different to him than for most anyone else. Having lost his sizable house to arsonists a decade ago, this smaller, more modest abode in the Garden District, with the emptiness left by Linda's departure, stood mostly as a symbol—perhaps of defiance, or struggle, or victimization—and less as a heartfelt dwelling. His remaining possessions also seemed trivial—nearly nothing had survived the fire. His soul didn't belong here. The dirge of silence in this home had forced him to seek the refuge of longer work days at the office. Even at night, he'd roam the quaint streets, block after block, to tire himself so he could evade the silence, the seclusion, the dead air in this house.

Sitting on his front steps, peering up at the roof ledge above him, and distilling the pros and cons of staying, he convinced himself that hunkering down would be nothing more than bravado, masked by whatever pretext he'd come up with—but bravado nonetheless—and it was not a compelling reason to risk his hide. He stepped back inside and spent the next hours packing. He'd evacuate by morning and head to Houston, which was far enough away to offer sufficient shelter from Katrina, he assumed, and it was where he might find Mariya.

*   *   *

Monday morning had come fast. In a matter of hours the wind had picked up substantially. The power had gone out, the phone lines were down, and he'd lost the signal on his cell.

Jonathan had gone through storms in the Crescent City since childhood, and this was just the norm, but every word from the radio seemed to point to more ominous signs of trouble. As he carried his two suitcases and duffel bag to the back door, he glanced at the spare batteries he'd lined up on the fireplace mantel next to the flashlight. He gazed past the hallway that connected the long, narrow living room to the kitchen. The room stayed dim, illuminated only by the candles he'd lit on the dining table. Some scattered slivers of daylight crept around the plywood nailed to the front windows, but it wasn't much light. Adding to the relentless whooshing sounds of the wind outside, the house creaked and crackled loudly, as if it were about to be ripped from the ground. The walls, the ceiling, the boarded-up windows, the wood floor, everything made noise. A popping sound echoed, followed by a rumbling that ended with a blunt thud on the side of the house. Something else from the yard had come loose.

The man on the radio was Jonathan's only connection to the world outside his cocooned abode. He worried about the tall trees in the backyard and his neighbors' even larger trees. Any one of them could crush his house if the wind picked up further.

The wind and hard rain battered the walls of the house with even more force than a mere hour ago. Every part of the house creaked. He had to leave now.

As he pulled out of his parking spot twenty yards from his house, an NOPD cruiser turned the corner a block away and headed toward him going the wrong direction on the one-way street. The Crown Victoria flashed its headlights twice as it sped straight for Jonathan's car. He slammed on the brakes and the police car screeched to a halt only a foot from his front bumper.

Sergeant Boudreaux sat behind the wheel, and his

somber face told Jonathan this was no social visit. Wearing a rain poncho over his large frame, the sergeant stepped out into the downpour and approached, his eyes narrowing. Jonathan rolled down his window and began hearing Boudreaux's loud voice.

"You making a fool out of me? Why you lying to him?" He was agitated, almost yelling. "I ain't got time to come chasing after you for this shit!" He spoke so hard that spit flew out of his mouth.

Jonathan couldn't get a word in.

"You asked me for a favor, and I did it, but now you pissed me off," Boudreaux ranted, his thick palm pressed on the windshield of Jonathan's car like an octopus. "And I've been calling you all morning, but you couldn't be bothered to answer."

Jonathan shrugged, trying to appear calm. "My cell phone isn't working."

"Yeah, right." Boudreaux pointed his finger at Jonathan's face. "You've got some explaining to do."

"Chill, brother."

"I ain't chilling till you start talkin'. Dead bodies are serious business, and you shouldn't..."

Fortunately, obese men can't yell incessantly for long. In between Boudreaux's winded breaths, Jonathan was able to take a stand.

"I have no clue what you're freaking out about."

The blue-uniformed giant slapped his palm against Jonathan's door. "Garceau called me saying you're full of shit about the corpse, that he doesn't believe you're representing a client, that there's something fishy about how this guy died, and, worse yet, that you falsely identified the body. That's what I'm talking about, and it makes me want to yank you from your seat and beat a truthful answer out of you."

Jonathan's heart was now racing faster than Boudreaux was spitting. The sergeant had turned things upside down, making Jonathan feel like both a victim and co-conspirator of Mariya's actions—no matter the fact that he didn't fully comprehend or control what had happened. He suddenly noticed that a neighbor walking his dog had stopped to observe the commotion.

Boudreaux turned to the woman. "What're you lookin' at? Get going and mind your own bu'ness!"

The neighbor did just that.

"You better have a good reason." Boudreaux said, turning back to Jonathan, his heated face leaning into Jonathan's open window. "Why d'you lie to me, of all people?"

"I didn't!"

"Get out of the car." Boudreaux opened Jonathan's door and pulled him out by his sleeve, his shirt tearing at the shoulder. "I'm taking you to the morgue right now for you to straighten things out."

"But they're closed. Haven't they evacuated?"

"No, Garceau is still there."

12

Stockholm, Sweden

THE AMBIENT BREEZE WHISTLED THROUGH A QUARTER-inch gap of the wood-framed window, venting the smoky air of room 609, a circular room atop the north-facing corner of the Radisson Strand Hotel fitted with rustic furnishings and a poster bed too short for Ron's long legs. He got up, lighting another cigarette before his bare feet touched the floor. He couldn't sleep and had no time to do so even if he tried.

He stepped to the window. At 10:40 P.M., the Blasieholmen section of downtown Stockholm resembled an evacuation zone. Ron stared at the empty sidewalks and glowing lampposts along Nybrokajen and Strandvägen streets that half-encircled the quaint Nybroviken Bay, a watery cul-de-sac connected to the city's more extensive and dispersed harbor. A dozen small white steamships, red and black smokestacks popping up from their roof-tops, were moored along its banks.

Leaning on the deep ledge that resembled more a slit in a castle wall, his cigarette stuck to his dry bottom

lip, he stared emptily at the floodlit façade of the Royal
Dramatic Theatre that bordered Bezerlii Park some two
hundred yards away. He elbowed the ashtray to one side,
next to a pair of binoculars, a cell phone, a walkie-talkie,
and his holstered Glock.

Ron inhaled the tobacco deep into his lungs and
counted the hours since he'd last gotten sleep after
leaving Arlington. The overnight flight, the incessant
worries over George Porter's mischief, and Sal's mysterious disappearance—all had left him sleep-starved and
edgy, despite having been upgraded to first and downing
enough scotch to kill a horse.

He'd arrived half-sober in the Swedish capital a few
hours earlier, after a stopover in Dublin, where he'd
circled the neighborhoods around Shannon Airport for
three hours in a bullet-proof SUV with the head of the
CIA's Clandestine Services for Europe to brief him on
what was planned in Stockholm, but mostly to get his
blessing on something Ron wanted: to put in charge of
the operation a man by the name of Tod Pendergast,
despite Glen's earlier disapproval.

Room 609 had been handpicked by Tod, the CIA
chief of station in Stockholm, the minute news broke
from Langley that the target, with his accompanying
delegation, had booked rooms at this hotel. With its
near-180 degree views, stretching from the west side of
Bezerlii Park to the waterway entrance into the small
bay, Ron could not have agreed more with the choice
of room. It would serve as a control tower of sorts if
the mission got the final green light. But the strategic
vantage would do nothing to quell his concerns. The

mission was flawed from the get-go, but not a damned soul at the Agency saw things his way.

Ron's phone buzzed. It was the umpteenth text he'd received in the past hour from the team, some of whom were in other rooms, some at the embassy's secured basement a mile away, and at least one other in a van parked near the theatre. He hadn't met them all, but most had been chosen by Tod, who had a good track record for assembling the right people.

"We're a go in thirty minutes. Are you coming?" It came from Tod himself.

"On my way," Ron texted back, and then clipped his holstered weapon to his belt, threw on his boots and flannel jacket and shoved the phone and radio into the pockets.

Tod was waiting for Ron in two adjoining rooms one floor down. A tray with remnants of sandwiches and fries scattered over several plates, empty coffee mugs and bags of potato chips, Perrier water bottles and four Coke Light cans lay by the door.

Ron was a bit surprised and shook his head. Other than hanging a banner on the door, there were few more obvious ways to advertise to hotel guests and staff that the room was occupied either for an orgy or a surveillance stakeout.

Ron knocked twice before being greeted by Tod. His dark brown mop of hair had turned almost entirely gray and he was chubbier than the last time Ron had worked with him back in the months following the 9/11 attacks.

Tod had spent his life orchestrating tricky operations, including a dozen defections in West Germany, Greece,

Spain and Belgium. The fact that he'd held a bureaucratic post in the Swedish capital the last three years hadn't reduced Ron's confidence.

"We're all set," Tod said, grinning, his hands at his waist. He closed the door behind Ron. "Come in and meet the family."

The sound of Tod's overconfidence echoed uncomfortably in Ron's head as he followed the man into the room past the open doors connecting the adjoining guestroom, where two tall, large-framed fellows, both in their mid-thirties, stood sorting through an assortment of surveillance equipment they'd scattered over their beds.

"That's Terry—from Iowa—and Brett—from North Dakota," Tod said.

Ron acknowledged them with a nod.

Tod turned and pointed to a younger, part-Asian man with rectangular glasses seated at the credenza behind him. "This is Jack at the controls—we borrowed him from ops in Seoul."

Jack briefly unglued his eyes from the laptop's screen and nodded.

"Do you speak Korean?" Ron asked, since he couldn't imagine that anyone else here did.

"He sure does," Tod interjected.

"Before I forget, the letter please."

Tod dug through his hard-framed Samsonite briefcase and pulled out a large manila envelope. "Our little Commie gave us this a few hours ago, but Jack didn't have time to translate more than the first two pages. I've sent a scan off to Langley, so we should have a translation sometime tomorrow."

"Uh-huh." Ron was unhappy that Jack and Tod had seen the contents of the would-be defector's letter, but he'd forgotten to tell them earlier to keep it sealed. Whatever the target had to share was for Ron's North Korea desk eyes only. Moreover, Ron had no clue what the vice-admiral had offered to share, and if any of it was even truthful, or if it had been done without raising suspicion from others in the delegation.

Perhaps reading Ron's mood, Tod added, "All went fine. He left it in an opened seam inside one of the curtains, just like we'd instructed him. We picked it up when they were out for dinner, and we did a second sweep of his room—all clean."

Ron was eager to know what Ri Ju-song had written, but he'd have to contend with only two pages in English for now. What concerned him most was that he didn't know Jack or the rest of Tod's motley crew, but neither did Tod, it seemed. They'd come from the States, some contractors, one or two borrowed from Department of Homeland Security, two from NSA, and the rest Agency—Clandestine Services, mostly. Eleven men in all. Whatever the letter said, the content had to remain secret until it had been thoroughly examined by Ron's team back in Langley. Tod should have assumed that. But it was Ron who'd placed Tod in charge, knowing full well that it contravened protocol. Chiefs-of-station rarely got their hands dirty in such operations, let alone directed one.

Ron had picked Tod because he'd seen his diligent work firsthand years ago, but also because he needed someone he could control well enough. But more importantly, he'd set up Tod to share the fallout if things went to shit. It would dilute Ron's role—and ideally, provide sufficient protection—though he conceded that his mere presence in the team still made him vulnerable. Tod, for his part, appeared too happy to take on the task, apparently either excited that something big was finally happening in sleepy Stockholm, or unaware of the risks—risks Ron had reiterated for months to George Porter and Glen Sanders, but not fully to Tod, in part because of the short timing.

Tod's confident air, rather than reassuring Ron, made him more anxious. There was nothing certain worth clinging to. Eleven guys had assembled in Sweden to enable the defection of a man with one of the smallest files in CIA archives. An unknown figure but for his rank, some loosely-vetted hearsay, a few clandestine exchanges with dubious proxies, and a few transcribed phone calls with a family member who'd now gone missing. It was an unusually weak collection of information for a man who'd risen rather fast through the ranks to reach the prestigious position of Vice-Admiral in the North Korean navy.

Tod smiled, motioning to Ron as he pressed his palm on Jack's shoulder. "Let the games begin."

Jack moved his mouse, and the monitor awakened from standby. His screen appeared divided into four equal parts, all black and white imagery, one bright, the other three dark and grainy—probably night vision footage.

"What is this?" Ron asked.

"Surveillance cameras we installed in each of their rooms," Tod said. "Nicely done, huh?"

Ron approached, his arms crossed, consciously camouflaging any hint of skepticism. "Don't tell me, in the ventilation ducts, right?"

Tod ignored the sarcasm. "Yes."

"Is that Ri Ju-song?"

"Yep."

Ron leaned over Jack's shoulder, measuring the live image of the prized target lying on his side on one of the beds, a reading light on the headboard turned on but pointed away from him.

"His room's almost right below us," Jack said, and then tapped the adjacent image with this index finger. "In the next room is his personal security—one guy, we believe unarmed. The rooms don't connect."

Ron leaned in. "Looks like the bodyguard's not in the room."

"He is! Right there, sitting up in bed," Jack replied, clicking his mouse to expand the window to a full screen. "See? His eyes are wide open." The infrared camera yielded only a grainy image, the man's upper body barely distinguishable in front of the headboard, but his eyes appeared open, staring into the darkness.

"Yeah." Ron knew exactly what was going on in that room.

"He's just staring blankly—kinda creepy, huh?"

"No, he's listening."

"To music?"

"To his neighbor," Ron said softly. "It's what they do best—spy on each other." Though he never bragged openly about his experience, he knew more about the North Korea's reclusive regime and their diplomats and military personnel than anyone in the Agency and perhaps more than anybody in the intelligence services worldwide. So it was no surprise to see this security member of Ri Ju-song's delegation fully awake, ready to catch anything suspicious in the room next door.

"He went into the hallway at least three times in the last hour," Jack said. "All that listening."

Ron sighed. "Yeah, but if all goes well with our plan, in a few days this guard's wife and kids will be summarily executed; his grandparents—if they're still living—will be hauled off to a prison camp to work on pig farms, where they'll likely starve to death or die from exposure by mid-winter; his apartment will be confiscated; his personal effects will be sifted through and burned; and the moment he lands back in Pyongyang, he'll be whisked off to an interrogation room for several weeks of torture before being killed by a firing squad. That's what's going to happen to this guy when his dear vice-admiral comes over to our side."

"Damn," Jack whispered as he glanced up at Ron, his brow edging high above the frame of his glasses.

"What about Ri Ju-song's family?" Tod then asked.

"That's for a later conversation," Ron said. He didn't want to share what he knew with the whole room. Ri Ju-song had let it be known through an intermediary that his wife was terminally ill and had returned to her birthplace of Sonbong, a coastal town near North Korea's border with Russia, but Ron had not been able to corroborate the claim. Getting information about anyone in the totalitarian nation entailed insurmountable danger for the few local CIA informants working within its borders, and dispatching one of them to a small town to track down a frail elderly woman was simply too risky.

Not having verified Ri Ju-song's claim was yet another red flag in a long list of concerns that gave Ron pause. He was convinced things were fishy. The North Korean Ministry of Foreign Affairs was one of the most vetted bureaucracies in the regime, with no diplomat or military official given the right to travel abroad without leaving behind something the regime could use as collateral, and ultimately create sufficient disincentive to defect. For the regime to allow Ri Ju-song to leave seemed bizarre if his wife was indeed terminally ill, no matter his high rank and the influence he apparently prided himself on having in the Korean People's Army. Ron's suspicions had grown louder a few weeks ago, when he'd learned that Ri Ju-song's son began studies at a university in Beijing. That left the vice-admiral with no immediate family back home. But his warnings to Porter and Glen back in Langley had fallen flat. That the guard would lose his family in an instant, while Ri Ju-song might get away free and clear just didn't pass the sniff test.

He eyed the first screen again and pointed at Ri Ju-song. "His light's on, but he looks asleep."

"He was in the john twenty minutes ago," Jack said.

"Well, now, he looks asleep. And he'd better damn well wake up on time, right?"

"Relax," said Tod, pulling his sleeves back with a calmness that further irked Ron. "He's got eighteen minutes."

"Hopefully he's not using the alarm clock to wake up."

Jack and Tod turned to Ron and then eyed each other. *Had they not considered it?* Ron thought, clenching his fists. "Guys, if the alarm rings, his security's gonna hear it and wonder what the hell the fella he's been told to watch like a hawk is doing waking up at midnight."

"Ron, Ron, Ron...definitely, no more caffeine for you," Tod said, reaching for a can of Red Bull from the mini-bar. "Take it easy, we've got this covered."

Ron took off his jacket. For a split-second he questioned if maybe he was unreasonably paranoid about all he'd seen so far. He stretched over Jack's shoulder to study the images on the monitor once more and asked, "Who's in the other rooms?"

Tod cut in before Jack could answer. "A mid-level diplomat from their U.N. Mission in Geneva," he said. "And the fourth guy is Pak Jong-ryul, a close aide—"

"I know who he is." Ron rubbed his watery eyes. His hands felt heavy, puffy. "I've been following Pak's career closely the last couple years, but haven't quite figured out what he really does. He's tight with the Russian clan."

"Russian clan?" Tod asked.

"A fringe group of military and political figures within Kim Jong-il's inner circle. They favor reviving deeper ties with Russia rather than growing more dependent on China. Pak is in that mix, but we just haven't figured out how he exerts his influence. He's usually in the shadows, barely seen in Pyongyang, and that's why it's puzzling to see him here in the West.

The two farm boys in the adjoining room came around and stood behind Tod to witness the on-screen uneventfulness.

Ron hesitated to ask more questions. The more he was told, it seemed, the more he feared things would go awry. "And what about Ri Ju-song's phone? Are you sure he can get to it, and that no one found it?"

"God." Tod inflated his chest and quickly set down his can of Red Bull on the credenza. It was as if Ron had called him a bad name. "It's secure! We strapped it to the back of a drawer in the bathroom."

How original, Ron thought, having expected a bit more creativity from Tod. "I don't like it."

"His security didn't find it, so what's the worry?" Tod grabbed one end of the laptop's flip-screen. "Do these folks look like they've got something up their sleeves? Look at 'em. They're clueless. Ri Ju-song's comin' over, and there isn't a damn thing they can do about it."

"You're talking as though it's a done deal." Ron glanced at Tod's colleagues. "It ain't done till we have him in the Gulfstream and it takes off." Ron had summoned the civilian-registered jet—the same one he'd sat in during an extraordinary rendition in Indonesia—to land early morning at Bromma, the smaller of Stockholm's two main airports, because of its proximity to downtown and the less onerous security, customs and immigration procedures. Ron knew that getting the North Korean vice-admiral out as quickly as possible was the best way to avoid any diplomatic fallout with the Swedish authorities.

"If you'd been here the last few days, you'd have seen how much effort we've put into this," Tod said, smirking. "Nothing will go wrong. We did a full sweep of his room when they were all gone earlier today. No bugs. Nothing. Everything will be fine."

Ron had heard that last phrase before, on countless occasions, over the years, and what it really meant was this: there's a real chance something will get fucked up but I'm going to bury my head in the sand and hope it goes well, and if it doesn't, I'll hope to still have my job by morning. This was disconcerting, especially since Ron had picked Tod, whom he'd thought—perhaps wrongly—was up to the task.

Tod pulled up a chair next to Jack and nursed his Red Bull.

As Ron pulled out his pack of Marlboro Reds, Tod craned his neck forward and blurted in mid-sip, "There's no smoking here."

It wasn't worth fighting over. Ron returned the pack to his jacket and mumbled, "The second-hand smoke is the least of your worries."

Tod revved his lungs. "Ron, all's going to be fine."

"I'll be back in a bit." Ron needed some air. He headed to the door, and during his short ride down to the hotel lobby, he recalled his conversation with Tod on the drive in from the airport. He'd asked about the preparations. The low profile of the team. The logistics. He'd queried about the precautions Tod had taken to avoid being spotted by the *Säpo*, the Swedish government's security services, whose agents were already keeping tabs on the North Korean delegation from a car parked along Nybrokajen. Ron had asked many questions, but few of Tod's answers had satisfied him. He now wondered if transferring responsibility for the operation to this man may have been imprudent given the inherent risks he'd advertised up and down the chain of command—and for that matter, putting Tod in charge, he thought, may now outweigh any benefits of shielding himself from a potential fallout. He pondered the issue some more and finally came to only one conclusion: he could not let the defection fail and put his entire career at risk. It had to be done right.

13

AT 11:28 P.M., RON OBSERVED THE PUDGY, BLACK-HAIRED vice-admiral pop his head up from the pillow and check his wristwatch. The North Korean turned off his reading light, but the grainy image plastered onto Jack's laptop screen showed him wide awake, standing in striped pajamas with cuffed sleeves and an oversized collar—the kind Ron's dad used to wear. He appeared careful not to make any noise. Even the way he walked seemed to minimize any sounds from the hardwood floor.

Ron and the others stared intently at the monitor as Ri Ju-song passed below the camera and disappeared from view, presumably headed to the bathroom to use the phone Tod's team had planted for him.

"Perfect!" Tod's loud whisper shattered the silence. "He's going in the bathroom and turning on the faucet." None of this was within view of the surveillance camera.

Tod quickly reached into his briefcase and pulled out a cell phone. "He's going to dial this any second." He checked that it was on and placed it on the credenza's glass surface, next to Jack's laptop.

Ron sat down at the foot of the closest bed, staring at the monitor. "Do you know he doesn't even have a cell phone back home?"

Tod shook his head, arching backwards onto his chair until only two of its legs kept him up. "It's 2005 for Christ's sake, are you telling me they don't have cell phones there?"

"Yep. Only a few hundred people have one—with only limited coverage within the capital—and Ri Ju-song ain't one of them."

Tod swung his chair back down. "You're kidding."

"I'm serious, I don't think the guy's ever used a cell phone in his life. Landline phones, of course. But a cell, not that we know of. So, I hope you guys didn't make it too hard for him." Ron now chided himself for not asking Tod about this earlier.

"There's only one number stored on it, and he just has to follow the printed instructions to enter a code—his son's birth year—and press the express-dial function. Simple. Any North Korean can use it. It's not nuclear physics."

"Actually, they're quite good at that, but not at using cell phones."

Ron secretly pictured a bumbling Ri Ju-song, sitting on the toilet, his pants down to his ankles, holding the device with the dexterity of a caveman and dumbfounded at how to flip it open.

It was 11:34 P.M., four minutes past the time the team had expected Tod's cell to ring.

For the first time, Tod looked worried. He sprang to his feet. "What time d'you have?" he asked Jack, who gave him the same time everybody else had. He then turned to Ron and with a harsher tone asked, "Are you serious? He can't use a cell phone?"

"I don't know for sure, but I'm telling you he's never owned one. My folks track all their communications. I'm assuming you left instructions in Korean, right? Or need I remind you, he doesn't read English?"

"No need for spite, Ron. We gave the instructions in Korean."

"Can we call him instead?" Jack suggested.

"Only if you set it on vibrate. If the guard next door hears a ring tone, it's *over*."

Tod frowned. "I don't know what the big deal is about that security guy." He was trying to pace about his small corner of the room but there wasn't much space between the furniture and the giant men from the cornfields. "If he finds out, who the hell cares? He's unarmed, and Terry can take him down in a second."

Ron couldn't believe what he was hearing. He too got up, threw his jacket on, began heading for the door, and said, "I told you from the beginning, Tod, we're not kidnapping the guy. Ri Ju-song may not defect. I hope he does, but he may not. We're not entirely sure he's not setting us up for something. Or maybe he's for real but still on the fence about defecting, and I can tell you, no one in any of our agencies, no one at State, and no one on Pennsylvania Avenue has the balls to kidnap a North Korean vice-admiral or have an open confrontation with his delegation. Either he sneaks away quietly, with no trace of our contribution, or nothing goes down. That's the rule, and I thought we were on the same page."

"We are," Tod barked, "but my point is that in case things get prickly, we can still get him—somewhat cleanly."

"Jesus! The answer is *no*. It's either clean or nothing happens at all. And the fact that he's not calling tells me just about everything I need to know." Ron now realized this was an opportunity to get his paws off this entire mission. And it seemed convenient to have Tod circumvent the rules at his own behest or to have Ri Ju-song change his mind and continue his career in the service of his beloved Communist wonderland.

Suddenly the cell phone on the credenza rang, and everyone turned.

Tod grabbed it fast, flipped it open and handed it to Jack, but it slipped from his hand and fell below the desk. Tod dove for the phone but tripped over his own feet and bumped into Jack's chair, yanking the laptop's power cord and flinging the device off the desk and into Jack's lap, with the battery falling to the floor. The screen immediately went black.

"Shit!" Tod blurted, just as Jack grasped the cell phone and answered in Korean.

If Ron's career weren't on the line, perhaps he would have laughed. Instead, a voice inside his head tempted him to pull out his Glock and take Tod out before anything else would go wrong—a worthy use of the 25-cent bullets in his magazine. Ron's confidence in Tod was now worn to the bone.

"We need the images back," Ron barked. "Quickly! And make sure the guard is still in his room."

Jack listened and then spoke his native tongue, stepping back to let the farm boys reposition the laptop and reactivate the imagery. His face grew serious as he pulled a notepad from the desk drawer.

"Hurry," Ron said.

Jack took notes on a pad, and every few seconds Tod crowded over it to read.

"Do you have anyone on his floor?" Ron whispered.

"No," Tod replied. "Only in the lobby."

Jack continued to communicate with the vice-admiral and wrote some more on the pad.

Ron approached and began reading Jack's notes over his shoulder as the computer reawakened and the images of the rooms came back online.

Suddenly Tod pointed at the screen. "Dammit, he's not there."

The guard, who moments ago was resting wide-eyed up against the headboard with the lights off, was gone, no longer in view of the camera, though the room was still dark.

"Tell Ri Ju-song to stop talking and hang up if he hears anything at his door," Ron said to Jack. "Terry, go down to his floor. If you see the guard in the hallway or anywhere out of his room, take cover and pull the fire alarm."

Tod turned to Ron. "What?"

Ron patted Terry's beefy shoulder. "Go now. If you have to pull the alarm, leave the hotel immediately after that and wait for us outside."

"What if I don't see the guard?" Terry asked.

"Then call us."

"Why?" Tod asked, as if Ron had lost his mind.

Ron swung his head in Tod's direction. "We need to keep the guard out of Ri Ju-song's room. The alarm will distract everyone, and hopefully save our man."

"He's asking what's going on," Jack said, holding the cell phone in the air with his hand blocking the mouthpiece.

"How many key cards was Ri Ju-song issued for his room?" Ron asked.

Tod looked at his colleagues. "Anyone?"

"Probably two," Ron said when no one answered. "That's quite common with some delegations—the security detail gets a spare key card for every delegate's room. And if that's the case, he could just walk into our guy's room any second."

Tod rubbed his jaw hard. "Maybe he's got the dead-bolt or chain locked."

Terry hurried out of the room.

"So what should I tell him?" Jack asked Ron, his face straining.

Ron grabbed the notepad and quickly finished reading Jack's notes. "Tell him we're confirmed for tomorrow and also that a fire alarm may go off momentarily but not to worry. Have him join his group and stay calm. It's just a precautionary move."

Tod chimed in. "Get a clear 'yes' from him about tomorrow, in the restaurant, as planned."

Jack spoke and a moment later nodded. "He's good with it. At about two in the afternoon." He hung up.

"Hurray, mother of God," Tod said, wiping beaded sweat off his brow with his palm. "He'll need to separate from his group at the restaurant, go to the men's bathroom, and we'll take care of it from there."

"That's still many hours from now," Ron said. "We all need to stay focused."

A high-pitched siren suddenly pierced the stillness of the floor. Terry must have pulled the fire alarm.

Tod looked at Ron. "Do we stay?"

"Yes, stay with Jack, but hide the gear in case they check on the rooms," Ron said, trying to stem his own worries over whether the operation had just failed. Perhaps the guard had overheard Ri Ju-song using the cell phone. Maybe Ri Ju-song now lay in his room stabbed or strangled. Perhaps a diplomatic catastrophe had already been unleashed and he and Tod stood only hours away from being fired. His worry was only overshadowed by his anger. An anger fueled by Tod's apparent missteps. And further flamed by Ron's own waffling decision to put Tod in charge. And by his disdain of George Porter for having sent him here in the first place. And all the loose ends he'd now had on his plate following Sal's disappearance. Ron's world was imploding. Nothing seemed in control. Not even his heart rate, his breathing.

Ron had raced to the stairwell past several anxious hotel guests, some in robes and others haphazardly dressed in whatever they could throw on. He needed to find Ri Ju-song. As he joined the throng of half-awake guests descending the dimly lighted stairs, he caught sight of four Asian men in pajama-style garments—one of them holding an attaché case tightly under his arm.

North Korean male fashion is best known by the attire of its fearless leaders, in particular the oft-seen olive green suit that is nothing more than an overall style zippered tunic that is as unglamorous as the uniform worn by prison inmates. But Ron's expertise on all things related to North Korea gave him an edge even in the rather mundane field of clothing. The Stalinist nation produced cotton pajamas in no more than three different patterns and two pastel colors, with only insubstantial variations in couture any given year. As they reached the ground floor, with better lighting, Ron gazed at the pajamas again and noticed that one of the North Koreans was wearing something different. It was high-end silk, Italian designed, expensive for sure. A garment like that would be impossible to find in Pyongyang, and in any event would cost hundreds of dollars. It didn't make sense that the man wearing it wasn't Vice-Admiral Ri Ju-song, but rather Pak Jong-ryul.

He followed them discreetly from a safe distance, remembering that he'd been warned a year ago that his own identity was most likely known by Chinese intelligence services, who may have passed it on to their North Korean counterparts. He stayed behind the crowd that had gathered in the lobby.

The two-strong Swedish staff ushering people toward the door, their soft voices inaudible over the wailing alarm, suddenly appeared confused. Three British male guests, apparently intoxicated, began arguing with them, insisting that they shouldn't be made to go outside since there were no visible flames or smoke. Another Swede joined his beleaguered colleagues but seemed unable to get a word in. The Swedish threesome at the door were overcome with excessive politeness—surely borne out of their orderly neutrality that was wholly unfamiliar with the behavior of Britain's belligerent blue-collar ambassadors—and rendered them utterly ineffective in dealing with them. Consequently, the agitated crowd of guests froze, waiting for the loud standoff to end so that they would either stay inside or be taken onto the street. *Thank goodness it's not a real fire*, Ron thought, shaking his head. The staff would have asphyxiated or burned from courtesy and caused everyone else to perish.

Ron headed outside and observed the crowd from across the street, on the sidewalk at the water's edge. The commotion had finally quieted when the drunken Brits walked out of the hotel, cursing, as they passed the North Koreans huddled near some parked cars facing the hotel, behind two fire trucks that had just pulled up.

Within a half-hour, the firemen had given the all-clear without having ventured far into the building. The guests returned to their rooms. Ri Ju-song went back to sleep, and his guard resumed his vigilant pose in the adjacent room.

Ron's operation had regained a strange semblance of normalcy, but things were a bit different. Now he suspected that Pak Jong-ryul was probably the cause of Ri Ju-song's fear and hesitation. It was a surprise that didn't add up, and it would bug him for hours.

14

DAYLIGHT HAD LONG CREPT OVER STOCKHOLM BY THE time Ron glanced at the 5:30 A.M. time glowing in red, though that was to be expected this far north of the equator in late summer. A sliver of light between the room's curtains had aggravated Ron's sleeplessness enough to make him get up after only two hours of deep sleep— wholly insufficient to ensure his best performance on this challenging day. He imagined for a moment the praises he'd receive from Sanders if Ri Ju-song defected as planned. The CIA might learn more than it ever had about North Korea's nuclear weapons programs or their proliferation networks, or even their ability to arm ships and submarines with nuclear devices and other unconventional weapons. There was a nearly endless potential windfall, if it was real, and if it worked. But Ron was swimming in doubt—about the mission in general, the team, Tod's leadership and the other members of the North Korean delegation—Pak Jong-ryul in particular.

From his high-rise vantage, he squinted, his tired eyes struggling with the dawn and studying everything, from the boats that began unloading early-rising passengers from their commutes across the city's serpentine waterways to the pedestrians, their purposeful postures and seriousness visible from afar, all beginning their work day with little fanfare, no noticeable conversations and drone-like duty. *How Swedish.*

An hour later the phone buzzed. He extinguished his cigarette in the ashtray, where rested the dozen butts from a long night of insomnia.

"All good," read the text message from Tod. "RJS+3 at table. Eating. Yawns. No prob so far." Ron was relieved.

"Don't let RJS out of ur sight," Ron replied. The operation's most crucial phase was about to start in earnest, a sequence of events that Tod had shared with Ron before the two went their separate ways a few hours earlier. Ron went to the window, and cracked it open.

A knock at the door broke Ron's meticulous observation of the nearby park. He opened it to find Terry with two large, hard side suitcases in hand. The linebacker-sized operative quickly beelined for the raw oak desk in the corner of Ron's room.

Terry set the luggage flat on the floor, opened it and began removing and assembling an array of communications gear: two large radio sets, bundles of wires, a laptop—larger than the one Jack had used the prior night—a military-style handset, a bulky headset and more wires. He plugged the power cables into the outlet but also connected an oversized battery pack similar to a car battery, as backup, which he hooked up to the laptop and radios. By the time Ron had chain-smoked three more cigarettes, the farm boy was done and seated at the desk with a headset around his neck. Everything appeared ready.

"What's that one for?" Ron asked, eyeing a second headset.

"For Jack, to listen in on phone conversations, in case Ri Ju-song or his colleagues make or receive calls. We're going to track it from here now, but the signal will be fed through the embassy. He should be here shortly."

Ron picked up his radio with one hand and the binoculars with the other. "This is SIERRA, are we all on?" Tod had asked Ron to be the key spotter for the crew, given the unobstructed, panoramic view from his hotel room.

"PAPA here. Loud and clear."

A quick glance through the binoculars confirmed that Brett, the other farm boy, was indeed where he ought to be—on a bench at the south end of Bezerlii Park, wearing body armor, concealing an Uzi, a pistol and at least two stun grenades under his light trench coat. Ron had admonished Tod for arming Brett for the apocalypse. Violence was to be avoided at all costs and being so heavily weaponized only heightened the chance of a miscalculation. Despite Ron's insistence, Tod had flatly refused to go light on weaponry.

"LIMA is on, too. All good."

Ron focused his sights on this spotter wearing a blue cap, who was leaning against the fence facing a narrow footpath that cut between the western edge of the park and the entrance to Berns restaurant. Ron hadn't met him and hadn't asked if he too was packing an arsenal, but it was this tall, fairly gangly operative who'd been tasked with extracting Ri Ju-song through a window in the restaurant bathroom when it came time. *Hopefully, Ri Ju-song's waistline is narrower than the window*, Ron mused.

"BRAVO, check," radioed another guy on the team that Ron hadn't met. He was carrying a yellow shopping bag somewhere in Norrmalmstorg Square, on the other side of the park and out of Ron's field of view.

"OSCAR here, all set as well."

Ron leaned forward and the other spotter, wearing a red cardigan and standing next to a ferry ticket booth. He was tasked with trailing the delegation the moment they exited the hotel, and in such a manner as not to attract the attention of the *Säpo* agents—code-named "roosters"—who would no doubt follow on foot as well.

Ron yawned and rubbed his watery eyes. He secretly wished the whole operation would be aborted. First, to get him off the hook in this risky endeavor. Second, to return to bed.

"Anyone else?" Ron asked.

The channel remained quiet.

"How are the roosters?" Ron then said.

"They're still in the car."

An entire minute passed before Tod finally signaled his indispensable presence. "Yep, TANGO here, with the others."

The binoculars were powerful enough to give Ron a visual of Tod shoving an oversized pastry into his mouth as he climbed into the back of a windowless van parked facing the theatre. The sight of Tod instantly annoyed him.

Ron felt an urge to take charge and lock Tod in a basement somewhere until everything was done, and he'd almost done so the prior night. But Tod's quasi-leading role seemed to still benefit him in case things were to fall apart, and that still made sense since nothing he saw the night before had eased his fears. *He must still be on the fence*, Ron thought of Ri Ju-song, *a mere breath from walking away*; no matter that the vice-admiral had committed to defecting the night before on the phone. Ron again checked his radio, all the while reminding himself of the alternate risk: What if Ri Ju-song had fabricated the revelations in the letter? What if he'd just played into the hands of an all-too-eager cadre of veteran sleuths in Langley who'd gush all over a few pages of astounding, game-changing revelations, only to discover much later that it was all make-believe. This too would soil Ron's career. He'd long learned that in this business there were rarely extraordinary finds, and when one surfaced, it was likely a sophisticated ruse that often wasted precious time and resources before being unraveled. He checked his watch and forced himself not to second-guess his earlier decision. Tod would stay in command, come what may.

*   *   *

"They're moving," a voice came in on the radio.

Ron was now sharing his room with Terry and Jack, both glued to the communications gear on the credenza.

The digital clock just changed to 12:36 P.M.

"Anything?" Ron asked Jack, who was listening in on only one earphone of his headset.

Jack shook his head. "Pak Jong-ryul's the only one with a cell phone. He only got one call, and it was brief and cryptic. We shouldn't expect much else."

Terry, on the other hand, had the more important gear that connected Ron's room to an operations team—including a CIA lawyer—at Langley and to the extraction team flying into Bromma Airport.

"Anything on your end, Terry?"

Jack tapped his colleague on the shoulder, since Terry didn't hear past his large headset. He pulled them off momentarily. "The jet's over Oslo now, will land shortly, and Team Blue's moved to the standby area."

"Team Blue?"

"Yes, you mean...Tod didn't mention—"

"No, he didn't." Ron grabbed the handset from Jack's hand. "TANGO, what's Team Blue?"

Tod didn't answer right away. "Let's talk off-line."

Ron didn't want more surprises. He picked up his cell phone and dialed, punching each number with almost enough force to break the keypad.

"Yeah," Tod answered.

"What is it?"

"Your buddy George wanted to have a plan B."

Ron began calculating why George Porter would do anything behind his back, and most of all using Tod. "What did he arrange?"

"It's just a little muscle if we need it."

"Tod, I want specifics."

"A full extraction team, mostly ex-Blackwater folks, with solid Iraq war zone experience, contractors—all clean, no ties to us whatsoever."

"Nationalities?"

"I don't remember exactly."

"How big?"

"Eight."

"This is nuts," Ron said and hung up.

Knowing George Porter's cautious nature, Ron suspected this was more Tod's doing, probably to ensure that the defection happened, regardless of whether Ri Ju-song made the move or not. At least that's what Tod's thinking might be, Ron surmised—that a defection at all costs would somehow help Tod's career over no defection at all. Ron nervously rubbed his face, wishing only that this was a nightmare that would vanish upon awakening. But it wasn't. Bringing in a bulldozer to perform surgery was completely contrary to what Ron had planned for this operation. "Quiet and under the radar," he remembered the Agency's European chief of Clandestine Services insisting during his stopover in Dublin. Team Blue sounded more like a SWAT team. Tod was now the most dangerous loose end in the operation. If anyone ought to defect it was Tod.

Ron dialed Tod again. "Don't you dare pull that trigger. We're not having a shootout in downtown Stockholm, is that clear?"

"It's not your call anymore, Ron. I didn't tell you precisely to avoid this debate. Someone above us— above Porter too—asked for this. This is from high up. I only put the guys together, I didn't give the order. And it ain't me who's going to unleash them." He hung up.

Who, then? We're the only ones here on the ground. Ron could not image Porter or anyone else thousands of miles away sending in that team. Ron was now certain Tod had set this up, and he was tempted to call Porter that very instant. But he didn't. Porter was not to be trusted either. *Watch your back*, Ron reminded himself.

A cold chill had rapidly descended Ron's spine, strangely killing his urge to smoke the latest stress away. Perhaps, he worried, Porter had set them both up for failure. The thought of Americans lighting up heavy weapons on the busy pedestrian streets of the capital of a friendly democracy could not be more insane.

Ron returned to the window and checked his watch.

Ri Ju-song had given only a rough plan of what he'd do in the morning after breakfast, though he confirmed for sure that by 11:30 A.M. the delegation would walk to Norrmalmstorg Square, do a bit of shopping at an electronics store and then they'd head back to lunch at Berns, adjacent to the park. The delegation had this day off before the two-day UN-sponsored conference on the Law of the Sea was set to begin the following morning. Tod had placed the men in such a way that Ri Ju-song and his entourage would at all times stay within sight of at least one member of the team.

"Guys, they're in the lobby," a voice came in.

"One rooster exiting car, and following."

Ron had expected this, but what worried him was whether other Swedish agents had gone unnoticed by Tod's team.

Ron moved to the other window of his circular room to survey the sidewalk closest to the hotel. The cluster of North Koreans came into view, the person walking ahead of the other three appearing to be Pak Jong-ryul, a cigarette in hand. None seemed to be speaking to each other, but they all walked slowly toward Berzelii Park. Ri Ju-song, his security guard and the other diplomat trailed Pak by five yards. As they continued north along Nybrokajen Street, Ron returned to his preferred window and opened it all the way, so he now had an unobstructed view of the target.

Tod radioed from the van that he had them in sight, as did another in Tod's team from a bench in the park.

The North Korean foursome walked at a casual pace to the path that deviated from the street toward the west boundary of the park, toward Berns Restaurant, with OSCAR trailing from a safe distance, as planned.

The streets that surrounded the park were bustling—-the norm in this upscale part of downtown Stockholm. The four men, Ron imagined as he followed them with his binoculars, were likely stunned by the beauty and charm of the pristine surroundings, a place that could not be more different than their dreary capital, Pyongyang. Ron lost sight of them momentarily to the foliage of the trees as they passed the restaurant, heading north out of the park to Hamngatan Street. Surely they'd gawk dizzyingly at the street's vibrant storefronts, Ron continued to imagine, and at the range of modern garments, gadgets, and other products the West takes for granted but which their compatriots back in North Korea would deem pure science fiction.

Ron shook his head. "Brainwashed," he whispered, his hand clenching the radio, and his eyes locked onto the North Koreans as he listened to the inputs from the spotters, who relayed their position every few seconds.

"They're passing near the McDonald's on the southwest corner of Norrmalmstorg square," reported one of Tod's boys.

"Keep your eyes on 'em," Ron instructed, though he knew the most important vigilance would come in a couple hours, after the North Koreans finished their lunch.

"BRAVO here. They're strolling north, along the east side of the square, close to the bank."

"Let 'em shop," Tod uttered.

"BRAVO again. Target's entering..." Static cut him off.

Ron brought his radio close to his lips. "BRAVO, repeat."

His voice came back but was barely audible over the scratchy noise. "...the flower shop."

"Alone?"

BRAVO replied what sounded like "yes," but the interference was too strong.

"Repeat." Ron began to think Tod's team had done something wrong with the communications. He glanced at his colleagues in the room.

Terry simply shrugged his shoulders.

"Yes, alone," BRAVO broke through the static but sounded as though he was shouting to be heard. "Having a smoke...kiosk..."

The intermittent sputter of loud, fuzzy sounds drowned his words and frustrated Ron. "And the others?"

Ron's question was met only by the steady sound of static. That's when Ron wondered why Ri Ju-song would stroll into a florist. He certainly wouldn't be buying flowers for his official meetings, nor to bring back a bouquet to Pyongyang. He searched for a reason but couldn't find any that made sense.

"Check on him now!"

BRAVO didn't respond.

Ron scanned the distance with his binoculars, but he had no way to see past the park. "Anyone else have a visual?"

There was only silence.

Ron shook his head.

"Want me to go in?" Tod said, but it would take him a good minute to walk the two blocks and Ron couldn't trust Tod to keep a low profile, so Ron didn't bother answering.

"LIMA, d'you have him?" Ron asked.

"Negative, but I'm headed there," he said, a lighter but noticeable static accompanying his reply. BRAVO must have a radio issue."

"LIMA, you're also getting interference." Ron glanced at Terry, sitting at the radios on the credenza, as if Terry could fix BRAVO's communications problem.

Terry threw his hands in the air.

"Does anyone else have a fucking visual? Anyone? Dammit!"

The airwaves suddenly began opening up, with Tod, LIMA and someone else talking loudly over one another and through the intermittent static, until the orders, questions and statements became a chaotic, unintelligible

chatter that threw Ron over a cliff. It was he who finally
had the deepest lungs. "Shut the hell up! All of you.
Now, one at a time, please, like the professionals we're
supposed to be."

Several long seconds of stillness returned.

"I'm in the store now," BRAVO said, the interference
dimmed enough to make his voice heard. "But I don't
see him."

"Someone cover the back of that building, on
Norrlandsgatan," Tod instructed.

"PAPA here, on my way."

Ron lunged for his map and spread it over the bed.
He searched for the street Tod had just named and stabbed
it with his index finger. "Something's going down."

"Let's not panic," Tod said uselessly.

"Shit, shit, shit!" Ron threw his binoculars across the
room with all his strength. They smashed into the wall,
shattering the lenses into tiny pieces, and ricocheted to
knock down one of Terry's empty suitcases lined up
along the wall.

Terry jumped to his feet, his chair falling back, and
pulled down his headset to his neck. "What the..."

Jack whirled around and silently stared at Ron.

"One of you stand by the window. Tell the spotters to
close in, and report." Ron then grabbed his jacket. "I'm
going there right now." He quickly adjusted his wired
earpiece, clipped the mic on the same wire to his shirt
pocket, and connected the other end to his radio, which
he concealed in the inside pocket of his jacket. Waiting
for the elevator, he removed his Glock, checked that
the magazine was full, and returned the weapon to his

holster, all the while reminding himself that not a bullet would—or should—be fired today, as it surely would mean careers would be over, beginning with his and Tod's.

"Goddamn idiots," he whispered only to realize a second later that the mic was on auto-activate.

"Who was that?" a voice sounding like Tod echoed through the airwaves.

Ron didn't answer and switched his radio to manual.

*   *   *

Four minutes was all it took to get down the elevator, across the lobby and out to the street facing the Strand Hotel. As Ron caught his breath outside, Terry's voice filtered in. "Careful...the other rooster's out on foot."

"I don't give a shit," Ron said as he kept a steady jog's pace toward the park.

"Behind you. Black trench coat, dark green shirt."

"I told you, I don't care. I'm heading to the square."

He might have thrown brave words at Terry, but he was worried. Being followed by a *Säpo* agent added yet another complication.

"We should only get Ri Ju-song out if we can do it unseen by his group," Ron said, marching briskly toward the pedestrian walkway along the west side of the park, the same path the vice-admiral's delegation had taken.

Terry's voice again came through his earpiece. "Your tail's walking faster—looks alarmed and still headed your way."

His heart racing, his breaths short, Ron now had the square in sight, fifty yards away. Cars and buses criss-crossed his line of sight as he approached, his legs now starting to tire.

Ron scanned the square from the bandstand/gaze-bo-looking structure on the west side across from where BRAVO had spotted the flower shop. He jaywalked across Hamngatan, eyeing the shop, which was squeezed between other retail shops on the ground floor of a sev-en-story office building.

A loud bang broke through the air. Pedestrians ducked and screams echoed. Another two bangs followed—gunfire for sure. Ron dove behind a slow-moving car and ran to take cover behind a stopped bus a few feet away off the square, patting his holster from outside his jacket but choosing not to reach for his weapon just yet. "You see anything?"

"Blue, go. Go!"

"No!" Ron couldn't believe what he'd just heard Tod say.

"We're not losing him."

Ron ran along the south side of the building, glanc-ing in all directions as stunned pedestrians ducked for cover.

Suddenly, ahead of him, he spotted a person lying flat on the ground at a traffic light. He rushed closer and pushed his way past two bystanders who'd come to the aid of the fallen person. He froze. The body was Ri Ju-song's. The vice-admiral lay face down at the edge of the sidewalk, his bloodied head twisted to his shoulder and resting on a drainage grate. Five yards ahead of him, on the same sidewalk, his security guard lay unconscious against the building, blood draining from his belly onto the pavement. A gun lay near his left shoe—he'd been armed, after all.

Ron heard the screeching of tires across the intersection. The side door of a van flung open and five burly black-fatigued, helmet-clad men holding submachine guns scrambled into the second lane of traffic forcing cars to brake and swerve wildly across the wide street.

"Tod, what the fuck are they doing?" Ron was beside himself. "Get them out of here!" He assumed they were the 'Blue Team' friendlies Tod had talked about earlier and now called into action so irresponsibly. "There's no point—our target's a goner."

"What?"

"He's dead. Someone shot him."

"Who?"

"I don't know."

The armed men, each wearing masks over their faces, raced toward Ron's side of the street, their weapons drawn in his general direction. A few high-pitched screams pierced the air, and the normally sedate Swedes who had crowded around the bodies scattered quickly, clearing the way for the stormtroopers.

The leader cautiously approached the bodies on the sidewalk, while his teammates behind him scanned the windows of the facing building, their weapons sweeping for possible targets. The leader moved in toward Ri Ju-song's body, turning him to see the extent of the wound. The vice-admiral's brain was visible from the skull and hairline that had been obliterated from the impact of the bullets.

Ron ducked down and held onto the light pole close to Ri Ju-song's body. "Get out of here."

"*Komma ner!*" the leader yelled back and motioned for Ron to stop and get down, clearly not knowing who he was. Ron recognized the American accent behind the man's command. And if he did, Ron worried, so would the bystanders.

Ron heard loud, fast footsteps behind him but had only turned part way before another armed man knocked him to the ground.

"I'm SIERRA—"

The force of impact knocked the air out of his lungs. He tried getting up, but immediately felt a massive weight push him down. The thought of being accidentally shot by his own team made Ron angry enough to want to reach for his own weapon. He tried, but another Blue Team man pinned him to the ground and shoved the barrel of his submachine gun into Ron's cheek.

"Motherfucker's armed," Ron then heard the man on top of him say. He then felt the man disarm him and saw him throw the Glock onto the street.

"I'm SIERRA, you shitheads!" Ron couldn't move. His face was firmly pressed onto the gritty, cold asphalt by the force of the asshole's knee on his upper spine. He'd lost his earpiece, mic, radio and phone. "Let go!"

At that moment Ron caught a glimpse of a man walking hurriedly on the opposite sidewalk, heading toward the square. The man looked familiar. Ron strained his head back to keep his watch on him. *Sal?* He squinted, trying to see more clearly. The resemblance was too great. It was Sal. Ron was sure of it.

"Get off me!"

The Team Blue man crushing him to the pavement paid no attention. Instead, he gestured at his colleagues and uttered short coded words into a radio.

The man Ron believed was Sal crossed the street and disappeared. A few seconds later, the weight came off Ron's back. The men hustled back across the street's center dividing line, the leader now yelling into his headset and his heavily armed buddies huddled around him in the middle of the four-lane street.

Ron, still on the ground, spotted two policemen running towards this chaotic scene from a half-block away.

The team leader waved frantically at the van's driver to pull a U-turn. The van whipped around. The cabal dove into the vehicle through the opened sliding door and sped away. They hadn't fired a shot, but they hadn't kept their mouths shut. Consequently, it wouldn't take long for the Swedes to figure out they were Americans.

Ron quickly got up, picked up his radio and sprinted back to the square, scanning every storefront, every car, every bus in sight. But Sal was gone. Ron couldn't understand what Sal would be doing here, in Stockholm, except perhaps to track him down.

Suddenly Tod's voice came in on the radio. "Guys, looks like Pak's vanished."

Ron was furious. The vice-admiral was dead, and his suspicions about Pak Jong-ryul had proved true, but he couldn't understand who would take him, or why Sal was here in Stockholm, and most certainly involved.

15

New Orleans, Louisiana

"THAT'S THE WHOLE TRUTH, I SWEAR," JONATHAN SAID,
his frustration mounting—most disturbingly because the
man accusing him was not just a cop, but his childhood
friend. Boudreaux had cornered Jonathan for over thirty
minutes outside their cars in the rain, on the narrow
street facing Jonathan's house, and he hadn't backed
down one bit.

"I'm trying to stop you from making things worse."

"I've done nothing wrong!" Jonathan slammed
his fist like a hammer onto the roof of the squad car.
Jonathan had tried to convince Boudreaux that there
was nothing sinister behind checking on the corpse at
the morgue. He'd told him about Mariya, about how
shady she was, about the limited favor he'd agreed to do
to encourage her to leave town without causing havoc,
all to no avail. Jonathan's sole cop-friend hadn't given
ground.

The driver of a pickup truck pulled up to them and
asked to pass by, but Boudreaux—still fixated on inter-

rogating Jonathan—barked at him to back up and go another way.

Jonathan took a step back from Boudreaux's car. "If my client doesn't tell me the truth—and if I don't know that—then that's not lying."

Boudreaux's face flushed, looking even more furious than when he'd first pulled up. "Go to the morgue now, or I'm taking you there in handcuffs."

Though tempted to drag out the argument to change the cop's mind, Jonathan ceded with a simple nod.

"Sort things out with Garceau, am I clear?"

"Yes! You'd rather I clear up paperwork at the morgue instead of evacuating."

"Don't you be smug," Boudreaux snapped, crossing his arms over his giant chest, which looked even larger with his bullet-proof vest. "I don't know what's goin' on here—frankly, I'm not sure I want to. Just get this sorted out right now, before you leave town. I don't want anyone pointing a finger at me later."

"I'll go now, dammit."

"I'm going to follow you to make sure."

"Fine, but after the morgue, I'm gone."

Boudreaux frowned, shook his head and returned to his squad car. He followed Jonathan for the ten minute drive to the morgue on Tulane and watched as Jonathan crossed the street toward the building.

*   *   *

"You were surprised by the body, weren't you?" Dr. Garceau said from the side of his mouth, having coolly greeted Jonathan a minute earlier in the lobby. "It wasn't who you expected, was it?"

They stood just outside the examination room. Jonathan knew he was in trouble but was trying to play it cool, hoping that Boudreaux had put in a good word for him. "Maybe you're right, Doctor."

"Then you lied to me."

"Honestly, I don't know. My client is hiding something, I'm sure of it, but I suspected this only after the fact. I told you the man's identity based solely on what she'd shared with me, and I had no reason to distrust her at the time."

"How would she even know he drowned?" the pathologist asked, standing in his long white lab coat, his arms crossed, apparently ready to debate this issue in depth. "You should ask her. How on earth could she have told you to look for a drowning victim when only a handful of first responders—and maybe a couple folks at the Port of New Orleans—and three people here in the office knew what happened? I only called around over the weekend. No one else knew about this drowning. Well, except that one reporter at the *Times Picayune* was told about it, but as far as I know he didn't publish the story."

If that was true, Jonathan had no explanation. He couldn't even fudge one. How could Mariya have known without perhaps having had a role in the man's fate? But then, why would she need Jonathan's help to find out what happened to the guy? Why inquire at all? Why ask so many questions if she'd killed the man herself or had witnessed the incident firsthand? Nothing added up. The logic behind her request now seemed shifty and troubling, and Jonathan suddenly felt like a fool in front of this seasoned forensic expert.

"Whatever explanation you have, Mr. Brooks, I don't appreciate you holding back information, and I'm concerned you're still not being completely straight with me. A death is a serious matter for a coroner's office."

"I should have shared my concerns with you from the get-go, and for that I apologize. I just didn't—"

"Say no more." Garceau raised his hand. "We'll deal with this at a later time, but you should understand that I've already notified the authorities, and will update them about our discussion now."

Jonathan felt a sudden chill. Even with Boudreaux's help, he might not be able to smooth this out. He met Garceau's gaze as an uncomfortable silence descended on the two men.

"I'm really sorry," Jonathan finally said.

Garceau shook his head. "Come see what else I found, for what it's worth."

"Have you done the autopsy yet?"

"No, but we plan to—everyone's gone now because of the storm."

They headed into the cold room where autopsies are performed. The body lay on its stomach, a white plastic sheet covering the buttocks and legs. The flesh from the neck down to the upper lumbar was of a scaly texture with a patchy, brownish-charcoal tint—almost the hue of an overcooked polish sausage—while the rest of the lower back was a more even pale gray.

As Garceau slipped on a pair of latex gloves, Jonathan's eyes traveled to the back of the cadaver's skull, the hair and scalp appearing fragile enough to slip off with a mild gust from an air conditioning vent.

Garceau reached for a magnifying glass on the nearby counter and held it over the middle of the man's back. "Look. Two small abrasions—equidistant left and right of his spine. See?"

"Uh-huh." Jonathan had a hard time distinguishing the abrasions from the decaying skin. He leaned further over the body and surmised Garceau's concern likely had less to do with the abrasions themselves than with the fact that they were identical and evenly spaced on the corpse's back. Each mark was about a quarter-inch wide and two inches long, extending out to the side. "Does this mean he was wearing something—something that might cause bruising or pressure?"

"Like a horse may have saddle marks," Garceau said, but then grimaced as if he'd caught the inappropriateness of his remark. "I mean, if he were, say, a hiker, you might find an abrasion from a backpack."

"What about scuba gear?"

"I hadn't thought of that." Garceau peered over the skin once again, holding the magnifying glass over the spots. "But why would anyone scuba dive the river? He wasn't wearing a wetsuit."

"The water's ninety degrees," Jonathan said. "There's no need for one."

Garceau sighed. "I suppose that's possible, but diving gear doesn't magically come off. The Harbor Police found him wearing only swim shorts—no shirt, no shoes, and no scuba equipment anywhere in the area."

The faint sound of footsteps filtered its way from the hall into the examination room.

"Doctor Garceau, you there?" A woman's voice called out, agitated and loud, her trembling words accompanying the louder, quickened noise of her heels on the tiled floor as she reached the other side of the door. She called out Garceau's name once more before barreling in, her large limbs fidgeting. "We gotta get outta here," she said through rapid breaths. "There could be flooding real soon."

"Calm down." Garceau grabbed her shoulders. "Flooding? Where?"

She spoke fast. "Someone on the radio said the 17th Street Canal was overflowing and water's heading south."

"No need to wait for us, Latisha. I really appreciate your concern, but Mr. Brooks and I are just finishing something up here. You go home now and stay safe."

"You better hurry." The woman shook her head and lumbered off, mumbling all the way till her footsteps were out of earshot.

"Shouldn't we go, too?" Jonathan asked, although his mind was buzzing with a handful of nuanced theories.

"This won't take too long."

Jonathan looked down at the body. "What if he took it off?"

"Took what off?"

"His scuba gear!" Jonathan pointed at the cadaver.

"Perhaps he was struggling in the water, took off his BCD—buoyancy control device—with his air tank and other gear, but somehow still drowned?"

Garceau tapped his chin with the magnifying glass. "Possible. Panicked divers can do strange things. But there's no reason for him to dive there. It's dangerous——lots of rip currents."

"I don't know, but he could be a pro. Look at his build. His muscles. His chest. His arms. This fella's a good swimmer for sure, perhaps a diver. I find it hard to believe he's a simple crewman."

Garceau observed the body silently. He then examined the file folder, scanning through the pages of preliminary lab results and other information.

"Regardless of why he was in the water—diving or not—we'll have to wait for an autopsy to determine what caused his death. But for now this looks like a plain drowning."

Two rapid thuds echoed down the hall, then a crash that sounded like something metallic falling to the floor.

"Latisha?" Garceau asked loudly and then opened the door, to find the hallway darkened. "Are you okay?"

Silence.

"Let me go check on her," Garceau said, heading out into the darkened hallway as a door around the corner squeaked.

Jonathan walked to the door as Garceau headed down the hallway calling for Latisha.

Suddenly, two dark-clad men jumped out from around the corner.

"Watch out!" Jonathan yelled, racing forward as the men lunged at Garceau.

They slammed the pathologist against a shelving unit, as a third assailant jumped over them and headed straight for Jonathan, who leapt backward into the examination room and slammed the metal door shut.

A thunderous thump shook the door, and a loud grunt followed. Jonathan, his body pressed up against the door, scanned for a lock on the handle. There was none. He pressed on the door with all his strength, but his feet slipped back, losing traction on the tiled floor. He felt more pressure pushing on the door as though the other two assailants had now added their weight.

His head, chest and hands were pressed firmly on the metal door, but still, his shoes slid further back another inch. He couldn't hold them much longer.

Jonathan glanced up at the lone window in the back of the room—it was small and too high up for a quick escape. He then spotted a large pair of scissors on a counter about ten feet away. *Can I make it across the room in time? And what then?* His strength weakening, he questioned how effective the scissors would be against three determined thugs.

The assailants were now throwing their bodies into the door, which moved back enough for one of them to reach his hand around the side. Jonathan hit it with his fist and heard a loud cry.

Jonathan's feet slid further. He eyed the scissors again and gave one hard push into the door, let go, and leapt sideways and darted for the scissors. He lunged for them but as he reached out, a horrendous pain bolted through his body. He collapsed onto the floor, tossed around in a violent, uncontrollable spasm. A shriek came from the depths of his lungs as another jolt hit the back of his neck, his body jerking as the pain faded. His view of the room blurred and two seconds later went black.

*   *   *

An earsplitting screech startled Jonathan out of the darkness. He awakened, scarcely conscious, the grogginess alarming him. The noise spliced through the room again. A woman's scream. His vision sharpened, and light began to fill his eyes.

A white tiled floor, up close, came into view. He was lying face down on it, a thick wetness covering his cheeks and mouth. He brushed his hand over his face and was relieved to discover it was simply drool, not blood.

He slowly moved his arm, and then his hands and fingers until he reached the main sources of his pain: a large bump on his head, and the back of his neck had what felt like a two-inch wide burn, its soreness spreading to a larger area of his skin as his bleariness receded. He peeled himself off the floor, trying to sit up but sharp pain coming from almost everywhere hindered his effort.

"My God, my God!" The woman's panicked voice, accompanied by clanging noises, came from outside the examination room.

Jonathan was barely on his knees, still struggling for

the strength to get up. He glanced at the examination table. "Dammit!"

The body was gone—taken by the thugs who'd knocked the crap out of him.

"Lord, help us," he heard the woman moan frantically.

Jonathan grabbed the edge of the table to prop himself to his feet and wobbled to the door, following the woman's voice in the corridor.

Latisha was huddled on the floor, a pair of legs sprouting from under her. Garceau's legs.

"How is he?"

She turned, startled, and her cell phone dropped to the floor. "I should ask you that."

"Some men attacked us. That's all I know."

She looked down at Garceau. "He's bleeding bad, real bad."

"Shit!" Jonathan hobbled forward and stumbled to his knees next to her.

"I tried to call an ambulance, but I can't get through," she said, breathing hard as she pressed a blood-drenched towel up against Garceau's temple.

Jonathan leaned his head onto the pathologist's chest and listened, only finding a faint heartbeat. "He's still breathing—barely."

"Was he shot?" Latisha asked.

Jonathan lifted the towel she held over his wound. "It doesn't look like a gunshot." The deep gash was uneven and the tissue around the wound was sizably swollen. He glanced up and spotted the bloodied corner of the metal countertop a few feet away. "Blunt force, that's what it was. He's lost a lot of blood. I'll go get someone."

"Don't bother. I think there ain't nobody left in this building."

"What do you mean? NOPD Headquarters is here."

"They cleared out earlier this morning and are setting up somewhere else downtown."

"How come you're still here?"

"I got no way to leave. The streets are flooded outside, and I can't reach my car."

Jonathan noticed her shoes and lower legs were soaked. He glanced at his watch, calculating how long he'd been out cold. He guessed about an hour. Garceau's blood had oozed across nearly the entire floor of the narrow corridor.

"Keep pressure on the wound," Jonathan said as Latisha grabbed the counter to stand up. He wrapped his arms around Garceau and slowly lifted him up to his chest and then over his shoulder, thanking his lucky stars that he was carrying the lightweight pathologist and not the heavyset assistant.

"He needs to go to a hospital right now."

With Latisha steadying him from behind, Jonathan carried Garceau into the connecting hallway. Latisha quickly elbowed open the emergency exit door and let out a gasp. They both froze, the strong wind swirling around them, as they stared down the steps.

The street was filled with almost two feet of water, both north and south of where they stood. The moderate rain accompanying the strong winds could not account for so much water. It had to be the overflow from the levee she'd mentioned earlier.

Jonathan spotted the top half of his Camry street-parked a block north, but the water already had reached the door.

"There, there!" Latisha shouted. She pointed at a police car making a speedy U-turn two blocks east, its tires squealing near where the flooding appeared to taper.

"Wave! Get their attention."

Jonathan, still bear-hugging Garceau's body off the ground, walked down the steps and into the lukewarm, murky water. He sloshed his way forward across the street, the foul-smelling water splashing over his thighs. Latisha stayed right behind him, her hands still pressing the towel on Garceau's head wound.

His foot suddenly caught an obstacle in the street, flinging him forward. With Garceau locked in his arms, he fell into the water, soaking them both from head to toe. With Garceau still in his grasp, he thrashed about, trying to find his footing, as Latisha pulled him up by his shirt until it started to rip.

Jonathan righted himself and continued to kick his way through the filthy water as Latisha waved her arms above her head, screaming at the squad car.

It slowed, its brake lights glowing.

"Thank God!" Latisha gasped. "Hurry...and what's yo name?"

"Jonathan."

"You doin' good."

Jonathan was nearly out of breath when he reached the two officers—one white, the other Hispanic—who'd stopped their car on a patch of dry pavement.

The officers gently placed Garceau face up in the back seat.

"He's not breathing," said The white, freckled cop.

Jonathan dove past the officers and examined Garceau up close. He began CPR. He pressed on Garceau's chest at a rapid pace as one officer rewrapped the crimson-stained towel around the pathologist's head.

"What happened?"

"We were attacked in the morgue," Jonathan replied He continued the compressions, his energy focused on saving the man's life.

"Looks bad..."

"Let's drive him to the hospital," Jonathan said, as Latisha elbowed past the two cops to peer into the back seat.

"Can't! It's flooded up Galvez, and along Perdido, too, and we nearly stalled going through some high water west of here."

"What about going down Poydras and cutting across?" Latisha asked.

The officer shook his head. "Impossible. The flooding's gettin' worse by the minute."

"Then call the paramedics!" Latisha shouted, her voice now trembling. "Call 'em now."

The Hispanic cop pulled a radio from his belt, flicked a switch and said, "Hey, lady, you see? The radios ain't workin'. The towers must be down."

His colleague jumped in the driver's seat and tried the squad car's radio mounted below the dash, but only a solid screeching sound burst from the speaker. The airwaves were dead, and Jonathan realized what that meant: a city whose first responders couldn't communicate was doomed for sure.

"Then drive, drive!" snapped Jonathan. "Figure out a way. Let's get him to Tulane Medical Center. It's only a half-mile away." But he knew that if the cops were right, the flooded streets would make it hugely difficult, if not impossible, to reach the hospital.

"You can't just let my boss bleed here," Latisha added, leaning into the front window.

"We'll try, but there's water everywhere." The cop started the car and his buddy jumped into the front seat.

"You got room for me?"

"Go back to the courthouse, lady," the second cop said to her. "Stay on a higher floor and hang a towel from the window and wait. It's too risky to stay in the floodwaters."

Latisha nodded. "Jonathan," she said. "You save his life, you hear me?" She closed the back door and stepped away from the car.

Jonathan continued the compressions, his arms beginning to tire, as the car swerved abruptly, the tires squealing with each sharp turn. He kept going, gazing at Garceau's bloodied, unresponsive face until the car suddenly screeched to a halt and propelled Jonathan to his side, his body slamming against the glass divider. "Why are we stopping?"

"Look," said the officer behind the wheel.

Jonathan sat up and stared ahead, out the front of the car. They were already in water, maybe a foot deep, but the rest of Gravier Street ahead was flooded deeper—up to the bottoms of first floor windows—as was Galvez Street just around the corner.

"We won't make it," said the cop at the wheel.

Jonathan turned and resumed the compressions. He pressed on Garceau's chest hoping he'd see a miracle: a sudden cough bringing the pathologist back to consciousness, his eyes opening, a mouthing of words, a noise of any kind. Any sign of life.

Nothing happened.

Garceau's face bobbed up and down as Jonathan persevered. The back door opened, but he ignored the officer squeezing into the tight confines, checking Garceau's neck for a pulse.

The officer turned. "You should stop."

"Come on, come on!"

The officer grabbed Jonathan's arm tightly. "Sir, you gotta stop. He's dead."

Jonathan froze as the officer closed Garceau's half-open eyes and gently patted Jonathan's shoulder.

Jonathan could hardly breathe. He stormed out of the car and stepped into the watery street, grabbing his own hair with both hands and yelling from the depths of his lungs. He breathed harder, staring at his hands drenched in Garceau's blood. *How could all this happen? How? The world's gone mad.*

His stomach in knots, he stared vacantly at the squad car in the middle of the street. The officers got out into the calf-deep water and pulled Garceau's body out of the vehicle. They carried it to the front of the car and gently placed it on the hood. One officer retrieved a blanket from the trunk and spread it on the front part of the hood, and the two then rolled the body onto it and wrapped it once around.

Jonathan returned to the car. "What are you doing?"

"We're leaving 'im here."

"What are you saying?" Jonathan felt an urge to punch them.

The officer shrugged his shoulders. "We're not a hearse."

"He's a parish coroner, for God's sake; have some respect."

The officers looked at each other stone-faced but said nothing.

"We can't simply leave him on the street."

"So what d'you suggest?"

Jonathan wanted to scream. Discarding a man's body like that—what has the world come to? His mind raced with possibilities—could they take him back to the morgue? What about the nearest funeral home? Or a cemetery that wouldn't be underwater? But he discarded every idea as quickly as it came to him. There was just too much water. It was impossible to drive almost any-where. And the rain was still coming down.

Defeated, he scanned both ends of the flooded street.

"Well?" the officer snapped.

"Over there." Jonathan pointed to an auto parts store one building down.

They carried Garceau's corpse to the alley adjacent to the store and lifted it onto a concrete loading dock about four feet off the ground. The officer then scribbled something on a citation and tucked in under the blanket.

The three men walked back to the police car as the water continued to rise around them. A moment later the car's engine died and it didn't restart.

Jonathan left the officers. The water had reached his

thighs by the time he'd walked passed the next block, his surprise anesthetizing him to the calamity of an entire city's slow drowning. He continued his trek, spotting a dead cat floating by, and two young men making their way in the opposite direction, one of them lugging an electric keyboard. He inhaled the putrid smell that rose from the water with no reaction. Two blocks' walk had become five. The water had risen waist-deep by the time he reached the westbound ramp of I-10 at Poydras.

He began walking up the ramp, eyeing a crowd that had gathered at the top. And when he reached them, the crowd was much larger, taking up a large swath of the raised roadway amid several abandoned cars. Men and women, some elderly or sick or both, were sitting and lying on the pavement, their gloomy, exhausted faces not unlike those fleeing a war zone. At one edge, near a guard rail, were two wheelchair-bound women, one of them screaming. Crying children and toddlers paced anxiously, some appearing dazed, some without parents. There was neither water nor food anywhere in sight. And no help, not a single cop or rescuer.

Jonathan gazed at the people around him and shook his head. He'd made it here, above the water, but it was hardly an ideal place to stay. All he wanted now was to find Boudreaux, wherever his friend might be. And this meant heading back into the flooded streets.

16

THE PARKING LOT OF THE NEW ORLEANS POLICE Department's Sixth District station was buzzing with cops, their faces etched with worry. Some conversed tersely in the light drizzle; others packed gear and weapons into their squad cars; others hurriedly headed into the station.

"Garceau's dead, you hear me?" Jonathan said, hoping to get a response from Sergeant Boudreaux.

Having listened to everything Jonathan could throw at him about what had happened at the morgue, Boudreaux stood silently, leaning with one hand pressed against the side of a police van, nervously chewing his gum, his eyes wide open and aimed vacantly at the pavement.

Jonathan's clothes were still soaked. He'd walked many blocks through the floodwaters, up portions of the elevated lanes of I-10, and then back into the floodwaters, walking the rest of his way to the station.

"I'm telling you, no one would storm a morgue and

steal a body unless it was real damn important. We have to do something."

"Yeah, like what?"

"I don't know, you're the cop."

Boudreaux quickly checked his watch, his face strained. "The city's falling apart; the last thing I need is to deal with your problem."

"My problem? A parish pathologist was just murdered. I thought he was your friend?"

"Not really, but that don't matter."

"Whoever attacked us and took the body might still be in the city."

"You think we can find them, just like that?"

Admittedly, Jonathan knew tracking them down was a long shot, but standing there doing nothing was the worst of all options. "Can't we—?"

An unmarked Crown Victoria suddenly pulled up and the uniformed officer at the wheel rolled down his window. "Hey, Claude, change of plans."

"Lieutenant?" Boudreaux wiped the sweat and droplets of rain off his face with his sleeve.

"Take some guys with you down to Wal-Mart on Tchoupitoulas."

"Now?"

"Did I stutter? Yes, damn it, now. They're looting the crap out of it."

"That's happening all over."

"Right, but Wal-Mart sells guns. Lots of them. I don't think we want them loose by nightfall."

"Fu..."

Boudreaux's superior handed him a note and said,

"The manager gave us the combination to the safe. Try to get there before all the guns are gone." The lieutenant drove off as quickly as he'd pulled up.

"Can you drop me off near the morgue on your way?" Jonathan asked.

"No. Besides, you said they got away."

"Yes, by the time I came around the bastards were gone, but there could still be clues. It's a crime scene, for cryin' out loud. You could find something—prints, security camera footage, whatever."

The sergeant shook his head. "Ask someone else here to take you."

"Please."

Boudreaux sighed. "Tell you what," he said, reaching into his pants pocket for his keys, "I can try to take you there when we're done at Wal-Mart."

"Fine, I'll stay with you."

"Only if you don't get in the way and do as I say."

"Promise."

Boudreaux then shouted at two colleagues standing near another police cruiser and told them to also head to Wal-Mart.

*   *   *

The tires screeched at each abrupt turn as they zig-zagged down a narrow, debris-strewn, pot-holed street that ran parallel to St. Charles Avenue. Boudreaux turned again and floored it down another vacant street, the siren wailing, the gyrolights flashing atop the car. The flooding had not reached this part of town—not yet, at least—but homes were already damaged nonetheless, by wind or perhaps by looters. Power lines were down. Trash cans, branches, pieces of wooden fences, street signs, all littered the ground. To Jonathan, it was the closest thing he'd seen to a war zone.

"That's some crazy shit you just told me."

"Damn right," Jonathan replied, testing his seat belt as Boudreaux picked up speed. "I'm lucky they didn't kill me—just a bump on the head and a burn from being tazed—but I don't want to die now in your car."

Boudreaux swerved the car around newspaper boxes littering the intersection. Jonathan hung on for his life as the sergeant pushed sixty miles per hour on streets not made for driving half that speed on a good day.

"You gotta find that woman—that client o' yours." Boudreaux rolled down his window and nodded at the glove compartment, "Hand me a cigarette."

"Now? Can't you wait?"

Boudreaux gave Jonathan an ugly stare as he maneuvered their speeding car around a discarded bicycle in the divider lane.

"Fine, but keep your eyes on the road." Jonathan took out the pack of Camels as Boudreaux reached for the lighter in his pocket. "The road!" Jonathan grabbed the lighter from Boudreaux's hand. "I'll light it for you so we don't die."

They screeched across another intersection, and another, then took a sharp right turn onto St. Andrew Street. Boudreaux suddenly let off the accelerator.

"Holy crap."

A dozen young black men—some carrying bats and

pipes—were running in the same direction, past a smol-dering pickup truck discarded on the sidewalk adjacent a small park bordering St. Thomas Street, straight ahead.

"Hold on."

Jonathan grabbed the dash. "Jesus!"

Boudreaux stepped hard on the accelerator. Their car bounced over the curb, tore through the shrubs—narrowly missing two of the thugs—and rolled over the grass of the block-long park, then scraped a parked car as the vehicle bounced off the sidewalk and rejoined the street on the other side.

Jonathan looked straight ahead and quickly realized that the real danger hadn't passed, but rather, it was dead ahead of them: the parking lot of Wal-Mart was swarm-ing with people—young, old, black, white, Hispanic, angry, agitated—most of them carting items they'd taken from the store.

"This may get ugly," Boudreaux warned, slowing down, turning off the siren, tossing his cigarette and rolling up his window. He locked the doors and tightly gripped the steering wheel with one hand as he rested his other hand on his holstered pistol. He inched the car forward.

The disjointed horde eyed them with ire before reluc-tantly clearing space for the squad car to ease through. Boudreaux drove into the lot that now was devoid of cars and pulled into the fire lane at the store's main entrance.

Jonathan scanned the lot. He couldn't count the numbers. A hundred, hundred-fifty, maybe more, all of them heading out with whatever stolen goods they could carry, some in bags, others using carts, another pulling a stroller with a flat screen television on it. Jonathan quickly gathered that the arm of the law at the very moment extended only to Boudreaux and him, and that wasn't saying much. There were no other cops around. The backup Boudreaux had called for at the station was nowhere in sight, and with the police radios and cell phones down, there was no way to summon others.

Boudreaux wheezed a deep sigh as he reached for the door handle.

"Shouldn't we wait?"

The sergeant shook his head. "Wait for these fucks to arm themselves inside? Not on my watch."

At that moment, it occurred to Jonathan that this might be his last day walking this earth.

"Here, only use it if you have to." Boudreaux handed Jonathan his Glock. "It's loaded."

Jonathan hadn't held a weapon in years but as he took the pistol, a strange comfort washed over him. Perhaps it was a survival instinct, given the frenzied looters outside. Or maybe the need to protect his friend. Whatever it was, Jonathan's hand felt one with the Glock. He released the safety and held it over his lap. "What about you?"

Boudreaux cocked his head back, stepped out and popped open the trunk. Jonathan had no choice but to follow his pal.

"This one's mine," Boudreaux said, pulling out a shotgun from the trunk. "A 12-gauge full of love." He began to load it while eyeing the entrance to the store. "We're going in carefully, you hear me?"

Jonathan nodded, his heart now pounding. He kept his weapon down by his thigh as Boudreaux slammed down the trunk.

"I don't know when the others will get here, but I don't want fifty freshly armed men inside which is what will happen if we wait too long."

"I don't like this one bit." Jonathan felt the adrenaline rush as he turned to the store with his weapon in hand.

"Good thing for you I'm a much larger target," Boudreaux quipped as he chambered his shotgun and held it across his belly.

A stream of young looters suddenly poured out of the entrance, only a handful of them even noticing Jonathan and Boudreaux.

Boudreaux glanced at his buddy. "We're a bit outnumbered."

"Uh-huh—by a hundred to one, I'd say." Jonathan stared tensely at the fine citizens making their way out of the entranceway with newly acquired possessions, trampling the shattered glass of the sliding doors.

"Put that shit down!" Boudreaux shouted at a middle-aged black man carrying what looked like two fax machines in one arm and pulling a heavy suitcase with his other hand.

The man—who looked as if he'd just gotten out of bed for this special sale—stopped and stared at the sergeant as if he'd just been insulted. "Go fuck yourself."

Boudreaux swaggered forward, his eyes narrowing.

"What chu gonna do 'bout it, huh?" said the shirtless man, who Jonathan instantly decided was either the bravest man in New Orleans or too dense to know what a two-hundred-eighty-pound, short-tempered, shotgun-wielding Boudreaux was capable of doing.

Suddenly a cadre of fellow looters—six of them—also with stolen goods in hand, came to the aid of their friend. Two were tall and lanky, one portly, and the others rather stocky—certainly not the group Jonathan and his law enforcement buddy would stand a chance of winning in a brawl and Jonathan realized there was no telling if the looters were themselves packing. The group was readying themselves for a fight for sure, silently staring at the officer and likely calculating their odds.

Jonathan tightened his grip on the Glock. "Claude, let these losers go."

Boudreaux raised his shotgun over his shoulder, spit on the ground, his angry glare telling Jonathan some folks might not live to sunset.

"They're not worth it."

"You punks." Boudreaux shook his head, walked backwards a few steps and then turned. "Human waste."

The looters started laughing and then shouted insults.

The sergeant headed into the store, and Jonathan shadowed him, his eyes still glued to the men outside who now numbered close to fifteen, their mocking taunts echoing in the store as the two retreated past the Customer Service counters, then past the destroyed cashier stations—not a single cash register was left.

Dozens of people were rummaging through the aisles. Boudreaux yelled at the ones he crossed. Jonathan followed him toward the back of the store, first down what was left of the cosmetics aisle—only a few items were still stood on the shelves.

Jonathan led the way through the next aisle—gift cards and books. "See, looters don't read," he said, turning to Boudreaux and pointing his handgun at the nearly intact racks filled with paperbacks and magazines.

"Does that surprise you?" the sergeant snickered. "But I bet the electronics department is wiped clean."

Jonathan laughed.

Boudreaux suddenly ran up to a young white woman carrying picture frames toward her cart already overflowing with DVDs, baby clothes and toys. "Drop that and get the hell out," he shouted, smacking the frames out of her hands with the butt of his shotgun. The frames shattered on the floor. "Get out or I'll handcuff you to the rack."

"You hurt me, motherfucker!" she yelled back.

"Damn right, bitch." Boudreaux straightened his back and raised the butt of his shotgun. "Next one will cost you some teeth."

She got the message and scurried, cursing her way down the aisle. But the commotion had no effect on two other looters just ten feet away, their hands also filled with household goods.

"You too, get out. Now!"

Jonathan walked past them, tapping Boudreaux on the shoulder, "We have something more important to do, don't we?"

The sergeant reluctantly disengaged, walking alongside Jonathan, until they reached the back of the store, where a crowd had gathered inside a small room behind the empty sporting goods counter.

"Everyone out!" Boudreaux shouted.

No one budged. A few looters glanced at the cop as if he were nuts.

Jonathan stood two feet behind Boudreaux, eyeing everyone near him. *Hope you know what you're doing.*

Curse words ricocheted around the room but no one moved to leave.

Jonathan peeked around the sergeant, eyeing the small space. There were at least ten unfriendly faces in there, one man holding a crow bar, and another a large wrench. The safe on the far wall looked scratched and dented, but it hadn't been breached—yet.

"If you know what's good for you, you'll drop those tools and get out of this store." Boudreaux sounded increasingly impatient.

They all stood there, motionless, returning vicious stares, and Jonathan realized that there was no way to predict what they would do, especially when cornered in a twenty-by-fifteen room. A shootout was the worst of all outcomes, but Jonathan felt ready to raise his gun and pump them with lead if he had to. He was already sweating profusely, his hands, too. His heart was racing. The men, some in scraggly clothes, jostled to form a human wall some ten feet in front of him, the safe now hidden from view.

Boudreaux shouted again, raised his shotgun higher over his bulletproof vest and moved a foot.

Jonathan's anger took over his fears. "Okay, that's it!" he barked. "The officer asked nicely, and now you've worn out the courtesy. You fucking scumbags are getting out of there either on your own feet or in a body bag. You decide!" He stepped back from the entrance to the room, raised his pistol at the ceiling and pulled the trigger, twice. "Get the hell out of this room, NOW!" he yelled as Boudreaux turned, stunned.

Jonathan pushed him to one side of the door as he lunged to the other. Reaching partly around the door, he then pointed his Glock at the ten feet of floor space that separated him from the looters. "I have one bullet left for each of you."

He had never seen men exit a confined space so quickly, the last one clearing the door in under five seconds.

Boudreaux pointed his shotgun straight up as the looters scurried through the aisles to the door. A loud blast followed as Boudreaux fired into the ceiling, making Jonathan flinch. Small fragments of debris rained down on them, and they both broke into laughter.

"The sale is over mothafuckas," Boudreaux shouted. "Wal-Mart is now closed. Get the fuck out!" He pulled the trigger again and the blast echoed across the store.

Jonathan could hear the commotion at the entrance. Finally, people were leaving.

They secured the guns in the safe—an arsenal of over fifty-five rifles, shotguns and handguns. But they knew that if they left, the looters would wander back in. So they stayed put and guarded the stockpile for another half-hour, until a six-strong police backup finally joined them in the back of the store.

Jonathan, Boudreaux and a few other cops then walked the aisles to ensure there were no weapons of any kind anywhere in sight.

"Holy shit," Jonathan said the second he walked outside.

The cavalry had arrived in earnest. The parking lot had been completely cleared of looters, replaced by dozens of police cars, police vans, Orleans Parish Sheriffs' cruisers and several unmarked Crown Victorias.

Before he'd left the store, Jonathan had taken a backpack and filled it with several water bottles, a flashlight and a hammer. And when Boudreaux had stepped away to use the bathroom, Jonathan had taken one of the handguns they'd rescued from the safe, along with three loaded magazines, guessing that the sergeant would ask for his Glock back—which he did the moment they stepped out of Wal-Mart.

Boudreaux walked over to his colleagues and began shouting orders, telling them to secure the lot's three entrances, the perimeter fence, the alley behind the store, and the loading dock.

Jonathan reminded himself of what the sergeant had promised. He walked to his pal and said, "Let's go."

"Where?"

"To the morgue, remember?"

"No way. We're hunkering down. Things have gotten really bad—lots of armed gangs roaming the streets. We're gonna secure this place as a base overnight."

"But you—"

"If you want to leave and get yourself killed, go right ahead, but I gotta keep my men safe."

"Then give me your keys." Jonathan was determined.

Boudreaux stared at him as if he'd gone nuts. "I'll be damned if I let you drive a police car."

Jonathan flung his backpack over his shoulder and began walking to the street.

"Shit, you're so damn stubborn."

Jonathan didn't stop.

"Fine!" Boudreaux shouted. "You win!"

Jonathan turned around as Boudreaux summoned an officer who'd just gotten out of a patrol car parked in the fire lane and told him to take Jonathan to the parish morgue.

"Just get your ass back here well before dark. Am I clear?"

17

OFFICER FLYNN DROVE UP SOUTH JEFFERSON PARKWAY TO the intersection with Walmsley Avenue, which was as far north as the car could make it through the deepening floodwaters.

He pulled a U-turn and stopped, checked his wristwatch and raised his chin at Jonathan, seated in the passenger side with his backpack. "I'll pick you up right here in exactly two hours—at 6:25. Not a minute later."

"How about 7 P.M. instead?" Jonathan wanted as much time as possible to investigate the morgue.

"No. I'll be on patrol from seven till midnight. Be here at 6:25 or you're on your own—and you certainly don't want that. The Sheriff's Office transferred inmates from the jail a few blocks over to a building across I-10 but several got away. So, in addition to having armed looters, you've got violent prisoners running wild through this area. Don't be late."

Jonathan stepped into the nearly knee-deep water and began walking as quickly as he could.

A few blocks north, he crossed Earhart Boulevard, noticing the water deepening. He continued his north-bound trek along the parkway, gazing at the extensive flooding across the south side of the Xavier University campus to his left and the dozens of warehouses on his right, along Euphrosine Street.

He eventually reached the overpass—and relished the brief respite from the water—that crossed a flooded section of I-10, but he was back in the floodwaters on the other side. His soaked path continued to Tulane Avenue near the morgue, where the water had reached nearly two feet in depth. His partly drowned Camry was still parked in the same spot he'd left it this morning. Opening the trunk, and finding everything as it was sup-posed to be, gave him much needed relief. He retrieved his passport, an envelope with a few hundred in cash, and his phone book, and threw these into his backpack along with a Polo shirt, a T-shirt and a pair of blue jeans. He then made sure the gun he'd taken at Wal-Mart rest-ed on top of the clothing, within easy reach.

Jonathan turned and eyed the eerily quiet building where only a few hours ago he'd been knocked uncon-scious and Dr. Garceau had been mortally wounded. The coroner's files, including pictures of the body, were all he needed. No big deal, he convinced himself. So long as the men who'd attacked them earlier weren't back in there going after the same things.

The quietness troubled him. He scanned the street and spotted a small dinghy a block east, at Dorgenois Street, inside it what appeared to be two rescuers with paddles. But there were no other souls in sight. No one.

The concrete building appeared to be completely abandoned, no sign even of Latisha. He cautiously opened the unlocked doors and proceeded through the empty lobby, which had stayed dry, and headed to the back of the building toward the coroner's office, hoping that someone had come to rescue her.

Dripping wet, his soaked shoes sloshing over the tile floor, Jonathan made his way through the darkened hallways with a flashlight in hand and soon reached Latisha's desk. There were several file cabinets lined up behind a row of workstations and it occurred to Jonathan that perhaps the file he needed was in there. He pulled out from his backpack the hammer he'd taken from the store, but as he did so, he realized that the locks on the first three cabinets had already been busted open. He aimed the flashlight at the other cabinets only to see the same thing, with some drawers left open and files scattered on the floor. Indeed, someone had already gotten to them. The idea of finding one particular file folder seemed daunting, especially he had less than forty minutes before he'd have to trudge back to where the cop had dropped him off—the last thing he wanted was to piss off Boudreaux by not showing up.

After rummaging through each of the file drawers and the papers on the floor, with no luck, he headed to the morgue's examination and storage rooms, quickly checking every cabinet, shelf and drawer he came across. Again, nothing.

Discouraged, Jonathan closed his eyes and tried to picture Garceau flipping through the folder earlier that day. Suddenly he remembered that before stepping into

the hall, Garceau had set the folder on top of a refrigerator next to the door. He retraced his steps into the
examination room where they'd met earlier in the day,
the beam of his flashlight glowing ahead of him until he
opened the room's door and the light hit the large white
appliance. Sure enough, on top was a stack of files. He
plopped them on a nearby counter and lifted a thick
folder on top, his hand shaking from the chill of his wet
clothes.

The folder had a typed labeled that read "John Doe
06" with the name Igor Yakin handwritten below it. He
flipped it open, barely containing his excitement to a
subdued mumbling. Inside were at least ten black and
white photographs of the body, various typed forms and
handwritten notes.

Jonathan shoved the folder into his backpack and
headed out as fast as he could. Within thirty minutes
he'd trawled through the floodwaters again and returned
to the spot where Officer Flynn had told him to be.
He was ten minutes early, and to his surprise, the cop
arrived on time.

*   *   *

Wal-Mart had been transformed into a fortress, with
officers holding shotguns and assault rifles stationed
along the perimeter fence. Dozens of police vehicles
blocked the points of entry and dozens more parked like
circled wagons in the center of the expansive lot.

A police van securing one of the entrances pulled
back to allow Officer Flynn's patrol car to drive in.

Jonathan leaned forward in the passenger seat, scanning the lot for Boudreaux. Now that he had the folder, all he wanted was to find a way out of New Orleans and attempt to track down Mariya somewhere in Houston, if that's indeed where she was. Mariya held part of the puzzle, he assumed, but the folder he'd found at the morgue gave him leverage. The dossier was most likely all she'd wanted from the get-go, and he could now use it as bait if only he could find her.

Boudreaux was comfortably seated in a folding chair under a large vinyl tarp fastened to an ice delivery truck at one end, to a Metairie police car at another end, and to two NOPD minivans at the other two corners. On a table set up under the tarp were several radios and cell phones.

"Can you believe this?" said the sergeant, tinkering with one of the devices. "Not a single radio works." He then held up a cell phone. "This is the only device that's working right now, off and on—of the fifty phones we've got around here. Apparently there are two cell towers still up, but the signal's weak and it's only with one service provider. Ridiculous, isn't it?"

Jonathan glanced at the ice truck, its engine running. "What's with that?"

"Our food's in there—from Wal-Mart and Winn-Dixie—in case there ain't nothing else to eat this week."

Jonathan heard a shopping cart pull up behind him and turned to see an officer, unloading wine, beer and water.

Jonathan laughed. "Gotta quench your thirst, too, I see."

"Goes well with frozen pizza," said the officer.

"Hey, we gotta stay hydrated, right?" Boudreaux added. "Officer Harton here was clever enough to hot-wire the truck and load it up with food."

Harton handed a beer each to Boudreaux and Jonathan, then cracked one open for himself. "We also jerry-rigged a manual pump to fill the gas tanks at the Chevron station down the street."

"Clever."

"Guess you underestimated the resourcefulness of New Orleans' finest, eh?"

"Uh-huh," Jonathan said, trying to gauge how he could pull off another favor from Boudreaux.

Boudreaux took a swig from his beer. "Grab a chair, chill out. It's gonna be a long night here at Camp Wal-Mart. We'll have a campfire soon, down some more booze and enjoy the fireworks that are sure to start after sunset."

"Fireworks?"

"There are thousands of folks behind that fence with scores to settle, and with few police on the streets, no 911 to dial, no electricity, no alarms, nothing. It'll be like a civil war."

"I was hoping to be out of town by now, but my car is still parked in two feet of water."

"Did you find anything at the morgue?"

"No, but that woman—my client—has the answer, and she said she was headed to Houston." Jonathan had no intention of telling the sergeant he'd found the file for the body. The last thing he wanted was to have Boudreaux confiscate it. "So I need to go to Houston, or at least Baton Rouge, where the phones probably work."

"And how the hell are you getting there?" Boudreaux said, grinning.

"You're going to tell me how and help me."

Boudreaux's grin evaporated. "Good luck."

"There's got to be a way."

"I-10 west of Kenner is closed, East Airline Highway is closed, and 18 is closed," Boudreaux went on. "The only way west, I'm told, is further inland along the west bank of the river—either Highway 1 through Thibodaux or Highway 3127. You could take 3127 to Donaldsonville, then U.S. 1 to Baton Rouge, and from there hop onto I-10 to Houston."

"Yes, but I need a car."

"How long are you gonna be gone?"

"A few days, tops."

Boudreaux sat up and grimaced. "You can't sit still, can you?"

"Not anymore. Something bad's going down. I need your help, but I can't offer anything in return, pal."

"I know. Even those Saints tickets are kinda useless now, huh."

Jonathan nodded.

Boudreaux dug into his pocket and retrieved a key-chain with a dozen keys attached to it. He hesitated for a moment but then threw the set at Jonathan. "You got thin fingers, so remove the Dodge key—it's my grand-mother's beater."

Jonathan pried it from the keychain and laid the keys on the folding table.

"It's twenty-five years old, and it's still runnin' fine, if you don't mind the rusted fenders and torn seats."

"She won't mind?"

"No, my brother took her to Memphis on Saturday." Boudreaux retrieved a map from the front seat of the police minivan and returned to the table, flattened the map and pointed at an area south of the river. "Here, this is your way out. At nine o'clock tonight a bunch of boats are pulling up to the docks about a block from here. They're going to Avondale Shipyards."

"What for?" The shipyard, located about twelve miles upstream from downtown, had been a client of Jonathan's former firm many years back when it was still a large defense contractor with a huge backlog of Navy vessels under construction.

"We're moving sensitive cargo out of the city."

"Sensitive?"

"Yes, money—lots of it—from the casino, from downtown banks, from a lot of places. I heard there'll be armored trucks waiting at the shipyard to move the stuff out of state. You can hitch a ride on one of the boats, then from the shipyard walk over to Bridge City. My grandma's house is on 14th Street—the third one on the left from the levee. You'll see the beater in the driveway."

"How d'you know it's still there, undamaged?"

"I heard the area's not badly hit."

Jonathan thought about how he'd get to Houston. He worried about having enough money for the trip, that he might not even find Mariya if she refused to answer his phone calls once there, that roads further west might be blocked. But he was determined to try.

18

A GUNSHOT RANG OUT A BLOCK NORTH OF WAL-MART.
Jonathan and Boudreaux glanced at each other. It was
the fifth time they'd heard a firearm discharge in the last
twenty minutes, all from different directions. There had
been many more since sunset, just like Boudreaux had
predicted. With every street in New Orleans dark and
filled with roaming looters, Jonathan was glad to be in
this secured compound on Tchoupitoulas in the company of about fifty well-armed cops.

It wasn't long into the night when Jonathan began to
think of Linda. At first he felt guilty for not contacting
her, at least to tell her he was safe. But the more he
thought about it, he realized that despite his earlier vow
to stop speaking with her, he missed hearing her voice.
He considered trying to reach her on the single working
cell phone in the makeshift camp but then talked himself
out of it. He'd find a better opportunity later.

At ten till nine, a shotgun-wielding Boudreaux and
five other officers convened near four large U-Haul

trucks that had taken refuge in the Wal-Mart lot since late afternoon. The civilian drivers slowly maneuvered the trucks out of the lot and into an alley that ran along the riverbank, as the on-foot police escort kept pace. Jonathan followed them about two blocks upstream, toward a dock. There they waited, chatting casually, their words interrupted now and then by the sounds of low-flying helicopters. They stuck to small talk, and that was just fine with Jonathan. He was exhausted and had seen enough on this Monday to numb him from more meaningful dialogue.

A tug boat and a large cabin cruiser arrived about twenty minutes later than scheduled. There were other boats nearby, but only the two had pulled up to the dock.

Jonathan watched the handful of private security guards and NOPD officers transfer the trucks' contents to both boats. There were dozens of suitcases, trunks and crates that he assumed contained cash, jewelry and other valuables, along with large framed paintings, what looked like a huge Egyptian vase protected top and bottom by Styrofoam and a metal frame.

Boudreaux leaned into Jonathan. "From some of the mansions on St. Charles and around Audubon Park. And those guys...two are Israelis, former military. When you got money, you can pay for the best to take your belongings to safekeeping." That's when Jonathan realized the clandestine delivery wasn't so much about getting the cash from banks out, but rather that New Orleans' rich and famous had arranged a flotilla to secure their most precious possessions. It filled him with disgust that resources were being used for this purpose while women in wheelchairs waited helplessly on expressway ramps and people like Garceau were left dead on the street.

Jonathan shook the sergeant's hand, boarded the tug boat and sat at the stern, observing the eerie, pitch-black banks of the river.

The flotilla moved upstream fairly slowly. Jonathan heard frequent thumps and thuds as the hulls hit debris floating down the river, but that was to be expected from a storm the size of Katrina. At one point, a man held a searchlight over the water, pointing out logs and other floating artifacts. As Jonathan walked over to join him, the man gasped. He'd flashed his light over two bloated bodies that slowly passed them downstream, in the opposite direction.

They continued for some forty minutes past the darkened riverbanks. A few more gunshots rang out, and occasional screams and yells echoed from shore along with the sounds of cars, perhaps merely joyriders in stolen cars taking advantage of a chaotic night.

Soon they passed under the Huey P. Long Bridge, whose unlighted metallic silhouette appeared ghostly. Jonathan then spotted lights about a mile ahead on the left bank. Two floodlights, probably powered by generators, illuminated the small dock adjacent to a large dry dock in front of the sprawling but dilapidated facilities of Avondale Shipyards. Jonathan knew the place well from his early years in practice, but now the shipbuilder was only a fraction of the commercial and military manufacturing giant it had been in its glory years, when it was Louisiana's largest employer.

A heavily armed contingent of private security guards waited at the dock as the boats pulled alongside. Jonathan stepped out, helping others unload a heavy metal crate to a waiting armored van. There was no commotion and little conversation, other than a guy who seemed in charge, methodically instructing as to which vehicles would take on which loads. It all seemed well choreographed, in sharp contrast to the disorder Jonathan had seen from the moment the flooding began.

Jonathan left the bevy and headed for the river path. It was a short walk to 14th Street, where Boudreaux had assured him the truck was parked. To Jonathan's relief, he was right. The old beater was there, with nearly a full tank of gas, and the engine started on the first try.

Highway 3127 was open but congested. It took him nearly an hour to reach Grosse Tete, a hamlet a few miles west of Baton Rouge where he'd planned to take I-10, but to his frustration, the interstate highway was closed. He headed north and took Highway 103 westward, driving past the dark streets of Opelousas, past Eunice, past Kinder, past barren, dark land.

When he finally arrived near I-10 again, in Saint Charles, it appeared to be open, but there was a more pressing problem: he was nearly out of gas and both stations at foot of the I-10 ramp were closed.

"I'm screwed," he whispered, frustrated at how far he'd gotten only to be stuck here with no gas. There was only one option left, and he had no choice but to try it.

*   *   *

"Thank you," Jonathan said two hours after hitching a ride. He stepped out of the man's Suburban, thankful to have made it to Houston. "I wish I could give you more." He offered the man a twenty, but the man refused, pushing back Jonathan's hand.

As the Suburban drove away, Jonathan chuckled, wondering how he'd even fit in the vehicle, which carried the man's heavyset wife, three kids, a large mutt, and loads of crammed belongings. He'd never hitch-hiked before, but these were exceptional times.

The half-lit "welcome" sign of the Smile Motel was hardly a comforting greeting, but it would do for now. The Good Samaritan who'd given him a ride to Houston was friends with the owner and had promised that a room would be waiting.

Jonathan checked into his room and immediately dialed Mariya's cell phone.

"Yes?"

"It's me—Jonathan."

"Hmm, it's about time."

"In case you haven't heard," Jonathan snapped, "the hurricane caused a bit of damage, and the phones are down."

"Honestly, I was very worried. Where are you?"

"In Houston. Are you here as well?"

"Yes."

"Then we need to talk."

"About what exactly?"

"I have everything you want about the body."

She paused—a long moment of silence that made Jonathan jittery.

"You hear me?"

"Yes. I'll come see you now—but only if you have what you say you do. I'm leaving in the morning."

"To where?"

"I'll tell you in person. Something serious—very serious—is happening."

Jonathan gave her the address to the Smile Motel. Then he jumped into the shower and scrubbed away what seemed like a lifetime's accumulation of dirt, sweat and blood.

*   *   *

Through a slim opening in the curtains, Jonathan spotted Mariya's car idling outside. She'd called him moments earlier, sounding surprisingly mellow.

Perhaps I should feel anxious, he thought. After all, she's the one who'd put him in a heap of trouble. But he didn't. Maybe his fatigued body couldn't muster the strength to be angry or worried. Instead, he felt a strange sense of relief that she was here.

He left the room with his backpack and got in her car.

"I'm glad to see you safe," she said.

"Safe is not the first thing that comes to mind when I'm around you, Mariya."

"Tell me you're happy to see me, even slightly."

Jonathan shrugged.

"You have the information?" she voiced casually, as if his answer wouldn't matter. But he knew there was only one reason she'd gone to the trouble of coming to see him this late in the night.

"Yes, I have the coroner's file in my bag."

"Good." She eyed his backpack. "So, I guess I can kill you now."

Jonathan took in her dry Russian humor as if it was a brief whiff of shit-flavored air. "After all that's happened since Friday, I almost don't care if you do."

He thought back over the past twenty-four hours—how it had started; how many steps he'd taken through filthy floodwaters; how the throbbing pain in his head and neck hadn't gone away completely since being clobbered at the morgue; how, despite best efforts, he'd watched a man die; how he'd narrowly avoided violence at the hands of an angry mob of looters; how he'd even made it out of New Orleans in the rust bucket that Boudreaux had let him use; how he'd managed to hitch a ride the rest of the way to Houston; and how he was still standing with such little sleep. The day had worn him down to where he could no longer trust his senses. *Killing me might be the relief I need*, he mused. He glanced at the clock on the dash. It was just past one in the morning.

"I want to go with you," Jonathan said.

"Don't be ridiculous." She tightly grabbed his left wrist. "You've helped me a lot already, and if you give me that file, I'll take care of things from here on."

"No, I'm going with you, and you're going to pay me for my time at my regular billing rate."

"Clearly, Hurricane Katrina has made you insane."

"I left New Orleans with only this backpack, my wallet, a little money, and my passport, just to find you. I can't go back there without answers. So, against my better judgment, I will follow you wherever that evidence leads." He closed his eyes, the fatigue wearing him down.

She sighed. "You want to go to Panama with me?"

Jonathan opened only one eye. "Panama? Why?"

"The *Nixos-Dakar* is sailing there as we speak and will cross the canal in two days."

"Tell me more."

"Why should I?"

Jonathan reached into his bag and took out the quarter-inch thick file folder. "*This* is why. It's cost a coroner his life and nearly got me killed, and it could cost me my law license, among other things. You owe that to me."

"I was wondering what happened to the back of your head," she said, her eyes now fixated on the file. She took it and flipped through the pages and photographs. "A few hours ago I received a coded message from home. I have instructions to inspect the ship before it crosses the canal. Apparently there's something boiling. Something big. Something serious enough to make my President summon an urgent meeting at the Kremlin at three in the morning and then have one of his most senior deputies give that order directly to me—not through normal channels, but only to me—with not even a whisper of details or reasons."

"I find it hard to believe that you don't know more. When your lips move, I hear the same cryptic bullshit, so pardon me if I'm a bit skeptical now."

"This is completely different. At this exact moment, a planeload of Russian special forces is on its way to South or Central America—they refused to tell me where. This has not happened in decades, if ever! Something very strange is brewing, and they're also going to extraordinary lengths to ensure that your country's intelligence services know nothing about it. So, I'm trying to piece it together, but my people aren't talking. We can learn things from that ship, perhaps. I sense a very sinister undercurrent but can't figure it out...*yet*."

"Take me with you. I can help."

"I'm already expecting help there, so I don't know what good you would be."

"Let me help. I need the money, and after all you've just put me through, you owe me a favor." Jonathan would never before have considered asking such a thing, but Katrina had turned his already drab financial picture into an ugly reality. He was nearly out of cash and had less than two thousand dollars available on both his credit cards combined; not much more in his personal checking account; only about twice that in savings; and around nine thousand on the firm's account—if Dino hadn't already withdrawn it. Regardless, with the city flooded and without power, his debit cards were unusable, and his credit card hadn't worked at the motel. Worse yet, Katrina wiped out all hopes of billable legal work for the foreseeable future.

"You're asking me to bring you along, and also to pay you?"

"That's right." Jonathan was doing his best to not appear weak, but he knew his bargaining strength was tantamount to zero if he handed her the coroner's folder. Then again, he thought, she could just shoot him and take it away free and clear.

She smirked. "I don't need legal advice, that's for sure. So, I'm not paying your hourly rate."

"Then a flat fee."

"You have balls asking me this."

"You have more balls than me, Mariya."

She gazed at him pensively. "Let's make it simple: five thousand for five days. You do exactly as you're told, and you don't interfere with my team. If I want to keep you longer, only I decide. So, take it or leave it."

"Deal. Thanks."

Jonathan quickly checked out of the motel and got back in her car. Mariya drove out of the pot-holed lot and headed north on the Eastex Freeway. She didn't ask anything, and he didn't volunteer anything, either. Instead, the quietness of the thirty-five minute drive to her hotel from the seedy motel on Washington Avenue where she'd picked him up had almost allowed him to fall asleep.

"We're here," Mariya said as she tapped Jonathan's leg with her hand. He jolted his head up and saw the beaming red Sheraton sign at the top of the ten-story building. They headed into the parking lot.

As soon as she had put the car in Park, she turned to him and said, "I need to ask you something important." Her voice was steady and deliberate, which warned him that she was about to tell him something he wouldn't like.

"Don't tell me...There's another body you'd like me to find."

She didn't smile like he'd hoped.

"Do you promise not to interfere with my work?"

"I promise."

"Don't mess things up for me. I'm already bending the rules like you wouldn't believe. And you'd better be helpful if I ask you to do something."

"Sure."

"I'm serious," she said, her eyes searching his face. "Can I count on you?"

"Yes, of course." Jonathan was tempted to spell out his reservations and disclaimers—as any lawyer should, he thought—but he held back.

By the time they reached Mariya's room, Jonathan could barely keep his eyes open. He crashed, fully dressed on the bed closest to the door and dozed off before the Russian sleuth could utter anything else.

I cling eccentrically to this fresh idea,
inspiration more frightening than solitude:
My heart stings logically from the battle
to keep cocooned and contorted to the tune of a lie,
a false longing I may bare, maddeningly, in my cradle
so your aloofness sends me not to die,
and your pride meanders untorn from its saddle.
My love, withheld...

19

A THRONG OF PASSENGERS HUDDLED AT ONE END OF THE bar by the departure lounge to gawk at the images as the agitated voice of CNN's Anderson Cooper muted the crowd, his somber gaze and bleak words muffled only by the occasional boarding instructions from the ground crew in the half-empty departure lounge. To Jonathan, Cooper's impassioned commentary mattered less than the shocking images.

The camera aboard the helicopter panned over the giant metal scaffold of the Crescent City Bridge that spanned the Mississippi River. New Orleans' Central Business District edged into view as the reporter's arm cut into the middle of the camera's focus, pointing at the Superdome, the white-colored coating of its huge bulbous roof shredded to reveal an unseemly grayish-brown steel core with several holes poking through the top, and hundreds of survivors loitering in the streets below.

Jonathan shook his head, his eyes glued to the appalling scenes of destruction. He thought of Sergeant

Boudreaux, hoping he had left Wal-Mart and gotten himself to better shelter.

As he attempted to process the images on the screen, Jonathan felt a hand gently caress his shoulder. Mariya had come to his side, her eyes fixated on the TV above the bar's liquor-filled shelves.

"I'm sorry," she said. "This must be hard on you."

The footage panned further west, past the Superdome and the Broadmoor neighborhood, and further still as the helicopter maneuvered over downtown and the Central City neighborhood, he presumed. His heart sank. He ran his fingers through his hair, skipping a breath the moment the images revealed a seemingly endless reflective glaze in the midst of the city's urban structures and greenery. Water. Water just about everywhere. He'd seen it from the ground, but the aerial footage gave him an apocalyptic sense of the tragedy. The flooding carpeted a vast swath west of downtown. The length of the elevated concrete of I-10 dipped in and out of the floodwaters over several miles, like a sea snake.

Anderson Cooper's narration thinned into a meaningless drivel. Jonathan knew exactly what the images meant. His home was but a quarter-mile south of the scene now flashing on the monitor. The disaster had devastated the city, his neighborhood, his street, and most likely his home, too.

The filthy river and lake water had dragged floating debris and refuse into thousands of homes and businesses. The stark footage numbed him. He could still smell the stench of the water he'd tread through while carrying the wounded Garceau. The thought of the same grimy water engulfing his home made his heart sink deeper. Had it reached his block? Had it risen higher than the two feet that separated the floor of his home from street-level, or higher yet, to the shelves of the file cabinet in his laundry room, where he'd kept his few valuables: the lone family album that had survived the fire, his childhood notebooks and diaries, and the photographs Amber had brought him from the office on Sunday? Had the toxic water risen to Nagi's painting in the kitchen? If that was the case, the home might as well be condemned.

The thought of losing another home suddenly slowed his mind. He studied the aerial imagery a few more seconds before it cut to a commercial. He had no way of knowing for sure, and there was nothing he could do about it now. Turning away from the TV and eyeing Mariya, he felt a strange calmness take over—just like when he'd boarded up the window to his home—the sense of loss seemed to have already been embedded, deeply, like a long-passed *fait accompli*, as if whatever possessions that had perished now had already been taken from him long ago. In so many ways they had: his marriage to Linda; the once flourishing law firm; the heirlooms that burned in the fire; the house Linda and he had carefully renovated; the good life—an uncomplicated contentment that had been real an eternity ago.

Jonathan resigned to stop second-guessing his future. He'd insisted on joining Mariya's call to arms, and that meant following her demands, wherever they might lead, and for now it felt like the dose of escapism he needed to stay sane.

He looked straight into Mariya's eyes and said, "It doesn't matter anymore." The words seemed to flush out his mind, though he still ached for his neighbors, his Crescent City brethren—all of them, rich or poor, who'd had the misfortune to not find a way out and were now cast into a horrible predicament. He feared for them what he'd experienced at the besieged Wal-Mart: the elderly owner of the convenience store near his house; the old man who'd walked his poodle tied to his wheel-chair: the woman who'd always waved when she passed by his house with her stroller. So many familiar faces, and such bad luck, such sadness.

"Let's board," Mariya said.

*   *   *

Mariya had arranged first class seats for the both of them. *She probably travels in first all the time*, Jonathan thought, wondering if she'd felt too guilty to send him to coach or if she just wanted to keep an eye on him. But even coach tickets were pricey and it reminded him of his precarious situation: he was headed to a foreign country a thousand miles away depending almost entirely on handouts from an unpredictable Russian hellion who'd likely sacrifice him if and when it suited her. *What am I doing?*

While the plane idled on the tarmac, he incessantly mulled over the dilemma of staying at Mariya's mercy, but he couldn't ease his angst. Linda also popped into his head, quite unexpectedly. He hadn't called her and his phone had since gone dead. Had she tried to reach him? Was she worried when the phone lines went down as Katrina swept over the city? How could he leave for Panama without having spoken with her? A feeling of guilt suddenly overtook him, until Amber's logic eased its way into his mind. He regrasped the reality that he was divorced, that he had no obligation to his ex, that he was on his own. But in some ways, he wanted Linda to worry. Perhaps seeing the same aerial images he'd seen before they boarded would help her recalibrate. Perhaps she'd miss him. She'd worry. For now, he'd fight his urge to call her.

Reclined in his first class seat, his eyes vacantly gazing at the lighted NO SMOKING sign above, and waiting for boarding to end, he lamented his imminent departure from U.S. soil. *How irresponsible*, he now thought. *If anything happens to me, no one will know where to look.*

The plane took off. His hesitation to leave Houston was now a moot point. If Mariya were to abandon him and his credit card didn't work in Panama, he'd have no way to return. He glanced at her. *I must treat you nicely,* he thought grudgingly.

As the plane leveled off, Mariya tilted her head against the half-closed window shade, and an off-white carpet of clouds behind her illuminated by the bright morning sun. She was immersed in a poetry book: *Ariel*, by Sylvia Plath. She looked at him and silently mouthed the word, "What?"

Jonathan shrugged.

"What?" she then voiced, sloping her head to one side and nudging her reading glasses to the tip of her nose. "Why are you looking at me that way?"

He shook his head. "No reason."

"Something's bothering you, so just say it."

"It's in English," Jonathan said, pointing at the book's cover.

"I enjoy reading in English, too, you know." Her tone hardened. "Almost as much as Russian."

Her feistiness, even for something as trivial as reading material, made Jonathan roll his eyes. "But poetry?"

"Yes, so what?"

"It doesn't seem natural for you."

"What do you mean? You read what I wrote you, right?

Jonathan shrugged. "What are you talking about?"

"Didn't you?" She looked at him puzzled.

"I read your four-word note, so what?"

She shook her head and her eyes saddened. "You didn't read it..." She ended the sentence with a sip of wine.

"Poetry's not your thing, hun." He'd always thought of poetry as the richest of the literary arts, and one that normally draws mankind's most sane, calm, and solicitous persons. Not a devious spy with an inseparable kinship with deceit; not a woman with a penchant for inflicting mayhem. He imagined Mariya as a child: running after boys with scissors; a hostile little creature lobbing Molotov cocktails to celebrate birthdays; and deflating ambulance tires on her way to school. "You are a violent person, Mariya, and I only had the distinct joy of meeting you after you hit forty. I can only imagine if it had been earlier, when you were in your prime, probably busy lopping off some poor man's testicles in a remote Cold War prison or poisoning a political candidate in some poverty-stricken sub-Saharan country, or some other form of malice. Am I far off?"

"Very far, my friend. You have me quite wrong. If you'd met me earlier, we'd be sitting here as lovers, or even as husband and wife." She said this with a seriousness that frightened him.

"I see you as someone who reads dark, violent fantasy, given what I assume was a traumatic upbringing in your former Communist utopia."

She leaned into him and whispered sternly, "You saw me kill one person who deserved to die, and you assumed I did the same with another man equally deserving of the same fate. But you've seen nothing else. So don't judge what you don't know. And as for my literary preferences, it is and always will be poetry. It's part of my soul—the real me that you haven't yet had the fortune of discovering."

Jonathan scoffed. "Poetry, huh. That seems as bizarre as seeing you nurse an infant." He could hardly contain the sarcasm rolling off his tongue.

"Verses soothe me," she declared, studying him. "I grew up with it on the radio and on TV. I often sat for hours listening to poetry readings with my mother, until my father came home from work and switched the channel to his comedy shows. How I despised his interruptions, especially with Mikhail Zhvanetsky."

"Mikhail who?"

"A popular comedian. My father was also addicted to *Vokrug Smeha*, a comedy show that drove my mother nuts, and he always turned the volume up so loud. Our apartment was nice—even by Western standards—but not large. There was no place to hide from the noise. By the time I was in my twenties, I'd heard every joke east of the Dnieper River."

"That explains your perpetual grumpiness."

She lightly slapped Jonathan's elbow. "Your words only show me how little you know me. What nurtures me is poetry. Always has. Funny poetry. Serious poetry. Revealing poetry."

"Murderous poetry?" he said, smirking.

"Obviously, you've never read Plath. If you had, you'd understand." She shook her head. "Poetry is richer than any other written expression, and in Russia it was always held with esteem—except for people like my father, I suppose. It's had a special place in me since my teens and still does to this day."

Jonathan was glad they were talking somewhat like normal folks, perhaps for the first time since they'd met.

"My closest friend was a poet," she added, fiddling with a corner of the page, and looking down as though trying to hide a saddened smile. "An amazing man—a few years younger than me—and a talented musician, too. He had presence, the kind that makes a woman weak at the knees. A beautiful human being, with adorable rounded cheekbones and piercing eyes and shapely, inviting lips." She glanced at Jonathan. "Lips like yours. You remind me of him, and in more ways than I like to think. Your smile especially, your body language, and your all-knowing, disarming, greenish-brown eyes."

She folded the dog-ear back and forth between her fingers a few more times and then closed the book, lay-ing it flat on her lap, her eyes fixated on the cover. She bit her bottom lip.

"What's his name?"

"Alexander Nickolaevich Bashlachev—or simply Sasha. Some friends called him SashBash." Mariya stretched her arms out and then ran her fingers through her hair. "Oh, Sasha," she whispered, shaking her head, and pulled the window shade all the way up and peered out the window. "He read me poems he'd written in a notebook. I sat for hours, mesmerized by each verse and craving the next, but also craving the tone of his voice that carried me into the clouds—to the moon, actually. Then, when he'd tire of reading, he would take his guitar over his knee, his soft hands touching the chords with gentle, flawless precision, his eyes locked on me the entire length of each song, until the echo from the last note vanished. I was his most important listener, it seemed. I felt like the most important person on earth. No one had ever held me in such a place, on the highest pedestal."

"Were you lovers?"

She seemed surprised and paused. "No..."

She downed the last of her drink, placed the book in the seat pocket and met Jonathan's intrigued gaze.

"I remember Sasha's slender arms," she continued, "as if they were holding me now. His long, disheveled dark brown hair. I can still recall the pattern of the veins on the back of his hand. His double-knotted shoe-laces. The exact shape of his eyebrows. The brusque, manly way he lit his cigarette. Every damn detail. And especially his enchanting verses, his songs, his soul..."

She turned to the window and began humming a tune, lightly, her eyes lost to the clouds below the plane. "His voice transported me far away from our dreary, gray Soviet existence. Far into a surreal, alien world that our imagination constructed merely from myths, hyperbole, music and poetry. Yes, poetry and music, the drugs I craved the most. More than even water and air. Our world could not have seemed more complete in those precious moments we shared. So long ago."

Jonathan rested his head back, still watching Mariya.

"I can still remember as if it were yesterday. My father was with me. We'd argued the entire way to the train station, in his noisy chauffeur-driven army vehicle. I was headed to Leningrad to see Sasha, and the only reason he'd agreed to take me to the station was to have more time to persuade me not to go. He hated everything that was new, fresh or had a semblance of counter-culture, or that even remotely pushed the boundaries of the social ineptness that was the USSR of my younger days. My father was the old guard. A staunch Stalinist. He had no tolerance for his precious daughter befriending a young, eclectic artist whose ways could be confused for those of a Brit or an American, he'd warned—though I had never befriended a Westerner in those days.

"Did he convince you to stay?"

"He deliberately told the driver to take side streets, yelling at me, humiliating me, nearly slapping me, until I arrived at the station fifteen minutes after the train had departed." Mariya's hands rose to her mouth. "I remember my face, full of tears. So wet I couldn't even see the empty platform and train tracks in front of me. I must have cried for hours. I had never been so angry and hurt all at once."

"Well, such is young love."

"No, I was in my early thirties!"

"What?"

"Yes, ridiculous, right? But I stayed with my parents when I wasn't on assignment overseas or in different parts of the Soviet Union."

"Are you still in touch with Sasha?"

Her head fell to one side, her eyes narrowing. "No." A heavy pause filled her breath. She reopened her eyes wide and picked up her book, cracking it open to the saved page. "The next day, Sasha fell from the ninth floor of an apartment building."

"I...I'm sorry."

She nodded, her mouth as straight as a hyphen.

Jonathan began to feel bad that he'd led her recollections down this path.

She raised her eyebrows. "And what do you read?"

"Pleadings, legal briefs, depositions, transcripts, affidavits, and other highly creative fiction from clients and adverse parties. Fun stuff."

"Hmm."

Jonathan could see the ghost of Sasha in her eyes.

"Have I ever told you how attractive you are?" she asked. "How it disturbs me that you are so untouchable?"

"No, you haven't. And that's probably a good thing."

"Do you even know what love is?"

Jonathan chuckled. "I should ask you that."

"Then ask me."

"I don't need your answer. If you somehow know

what love is, then at best you are bipolar and there's medication to treat you, and therefore some hope."

"Love is violent sometimes; it can be chaotic; it can be destructive; but that's what makes it the most misunderstood human emotion."

"I know what it is *not*."

She shook her head and sighed. "You wouldn't see love even if it stung you in the face."

"We are very different people..."

She looked down and turned to a new page of her book. The conversation was over, apparently.

An odd, unanswered question lingered—not in any form that could easily be voiced, but rather sensed by its absence of words—and he felt it creep into the space between them. A question he simply couldn't answer: how could she accept him tagging along with her? He was no spy. He'd had one lucky spell ten years ago when he'd made it out alive from a maddening international espionage plot, but he'd done nothing of the sort since then. His key skills—knowledge of the maritime industry and of admiralty law—would be of little use to her in Panama. He had no fancy gadgets, no weapons, and couldn't kill anyone with a simple gesture of the hand. *My Spanish,* he then thought. That was the only skill he could think of that had any value to her, but he didn't really speak it that well.

*   *   *

The captain's voice screeched through the PA system. The plane would be on the ground in thirty minutes.

Mariya closed her window shade, dragged her oversized purse from under the seat in front of her and unzipped the main compartment. Jonathan was amused to note that the interior was sheer clutter, its contents clunking loudly as she wrestled to keep it steady on her lap. There was no telling what was inside, but it had cleared security. She seemed, at that moment at least, like any other woman, using a purse of limited dimensions as an armoire with a strap. This was the first time Jonathan had ever had some assurance that she wasn't carrying a firearm.

Mariya lowered the tray in front of her and tossed onto it a small vinyl pouch she'd pulled from the depths of her purse. She threw Jonathan a frown, as if she wasn't pleased he was there, prying into her business.

She pulled the zipper back and shook the contents out of the pouch and onto the tray.

Jonathan peered wide-eyed at what had fallen out. Five different passports—their varied colors forming a sort of rainbow—and three ID cards, and a half-dozen credit cards strapped together by a rubber band. She quickly tossed the cards and three of the passports back into the pouch and seemed to ponder which of the remaining two to use—a British one or a dark green one with the words DIPLOMATIC PASSPORT embossed in gold at the bottom, under the Cyrillic spelling of Ukraine.

She covered it with her hand when she noticed him leaning over to look. "Stop."

"So much for the innocence of poetry."

She curled her lip. "Read a magazine and shut up."

"You could use the Pope's passport, for all I care. Just don't drag me down with you if you get caught."

Her brow hardened. "I've never gotten caught."

"Uh-huh. I see you're still drunk on Soviet-era bluster. Enjoy your Panamanian jail cell alone."

Mariya blurted something in Russian, tossed the UK passport into the pouch and then began filling out her immigration form with her Ukrainian passport opened to the picture page.

Jonathan stretched his neck over her shoulder and read out loud the name on it. "Tanya Morosh?"

"Don't push your luck."

The volatile Russian sleuth turned her shoulder, blocking his view, and then huddled over the documents until she was done. She slipped the passport into her purse and returned the pouch deep into the pile of clutter, her elbow planted on the wide armrest separating her seat from Jonathan's.

"You *are* dangerous."

She shrugged her shoulders. "Maybe, but today I'm a Ukrainian diplomat, so if you didn't want to have sex with me before because I was Russian, this is the best excuse to finally do me now." She half-smiled.

Jonathan studied her. She'd always had a mysterious, wicked something about her that drew him close. But nothing had ever happened back then, for many reasons, Jonathan recalled, and principally because he was married, and Linda mattered more than anything. Now, he sensed Mariya was availing herself of the opportunity again. Linda was gone. Jonathan was in a different place. The temptation lingered in his head for a long minute.

"That's too bad," he said, smiling. "I would have considered it if you'd chosen to be British." But now, his mockery only made him recall that awkward moment years ago. Mariya had just blown a man's head off and almost immediately after, still seated in her chair, lit up a cigarette, the scent of gun powder mixing with the tobacco smoke in the small confines of the dead scientist's dacha. She'd grinned, gloating over her kill. Her cigarette half-finished, she'd ordered Jonathan to the bedroom at gunpoint and demanded he have sex with her. *Demanded.*

He'd decline then and he'd decline again now. Divorced or not, he wouldn't be lured into the freakish world of a woman who got that turned on by her own violence, no matter how remotely curious he might be about her sexual prowess. Quite simply, Mariya was nitroglycerine, and for the love of sanity—and if you value your life—you don't fire it up or have sex with it. Ever.

20

JONATHAN KEPT HIS DISTANCE FROM MARIYA THE MOMENT they left the plane as if she'd contracted leprosy, and even more so when they shuffled through the hall leading to Passport Control at Panama's Tucomen Airport.

He observed her casually meander to a line reserved for cabin crew and diplomats, her strides long, her confidence unwavering, it seemed. To his amazement Mariya had gotten only a brief glance from the officer, who in a matter of seconds had stamped her papers and waved her through as she gave the man a glowing smile and eased away with the flair of a rock star. After clearing the booth, she lobbed a gloating nod at Jonathan.

He calmed down as soon as he'd cleared customs, shortly after Mariya had done so. He cautiously rejoined her in the arrivals lounge.

Mariya swept the thin shawl she'd worn in the plane off her neck, tucked it into her handbag and turned to Jonathan.

"You weren't afraid before." She leaned her long

plaid-patterned suitcase against her beige linen pants. "When you were in Moscow, you dazzled me with your courage, innocence, and a charming naïveté that is so foreign to us Russians. You really did. Back then..."

The compliment surprised him, but, he thought, it was her choice of past tense that was the real message she'd just conveyed. *Does she now think of me as timid, or even cowardly?* All the while he told himself his prudence was borne out of hardship. Adhering to a well-justified, sane caution was imperative—something she'd hardly understand. *That's what happens when you've been burnt enough in life,* Jonathan told himself.

Perhaps Mariya was not altogether fearless herself, no matter that she'd always done her utmost to display an unshakable image of resilience. But he couldn't prove it. She wore her strength on her sleeve, in her eyes, in her stance, in the way she moved, the way she scrutinized everyone and everything within pistol range of her. She wasn't about to let herself be pried open for Jonathan's inspection, but he had seen a glimpse of vulnerability on the plane.

"We must wait," she said coolly.

Jonathan gazed at her, at her erudite pose, her large designer purse dangling at her hip, her silk blouse no doubt fitted by the finest couturier. Mariya looked like an ad in a travel magazine, her arms loosely crossed but relaxed, a strange, confident but soft aloofness crossing her face as she looked away from Jonathan—purposely, it seemed—and out the window. If she were fifteen years younger, anyone would have confused her for a model heading to a photo shoot deep in the tropical rainforest.

She could also have passed for an esoteric jetsetter, escaping urbanhood to a remote cabana on the desolate Panamanian shore, palm trees casting shadows over her slightly lined cheekbones, her body stretched across a catamaran, a bubbly flute glass in hand. No guns. No secrets. No scheming. No one to threaten or injure. No battlefield to plant the flag of her Mother Russia. The farfetchedness of this illusion made him chuckle. Such a passive, inert purpose to a journey would send this woman into cardiac arrest.

Everything that had happened from the moment he'd scrambled out of New Orleans to this very moment here in the middle of this Central American airport terminal had passed with such speed that he'd not allowed himself time to reconcile and reset all that he'd witnessed. Every second recycled mental images of the dark, flooded streets, the silence broken by random gunshots and unanswered cries from rooftops. The sounds piercing the dense night air. He touched the back of his head, feeling the tender bump on his scalp. His mind honed in on the attack at the morgue and the moment he'd regained consciousness to find Dr. Garceau bloodsoaked and near death. The adrenaline rush had endured nearly nonstop through the pitch-dark siege in the barricaded Wal-Mart. He couldn't dilute the mental aftershocks as fast as they popped into his conscience, along with the hundreds of questions piling up with no answers to quell the onslaught. Troubling questions. Whether he'd done the right thing. Whether he'd regret following Mariya. And if not, had he the courage to stay with her? He knew the answers could not come fast enough. He yearned to put all this into a logical framework—something, anything that made sense—or he might just lose it.

Jonathan picked up his duffel bag, swung it over his shoulder and faced her. "Don't keep me in the dark." There was no telling what he'd get for resurrecting the issue, but staying silent was no longer tolerable.

"What?"

He dropped his bag hard at her feet. "I need to know what we're doing here," he snapped in a loud whisper. "You owe me the truth."

"We'll see," she replied, nodding her head as she looked at him out of the corner of her eye.

"Yeah, just like last time. Your silence ten years ago nearly got me shot by snipers and mauled by dogs. Your silence this weekend nearly got me killed in a morgue. You shouldn't be surprised that I want answers."

Mariya looked over her shoulders and scanned the arrivals lounge. "This isn't the time."

"It never is."

"Why don't you appreciate the fact that I've taken you away from the hurricane...for a little adventure?"

"Adventure? Are you mad?"

"I know the shithole your life has been lately, and that's before Katrina turned your city into a sewer." Her voice hardened. "You should thank me."

"You're being ridiculous. My life is normal, no more or less chaotic than anyone else's. No richer, no poorer. Just normal."

"I know what you've gone through the last five years. I've kept an eye on you."

"Explain, because I'm getting annoyed."

"You've gone through hell. Your last law firm went out of business, and you were just about broke. Remember when you emptied your office, lugging your belongings through the pouring rain to the U-Haul outside; when you had so much debt you could barely pay for the gas in your car; when Linda walked out on you; when you were...lost? When all that shit happened, who was there? Who do you think *was* standing there, near you, with an umbrella in hand, watching you load the boxes onto the back of the truck from across the street? Your blue shirt and black slacks were drenched. Your face looked numb from the shock, from your battered ego. You moved like someone who'd been drugged. I know how you felt. I heard your phone calls. Who do you think was there feeling sorry for you? And where do you think that cash came from?"

"Cash?"

"You know exactly what I mean—the money in that bottom drawer."

Jonathan's mind quickly spun back to that week, to that Tuesday morning when three of his law partners strolled skittishly into his office to inform him they were leaving—but not with just a simple departure. They'd gotten into so much debt that they were taking the entire firm down with them. Jonathan's prestigious, eighteen-lawyer admiralty practice, established in the 1950s by admired mentors, had suddenly tanked. It would make the papers. It would become the brunt of jokes around courtroom halls for months. The collapse had come only weeks after Linda had thrown in the towel and moved out to a small apartment in Lafayette before leaving the state altogether.

The speed with which his firm had caved had been all the more bruising. In a matter of eight days, the once sleek, high-rise office space lay vacant, with stained carpets and a scattering of cables and wires as the only reminder that people had worked there. People. People with pride, with souls, with families to feed, parents to care for, hearts to shield, and bills to pay. Real people. All thrown into chaos by three reckless partners.

Jonathan had gotten rid of all his office furniture except for his desk and his client file boxes, the latter a testament to fifteen years of legal advice and a legacy quickly condensed to the form of paper and memories. He'd taken the desk and boxes to a shoddy storage space in Gretna until he'd found his bearings and tried to get back on his feet. But with few clients of his own, and a difficult economic climate, none of the other admiralty practices in the city were willing to bring him on. Finally, with no viable options, he'd thrown up a shingle with Dino. Jonathan had fallen. He'd fallen hard, pride and all. It had hurt then, as it did now to recall that deeply buried defeat—a professional sucker-punch like he'd never thought possible.

"You remember?" Mariya said.

He didn't want to, but the revelation set the wheels in his mind spinning.

The surprise seeped in further as he remembered the moment he'd unloaded his oversized desk from the truck. A thick, sealed manila envelope lay at the bottom of an empty drawer. He'd opened it to find nineteen thousand three hundred fifty-two dollars. When you're desperate and a windfall lands on your lap, you keep your mouth shut and don't trace the source.

"Yes, I remember...a lot of money," he said quietly.

"I had intended twenty thousand," Mariya said. "But I bought a pair of Manolo Blahnik shoes—they were on sale." She shrugged her shoulders and smiled.

The money came from her. He felt goose bumps snake up his spine.

"That was you?" he asked timidly.

She nodded. "I've been around."

"Why?"

"Also when Linda moved out, I sent someone to check on you. I was worried. I thought..."

"But why?" Jonathan asked because he could not imagine a worthwhile motive, and it suddenly disturbed him to picture Mariya as a giver when all along he'd cast the devil's shadow over her.

"Because I've always..." Her phrase faded into an inaudible mumble. She suddenly looked over Jonathan's shoulder and blurted something in Russian.

A burly, sandy-haired man edged past Jonathan and grabbed her luggage. She pointed at Jonathan's duffel bag, and the man quickly picked it up as well.

Mariya's smile returned. "Come on," she uttered, playfully punching Jonathan's chest. "Boris will take good care of us."

Jonathan followed the large man and Mariya to the far curb outside the terminal, where a dark blue Nissan SUV was parked with its engine idling and a blond-haired man half Boris' size leaning on the front grill.

"This is Gennadi," Mariya said to Jonathan.

Boris pointed to the American. "You, in front." The large-framed Russian squeezed into the driver's seat and rolled up the windows, as his smaller colleague and Mariya got in the back.

Jonathan sat silently, trying to dispel Mariya's revelation with questions and doubts, but there was nothing truer than what she'd described on the day he'd left his floundering firm five years ago. The astonishment was still seeping in, but he warned himself not to be swayed by one anecdote of her generosity, not to be lured into bad decisions, and to stay cautious, eyes wide open.

Once away from the airport grounds, Boris reached under his seat and took out a small satchel. He tossed it on the back of the center armrest and said something to Mariya, who reached into it and retrieved a pistol and two loaded magazines.

"*Spasibo*," she said, winking at Jonathan.

Here we go again, Jonathan thought. The relative calm he'd felt with her on the plane was now gone. She was once again armed and back into her comfort zone.

Mariya pretended not to notice his frown. She quickly slid a mag into the well at the base of the handgrip, reached for the top of the weapon, pulled the slide back, and then slid the loaded weapon and the spare mag into her handbag.

They'd taken the highway straight from the airport. Jonathan spotted a handful of tall high-rises in the distance, along the waterfront. But the highway soon turned into the inner city, away from shore.

With Boris driving below the speed limit—no doubt to reduce any chance of encountering police—they'd merged onto the Corridor Norte expressway. The smooth, multilane highway continued a few miles north from the city, but they soon exited to a poorly paved road that alternated between two lanes and four. They headed down the shoddy road, through dense tropical forests and economically deprived hamlets lined with unglamorous storefronts, abandoned cars, run-down tractor trailers, converted U.S. school buses and stray dogs.

Jonathan glanced over his shoulder. Mariya was asleep in her corner of the backseat. He'd never seen her with her eyes closed for any length of time, and it almost disappointed him. Gennadi, next to her, was intensely absorbed by whatever documents he was reading, paying no attention to anyone else in the car.

After thirty minutes in the front seat, and having driven through the dimly lighted town of Chilibre, which seemed as fascinating as watching grass grow, Jonathan gave up his search for the journey's redeeming qualities. For the next forty miles, only the occasional pothole jolted him back to consciousness. He was tired, and it made no sense to fight it.

*   *   *

"We arrive," Jonathan heard in heavily accented English just as Boris bumped his hefty knuckles into his shoulder.

They turned off the main road and headed onto Randolph Avenue. It surprised Jonathan to see street names in English. Street lamps were few and far between on this desolate stretch of pavement. Boris then veered onto another forest-lined road and before long they crossed an abandoned checkpoint.

"We're entering an old American army base," Mariya said, stretching her arms out and yawning.

"How nostalgic. It must have great sentimental value for Russian spies like you," Jonathan said, drawing a scornful look-down from Boris.

Some dilapidated, box-shaped buildings came into view.

Gennadi spoke up, reaching over the center console and pointing with papers in his hand.

"That's the old movie theatre," Mariya said, translating for Gennadi. He spoke again. "The large building coming up is where we're staying."

It was a large, elegant yellow-colored building surrounded by tropical foliage.

"I assume the State of Russia is picking up my tab?"

Mariya chuckled through her yawn. "I think you may have a bigger net worth than my government at the moment."

"That's scary."

Jonathan followed Mariya and her crew into the three-story high atrium that featured soft yellow walls, arched hallways, and a long balcony in the mezzanine overlooking the lobby.

"Do you want your own room?" Mariya whispered, "or do you want to save my country money—"

"And conserve water, and electricity...Yeah, I get it. But no thanks."

Her suggestion didn't surprise him. She kept trying. And perhaps in a different life, in a different place, under different circumstances, he would be truly tempted. Really tempted. But turning her down again amused him, though he felt it was the only real power he could wield over her.

"As you wish." She shrugged her shoulders, pausing as if to give him an opportunity to change his mind. "You don't know what you're missing."

"Oh, I do." *A crazy, armed fifty-year-old-ish nutjob with a penchant for destruction*, he thought. A woman who'd once drugged him in a Moscow hotel room while seducing her lesbian lover right on the bed in front of him. A ruthless spy capable of enough mischief to kill any romantic mood he could ever muster, even if he'd do the unthinkable and relinquish. *Yeah, I know exactly what I'm missing.*

Jonathan reached his room uneventfully, unpacked his meager possessions, and opened the blinds to see the darkness of the forest. The tiredness he knew was there before had not yet returned—even now, just shy of midnight. He heard a knock at the door, followed by Mariya's voice.

"What?" he asked through the door.

"Open."

As soon as he'd cracked the door, Mariya nudged it open with her elbow and took a step forward, her hand pressed on the door frame. "One more thing about what I said at the airport..."

Jonathan was now ready for almost anything.

"To be clear, I wasn't stalking you. Nor was I intruding in your life. I only wanted to help. I have been..." Mariya frowned and took a deep breath. "Never mind. You wouldn't understand."

He was about to speak when she raised her hand to his lips.

"And I also want to remind you that we're meeting Gennadi and Boris in town at eight in the morning, so be ready downstairs twenty minutes before."

It didn't surprise him to see Mariya at his door with a lame excuse.

"Why aren't we going together?" he asked.

"They just left. They're staying at a hotel in downtown Colón, right on the water, where they can watch the ship. It just anchored a half-mile offshore."

"Then why are we staying here?"

"It's safer to split up the team. Besides, this hotel is much nicer."

She paused, standing and gazing, perhaps in wait for Jonathan to make a move. But he didn't.

"Good night," he said.

She left, but it took a while longer for her freshly applied perfume to dissipate.

21

"Hurry!" Mariya barked from the driver's side of her SUV as it idled under the entrance canopy of the hotel.

Jonathan felt tense the moment he got in the passenger side, unable to lean back in his seat.

She greeted him coldly, most likely, he guessed, because he'd rejected her advance the prior night. She wore a short black skirt and dark blue blouse, all of which revealed more fleshy real estate than anything he'd seen of her before. From the corner of his eye he studied her slender, toned legs, and wasn't surprised to see her wearing four-inch heels—inexplicable apparel to begin a second day in the rugged, humid tropical environment of north-central Panama. She abruptly shifted into Drive and sped out from the shadow of the hotel.

"Are you upset with me?"

"No." She kept her eyes on the road.

"Your words are not lost on me," Jonathan said as he recalled some of the things she'd mentioned the previous day: the money she'd loaned him; her references to his resemblance of her Russian poet-musician friend; and other tidbits that had made him uneasy and confused. He didn't want her to brood the rest of the day, so he felt it important to clear the air, or at least attempt to do so. "Right now I can't trust your intentions, and certainly not your words, given our past...and the fact that you still lie or withhold information from me is a problem. If I don't give you the answers you want, or allow myself to be seduced by you, or respond to whatever strange signals you give me, it's *not* because I don't find you attractive. There are reasons, lots of them, and I think for now we should just leave this topic alone. This way, we can concentrate on your mission."

The pause that followed gave him no clue about how his words were received. It felt as if he'd said nothing. Her eyes stayed focused on the road ahead, her body language unchanged, and not a word exited her lips during the ten minute drive to downtown Colón.

They drove up Paseo del Centenario, a divided four-lane street with a grassy, tree-lined median where people seemed to loiter. The homes and businesses were a mix of old and slightly less old, most of them run down. Mariya turned left onto a smaller street lined with two- or three-story colonial-style brick buildings with stylish wrought-iron balconies and arcaded storefronts, which made Jonathan think of Chartres and Toulouse streets in the French Quarter. The resemblance in architecture, however, didn't overcome two striking differences: historical Colón was smaller than the Quarter and suffered from significant decay, with many buildings abandoned, gutted or boarded up as if a storm were headed this way too—but none was.

"Have you been here before?" he asked.

"Once."

"For work or for fun?"

"What do you think?" she said with a vacant glance in his direction.

Mariya passed the crossing at Amador Guerrero Avenue, where on the corner stood the faded bluish-gray facades of the city's two-towered cathedral. They then turned right onto Avenida Bolivar, with its similarly worn feel, until they reached their destination a few blocks further.

The Washington Hotel was the jewel of a bygone era, when Colón had earned its rank as a major transit point for Americans, both military and civilian, associated with the construction and operation of the Panama Canal. Jonathan had read about the hotel in old maritime law cases he'd researched for a dispute years ago.

Mariya turned into the extended driveway leading to the beige-brown facade of the hotel, with its ornately crafted masonry and white-painted accents. She parked at the front of the building a car-length down from the four-columned, arched entranceway.

Jonathan was still bothered by her withdrawn attitude. He followed her up the steps to the lobby—which was surrounded by four opulently carved pillars rising from the stone floor to form archways above the balconied mezzanine before blending into the vaulted ceiling.

Gennadi sat under an oversized metal chandelier that held multiple tube-shaped glass fixtures. His pale skin

contrasted sharply with the dark velour of the brown col-
ored chaise. Some twenty feet behind him, glass doors
led to the back of the hotel, where there appeared to be a
large open space with palm trees and a swimming pool–
–but most importantly, the seawall with a view of cargo
ships waiting their turn to head into the Canal.

Gennadi got up lethargically and barely acknowledged
Mariya and Jonathan as he took a bulky pair of
binoculars from his lap. He escorted them out the back,
along the green-painted concrete terrace that extended to
the stone and cement seawall, where every few seconds
a large wave washed over it. The strong breeze vented
the salty air, throwing their hair back as they faced the
Caribbean waters.

There were thirty or forty ships anchored offshore,
Jonathan guessed, stopping his count at ten. Some were
anchored a few hundred feet from the seawall, while
others were scattered in the distance, nearly half of them
more than a mile away.

"Over there...that's our baby," Mariya said when
Gennadi pointed at the *Nixos-Dakar* before handing her
his binoculars. The vessel was exactly as it appeared in
the pictures Prasanth had pulled up online for Jonathan:
long, black-hulled, with three cranes, and a sizeable
multistory bridge castle painted mostly gray. Her port
side faced the bright, late morning sun, which showed
the well-worn black paint of her steel hull. Toward her
bow, several rows of shipping containers were stacked
two and three high as far forward as the front lift rig atop
the forecastle, but just as Jonathan had gathered from the
photos and data on the ship, the majority of its cargo was

not containers, but rather bulk, kept in the holds below deck and accessible through the large hatches that took up much of the main deck's surface area.

Mariya let Jonathan look through the lenses. He saw no crew on the bridge, nor on the monkey island—the open air deck above the navigation bridge—nor on any of the ship's other decks. Above the bridge castle, the ship's angled, black funnel had a red-painted logo: a snake forming the letter *S*, with one head at each end. From the pictures he'd seen of the ship previously, Jonathan had not noticed that there was more to it than a mere letter. The snake motif made him think of the dead man's tattoo back in New Orleans.

Gennadi and Mariya spoke for some time before she returned to Jonathan, took his binoculars and said, "They are entering the canal tonight. Gennadi listened to radio traffic all morning and, luckily for us, their initial afternoon crossing time was pushed back to 11:15 P.M."

"Why is that lucky for us."

"So we can inspect the ship under cover of darkness."

Jonathan tried to convince himself that somehow she might change her mind.

"I'm serious. We're doing it. Boris is at the warehouse getting the equipment ready."

He shook his head. "Just the three of you?" he asked, looking again at the ship. "Either you are incredibly brave or immensely stupid, or both."

"I have two other specialists flying into Panama shortly, and you're going to help as well."

"What will I be doing?"

"You'll be in a small boat with me. But for now, we just wait."

For about an hour they sat outdoors on cheap plastic chairs near the pool, which looked like it was in bad need of a fresh coat of paint and new tilework. Mariya spoke of her disdain of tropical climates and how she'd always avoided coming to South America if at all possible. Jonathan said little as he held a lukewarm beer in his hand. Gennadi said even less, his face looking paler than normal. He didn't even touch his water.

A text message had reached Mariya. She looked agitated while reading it and even more so after she put down her cell phone. "Boris will be here momentarily," she said, "but there's a problem."

She got up, said something to Gennadi and then leaned into Jonathan. "Stay here with him. I'll be back this afternoon. Don't make any calls. Don't send any emails. We have to stay under the radar."

*   *   *

"How can this be?" Mariya was so enraged she'd almost slapped Boris across the face as he drove out of the hotel's lengthy driveway, though she understood he was merely the messenger. It wasn't his fault. "Is that asshole there now?"

"No," said the large Russian, his cheeks beet red. "I'm telling you, much of the equipment is unusable. I don't know how we're going to get onto that ship."

Boris had spent an hour at a secret warehouse near Gamboa inspecting pre-positioned equipment that

Mariya had intended to use that night. The local SVR *resident* in charge of maintaining it had not done his job, at least not according to Boris.

Mariya needed to see for herself. "Call Oleg now. I want his ass there when we arrive. Tell him I'm with you but don't say anything else."

Boris dialed with his beefy right hand, his other hand gripping the steering wheel.

"Faster," Mariya said, glancing at her watch. "I don't know how he managed it, but he's been at the embassy for nine years." It disturbed her that Oleg had stretched the average five-year stint for Russian intelligence station chiefs working under diplomatic cover at overseas posts.

"As Cultural Attaché?"

"At first, yes, and now he's some kind of special assistant to the Ambassador, but the CIA has already flagged him, and so have the Mexicans and Colombians. His cover's been blown long ago."

"He must have either power or money back home."

She shook his head. "He has neither. He's just been savvy enough to work the system to stay here longer."

"Be careful, Mariya. He may have someone in Moscow covering his back. And we need him now."

She raised her brow. "If he's anything like what you've told me—and he's left the equipment in that condition—I'm going to kill him."

22

THE SMELL OF DEAD ANIMALS AND ROTTING WOOD WOULD have made most men puke, but Mariya had a stomach of steel. She casually followed Boris—who briefly covered his mouth and nose with his sleeve—into the stench-filled warehouse, a structure large enough to fit seven or eight cars.

The small, filthy windows high up on one end of the corrugated metal siding let in just enough light to display the mess that Oleg's mismanagement had caused: dozens of wood shipping crates stacked high, many cracked and three knocked over on their sides and shattered; a tall pile of broken metal and plastic carrying cases; old tires; torn sleeping bags; rotted ropes; rusted cables and chains dangling from hooks on the wall, next to two worn, dust-covered tarps that lay over other equipment. Spider webs were everywhere.

"Look at this," Boris said to Mariya.

He pointed at a box he'd opened earlier. It was filled with portable military radios that had succumbed to humidity, their olive-green exteriors mostly rusted. The rubber padding of the matching headsets were torn or deflated.

"And look here..." Boris lifted the lid of a crate with one hand, and with the other pulled out a tarpaulin that covered the contents, then glanced over his shoulder at Mariya. "Would you dive with this?"

Mariya leaned over and examined the scuba gear. Boris knew almost everything about special weaponry. With over twenty years' experience as a sniper-diver in the Soviet—and then Russian—*Spetznaz*, and the last three years supporting the SVR's clandestine operatives in fifteen countries, she trusted his opinion. He had her back, and she saw in him a good man whose loyalty she yearned to see in others.

"These closed-circuit re-breathers should have been kept dry in special bags and properly disassembled." They were lightweight combat-rated underwater breathing devices that permitted trained infiltration teams to approach enemy ships and ports without releasing tell-tale air bubbles, but they both knew these were fragile pieces of equipment that required care in long-term storage, where a minor defect could kill a diver.

"How are the weapons?"

Boris chuckled. "They are the only things that look fine."

"Come in here," Mariya shouted at Oleg, who'd been waiting outside since Mariya and Boris had arrived.

The short, pudgy Russian bureaucrat—who'd left his condo wearing his best suit and tie probably to impress Mariya—strolled in, his face sweaty and red.

Mariya stabbed him with a withering glare as he stopped ten feet away from where she and Boris stood and nervously removed his jacket.

"Is there a problem?" he asked hesitantly, his voice softer than the noise of the wind-ruffled trees outside. It didn't help Oleg that he was fat, bald and from Irkutsk, Siberian—three things that reminded Mariya of her former boss, the head of Directorate R at the SVR. More importantly, Oleg made her think of all the former SVR and KGB field operatives who'd taken the fall of the Soviet Union as a license to graze at their foreign posts and feign some usefulness from afar. Since 1991, she'd chanted the same song to countless *residienti* who'd crossed paths with her. But that tune had become old, and fewer cared to listen, even in the corridors of power back home. She suddenly felt more alone than ever, dwelling on the things she feared the most: irrelevance—being the lone voice. An anachronism of the once great department. With people like Oleg, she thought, the SVR would soon atrophy its HUMINT skills to something no more threatening than the spy agency of Luxembourg.

Oleg loosened his tie and opened the top button of his shirt, silently taking in Mariya's loathing stare.

"You're in charge of this shit, and this is how you leave it?" She was getting angrier by the second.

His mumbled response fell inaudibly.

Mariya quickly reached into her purse and pulled out her Beretta Nano. Her rapid strides barely gave him time to flinch. With one hand yanking him by his tie, she shoved the 17 ounces of gun metal into his neck, the stubby barrel disappearing into the fat below his jaw-line. "Aside from your cocktail events and daylong fuck sessions with your Rosita—that is your tramp's name, right?—you could at least make sure this expensive material is kept ready."

He tried raising his head.

"Don't you move, ungrateful asshole. The Russian Federation is, after all, paying for your parties, your suits, your SUV, your whore, your lavish dinners, and your condo, which I'm sure is undeservingly opulent."

"Mariya." Boris never said her name unless he was on edge.

"I'm tempted, Oleg Vadimovich, to add only one more expense—your funeral." Mariya's finger flirted with the trigger, her weapon still pushing into the station chief's throat.

He swallowed hard but didn't move.

"*Dolboyob!*" She headbutted his face, let go and backed away, drawing down her pistol.

Oleg anxiously touched his lips, which had begun to ooze blood, and shifted his eyes rapidly between Mariya and Boris. "Don't blame me! I didn't do anything." He dabbed his mouth with a handkerchief.

"Exactly!" Mariya sighed. "It appears you have some skills left to decipher the obvious. You were supposed to maintain all this, not do *nothing*. Were we asking too much of you?"

Boris walked behind Mariya and pulled back the larger of the two tarps with a strong tug, throwing a thick cloud of dust into the stuffy, malodorous confines of the warehouse, the dust particles illuminated by the stream of sunlight that sliced in from the far window. The air settled on what lay under the tarp: a rigid-hulled inflatable boat—a RIB—all black, specially designed for maritime assault and able to hold an eight-man team.

"This won't get us across a bathtub, let alone the canal," Boris said, tossing out a loose steel tube from inside the boat.

"This is completely unacceptable." Mariya tapped her weapon against her thigh, contemplating filling Oleg with lead and dumping his sorry ass in the canal.

Oleg paced a small figure-eight and then stopped as Mariya again strode up to him.

She pointed a finger at his face. "You were told—"

"*Otvyazhityes!*" he interrupted, his eyes narrowing. The redness of his face now matched his neck, and his skin beaded with sweat. "The Cold War is over! Not one Russian naval vessel has passed through the canal in years. Not one!"

"We must always stay prepared."

"Nonsense. Why are we keeping this junk? I say get rid of it, sell this building and save the money."

"What, so we can spend more on your lifestyle. And now we finally need this equipment but your incompetence has put us in jeopardy."

She turned and glanced at the RIB, its rubber sides deflated, the glass windshield over the center console cracked in two places, some of the metal support bars and handles rusted. The boat was filled with piles of metal pipes, wires and wood planks, any of which could further puncture the rubber sides. From the looks of things, Boris would have to use miraculous jerry-rigging skills to bring it to working order.

Mariya shook her head. In the old days she'd have either shot him or sent him off to a camp in Russia's Far East. Today, she could only write him up in a report and stare at him with disgust, an imposed impotence that only augmented her rage. That moment, she promised to find a way to get him fired, no matter what it would take.

"You're done, Oleg, the moment I'm back home."

He looked as if he'd finally crapped his pants.

"Give me your keys," she demanded of him. "I'm using your car until tonight. Boris will take you home later. And whatever Boris tells you to do, you better act upon it, without question. Next time I pull out my weapon, I'm using it."

*   *   *

The A/C was cranked, but Mariya was still sweating. "Keep a close eye on him," she said to Boris on her cell phone, as she headed north toward Colón in Oleg's Lexus GX 470. "Don't tell him anything more about the operation, and don't mention Gennadi, Jonathan or anyone else. The less he knows, the better." She'd abruptly left the warehouse near Gamboa, choosing to give Boris instructions by cell phone, away from Oleg's earshot. She also told him to get the equipment repaired by late afternoon, with or without Oleg's help.

After Mariya hung up, she scrolled through the text message she'd received during her call. One was direct from Moscow. "You must open the account," it said.

She knew what that meant: They had to raid the *Nixos-Dakar*, at all costs.

Mariya had come to Panama for the risky mission, but until that text came in she'd assumed—mistakenly perhaps—that she could abort it if things got screwed up, which they had. But now the mission was on, regardless of the equipment issues. Something immensely serious had led to this order, she realized, and it had to have come from far up the political ladder. But the details were absent. They were keeping her in the dark, no matter that Mariya was the most senior Russian intelligence operative currently on Central American soil. *This can't be good.*

*   *   *

Forty minutes later she arrived at the Washington Hotel. A nerve-wracked Jonathan greeted her in the lobby.

"Your buddy's sick, really sick," he said, leading her to the elevator. "He's been puking his guts out for the past hour. Did you poison him?"

"That doesn't amuse me." Mariya snarled.

"Few things do, apparently."

"Did he eat something bad?"

"I don't know. I'm not his chaperone while you go sightseeing."

"Actually, you are. And you should have called me."

"He didn't let me use the phone."

"You both need to be ready in one hour."

"Are you still sticking to your ridiculous plan? "

Mariya looked at Jonathan with surprise. "We're boarding the ship tonight, as I've been saying for two days."

"You're kidding, right?"

"I never joke about such things."

Jonathan opened the door to the room with a key card Gennadi had given him in case he'd gotten too sick to get up. A loud cavernous howl came from the depths of the room. Gennadi was throwing up into an ice bucket by his pillow.

"Yeah, a raid on the *Nixos-Dakar*," Jonathan said curtly and gazed at Gennadi. "He's going to be real helpful."

Mariya stared at her colleague curled up in his boxer shorts on top of the comforter, his face sweaty and pasty white. There was vomit on the carpet and on the edge of the nightstand. She said something to him in Russian, but he barely had the wherewithal to open his eyes.

"He needs a doctor."

Mariya half-kneeled onto the edge of the bed.

Gennadi forced a few words from his mouth.

"He thinks it's something he ate," she told Jonathan. "But we can't jeopardize the operation. He's an experienced agent; if he needs help, he'll find it himself."

Jonathan shook his head. "You'd make a great nurse."

At that moment Gennadi lifted his torso, grabbed Mariya's arm and leaned his chin over the ice bucket and again heaved what little was left in his stomach.

She uncoupled his grip and stepped off the bed, dropping her forehead into her hands. "*Chert poberi...*"

23

Near Saint Petersburg, Russia

I WALK ALONG THE NARROW PAVEMENT THAT STRETCHES between a cluster of birch and fir trees to my left and a grassy meadow on my right. My grip tightens on the bouquet in my hand. I continue, my nerves crackling, my breaths unrhythmed, past the five stone statues overlooking the open flame—a memorial to a far distant national trauma that was the Siege of Leningrad. If only my heartbreak had such distance.

Sorrow. Pain. Revenge.

My spinning mind compresses the chaos into more chewable pieces. Enough so I can endure each step, barely, with a heart so heavy that gravity could tear it from my thorax. I look down at the tall weeds that creep through the cracks in the pavement—a sign that too few visitors have made this journey.

The path leads to another meadow on the east side of the cemetery, where three rows of headstones catch the corner of my eye. Their proximity begins to slow my steps. The strength to look straight at these sacred monuments is still gathering. Sacred because below them lay the heroes—long forgotten ones—who persevered, who followed their conscience, who grasped on each morsel of hope and served their duties with loyalty and camaraderie to the very dark, cold end that greeted their demise. This hallowed ground is theirs, and each step I take amongst them further humbles me. They will find comfort soon.

The tranquility of Serafimovskoye Cemetery duels with the rage that fills my veins. I hear only birds chanting in the trees and shrubs. Then my eye catches the large black granite cube, raised on a stone incline. It is the memorial to the submariners of the *Kursk*, the vessel's name etched in gold leaf on one side and topped with the statue of a petrel seabird, a symbol for the souls of drowned sailors. I walk around, my head down but my courage mounting. I read the inscribed words, as I have many times before: "Do not despair."

Pain, revenge.

I admit, the importance of this monument to me does not arise from the monument itself. Nor from the scattering of flowers at its base. Certainly not from the eight hundred thousand rubles the State had given me along with their insincere condolences. Neither did the parade of dignitaries that assembled in far-flung towns across Russia on the anniversaries of the tragedy. What mattered to me most was much simpler—that the soul of my Nikolai, senior midshipman, who'd been robbed of his future at the mere age of twenty-three, can finally rest.

I sense his closeness. My shoes tread the cobbled

path, past identical black marble headstones, each with uniformed busts of the dead carved into the facades.

My steps slowing, my lungs taking in the flower-scented air. Having wrestled the demons of fear and mournfulness out of this instant, I approach. I hear the lone groundskeeper rake leaves a short distance away, close to the last row of graves that now stand before me, and the one I came to see. How sterile it is to observe his monochrome image. The yellow and orange carnations in the white vase bring me a smile.

"I miss you, Nikolai," I whisper. But the quieted sound of my son's name is deceptive. My whisper is meant to be a scream. This faint air that exits my mouth should instead be the loud cries of a mournful father heard blocks away. The soft nudging of my diaphragm should instead rip my lungs to shreds.

Revenge.

My eyes begin to fill with tears. My lips shake. My hands too. The black granite with his name carved in gold leaps out at me. Nikolai Yuryevich Chermayeff. I scrounge to find the peace that he supposedly has found in death, with his fellow crewmen who'd perished with him that day in 2000. I plead to believe in an afterlife; I want it for him. Is he smiling with his compatriots? Is he gazing down at me walking this path, heaven's doors opened for his brief peek at the saddened mortal that I've become? Can he sense my fury?

I place the flowers in the vase, mixing them with the others and again lay eyes on his image, his rank and the years he'd walked this earth—all inscribed on the dark stone. My friend, my hero, my treasured son. I stare, because that's all I can do here, where my anger is controlled—an anger compounded by the reality that my other son lies in a coma.

I sense Nikolai's heart pounding in fear that fateful day. I imagine his struggle to maneuver around his compartment, the air thickening, the lights gone, the cold water and carbon dioxide filling their breathable space with demonic speed. My heart continues to race as I see him sloshing through the passageways, the water rising, his body trembling from the cold.

"There is a time and place to even the score." I rest my palm on the cold stone. "This time will come soon... and your soul will be at peace."

I cannot measure how deeply entrenched the scar remains from the exact moment the news from the Barents Sea reached my laboratory in Chelyabinsk-65 that August day. The uncertainty first. Then the reckless promises from the authorities. The false hopes. And finally, the cadre of malevolent leaders spat out the truth, grudgingly, when it was all done, all gone, all over.

My hand caresses the marble one more time, and my eyes leave the stone. *Nikolai, I'm doing all this for you.*

I stroll back toward the cemetery gates. The long walk carries with it a bit less pain, but my thirst for vengeance stays strong, precise. I gaze at the stone arches on each side of the open metal gate. Leaving is hard. I can't help but feel that I'm abandoning him. I walk past the gate, the sounds of traffic throwing me back into the real world. The emotional cacophony that accompanied me into the graveyard is now gone.

The sidewalk is barren. I see my car, my bodyguards,

the dark tinted windows that hide me from the world.

The cell phone vibrates in my pocket, and I answer.

"I did it."

I recognize the monotone voice and subtle accent as Sal's. His words reignite my anger—he is American, of the same cloth as Nikolai's killers—but I must tolerate him for now. And I remind myself of my pledge, which I will keep. This man could have terminated me when he had the chance. He also could have killed my last surviving son. But he didn't.

"Did you hear me?" Sal asks. "I went to Stockholm; it's done. I also finished the job in Marrakesh."

"Yes, but that doesn't secure everything."

"Maybe not, but I assume you took care of the New Orleans problem."

"Yes, the body is recovered."

I cannot trust this double-dealing CIA-Mossad turncoat, no matter the deeds he has done on my behalf. For now I must control him until it is the right time. "What about Caldero?"

"I'm taking care of that tomorrow night."

"Do it, and clean the place up."

"Of course...but then what?"

"Finish off my partner."

"When?"

"He will be in Caracas on Friday." It is all Sal needs to know about Bo Huang. Things have been unraveling. Bo Huang's warehouses in Vladivostok have been raided. The North Korean specialists have not performed as he'd promised. The errors under his watch have multiplied. "Do it, and don't call me until I read his obituary."

24

Colón, Panama

THE STENCH OF VOMIT STILL LINGERED IN JONATHAN'S lungs as he and Mariya left Gennadi's room and headed down the single flight of stairs to the Washington Hotel's domed lobby, all the while bouncing in his head was the most serious question of all: how on earth could they inspect the *Nixos-Dakar* without assistance from the Panamanian authorities.

"A new ride?" he asked as Mariya unlocked the Lexus.

"One of our diplomat's cars."

"Living large, huh?"

"Quiet!" she barked, handing him the keys and stomping around the passenger side.

She made Jonathan drive, which seemed safer to him anyway, as she was constantly texting and her mind seemed to be elsewhere.

"Hopefully, Gennadi won't pass out and choke on his own puke," Jonathan said.

"I got more news on the ship." Mariya could switch

topics and moods on a dime, and when she did, it reminded Jonathan of how expendable he was, just like Gennadi, or whoever else served her temporary needs. "It's Liberia-flagged, has a 25-man crew—mostly Asian—and called on Caracas before docking in New Orleans. It then stopped in Houston, before heading this way."

"Did you see it in Houston?"

"Only from a distance, but I didn't spot anything unusual."

"It's owned by an obscure Chinese company."

"I know." Mariya scrolled through her text messages. "A firm called Echis Global; it also apparently has an address in Havana."

"It's a shell company—for tax purposes, no doubt."

"Perhaps, but I suspect a more sinister reason. I'll know more soon, I hope."

The drive south was more interesting than the night before, since it was daylight. Thick tropical foliage surrounded both sides of the road.

Mariya's cell phone rang. She spoke in Russian, her voice stern. She frowned, clenched her fist, argued for a couple minutes and then hung up.

"What's wrong?" Jonathan said as they drove through a village in the lush forest, still heading south toward Gamboa.

"They got detained."

"Who?" He glared over and saw her jaw working back and forth as though she was holding back angrier words.

"Two other guys who usually work with Boris.

They're good, perfect for this type of operation, but for some reason airport security arrested them in Caracas as they were boarding the flight to here."

Jonathan couldn't believe what this meant. "You're telling me it's now just you, Boris and me? And with no help from local law enforcement? Are you insane?"

"Looks that way," she said with a tone of surrender, something he wasn't used to hearing from her.

"You realize," Jonathan continued, "that this mission is crumbling. Shouldn't we pull the plug before this whole thing blows up in our faces?"

"We're going as planned—to the warehouse first. We have a lot to do in the next few hours. Turn right over there. We're close."

The paved road soon faded into a dirt road, which S-turned under large moss-covered trees that blocked much of the sunlight. They crossed a small ravine and continued down the road through the heavily wooded area.

Mariya pointed left. "Turn here."

A shoddy metal gate with barbed wire at the top secured a dirt path into the property's fenced-in perimeter. Mariya stepped out and pushed it open for Jonathan to drive through. A hundred yards further, past another turn, they reached a box-shaped metal and cement warehouse with a sloping metal roof. Boris' black SUV was parked facing the closed doors.

Jonathan was surprised to see what was inside: a RIB, dozens of opened crates with weapons and military gear around them. "There's enough here to overthrow the Panamanian government."

"Hardly," Mariya said. "Most of it is unusable."

She huddled with Boris behind the boat as Jonathan strolled through the space, inspecting the collection of weaponry. He couldn't understand their words, but from the looks of it, she and Boris were not on the same page.

"*Eto bezumiye!*" Boris suddenly threw his hands in the air and then pounded a crate.

Mariya didn't flinch. She straightened her spine and abruptly pointed her index finger at Boris' chin—which she could barely reach—and barked a sentence-full of spiteful sounding words.

Whatever she'd said made Boris step back, droop his shoulders and shut his mouth for a solid minute. The next words out of his lips were unsettlingly mellow and accompanied by a look of defeat.

Jonathan walked to them. "Why doesn't your country send an elite SWAT team to raid the ship *after* it crosses the canal, somewhere out in the Pacific, where there's no one to catch you and no political mess to deal with?"

"What are you talking about?" Mariya snapped "Boris here *is* the elite force...the very best."

"But he's alone."

"He has me and you to help."

You've lost your mind.

"We can't wait. We are boarding the ship tonight. Besides, your suggestion is not possible."

"What do you mean? You're a nuclear power. You've got a huge navy. You can—"

"No, we can't. We don't have a single naval vessel anywhere in this part of the world, and the nearest one is a spy trawler near Hawaii with no assault force on board, probably crewed by a bunch of lazy, overweight drunkards."

"But it's 2005!" Jonathan shook his head. He hadn't imagined that Russia would not have rebuilt its forces since the fall of the USSR fifteen years ago. "Maybe use that planeload of Special Forces you told me about?"

"Forget it. Panama would never let them land, and Moscow would have told me if they were headed this way. They're going somewhere else in the region, maybe Cuba, but not here." Mariya crossed her arms, her voice sharpening. "This is our only shot at understanding what's happened on that ship. The next window of opportunity may be only when it's in the Yellow Sea or South China Sea, and that's more than ten days from now, and we might not be able to do much there. Anyway, timing is critical."

"Then how about telling the local authorities? If it's that serious, they too will want to raid the ship."

"No, this problem is too sensitive to share with any other country."

"Nothing I've seen so far tells me this is urgent," Jonathan said. "You're hiding too much from me, so unless you tell me more, the only finger I'm lifting to help you is my middle one."

"We *need* your help."

"I'm here, aren't I? But that doesn't mean I'm willing to get myself killed raiding a ship in the middle of the night in this Central American armpit." He marched toward the warehouse door and pushed it open. "Either you tell me what you know, or I'm out."

Mariya ran up behind him and grabbed his arm, but he shook her loose.

"What is so fucking urgent?" he demanded as Boris began dragging more crates to the center of the storage space.

She leaned into him and said quietly, "We found a dead Asian man with an identical tattoo at a Russian port a month ago, and we think he was part of a sophisticated smuggling ring, but we're not sure what exactly... drugs, weapons, organs, diamonds—I just don't know. But there are powerful people in Moscow who are very nervous. I don't know more than this, and I have no clue why they are so worried now—and I mean *really* worried. They're pressuring me for results, and fast, and they're convinced there's vital information on that ship. I promise this is *all* I know."

"Who are they, those powerful people?"

"Why do you keep asking question after question?" Mariya slapped the corrugated steel panel that made up the door to the warehouse, the loud sound catching Boris' attention. He said something to her in Russian, but she shook her head then turned back at Jonathan.

"I'm not risking my life *again* for you, your country or whatever else, unless I can make an informed decision. It's as simple as that."

"If we can get to the ship, we may find a lot more information about the Asian sailors who have the same tattoos, their backgrounds, all of which could help you, too."

"What do you mean?"

"If those men are involved in something very bad, no

one is going to care that you made a false identification of the body back in New Orleans."

"That happened because you lied to me."

"Regardless, your proof may be on that ship."

"Why should I believe a thing you say now?"

"Jonathan, you're the one who wanted to follow me here. You insisted, remember? I was very clear: you come along if you do as I say, and on top of that, I'm paying you!"

"Not enough to die for no good reason."

"Whatever is happening is serious. There could be implications for you and your country as well, especially since there's clearly a connection with New Orleans."

"How did you know the man at the morgue had anything to do with this crap, or for that matter, that he had a matching tattoo with the guy you found in Russia?"

"We hacked email servers in more than a hundred major port cities around the world and installed computer viruses in police departments, harbor authorities, coast guard offices, and other agencies, mostly in Europe and the U.S. We then intercepted emails between the Orleans Parish coroner's office and the NOPD."

"Who's 'we'? You still work for the SVR?"

"Yes, of course."

"You've never told me precisely."

"Does it matter?" She sounded exasperated. "I wear many hats, and you know exactly what line of work I'm in, so why dwell on it?"

He stared at her. "Maybe because I don't trust you?"

"Look, I've already told you more about this case than any other intelligence agency knows, including your own CIA." She pointed at Boris, her eyes still locked on Jonathan. "Are you going to let this man and me raid the cargo ship alone? I would never have imagined you being afraid. You're not the man you were ten years ago. Back then I had never met a civilian more determined, more brave, than you. Be that man today, even if you have to pretend. Help us, because we have a shared interest in solving what's going on here, and the answers hopefully are on that ship. That's all I ask, and then you can go home, to the many challenges that await you there."

Jonathan pulled his shirt collar to one side, exposing his collar bone and a circular scar the size of a quarter. "See this?" He tapped it with his finger. "This bullet was from the last time I got involved in your stunts a decade ago." He turned his head and pointed to the still raw burn mark on his neck. "And this is from being attacked at the morgue two days ago when I was dealing with your supposedly dead nephew." He then stabbed Mariya with a stern gaze. "Yeah, I'm still alive, but I may not be so lucky next time."

"Being brave comes at a price," Mariya hissed.

"And being foolish?"

"It's impossible for only two people to pull this off," she pleaded. "We need at least three."

"How will one more make a difference? I'm not trained to storm a ship, for God's sake."

Mariya joined him outside. "You'll do fine." She put on her sunglasses and lit a cigarette.

"Fuck you."

She shouted something at Boris and then said to

Jonathan, "Get back in there, please. We need you, and if you knew how I feel about you, you'd understand that I would not ask you to risk your life for nothing. Go back in. Please. Boris will help you get set up."

Jonathan was angry, but after a long minute of deliberation, he realized that his options were limited. And he couldn't be sure that if he tried to leave, Mariya wouldn't shoot him in the back. He grudgingly walked to Boris, who towered over him and frowned.

"We are doing this," the Russian giant said in his dungeonous, heavily accented voice. "I do not like it; equipment is shit; timing is shit; place is shit, but *she* wants to do it, so we do it. Okay?" A long sigh followed.

"You know I'm not..."

Boris smirked. "Yes, your skills are shit. That makes one more problem. But I help you with equipment and weapons." Boris' authoritative voice had somewhat calmed Jonathan, but in truth, the fact remained that they were only a force of three.

"You know how to use assault weapon?"

"Sure." While Jonathan wanted Boris to know he wasn't a trained killer, he also didn't want to seem incapable of doing his part.

"*Horosho*." Boris stepped back to the crates, leaned into one and returned carrying an automatic weapon. He then brushed the dust off it and held it out in front of Jonathan. "From Russia with love."

The rifle was heavy, a bit bulky too, and had a short, fat barrel that appeared to include a silencer.

"We call it *Ksyukha*."

"It's a version of the AK-74U, with a compact

suppressor," Mariya added. "Your soldiers in Iraq call it a *Krinkov*. It's rugged and forgiving, even for a novice like you."

Boris came back again, carrying a pile of gear in his arms. "Your ballistic vest, helmet, radio and knife."

"There are fatigues, belts, and boots and other things in those crate over there," Mariya said. "Find what fits you. We're deploying at 22:30."

*   *   *

Jonathan had slipped into all-black fatigues. He'd loaded the weapons and checked the rope-climbing equipment, lining everything up for inspection on a canvas mat near the front of the warehouse. The radios were preset to a channel Mariya had selected. He then joined Boris at a table behind the boat, where the Russian had laid out pictures of the *Nixos-Dakar* and a detailed map of the canal.

Boris pointed at the map using a loaded magazine. "We start here, go there, and then approach when it crosses here. Then we climb ship from stern—the back."

"I know what stern means," Jonathan snapped, turning to Mariya. "Did you tell him I know a thing or two about ships?"

She said something to Boris in Russian.

"But if we see people on deck when we get closer, we will instead move to front, on starboard side," Boris added.

"That's just great." Jonathan imagined how hard it might be to rappel up the side of a moving ship, at night, loaded with heavy weapons and gear, and possibly with a hostile crew to greet them with gunfire. The idea of climbing quickly now sounded daunting, all the more so given his less than optimal physical condition.

"Don't worry," Mariya said, apparently sensing Jonathan's discomfort. "If Boris—twice your size—can do it, so can you. Think of it as your first workout in a long while."

"A gym would be safer."

"But not the same adrenaline rush."

"With you around, who needs any more adrenaline?"

Boris rested his beefy arms by his waist. "Very important: we *must* climb fast and go quickly to command deck. If not, they have time to destroy information—computers, files, cell phones." His eyes narrowed as he gazed at Mariya. "That is why it is difficult with only *two* instead of a full squad, and only one trained specialist. Crazy..."

Mariya raised her hand, palm out toward Boris, gesturing for him to stop his griping.

"If they are indeed the bad guys," Jonathan said, "aren't they going to be armed, too? I mean, it will be me and Boris up there against how many?"

"The crew is mostly legitimate, I think," said Mariya, "but you should expect a few infiltrators hiding among them."

"But you can't be sure."

"Yes, I may be wrong—the whole crew could be dangerous."

Boris crossed his arms. "If that is true, we may have to leave ship fast or die."

"I'm really unimpressed with your planning," Jonathan said as he threw his hands up and shook his head. "You must have a death wish."

25

THE LOOK ON MARIYA'S FACE SAID IT ALL: WE ARE screwed. At least that's what Jonathan took from her cringing expression. Unloading the equipment from the SUV, he kept glancing at her sitting under the dome light in the back seat and fiddling with her GPS device. "Are you coming?"

"In a minute," she answered hurriedly without looking at him. "Gennadi texted me: the ship is now heading through the Gatun Locks." That meant it would be in this area, near Gamboa, in a matter of thirty or forty minutes.

Jonathan pulled the empty boat trailer off to the side of the dirt road and returned to the waterfront.

Boris tugged the line, bringing the RIB back toward the sloping grassy slip that he'd just used to launch it into the water. The only light cast onto the motley crew at the banks of the canal came from the star-filled sky and the red-colored beam of the flashlight Boris had strapped to his chest.

As soon as Mariya joined them, Boris got in the boat first, and Jonathan followed carrying the heavy weapons. The other equipment was already onboard. It was ten after eleven.

Mariya stepped in and donned a bullet-resistant vest that reached her chin and seemed to dwarf her. Jonathan slipped into his as well. Boris had been wearing one since they'd left the warehouse, though his was bulkier, reinforced by ceramic plates over the mid-chest and back.

"Hurry," Mariya said. "We have fifteen minutes to be in position."

"Put your helmet on," Boris told Jonathan.

"No, I can't see well with it." Jonathan had enough weight on him, and he worried that he might not have the strength to climb the forty-plus feet to the ship's main deck.

Boris threw his hands in the air as if to say, "Get your head blown off it you must."

The engine awakened, the exhaust fumes filling the humid air. Mariya took out her flashlight and aimed it at a creased map flung over the RIB's center console of the boat. "Remember, when we're in position, Boris will go in front with the climbing gear and you will steer us to the ship. I'll cover you both with my sniper rifle while you climb."

"Lovely," Jonathan said. He could hardly believe where he was and what they were about to do.

He connected his communications gear, which included an earpiece with an attached mic extending half-way over his cheek and hooked up to a secure radio not much larger than a soda can and that fit snugly into the vest pocket. Boris handed Jonathan night-vision goggles and then threw on a balaclava and strapped his own goggles over it. Jonathan followed suit, omitting the balaclava.

"Can everyone hear each other?" Jonathan asked, the radio crackling as it came to life.

"*Da,*" Boris said.

"Yes, all good," Mariya said. "Now let's have fun."

Boris pushed the throttle full forward. They headed into the vast, dark expanse of Lake Gatun, the main body of water that makes up the Panama Canal.

Jonathan kneeled down and took in everything the noxiously surreal feel the night had to offer: the warm, dense air that felt as if they were sailing through glue; the roaring outboard motor; the sounds of the water rushing by; the eerily-dark jungle looming in the distance; the dark silhouettes of the Russians. He looked up at the sky and again grappled with Mariya's insistence that they raid the *Nixos-Dakar* undermanned and blind to the underlying urgency claimed by her bosses in Moscow. Like in the swarm of looters at Wal-Mart, he again felt unprepared for the danger he'd walked into. He glanced at Boris, at the man's assault rifle slung over his shoulder, at his pistol strapped to his thigh, and then at Mariya loading a magazine into her Dragunov sniper rifle, its long night-vision scope key to protecting both him and Boris during their vulnerable ascent up the side of the cargo ship.

A few minutes passed before Mariya blurted something in Russian. Boris reduced speed, swerved left, then slowed to a crawl, the motor's sound quieting to a subdued growl. They'd reached a marshy area. The boat brushed up against the high grass that now surrounded them before Boris reversed course to prevent the prop from getting stuck. Then he stopped, the motor idling.

"Now we wait," Jonathan heard him say.

Mariya glanced at her GPS device and surveyed the north part of the waterway for several minutes using her rifle's scope.

Suddenly she took two long strides to the other side of the boat and kneeled down, placed her elbows onto the inflatable rubber side and stabilized her weapon. "I see it, about four kilometers ahead."

Jonathan squinted. Very dim lights dotted the darkened horizon. He was impressed at Mariya's skills.

Boris reached down to a half-open bag and turned on an electronic gadget the size of a laser printer, with a four-foot flexible antenna coming out of it.

"What's that?" Jonathan asked.

"A jammer—to prevent the crew from making an emergency radio or cell phone call," Mariya said.

Boris revved the engine once and returned it to idle. "You take controls now."

Jonathan got up and took over, grasping the throttle with one hand and the wheel with the other. He could feel his heart beating rapidly under his thick vest.

The distant lighted object headed south at a relatively low speed—no more than five knots, Jonathan guessed—but it soon morphed into a recognizable shape, its decks well lighted and overall looking larger at night than it had in daylight back in Colón. Jonathan then wondered how many unfriendly armed thugs might riddle Boris and him with bullets before they could even reach the deck.

"Let's wait until it passes us," Mariya said, her voice rising slightly from excitement.

Boris grabbed the assault pole and the rope, while simultaneously extending the stock of his assault rifle and strapping his tool bag to his back all at the same time as Jonathan marveled at the Russian's ambidextrous skills.

"Now," Mariya said.

Jonathan eased the throttle forward, propelling them gently toward the back of the vessel. They soon crossed the ship's wake and took a position in the centerline, about three hundred yards behind the vessel.

Jonathan tensely eyed his approach to the ship, while at the front of the boat Mariya scanned the ship's decks with her scope.

Two hundred yards. One hundred-fifty yards. One hundred yards. His adrenaline gushed through this veins.

"No—go around," Mariya suddenly said on their shared radio channel. "Two men on upper deck."

Jonathan scanned the stern but didn't see them, though he knew that this meant plan B: boarding the ship from the side. He maneuvered right, back over the ship's wake and accelerated along the starboard side of the ship. About fifty feet separated the inflatable rubber sides of their much smaller boat from the freighter's huge steel hull. He hoped the crew would not hear them pass by.

"Closer, closer," Boris said, kneeling forward over the front of the boat to properly position the ten-foot assault pole.

As they crossed the midlength of the vessel, Jonathan pulled back on the throttle and lined up parallel to the hull by less than ten feet. They were still going a few knots faster than the ship.

"Make contact here," Boris said, now standing and holding the assault pole straight up. "We can't get too close to the forecastle."

They abruptly bumped into the hull twice before finally rubbing up into a fixed position.

The Russian held the pole steady.

Whoosh.

He had triggered the extension of an inner metal tube, which ejected upward and doubled the height of the pole. This allowed Boris to better aim the four-pronged steel hook assembly at the tip of the pole. A loud pop rang out. The hook shot upward, arced over the side of the deck and apparently connected. Boris tugged on the rope, saw it was stable and discarded the pole into the water. He then secured the end of the rope to a bracket at the front of the RIB.

Mariya took the controls and kept the boat steady while also raising her rifle at the upper deck, using the center console as a pivot.

Boris began climbing the rope. He grunted loudly but didn't appear to have any problem keeping a speedy rate despite his size.

Jonathan followed. Only a few seconds into the ascent, he felt his arms tearing. He struggled, his biceps nearly on fire, his breaths hard. With his vest, assault rifle, six 30-round magazines, thick boots, goggles and other gear, he wasn't sure he'd make it. He gripped the rope tightly, pulling his body up, and twisted his legs around it for more traction.

"Hurry," Mariya said.

The rope was knotted every three feet, but it didn't make the climb much easier. The boat momentarily separated from the ship. He looked down just as Mariya steered it back and again made contact, but the maneuver snapped him back toward the vessel, slamming him into the hull. The rope slipped out of his right grip, but he quickly regained it. His arms were tiring, but the distance shortened. Eight feet. Five feet. Three feet. He threw himself over the guard rail and fell to the floor. The grueling one-minute ascent left him panting, lightheaded and barely able to move. But he'd made it.

"Get up!" Boris gestured toward the stern. He took off his goggles and clipped them to a harness on the side of his vest and signaled for Jonathan to do the same, since the deck was sufficiently illuminated.

Jonathan quickly regained his focus.

Pop, pop, pop.

"Holy crap!"

Loud dings followed—bullets ricocheting off metal surfaces all around them. Jonathan ducked and took cover behind one of the containers. Two short bursts of gunfire rang out again.

"Follow me," Boris said, his voice straining. He raced to the port side of the vessel using the row of stacked shipping containers as cover. He turned the corner, and Jonathan followed, both of them racing to the ship's main seven-floor bridge castle at the stern. The

Russian huddled near an assembly of pipes, aimed his weapon to starboard and waited.

All of a sudden a man appeared out of a doorway two flights up a stairwell to the right and above Boris and aimed his rifle at the Russian, who didn't see him.

Jonathan instantly aimed and fired two long bursts in full-auto. The man, wearing only shorts and a T-shirt, jolted forward, twisted to one side and collapsed down the steps, his body crashing in a heap at the bottom.

Jonathan lowered his weapon, his stomach suddenly feeling nauseated. *Fuck*. He'd just killed a man.

Boris turned and gave the American a thumbs-up and then climbed the same stairs. Jonathan followed, almost automatically, his head now feeling numb.

"What's happening?" Mariya asked, her voice barely audible.

"*Ya v poryadke*."

"Jonathan?"

"One target down; we're okay."

"*Ostalos desyat minut,*" she said, sounding increasingly hyper.

"In English, for Christ's sake!"

"Sorry. You have about ten more minutes."

As Jonathan raced up the steps, he heard Boris yell inside, "Down, down!"

Jonathan stormed in seconds later to find four unarmed men face-down on the floor of the bridge, but one was still on his knees. "You heard him, get down." He lunged forward and kicked the man to the ground.

"*Que mierda pasa!*" the man shouted as he hit the floor. The Spanish words gave away his role. Gennadi had told Jonathan that the rules required that there be at least one local Panamanian pilot navigating the ship through the canal, in addition to the ship's normal crew.

Boris motioned for Jonathan to keep his rifle pointed at their heads. As Jonathan moved into position, Boris pulled a series of plastic ties from his pocket and secured their hands behind their backs, except for the pilot, whose hands he left free. Boris then patted down the pilot and the others while Jonathan kept watch.

Jonathan stepped over one of the three men in uniform, and when he reached the one who appeared to be the captain, he said, "Where's your phone?"

The man peered up but hesitated.

Boris kicked his ribs hard. "Your phone!"

The captain nodded toward the far end of the console.

Jonathan held his finger on the trigger as he shuffled past the other men and grabbed the cell phone, putting it into his pants pocket.

Boris grabbed the Spanish-speaking pilot off his feet and shoved him toward the controls. He secured the man's right hand to the wheel with a plastic tie. "Navigate!" The Russian then looked down at the captain. "Tell your men everyone stays on floor. No one moves. Understand?"

The captain nodded nervously and said something to his men in what sounded like a Chinese dialect.

Jonathan shadowed Boris who'd just turned into a narrow corridor. They headed up another flight of stairs, the noisy clanging on the metal steps defeating whatever stealthiness they still had left.

"Stay calm." Boris' heavy breathing accompanied his words in Jonathan's earpiece.

"Easy for you to say."

Boris hurried up the stairs and reached the top when suddenly a loud burst of gunfire erupted.

"Ahh!"

Boris exchanged fire but fell backward, crashing onto Jonathan, who then peeled himself from under the Russian's weight and immediately aimed his weapon at the top of the stairs.

"*Blyat!*" Boris frantically began patting his stomach, then his chest, looking down. "Good—only my vest." He pointed at the damaged fabric where he'd been hit, but the bullet had not penetrated the ceramic plate. He shook his head and again raced up the stairs, cautiously pointing the barrel of his rifle above the last step. "It's okay—he is dead."

Jonathan joined him. An Asian man's shirtless, bloodied body was sprawled across the floor, a rifle at his side.

The Russian pointed to the far end of the corridor. "Check the captain's quarters; I will look at these cabins." He disappeared into the other compartment.

The door was locked. Jonathan kicked it three times before it burst open. There was no one inside. He scanned the meager furnishings of the L-shaped cabin: a cheap wood desk with an open laptop on it, a worn leather chair, three metal file cabinets and a double bed. Jonathan opened the cabinets and sifted haphazardly through the papers, but the documents appeared to be in a Chinese language.

Boris barged in with his tool bag open. He grabbed the laptop and threw it in the bag. He did the same with two cell phones on a shelf above the desk.

Jonathan tossed in a few folders he'd pulled out of the file drawers. "Anything else?"

Boris moved the desk partly to one side. He then tilted each of the cabinets, one at a time. He pushed the bed aside, and then pulled away from the wall the large framed aerial picture of the *Nixos-Dakar*. "Ha!" He'd found a wall-mounted safe, locked with a digital keypad. He pulled out a small device resembling a hockey puck and tore off the self-adhesive patch on one side and stuck it to the keypad. He then motioned to clear out.

Jonathan quickly exited the room, followed by Boris. They both leaned against the wall, the opened door separating them.

Bang!

The device exploded, the thunderous noise momentarily numbing Jonathan's eardrums.

Boris headed back inside and filled his bag with whatever he could grab from the safe, though the contents—mostly papers and money—had been thrown about the cabin.

The radio squawked. "You okay?" Mariya asked.

"Yes, we're checking the crew quarters. Almost done on this deck."

"Hurry."

While Boris inspected the cabin next to the captain's, Jonathan headed one floor up through a different stairwell. There were only two doors in this corridor, and both were locked. He kicked open the first one, his weapon pointed into the dark darkened room, and then switched on the light.

The spacious cabin looked more like a storage room messily filled with diving related equipment. Scattered near the door were two piles of scuba gear and a strange all-black tube-shaped object about five feet in length. He heard Boris come up the stairs. "What's all this?" he asked as the Russian walked in.

"An underwater propulsion vehicle," Boris said, sounding surprised, "and rebreathers, BCDs, air tanks, waterproof canisters." The Russian rummaged through the equipment.

"There's more," Jonathan said, pointing at another pile hidden in a large closet.

Boris brushed by him and surveyed the piles.

"What's that noise...the ticking noise?" Jonathan asked.

The Russian cocked his head, then quickly twisted around his waist, reached into a pouch strapped to his belt and pulled out a small handheld device as the clicking sound grew louder.

"A Geiger counter?" Jonathan asked. He'd only seen them on television.

"Yes." Boris removed his balaclava, exposing his flushed face. He held the device toward the three rebreathers on the floor. The clicking sound didn't change in intensity. He reached over the air tanks and wetsuits, and nothing changed either.

Crrr, crrr, crrr...

The loud scratching sound replaced the earlier clicking noise the moment Boris had waved the device over a three-foot high pile of neoprene, vinyl and plastic gear. He leaned farther, peering curiously at the equipment as the counter continued to signal wildly.

Jonathan poked the pile with the tip of his boot. "Looks like large bags."

"Step back." Boris used the stock of his rifle to separate the gear. "Heavy duty lift bags, salvage flotation bladders, waterproof utility bags—I don't know why all this is here, on a commercial vessel." Still using his rifle, he dislodged another large bag from the pile. "See these heavy duty straps? Urethane-coated nylon—used for carrying big things underwater."

Jonathan shrugged. "Cargo crews don't normally need this stuff." The Asian cadaver at the New Orleans morgue jumped to mind.

Boris appeared bothered by the readings. "It is *not* possible," he said. "This means the bags touched radioactive materials."

"Take pictures," Mariya said, having listened to everything they'd said in their mics.

"I forgot the camera," Boris said before cursing in Russian.

Suddenly, gunshots rang out from a deck or two below, perhaps on the bridge. A man yelled, and three more shots followed.

"I see flashes—someone on the bridge is shooting," Mariya said loudly.

Jonathan grabbed Boris. "Time to go!"

The burly Russian nodded and headed through the door. "Let's get out, but be careful."

26

FEAR HAS MANY TELLTALE SIGNS, AND EVEN THE BRAVEST bad-asses can't completely camouflage it from others, not even a burly, well-armed, seasoned Russian special forces operative like Boris. So when Jonathan caught a glimpse of his wide-eyed scowl on their way down the stairwell, he knew they were in trouble. The bursts of automatic fire they'd heard seconds earlier made it clear that others aboard were still armed and could kill them both.

Suddenly the corridor lights went out and the tight confines fell into near-complete darkness.

Boris gripped a flashlight under his rifle's barrel and used the powerful beam to clear his way down the last few steps and then turned the corner, cautiously heading back to the bridge.

Jonathan strapped his goggles back on and followed the Russian. The lights and monitors on the bridge were also off, and from the looks of it, all the freighter's lights outside and on the main deck had been shut off as well.

"We have problem," Boris said through hard breaths.

Jonathan adjusted his lenses and stopped. *Shit!* He jolted back the moment he saw the grim sight at his feet. Whoever had been on the bridge moments earlier had gunned down the crew. The transit pilot was dead, his body balled up at the base of the control console, his right arm pointing up as it was tied to the wheel. The others lay motionless nearby, all shot and bleeding. The captain was dead, too, his torso twisted at the foot of the chart table, his head facing the ceiling, with blood gushing from his neck.

Boris darted to the far port side exit, sliding his large frame tightly along a wall to ensure some degree of cover. He lowered his weapon momentarily, turned off his flashlight and reattached his night-vision gear.

"Change your magazine," he said to Jonathan, doing the same with his own rifle.

Jonathan toiled with more difficulty than his Russian ally because he wasn't used to doing things while wearing cumbersome goggles.

Meanwhile, Boris surveyed the dead crewmen. He removed wallets from their pockets and tossed them in his bag that contained papers from the ship's safe, the captain's laptop and the cell phones.

"Done." He'd replaced the magazine but now feared he might have to fire every remaining round—including those in his other magazines—to make it out alive. *I might even run out.*

"Keep an eye out while I try to straighten the ship," Jonathan said. He estimated the ship was moving at about five knots into an increasingly narrowing portion of the canal toward to the Gaillard Cut, and without a pilot it would run aground soon. "Someone has to navigate it—"

"No time," Boris blurted. "There are two or three shifts for bridge operators, so others will replace them."

"But they're probably hiding below deck, or they're dead."

Boris shrugged. "Let it crash."

"If a freighter this size runs aground or capsizes here, it could close the canal for days, even weeks."

"Not my problem," Boris replied, pushing Jonathan forward. "Go that way, stay low and keep your weapon ready."

"Who turned the ship to an easterly heading?" Mariya said into the airwaves.

"I don't know," Jonathan replied. "The crew's dead."

"Because it's going to hit the shore."

Jonathan glanced out the windows. "I can't see." Nothing on shore was visible from the bridge, not even with his goggles. He flipped some switches at the control console and turned the wheel right a bit, but it was a complete guess. The digital screens with the heading indicators and other displays were all switched off, and he realized that the ship's entire electrical grid was shut down.

Boris grabbed his arm. "Let's go!" he said harshly, pushing Jonathan out in front of him.

As he headed to the side stairs, his rifle tightly in his grip, Jonathan scanned every possible angle from where a person could take a shot. He knew they'd have to dodge whatever gunfire might come their way through the darkness across the seventy yards of deck space that separated them from the rope they'd used to climb onboard and with which they would exfiltrate.

Boris cut in front of him and quickly headed down the open-air staircase, his weapon out in front. They took turns covering each other as they made their way down to the main deck. Neither had spotted any crewman.

"Boris!" Mariya's voice crackled into Jonathan's eardrum.

Pop, pop, pop.

A deafening cry tore through Jonathan's earpiece as bursts of gunfire came from somewhere far forward on the main deck, past the bulk cargo hatches, perhaps even as far as the first row of stacked containers, which was near where they'd climbed aboard.

Pop, pop.

"There, behind the closest container!" This time Jonathan spotted muzzle flashes before he ducked to safety right behind Boris. The bullets hit metal a short distance behind him.

Boris jumped up. "Cover me."

Jonathan began firing in the direction of the containers as Boris raced along the starboard side, jumped over the first of three oversized hatches and ducked into a blind spot before the next hatch.

Boris covered with several bursts as Jonathan raced along the same path.

The armed figure reappeared in green color through Jonathan's goggles, but only briefly and then vanished. Jonathan fired a few shots but again missed. The ricocheting bullets pinged loudly off the containers.

The Russian continued to fire while running forward. Bullets bounced off all the surfaces.

"Mariya, are you okay?" Jonathan asked, his heart racing as he lurched to take cover from the hail of bullets.

She didn't answer.

Jonathan quickly replaced his magazine and took a deep breath. *This might be it.*

Boris disappeared behind the closest double-stacked containers. More shots rang out and then silence.

"Boris?" Jonathan aimed but saw no one. Hearing only his own fast, deep breaths, he charged forward ready to fire in full-auto, turned the corner and slammed into Boris, who was on one knee perched over a body beneath him.

"I got this asshole!" Boris pointed his flashlight at the dead man's face.

After removing his goggles, Jonathan quickly studied the dead Asian. He wore dark camouflage cargo pants and a beige tank top. Boris had shot him in the chest and thigh.

He grabbed the Russian's flashlight and aimed it at the dead man's arm. "I'll be damned!"

The man had a tattoo identical to the one on the body he'd seen in New Orleans—the same snake-wrapped anchor with a black dot above it.

Boris yanked Jonathan by his vest. "We go."

They quickly headed to the rope that was still secured by a grapnel to the vessel's railing.

Jonathan leaned over the edge and peered down at the boat. "Mariya?"

Still no answer.

The small boat clung alongside, bobbing violently from the wake of the much larger ship. Mariya lay on her side at the front, but Jonathan saw that she wasn't moving.

"Go down," Boris said, motioning with his rifle. "I cover you."

Jonathan grabbed the line, threw one leg over and then his other. He rappelled down, bumping clumsily into the bow of the ship as he slid the rope between his hands and boots. All of a sudden he lost his grip and tumbled down to the boat from about ten feet up. He landed hard, knocking the wind out of himself. The boat jostled precariously in the wake of the giant vessel at its side and seemed on the verge of capsizing.

Jonathan took off his bullet-resistant vest and rushed to Mariya, grabbing her shoulders. "What's happ—"

She let out a loud cry and her head dropped to her shoulder.

"Where are you hurt?"

Mariya was unresponsive but at least was still breathing. He removed her bulletproof vest and searched for a wound just as Boris jumped into the boat behind him and grabbed his arm. "We're going to hit shore!"

Jonathan glanced up. The obvious was now apparent, even in the dim light. The brush-filled canal bank was fast approaching and if they didn't unhook themselves from the *Nixos-Dakar*, the ship was going to crush them to a pulp.

"Untie it!" Jonathan heard Boris shout. But he froze the moment he saw the bloodstain the size of a pizza on Mariya's abdomen.

Boris lunged to the front of the boat. "Do something! Take the controls!" He struggled to untie the knot, then whipped out a long-bladed knife from his tool bag and sawed through the rope until the boat was freed.

Jonathan jumped to the control console, slamming the throttle forward, steering a hard right away from the ship. Tree branches extending out yards over the water from the river bank began to swipe the boat, hitting both Jonathan and Boris even as they tried to duck. The vessel's wake jolted them hard, throwing Boris onto Mariya.

"Go, go, go!"

"I'm trying!" Jonathan was at full throttle, attempting to overtake the bow of the ship before it smashed them against the shore. He steered through the rough wake, which forced the boat to again smack into the hull of the cargo ship. He veered right again, his hand jamming the throttle as far forward as he could. "Shiiii..."

Boris pulled Mariya's head down and grabbed onto her as a large branch swooped only inches above their heads and smashed into the console. It ricocheted upward and bashed Jonathan's chest, knocking him to the floor. He got up, half dazed and in pain, but managed to clench the controls once more. The wake threw them sideways as the boat sprang up at a sharp angle, but he again stabilized it.

With the throttle again on full power, he finally cleared the vessel's bow, overtaking the ship by less than ten feet. He glanced over his shoulder as the giant, ghostly-dark cargo ship rammed the tree-lined riverbank. The shrieking sounds of grinding metal and uprooted trees cut through the noise of the smaller boat's motor. They'd barely made it, but they weren't safe yet. Jonathan's heart was still racing as he quickly planned their next move, while Boris carefully straightened Mariya's body and loosened her clothing, lifting her blouse to see the injury up close.

"It's bad, isn't it?" Jonathan asked.

Boris nodded and held up Mariya's assault vest. "The round penetrated near the bottom." He then tucked it behind her back for support.

"We need to find a hospital right away," Jonathan said. He picked up the GPS device off the floor and located their position. They were three kilometers north-west of their launch point.

Within minutes they'd reached the site. Boris jumped into the water and secured the boat to a tree. They both lifted Mariya out, and Boris took her to the SUV, while Jonathan collected what he could from the boat, including the rifles and the bag of items the Russian had confiscated from the freighter. Soon, Boris was speeding through the thick jungle road, with Jonathan in the back seat caring for Mariya as best he could.

Minutes later the vehicle suddenly swerved violently, throwing Jonathan against the rear passenger door. Mariya, still unconscious, slid off the seat.

"Slow down, dammit." Jonathan pushed her back.

"Sorry, but I must." Boris' voice was shaky for the first time.

Finally, Jonathan saw buildings and lights passing by as they moved into a denser urban part of Panama's capital. He gently added pressure onto Mariya's lower abdomen with a wad of gauze Boris had given him, but the blood kept oozing through.

"You're going to be okay," Jonathan said to her, even though he knew the wound would be fatal if untreated, and her chances looked slim. But he wanted to comfort her in a way a spy knew best: with a lie.

"We are close," Boris shouted.

Jonathan held her body firmly as Boris continued his rough driving, the tires tearing through each turn. He suddenly recalled that 48 hours earlier he'd been in the back seat of another vehicle frantically trying to save Dr. Garceau's life. He shook his head, coming the grips with the craziness and incomprehensibility of the circumstances, both then and now.

"Okay, hospital is there, one hundred meters."

"Don't go in front," Jonathan said. "Pull over here."

Boris stopped at the curb, by a fire hydrant, in between street-parked cars.

Jonathan cradled Mariya out of the vehicle until Boris came around, and they both carried her to the sidewalk where they lay her down near a storefront. "They can come get her—this way we can leave unseen." He quickly checked her pockets to make sure there was nothing that could help authorities identify her. He handed her cell phone to Boris.

"But I can get them now," Boris said already sprinting toward the hospital entrance.

"No, come back!" Jonathan stood up. "We can't risk you being arrested or identified."

The Russian stopped and turned.

"There's a better way."

"How?"

"Do you still have grenades?"

"Yes, a few," Boris said, returning with a puzzled gaze. "The green bag in the back seat."

Jonathan returned to the SUV and dug into the bag. There were three grenades. He only needed one. "Back up to the corner and wait for me." He watched Boris steer the vehicle in reverse to the prior intersection and checked that no one was on the street. He then tightened his grip on the grenade, pulled the pin and threw it about twenty yards down the center of the street, halfway between Mariya and the hospital entrance.

Boom!

The blast shook the ground and shattered windows of the parked cars. Car alarms blared. Jonathan heard shouts some distance away, and then a faint cry near him. Mariya was conscious again, barely, under glass shards of the storefront windows that had broken from the blast. He kneeled to her side and held her hand as she coughed and cringed in pain. He then spotted people rushing out onto the street. "Hey, this lady needs help!"

"Don't move. You're right next to the hospital." He kissed her forehead and ran back to the vehicle.

*   *   *

The doorman behind the counter threw his hands in the air. "I'm telling you, he's not home."

"*Mentiroso*," Jonathan snarled, shook his head and turned to Boris. "He's lying."

He noticed the armed security guard entering the

lobby of the posh high-rise, no doubt having been drawn by the commotion Jonathan had stirred after the doorman called Oleg's condo and pretended that the maid had answered and that Oleg wasn't home. Jonathan had distinctly heard a male voice on the other end of the line.

Boris leaned into Jonathan and whispered, "Oleg's scared, but if we insist he may become dangerous. He could call the police, so we must leave."

The security guard asked the doorman what was going on and seemed alarmed at the sight of two men in black fatigues.

As calmly as he could, Jonathan said in Spanish, "No problem, guys. It's okay. We're leaving. We'll see our friend Oleg tomorrow." He then patted Boris's shoulder. They left and walked two blocks to a convenience store where Boris had parked their SUV.

27

Washington, D.C.

THE AROMA OF GRILLED MEAT GREETED THE MAN WHO'D just passed under the white awning of the Peacock Café with a satchel in one hand, his wet umbrella in the other.

"Good day," the hostess said, smiling and motioning discreetly for her familiar guest to ease his way through the dining room to the usual table, the one at the end of the long bench seats, under the musical note—a colorful framed artwork in the form of a bass clef mounted on the wall. An avid piano player, Glen Sanders had always been drawn to this table and as he sat down, he noticed that the maître d' had timed it right today; there was a chilled bottle of San Pellegrino waiting for him.

Glen took his seat, alone, facing an empty chair on the other end of the narrow table, as he always did every other Tuesday for lunch in this Georgetown eatery, before or after his alternating biweekly meetings with the Senate Select Committee on Intelligence and the National Intelligence Council. He'd often catch faces of other Washington power-players dining at nearby tables, but he secretly thrived on being seen but not approached, contenting himself with the whispers his presence would bring, and on occasion a discreet nod. As Director of the CIA's clandestine operations, Glen thought himself a man both to fear and respect, no matter which side of the political aisle one sat, and he drew strength from this constructed aura. Alone. Powerful. Hungry.

But on his third sip of the sparkling water, a tall, goateed man in his fifties wearing a gray suit and black-rimmed glasses walked up and grabbed the back of the empty chair, casually sat down as if he belonged, and tossed a card onto Glen's bread plate.

"Relax," the man said. "Read the name."

Glen glanced down. It was a Maryland driver's license.

"Kolkin...Jeremy Kolkin," the intruder said, holding an icy stare. "Does that ring a bell?"

"Who the fuck are you?" Glen whispered hard, surmising that the man's accent was Middle Eastern.

"I apologize for the rudeness, but it's urgent. Elad told me you'd be here."

Elad? Glen looked up but said nothing.

"I finally meet the esteemed Mr. Sanders." The man seemed to relish the discomfort his presence had created.

As any spy should, Glen studied the man's face. He subtracted the glasses and the bristly shadow around the goatee; he straightened the wavy pewter hair; he took in the Hebrew accent; and then it hit him. *Yishai Ivri.*

The audacious breach of protocol perplexed him. The recently appointed secretive number three in Israel's venerable Mossad had taken a seat at his table an ocean away from his home turf. *Has this man crossed the pond merely ask this?* Glen thought but then doubted it.

Glen glanced over Ivri's shoulder at his bodyguard, who zigzagged through the dining area toward them, as patrons eyed his table.

Ivri didn't flinch. "No need to call your pit bull."

Glen's plainclothes security reached the table and assumed a near-fighting stance immediately behind Ivri, and asked, "Is there a problem, sir?"

Ivri looked into Glen's eyes. "Are you going to kick me out or discuss our issue?" He then took a piece of bread to his mouth and chewed it gruffly.

Glen waved off his guard. "It's okay, wait at the door." He leaned over his plate, crossed his fingers and stared Ivri. "This is not the way we do things. What you have to say better be interesting or my assistant will knock that bread out of your mouth."

"Such machismo," Ivri snarled. He wagged his index finger in the air. "You've made some people very angry."

"If Elad wants to talk—"

Ivri slammed his hand onto the table. "Why did you take him down?" he said in a strong whisper.

"Who?"

"Kolkin. We know it was your work."

"I don't know what you're talking about."

"His throat was slashed in a Moscow night club, and there's cell phone traffic pointing to your people."

"It wasn't us," Glen blurted. "Maybe he pissed off a hooker." Ivri's accusation spun wildly in his head, but Glen had never heard of anyone named Kolkin, and, regardless, the CIA hadn't taken anyone down in Russia in more than two years.

"Let's not talk fiction."

"Let's not talk at all. Besides, if there's an issue, Elad can reach me directly—without rude proxies like you."

"You expect us to believe it's mere coincidence—after you've lost your asset?"

Glen shook his head. He wasn't about to admit a scintilla of information. "Lost?"

"Your rodent in Morocco."

That Ivri apparently knew of Hasan Okyar was not unimaginable to Glen. The Mossad's tentacles were good at discovering other folks' mischief. But what shocked Glen was how fast word had gotten out.

"We don't—"

"Kolkin was tracking Chermayeff," Ivri blurted, "and so were your assets. Perhaps your guys got careless."

"*If* we lost someone, I need to know now whether your hands are clean or not."

"What's in it for us?"

"Depends on the answer."

The Israeli scratched his head and gazed at the ceiling for a few seconds. "Why was Ron tracking Kolkin's movements? And what's with Brusca?

"You mean Sal?"

"Yes, and I hear he's gone missing."

"We've done nothing more than mere surveillance."

"Then perhaps Ron has his own agenda."

Glen raised his chin. "I'll be sure to ask him."

"Don't wait too long. He's on his way to Caracas under an alias and seems keen to stay below your radar."

As the city's name left Ivri's lips, Glen shuddered. There was no reason for Ron to set foot in Venezuela, especially a day after the fiasco in Stockholm. Glen had gotten a tongue lashing from the White House, which was now engaged in damage control with the Swedish government, and he'd ordered Ron States-bound for a serious debrief. If Ivri was right, Ron had defied the order and was traveling without the required clearance.

Ivri pulled his chair back but stayed seated. "Did you knock off Kolkin? That's all I want to know."

"No." Glen was livid.

"I think it was someone under your watch. You'd better put your house in order before anyone else on our side gets hurt. We're supposed to be allies, remember?" Ivri got up and left unceremoniously.

As soon as the Israeli had reached the sidewalk, Glen dialed Porter. "We've got a fucking mess," he said, barely containing his rage.

"What's going on?" Porter said with a calmness that further irked Glen.

"The Mossad's lost an agent named Kolkin. Does the name mean anything to you?"

"Uh, no."

"And Ron's apparently made a detour to Venezuela for no good reason. Monitor his accounts and get a hold of our station chief in Caracas. Get Legal involved and alert FBI and DHS. Find that son-of-the-bitch. Pull up everything he's been working on—I mean *everything*."

"Will do. I told you he's gone off the deep end."

"I'm headed back now. Meet me in my office."

୫୬୯୪

No prize waits on this one-way street.
My solitude roams, strangely scabbing itself.
You're safe from demise so steep;
this crude yet grand reverie
coolly passes, as we do in the night.
For eyes so knowing, yours still don't see
the gash that's bled without respite,
My love, solemn...

28

Panama City, Panama

BORIS HAD BEEN ON HIS CELL PHONE FOR ALMOST THIRTY minutes, the last five with a map spread over the hood of the black SUV. Every second that passed with the absence of a clear plan was driving Jonathan berserk. They needed to do something more than stand there in the brightly illuminated parking lot of a convenience store in Panama's wealthiest urban neighborhood. There was no telling how quickly the cops would connect the dots and track them down—something all the more likely after Oleg's refusal to receive them.

Finally, Boris hung up, a transparent worry carved into his face.

"We go south," he said.

"That's it? That's the genius plan?"

"*Da.*"

"Don't you guys have a safe house where we can hide, or a private jet to get us out of here?"

"This was our only safe house," the Russian said, glancing dismally at Oleg's glitzy all-glass tower two blocks away. "And if police know, airport is bad idea."

"What about your embassy?"

"That is also bad because of Oleg."

Jonathan looked at the sky, still grappling with how things had gone so wrong, so quickly. *Perhaps ditching Boris might be better,* he thought momentarily. He then considered finding refuge at the U.S. embassy, but a few seconds of lucid thought dispelled that option. The objective was to get the hell out of Panama as quickly as possible, and for that Boris surely had access to more resources than anything Jonathan could conjure up.

"Get in." Boris pulled the keys out of his fatigues and handed the map to Jonathan. "I drive; you give directions."

"Hopefully our escape will be more successful than that of the Romanovs."

Boris' eyes narrowed.

"Sorry," Jonathan said. "Kidding."

"We go first to La Chorrera, on west side of canal. Find it on map."

They left and headed toward the Casco Viejo—the Old City. Boris weaved their large vehicle through the light 1 A.M. traffic to Avenida Central España, then to the Panamá-Arraiján highway, and shortly thereafter crossed the huge Puente de las Americas bridge over the entrance to the container harbor and the canal.

"You know what you're doing?" Jonathan asked, glancing at Boris' darkened profile, the Russian's attention staying strictly on the road ahead. Jonathan wasn't looking for a response any more complicated than a simple, confident "yes." He just hoped Mariya's go-to guy had it in him to get this right.

The Russian scoffed. "Why, do you have better plan?"

"I just want to know."

"Don't worry," Boris said, checking his cell phone for text messages. "We go southwest, then south to coast."

His continued evasiveness told Jonathan that whatever plan he'd concocted, if any, would have a razor-thin chance of success.

A troubling scene suddenly gripped his imagination: a squad of short, tanned men in uniform, lined up with rifles aimed at his head, his hands tied uncomfortably behind a pole. And then the order to shoot. Though he realized that his notion of Panamanian justice was probably a bit exaggerated, his anxiety rose as he glanced at a sweaty-faced Boris clenching the wheel with both hands. The thought of getting caught in this Central American country after causing such havoc in the middle of their prized canal terrified him more than anything he'd gone through in the pitch-black hell of Katrina-ravaged New Orleans.

"Are you sure heading south is a good idea?" Jonathan asked, knowing that going deeper inland gave the police more time to identify and catch them.

"I told you, we have chance—small chance. We go south." Boris then pointed at the map. "Find Capira. We go there."

A half hour later, they got off the highway and followed a local road instead, crossing La Arboleda and

Villa Diana and then La Chorrera, each a mirror image of the small towns Jonathan had seen the prior night on their way north to Colón: one main road; battered trucks and cars parked in front of shoddy single-story commercial buildings; a few half-lit neon signs on windows of run-down eateries or bars; and a few people and dogs roaming the dirt road shoulder in the dark.

About a mile from the last paved cross street in La Chorrera, Boris insisted that they park for an hour and a half at the end of a dirt road to give time for his contact to call him back with further instructions. The cryptic information was hardly comforting. During the wait, Jonathan asked a few questions, but Boris continued to dodge them.

Finally, when the requisite time had passed, Boris got on the phone with whomever he'd chatted with earlier, and soon they were off again. They rejoined the four-lane Panamerican Highway, as there was no other road south. After about ten miles, they reached the hamlet of Capira.

"So, now where?" Jonathan asked.

"We continue on this road," Boris said, his eyes fixated ahead. "Look for Santa Cruz, and then the turn for Punta Chame."

Jonathan followed the route on the map with his finger. Shortly after Santa Cruz they'd have to exit the highway and head east along Carretera Bejuco-Punta Chame. He followed the mapped road further and gasped.

"It's a dead end! Why are we going there?"

"Trust me," Boris said, accelerating fast.

Jonathan could have strangled him if it weren't for the fact that the Russian could demolish him with one swipe of his arm.

Boris glanced at his watch. "Someone will meet us there."

Jonathan studied the map to make sure he wasn't mistaken. He wasn't. The road snaked southeastward for about fifteen kilometers before turning parallel to the coastline for a shorter distance, and then it ended at the water. "I don't understand. Is there a boat waiting?'

"No, a plane!"

"But there's no airport."

Boris raised his chin at Jonathan. "You underestimate Russian planning."

"Underestimate?" Jonathan threw the map at the console. "Are you kidding me? Did you see the crap we went through tonight? I'd say I overestimated, and by far."

The near desolate highway and the quietness of the dark, forested surroundings did nothing to improve Jonathan's confidence as they continued south several more miles to Santa Cruz.

"*Chyort!*" Boris blurted, slamming on the brakes and bringing their truck to a sudden screeching halt, the tires dragging across the road's gravely shoulder.

Jonathan braced himself on the dash.

There were cops. A bevy of blue lights flickered a quarter-mile down the road. It was a checkpoint for sure.

"We should turn back," Jonathan said.

"No."

"I'm trying to stay calm here, but you're making it hard."

The Russian opened his door and squeezed his large frame out of the vehicle. He crossed the beams of headlights and reentered on the passenger side.

"What are we doing?" Jonathan asked, scooting over to the driver's side.

"We have to try," Boris said, retrieving a submachine gun from behind the seat and quickly loading a magazine into it. "It's our only chance." He then removed two grenades from a bag in the back seat.

"Oh, no you don't..."

Boris ignored him, rested the weapon and grenades on his lap and grabbed the map.

"We're not running a checkpoint, no fucking way!" Jonathan couldn't believe what he was seeing: that his forty-five years of walking this earth would now end gangland-style on this dark, remote near-jungle road in the backlands of central Panama.

"Go," Boris said.

"We can't do this. I'm turning back."

"There, you see?" Boris stretched the map over the steering wheel in front of Jonathan. "It's only fourteen kilometers, and then we are in plane."

Jonathan's limbs froze from fear or anger or confusion or just plain astonishment that they'd reached this far only to run into an impenetrable police roadblock.

"I can't believe you think this will work."

Boris looked away, pulled out his cell phone and quickly dialed.

"*Gdye ty?*" the Russian said as he nervously ran his hand through his greasy hair. "*Horosho. My sovsyem blizko. No politsiya ryadam.*" He listened tensely and then hung up. He placed his weapon at his feet—still within easy reach—and then sat back, a long sigh exiting his mouth.

"What exactly are we doing?" Jonathan prodded.

Boris again pointed at the map with his pudgy finger, his eyes narrowing. "You go straight and do not stop. There is calm water at end of road, at Punta Chame. When we stop on shore, you get out and swim to plane, okay?"

"What?"

"Yes, plane will land on water."

Jonathan guessed he meant a floatplane of some sort. He felt he could now cut Boris some slack. *Clever*, he thought, but getting there alive was the big question. Running a police checkpoint still seemed ludicrous. Suddenly, the thought of spending years in a Panamanian prison sounded somewhat more appealing than getting gunned down like common criminals. Judging by the number of blue lights, Jonathan knew they were outnumbered and outgunned—it was tantamount to suicide.

"We go now!"

Jonathan pulled the SUV from the curbside, his heart almost thrusting out of his chest. He drove the quarter-mile at a normal speed, his eyes studying the four police cars dispersed across a fork in the road. Two officers stood near the closest squad car, and one held a flashlight, signaling Jonathan to slow down.

"Drive around them now. Go! Don't stop!"

Jonathan floored it and swerved left and then right and left again.

Boris hurled a grenade at the second to last patrol car and began firing at the last one.

"Jesus!"

A loud blast echoed. Bullets began hitting their vehicle. Jonathan swerved again as the back window blew out and two rounds burst through the front windshield from behind. He raced down the winding two-lane road at over ninety miles per hour. With only the headlights showing the way, he barely made the turns in time to avoid crashing into trees.

"We have a good lead on them," he said, glancing in the rearview mirror. "Are you sure the plane is waiting?"

Boris spun in his seat, scanning the road behind them. "It will land in two minutes."

"We may not have that much time."

The road snaked through the forested area, passing a few small homes and farmhouses.

"Slow down. We are close."

The high beams lighted a hairpin turn a few hundred feet ahead, forcing Jonathan to slam on the breaks.

"Stop at the turn!"

The SUV screeched over the pavement and halted only a few feet from the water. The stench of burning brake pads vented through the open windows.

Jonathan got out and scanned the dark emptiness behind them. There was no sign of the cops, but it wouldn't be long before they'd catch up.

"Take this and swim fast." Boris handed Jonathan his weapon and a flashlight and quickly returned to the SUV and retrieved a more potent assault rifle for himself.

As Boris took cover behind shrubs at the water's

edge, Jonathan entered the sea as fast as he could, holding his submachine gun above his head. He advanced about thirty yards and stopped, his feet still touching bottom as the temperate water reached chest-level.

"Point the light that way," Boris shouted.

A faint hum filtered through the dense air with the distinct sound of a prop plane. Jonathan had no idea how the aircraft would land in the near pitch-darkness, but it couldn't happen soon enough for him.

The plane's engine grew louder. He pointed the light in the general direction of the noise and waved it in a circular motion. The aircraft flashed its landing lights once as it came in low over the trees and whooshed overhead. He heard several loud splashing sounds as the nearly invisible silhouette touched the water and maneuvered in the distance.

Jonathan signaled again with the flashlight. As the seaplane drew nearer he spotted its spoon-shaped tail. It made a U-turn, its single engine puttering loudly and its floats, fuselage and high-wings came into view. It was a larger seaplane than he'd expected.

The wake reached him, making his trek through the waves more challenging. As each wave hit, he gasped for air but ingested salt water, and when he could no longer touch bottom, he ditched the weapon and removed his shoes to ease the effort.

He was halfway to the plane when the gunshots rang out. Jonathan whipped his head back and spotted Boris firing at two police cars approaching at a high rate of speed. Both vehicles squealed before stopping some twenty yards from Boris, who kept firing.

The airplane halted close to Jonathan, its prop idling loudly. He lifted himself onto the starboard float, got up, pulled the door wide open, threw his shoes in, and quickly climbed into the empty co-pilot's seat, next to a helmeted pilot wearing night-vision goggles and an olive-colored one-piece flight suit.

"You okay?" the pilot shouted through the noisy cabin.

Jonathan returned a thumbs-up just as he realized the pilot sounded like a woman.

The plane maneuvered an S-turn in the water, shortening the distance for Boris.

Jonathan peered through the pilot's side window, gauging what was happening onshore. It seemed Boris had shot out all but one of the patrol cars' headlights. The large Russian's shadow moved quickly toward the cars, the muzzle flashes lighting up in front of him.

"Holy shit." Jonathan spotted Boris circling one of the vehicles. Clearly, he'd killed the cops, since there were none left standing.

The pilot stayed focused on Boris, who then ran to the SUV, retrieved what looked like the bag with the evidence and darted to the water with his weapon strapped over his chest.

Jonathan glanced at the pilot's hands pulling back on the yoke and its large wishbone-shaped support. The slender manicured fingers with dark red nail polish and the silver and leather bracelet clasped over the right wrist left no doubt that the pilot was a woman. But he wondered who she was.

She turned her head to Jonathan, tapped the window

with her hand and pointed at the road. The danger had returned with a vengeance: blue lights illuminated the darkened horizon, and this time there were more than two police cars—it looked like ten.

Boris was near but out of Jonathan's sight. The pilot leaned to her side, attempting to locate him in the water.

Jonathan quickly stepped back to the eight-seat passenger cabin behind the cockpit and peered out the windows. Boris was nowhere in sight.

A loud noise suddenly came from the back of the cabin. The rear door flung open. Boris barreled in, dropped his rifle and bag and collapsed on the floor, soaked and breathing hard. He looked like a beached walrus.

"You all right?" Jonathan asked as he pulled Boris' legs into the plane and shut the door.

Boris nodded. He crawled forward, grabbing the back of the nearest seat for support.

The pilot shouted something in Russian and then pointed at Jonathan to get back to the front, which he quickly did.

Boris slumped into the seat closest to the cockpit.

Tunk! Tunk!

A back window shattered. Glass shards sprayed across the seats and floor.

"They are shooting!" Boris said, moving to another window to observe the cops that had pulled up to the shore. "*Speshitye!*"

Tunk!

Jonathan heard more bullets hitting different parts of the plane, the thumping sounds echoing into the cockpit.

The pilot revved the motor, turning the plane a hundred-eighty degrees. She pushed the tall throttle forward and fiddled with other switches and knobs, while keeping the nose up.

Several more rounds struck the plane. The engine roared louder—louder still because a window in the back was blown out. The plane gained speed and began to skim off the water's surface, bouncing twice before getting fully airborne.

The pilot made a sharp right turn, but suddenly the fuselage began vibrating violently.

"What's happening?" Jonathan had never before been in a seaplane but he knew this wasn't normal.

"I don't know."

Her hands tightly clenched the yoke until she had completed the turn. They headed due west and leveled off at 700 feet. The vibration diminished but didn't disappear completely.

The pilot sat back in her seat, slipped off her goggles and flight helmet and put on a normal headset.

Jonathan tried to conceal his surprise. She was a brunette, in her late twenties, he guessed.

"You speak English?"

"Of course," she said as if he were silly to ask.

Pale, slender, and with soft features—and even a dash of lip gloss—she was hardly what he'd imagined would be rescuing him in the middle of the night under a hail of gunfire.

"Welcome to my Otter," she said, half-smiling. "But there will be no food or beverage service on this flight." The cockpit was too noisy to discern her accent, but her

English sounded quite good, and her humor was refreshing given the circumstances.

Jonathan nodded and returned a smile.

"Make yourself comfortable," she said, handing him a spare headset from behind her seat. "We have a tricky flight ahead."

He plugged in the cable, slipped it over his head and asked, "What's your name?"

"Natasha."

He could hear her better now that the background noise was muffled. Her Russian accent was subtle: she reminded him of Mariya, though he hoped that she wasn't as psychotic or prone to errors in judgment as her elder compatriot.

"Aren't they going to pursue us?"

She tilted her head. "Panama has no air force. Costa Rica has one but it's not much better than strapping wings to donkeys. What worries me are the *gringos*. They routinely intercept drug carriers over both countries. The radar jammer in this plane works quite well against locals but not well against the more advanced hardware of the Americans."

"Where's the jammer?"

"Welded to the fuselage, right under us."

How ironic would it be, he thought, *to be shot down by my own countrymen after all I've been through since leaving New Orleans?*

Within a half-hour, the strong vibration they'd felt during takeoff had returned. Natasha chewed on her lower lip and clenched the yoke.

"What's happening?" Jonathan said.

"Maybe the gunfire damaged something. I can't tell. Perhaps it's a structural problem—the floats or the tail." She scrutinized her gauges and added, "The engine appears fine."

"Did they hit the prop?"

"No, the vibration would be brutal—we would have already crashed." She then pulled and pushed on the yoke and kicked and released her pedals, momentarily changing the aircraft's pitch and heading. "The control surfaces feel okay, so it's something else."

He glanced out his side window but didn't spot anything blatantly wrong from his vantage, though it was too dark to see well.

"My wing is still attached, just so you know."

She chuckled. "No matter what, we need to get rid of unnecessary weight. Throw out the two black cases in the back. It's radio equipment we don't need. And the weapons, too."

"You serious?"

"If we don't lighten the load, we'll have to ditch in Costa Rica, or worse, Panama, and none of us wants that, especially after what you guys did back there."

"Yes, it was bad. But don't blame Boris or me. Mariya insisted that we raid the ship, and then she's the one who got shot."

Natasha's face crumpled. She removed her headset, turned to Boris and began shouting at him. They argued for several minutes—at one point it seemed she might slap him.

"Cool it!" Jonathan said. "I don't know what you're saying, but I suggest you focus on flying the plane." He turned and said, "and you, Boris, help me get rid of the excess weight."

Natasha shook her head and got back to piloting, but the anger had not vanished from her face.

"Do we throw the stuff out right now?"

"Yes." She met Jonathan's gaze. "With full tanks this Otter can fly about 820 nautical miles without refueling. But that's only when flying at normal altitude, in fair weather, and with just a few passengers."

"How far did you fly to get us?"

"415 miles, straight in at about 9,000 feet, most of it over water. Now we're heading back at 800 feet above ground, which burns more fuel, and we have to fly a longer overland path, including over mountainous areas and through an incoming thunderstorm."

"Can't you go higher?"

"And risk getting tracked by radar?"

"What about making a refueling stop somewhere?"

"The closest friendly fuel pump is at my home, on a lake 430 miles away. Between here and there we may run out of fuel; we may get shot down by one of your country's drug interdiction aircraft; or there may be structural failure and we crash."

"Do you Russians always focus on the positive?" he joked, though it did nothing to diminish his own anxiety.

"Come on, open the door and throw that stuff out."

"Just like that?"

"Yes, downward so it doesn't hit the tail. I'm slowing down to help." Natasha instructed Boris in Russian as she pulled back on the throttle and signaled Jonathan, who then headed to the back of the cabin.

He pushed his shoulder into the back starboard door. The force of the wind pushing on the other side made it hard to open. He grabbed a handle above him and pushed harder. A small space emerged. As it opened further, he stuck his foot out to hold it open and then his knee. Boris set the first heavy case onto Jonathan's lap. It weighed at least forty pounds.

Holding the door open with his shoulder, Jonathan slid the case out and pushed it downward before letting go. It fell from the plane, barely clearing the tail. He did the same with the second case, which felt heavier.

"The weapons, too," Natasha shouted.

Boris handed him the rifle, which Jonathan threw out with the same care so as not to damage the aircraft.

"Thank you," Natasha said as Jonathan returned to the co-pilot's seat. "What about that bag Boris brought in? It looks heavy."

"No, that's evidence we need to analyze."

"Fine, but there's one more thing: the bag behind your seat."

Jonathan reached down and grabbed the bulky blue nylon sack that weighed about twenty pounds and had several blunt objects inside.

"What's in this?"

"Tear gas, grenades, flashlights, tools, lipstick, toothbrush...the usual travel essentials." She didn't appear to be teasing. "Throw the fire extinguisher in there, too."

Jonathan unstrapped the extinguisher from the bulkhead behind her and quickly tossed it into the blue bag. He then opened his cockpit door, pushing his shoulder and knee into it with all his strength. He scooted the sack to the bottom of the opening, grabbing the fabric tightly, and eased it out of the cockpit. He released it, and it safely cleared the float below him and disappeared into the dark abyss.

There was no telling how much more distance they would gain from the weight they'd just thrown out, but he felt useful for the first time since Boris had taken control of their escape.

He turned to Boris and asked, "How much do you weigh?"

"One hundred twenty-nine kilos," Boris said, his eyes widening.

Natasha gave Jonathan an evil gaze.

"How much fuel would that save us?"

Natasha laughed. "Good luck pushing him out."

Boris shook his head and sat back in his seat.

They were cruising at about a hundred knots, still at an altitude of just under 1,000 feet, and everything seemed normal except for the persistent vibration that seemed to come from the lower fuselage.

Natasha turned to Jonathan with a frown, her eyes scornful.

"You okay?" Jonathan asked.

"No. I don't understand how you didn't take Mariya into the hospital."

Jonathan guessed that's why she'd argued with Boris moments earlier. "If there was security in the emergency room, then we risked getting caught or identified."

"That's not a good enough reason. You wasted time with your grenade stunt."

"You would have done the same thing under the circumstances."

The vibration suddenly worsened, violently shaking the plane.

"It must be the floats," she said.

Jonathan again glanced out the window. "Mine is still there—it looks perfectly fine."

"Yes, but the struts could be damaged."

"Can we still land normally?"

"I hope so. We're heading to a lake in Nicaragua, but it's still three hours away."

The thought of crashing now, after all they'd gone through, made Jonathan more angry than anxious.

29

THEY FLEW LOW THROUGH THE DARK, TURBULENT SKIES for over two hours, crossing the Panamanian jungle right into a thunderstorm as they entered Costa Rican airspace. No missile blasted them out of the sky. No fighter plane sprayed them with explosive rounds. Nothing of the sort. Not even a single call from an air traffic controller. Perhaps their fairly low altitude had accounted for their stealthiness, or the radar jammer that Natasha had mentioned had done its job. Or maybe it was simply luck. But they weren't yet out of danger.

Jonathan sat half awake—the loud engine noise, the abnormal structural vibration, the draft swirling in from the shattered rear window, and the rough weather they'd encountered for the last hour made it impossible to sleep. He gazed emptily outside, at the faintly visible tree tops.

Suddenly Natasha banged her fist onto the top of the instrument panel and cursed in her native tongue.

Jonathan straightened his back. "What's happened?"

"We're not going to make it."

She ran her fingers through her long, straight hair, pulling the strands in frustration. She checked the instruments and the portable GPS device strapped to the yoke.

Jonathan's heart began to race all over again.

Natasha shook her head. "We're going to be just short—by about fifty or sixty miles, maybe more."

"How much more do we have to fly in this storm?"

"It should clear soon, but it will make no difference."

The weather subsided about thirty minutes later. When the last clouds passed, a very thin crescent moon appeared just over the horizon. Jonathan squinted, spotting a faint reflection of the moonlight.

"There, straight ahead, isn't that your lake?" he said, pointing.

"Maybe, but it's far," she said, rechecking her GPS.

The altimeter read 1,400 feet. He hadn't realized that they'd climbed. "We're higher."

"Yes, we had to clear hills. We've stayed less than a thousand feet above ground the whole way so far. You didn't notice, but we reached 5,000 feet twice to clear mountain ranges."

Natasha craned her neck to see more clearly over the cowling and then scanned the various gauges. "The lake begins about sixty miles from here, but my landing site is another thirty miles north on the same lake and there's not enough fuel to get there. Let's just hope we at least make it to the southern end of the lake."

Five minutes later, she started to pitch up. "We're nearly in Nicaragua. I'm turning toward San Carlos. It's the closest lakefront town across the border."

"How far?"

"Twenty nautical miles."

She flipped some switches and then pushed the throttle forward, the engine growling louder. The airspeed indicator showed they were flying at around one hundred ten knots.

"Anything I can do?"

"Pray. Isn't that what Americans do?"

The vibration became stronger, shaking the instrument panel and just about everything else in the cockpit.

"I hope it doesn't rip apart," Jonathan said.

Natasha shrugged her shoulders. "I want to gain as much altitude as possible so we can glide farther if the engine quits."

Jonathan eyed the dim surface of the water in the distance.

A few minutes into her climb, just as they'd reached 7,200 feet, a sputtering noise came from the engine. The propeller slowed as the engine began to choke.

Natasha glanced coolly at Jonathan. "That's it."

The sputter cycled a few more times and then ceased. The engine went quiet, the propeller now rotating slowly, powered only from the force of the plane gliding through the air.

"Tell air traffic control we're out of gas."

"No, we don't want emergency services looking for us, no matter what happens."

She then said something to Boris as she set the aircraft to a slow descent, flipping several switches and turning off some of the electronics.

Boris' body was too large to strap his seatbelt, so he grasped the edge of the bulkhead with his chunky hands and dipped his head as if to pray.

"If the plane begins to sink, he's going out of the back door," she said to Jonathan. "And you'll go out of your door as quickly as possible. Unlock and crack it open now already. And if you want your evidence bag to survive, put in on your lap."

Jonathan grabbed the sack Boris had brought to the plane. Without it, the raid on the freighter would have been worthless, and he wasn't about to let it end up at the bottom of a lake.

The fuselage continued to shake. He held his door slightly open and peered out the window.

"The float on my side is wobbling. A lot!"

"We need to make water, float or no float," she said. "My plane won't do well landing in trees."

She added twenty degrees of flaps and tightened her seatbelt straps, as did Jonathan.

The lakeshore appeared ahead, but they were losing altitude fairly fast and the trees below them would make for an unforgiving landing. The seconds passed as Jonathan felt his own hard heartbeats even through the plane's vibration.

Four hundred feet.

Three hundred.

Two hundred.

The forested abyss below became more granular.

Natasha pulled the yoke back. The floats sliced the top of trees as the stall horn began to blare. More tree-tops smashed into the floats, but then, suddenly, they cleared the tree line, skimmed over a stretch of swamps and touched down on the water with a hard bounce.

They bounced a second time, but the right float instantly broke off and slammed upward onto Jonathan's side of the cockpit, and the aircraft plunged down, the wing catching the water and thrusting them sideways. A loud crackle pierced the cockpit, followed by the sounds of tearing metal. The abrupt stop threw him forward, his seatbelt expelling the breath from his lungs. Glass shattered, and he felt upside down but wasn't sure.

The cockpit quickly began filling with water.

"Go!" he heard Natasha shout.

The plane was sinking fast.

Jonathan unbuckled himself and kicked open the twisted door as more water rushed into the cockpit. Holding his breath, he squeezed through the opening and swam downward, grabbing the bag filled with cell phones and the *Nixos-Dakar* skipper's computer and documents. He slipped under what felt like the wing and propelled himself away from the aircraft as best he could in the pitch-black water. At the end of his extended breath he surfaced and gasped for air. Only the tip of the port side wing remained above water. Over his panting he heard someone else surface behind him.

"Natasha?"

"Yes, I'm okay. You?"

"Fine, but where's Boris?"

Natasha shouted her Russian colleague's name, but there was no reply.

The wingtip slipped below the mild wake. The plane was gone.

"Boris?"

Jonathan treaded water, still gripping the evidence bag. He'd survived the crash but apparently the Russian special forces operative had not been so lucky. The reality seeped in uncomfortably.

"I'm going back down," Natasha said.

He heard some splashes and then complete silence but for chanting crickets onshore. More than a minute passed before she resurfaced.

"I can't reach the back of the plane," she blurted, sounding out of breath. "It's too far down. Maybe the rear door jammed on impact. I'll try one more time."

She tried, three more times, until finally Jonathan convinced her of the obvious. Boris was gone, trapped somewhere in or under the carcass of the single-engine floatplane.

The closest shore was nothing but swamps, she'd said. Their only option was to reach San Carlos and its narrow waterfront at the junction of the San Juan River and the lake. The town's distant lights told them it would be a long swim. And it was. Some thirty minutes later they reached the shore, which was lined with shoddy buildings on stilts.

Jonathan climbed onto the wooden pier and helped Natasha up. They were both exhausted and barefoot—-she'd removed her boots for the swim; Jonathan had left his on the plane. They loitered a few minutes to catch their breaths before venturing into the small town. There, Natasha found a man willing to drive them to Granada—a 150-mile counterclockwise journey around Central America's largest lake—in his tattered Toyota pickup, for a steep fee of three wet one hundred dollar bills.

By eight-fifty in the morning, the sun now roasting them, they made it to some semblance of safety. The driver had dropped them off at the Iglesia Corazon de Jesus, a church on the north side of Granada, across from his relative's home and as far as he was willing to drive. From there Jonathan and Natasha took a cab over the remaining five miles to a dock south of town, where a water taxi shuttled the pair into the *Isletas*— -a 365-island archipelago on Lake Nicaragua where, Natasha explained, a growing number of wealthy families were driving out the *campesinos* in order to build lavish vacation homes.

The boat rounded a corner, toward a single-home island partly obscured by the lush foliage and tall trees.

"There, that's my place," Natasha said.

"Your own island?"

"Not quite. Just a small isthmus."

It looked cozy but palatial nonetheless, surrounded by water on nearly all sides. With no neighbors and no vehicular access, the hideout seemed like a perfect spy lair.

The boat pulled up to a dock, right behind a small motorboat.

"Yours?"

"Yes, mainly to shuttle back and forth to the main dock or to get groceries."

"And why two gas pumps?"

"One for my plane, one for boats."

"You won't need both now," Jonathan said, though he didn't mean it as a joke. He followed her along the cobblestone path to her abode, where he could finally rest his feet, which were blistered and sore. The coolness of the foyer's oversized marble tiles helped soothe the soreness.

She turned on the recessed lights, and then sped ahead into the living room and slipped off her flight suit. Jonathan caught only a glimpse of her nearly naked silhouette as she walked briskly into a darkened hallway toward the back of the house.

"I'll be back," she said.

Jonathan walked up to the expansive windows that stretched across the entire length of the immense living room facing the lake. Large wood beams sliced upward along the vaulted ceiling, but this was the only rustic addition to the space. The furniture was minimalist and contemporary, resting on dark cherry-stained hardwood floors. There were no picture frames, no ornaments, no flower vases, as he would have expected in a woman's home. Nothing cozy. Nothing personal. Only candles. Lots of them, on all the shelves, on the coffee table, on the end tables, on the ledges above and to the side of the stone fireplace, almost everywhere.

The lake was a mere five yards from the windows. The gently-rippled surface glistened in the intense morning sun, yielding a peaceful, picturesque setting for a body of water that had greeted Jonathan in a wholly unpleasant way only a few hours ago. He shook his head. Somewhere in those waters were a wrecked seaplane and a dead Russian who'd saved his life. The guilt of having survived crept in. Boris didn't deserve his fate. But it hadn't seemed to bother Natasha.

She returned, her hair towel-dried and loosely brushed, dressed in a black tank top and sweatpants. She held out a neatly folded pile of dry clothes and gym shoes.

"These may fit you," she said coolly, dropping them on the gigantic U-shaped sectional leather couch that had likely cost the hides of at least a dozen cows.

"Thank you." He had much more to thank her for, but even the relative calm of this home had not yet made Jonathan comfortable enough to open up more.

"The bathroom," she said, signaling with her chin.

"Did I do something to upset you?" Jonathan asked. "Or are you usually this distant to people you rescue by plane?"

He thought he saw a tiny smile.

She shook her head and sighed, her arms sliding against her slender hips. "I don't have much in me to talk right now."

"Were you close to Boris?"

"No."

"Is it the plane that upsets you? It's an expensive loss."

"Don't be silly. I can't explain now."

Her Russian accent laced her English words so sub-tly that Jonathan had to recall all that'd happened the past few hours to believe she really was from that Slavic land. He hadn't paid close attention to her in the aircraft, nor in the truck, nor when they'd been on the ten-min-ute boat ride to her home. Instead, he'd been locked in survival mode, coping with his wet, cold clothes and the sense of bewilderment that had consumed his every moment since Mariya had conned him into unwisely doing her a favor.

He'd seen only Natasha's flat, shoulder-length jet black hair, her pale face, thin build, and deep dark eyes. Nothing more. Not until now. Not till she coiled into repose at the far end of the couch, a blanket yanked up chest-high and a cell phone resting at arm's length.

"You'll catch cold," she said quietly, without looking at Jonathan. She peered out the window over the back of the couch, resting her head on her palm. The sun drenched the room with light and revealed her worried, pensive gaze.

*   *   *

Jonathan glanced in the mirror over the sink as he gelled his hair back. Colorful lighted candles decorated the counter. He rinsed his face with a hot washcloth, as if the shower had not fully cleansed him. Only a few small cuts on his left cheek and neck betrayed a night of chaos. He gazed vacantly at his reflection. The clothes she'd given him fit fine. Perhaps from an old beau? Or a current one? One who might not appreciate seeing another man at his woman's house, with her hair damp, her body tired, as if they'd just ended hours of sex. With all that had happened, the thought of being shot by a jealous boyfriend didn't seem farfetched. So, stepping out of the washroom, he thought it wise to clear the air.

"Are you okay with me being here?" he said.

Natasha was still elsewhere, staring out the windows.

Jonathan asked again, joining her on the couch, but at the other end. Only then did she snap out of her thoughts.

Natasha tilted her head and bit her bottom lip. Her solemnity seemed portentous, though he hoped it also held answers. He'd settle for even bits and pieces of certainty—anything to give some sense that someone knew what the fuck to do, because at that very moment he had none nor the strength or wisdom to concoct any solution.

She turned to him, the light striking the back of her silky hair and an edge of her delicately chiseled jaw. Her blanket fell to her lap, revealing her open shoulders—thin, pale, toned. Her demeanor added a few years to her age, which he now guessed was about twenty-eight.

"You're Jonathan, right?" she asked suddenly.

"Yes, I already told you."

She nodded, gazing at the ceiling. "A friend of Mariya's, huh?"

He chuckled. "I wouldn't call us friends, but I know enough about her." He stopped. Although Mariya had given him plenty to complain about, he couldn't bring himself to disparage her.

Natasha got up. "I'm going to get wine while you tell me more. And if what you say is remotely true and interesting, I'll allow you to sleep in the house until you get your bearings, and then you will leave to wherever you came from and forget me, forget everything that's happened, and especially forget that you were ever here."

"And if I don't?"

"I will toss your organs to the hungry lake fish."

Jonathan didn't sense a scintilla of wit accompanying that ominous reply.

"Mariya helped me find my brother many years ago. I don't want to explain. It's too painful and pointless to recycle now."

The sound of a violin came from speakers near the fireplace. Vivaldi. He welcomed the opportunity to escape from his thoughts into some music.

Upon returning from the kitchen with glasses in one hand and an opened bottle of Sauvignon Blanc in the other, she paused, frowned at him and asked, "Your last name is Brooks, right? The lawyer?"

He tried to recall if he'd previously told her his last name, in the plane perhaps. He hadn't, but had Boris? Jonathan simply nodded.

"Do you work for Mariya?" he said, trying to change the topic.

She filled his glass. "I'll ask the questions for now. Remember, you've got some talking to do, or the fish will have a treat."

"I didn't ask to get involved. I only wanted to help, in a very limited way, but Mariya sucked me into this mess."

Jonathan had not wanted to travel down the charred path of memory lane, but he soon did, and she listened. The wine greased the mental wheels and Vivaldi's melody coaxed him further, as did Bach and Chopin.

Natasha sipped and listened coolly and her voice became a soft, accented tune that filled the air with an inviting sweetness so diametrically opposite from the wintry body language she'd signaled to him since his rescue. As he took the last sip, he began to shed his first tears. It all came back. Every detail about his brother, Matt. Jonathan's tormented journey through the Russian capital in search of his kin made the failed raid on the *Nixos-Dakar* and the crash-landing on a lake all seem like child's play. He told Natasha everything, with the granular detail he'd never expected was still lodged in his memory.

She said nothing, choosing instead to listen attentively till he was done, well into the afternoon. She returned to her pose, staring intently at the lake, deep in her own thoughts. Every now and then, she checked her phone for messages. Her nervousness became contagious.

Jonathan did not budge from the couch. He assumed he'd spilled enough of the past to allow him to stay the night, but he was not comforted by his near-inebriation nor by the pensive and silent Russian sitting across from him.

They both rested on the couch, silently, for a long while.

"I'm going to take a nap," Natasha suddenly said. "If you want, there's a blanket and a pillow in that hallway closet."

Jonathan eyed the clock on the wall. It was 4:20 P.M. He watched her leave to her room.

30

THE BIRDS CHANTING IN THE TREES GAVE THE ILLUSION OF tranquility that Jonathan had last felt only back in New Orleans, long before Katrina had struck, and before he'd gotten embroiled in Mariya's pursuit of the drowned Asian and the *Nixos-Dakar*.

He gazed at Natasha's island-like refuge, made more impressive now by the sunset over the distant mountains to the west. He stared at the calm, expansive lake—large enough that the opposite shore was only faintly visible as a green sheath layered over the watery horizon. His false sense of comfort continued to sink in, as it had the moment he'd taken a seat on the porch a half-hour ago after awakening from a much-needed nap. The prior night's turbulent canal raid, the shootout with police, the narrow escape, and the plane crash were all locked away in his tired head. He also ignored, as best he could, the reality of his predicament—he had little money, no passport, and no way to go home. Besides, home was whatever was left post-Katrina. He consoled himself with only two positives: he was alive and in a relatively safe place for the time being. But he had to plan his next move.

The sliding glass doors opened behind him, startling him. Natasha, dressed in jean shorts and a tank top, her skin white as Russian snow, joined him on the porch.

"Is that what you took from the ship?" she asked coolly.

Before going to the patio Jonathan had laid out on the kitchen island everything Boris and he had taken from the freighter during the raid: a laptop, a Palm Treo, two cheap cell phones, the ship's log, three wallets, and pile of papers, all of them still wet.

"Yes, evidence," he said. "Do you know someone here who can extract the data?"

"I know how to do it, but come here first."

She led him to her study, a cozy room with draped windows, a small couch and a chaise, empty bookcases on two walls and a flat screen on the other. The television was set to CNN's Spanish-language channel, and Jonathan instantly saw the images he'd only seen from the ground in the dark.

Aerial footage of the *Nixos-Dakar* listing to its port side along the bank of the canal took up the whole screen. Dozens of tug boats and smaller patrol craft were docked alongside, and countless emergency vehicles speckled the shore. The commentator spoke of the incident's grim facts but only in the most general terms: a suspected terrorist strike with seven crewmen fatally shot; the ship lost power and ran aground; and the canal would stay closed for at least two more days.

"We only killed two, and that's because they shot at us," Jonathan said, feeling upset at how the event was portrayed. "A crewman shot the others—we didn't."

The news segment made no mention of a wounded female assailant. No word of nationalities or descriptions of the suspects, nor anything about a grenade going off near a hospital in downtown Panama City. Nor any mention of a shootout near Punta Chame or fugitives escaping by seaplane.

Natasha stepped in front to block his view, her hands at her hips, and said, "Mariya would not have let this get so out of hand. It's a disaster."

Jonathan couldn't believe his ears. "It was her call. She was in charge, and it all went to hell."

She took a long breath. "Then I'm surprised."

"They're keeping things close," Jonathan said, looking again at the TV images.

"Close?"

"Obviously, the authorities haven't shared much with the media, and that puzzles me. Why didn't they mention the two armed crewman? Or the grenade going off near the hospital, or the shootout at the checkpoint?"

Natasha's serious gaze didn't change. "Come."

Jonathan followed her to a room at the other end of the house. The outside shutters were closed, and the dark curtains half-drawn. A long workbench ran along a wall, and on it were two top-of-the-line desktop computers, each with a large flat screen monitor and a high-speed printer, all of them new—the kind of office equipment Jonathan only dreamed of having at his firm. There was also a high-capacity copier, a flatbed scanner, two strange-looking desk phones, a high-end Nikon camera and a double-stacked military radio with headset.

"So you've been following this case closely," Jonathan said as he spotted several black and white pictures of ships and buildings and handwritten notes pinned to a cork board on the wall.

"No, these are other matters. Nothing to do with the *Nixos-Dakar*."

He then peered into the open closet. Several assault rifles and what looked like a grenade launcher were mounted on a rack, and three large cases on the floor probably held more weapons or ammunition.

"This is my workplace," she said straightforwardly, as if it was perfectly normal to have such weapons and equipment in one's office.

"Should you be showing me all this?"

"Probably not, but Mariya said you're trustworthy."

He was surprised. "Did you speak with her?"

"Only before the raid," replied Natasha as she lay her hand on his shoulder. "So, is she right—that you can be trusted?"

"She may be dead."

Natasha's face froze. "Don't you worry about her," she snapped, pulling back her hand. "I've checked. She's alive. I don't want to talk about her."

The relative safety he'd felt for the past few hours suddenly seemed shaky. Maybe it was the equipment, the weapons, pictures or the cryptic notes on the board. The whole room seemed wrong.

"What the fuck is this place?" Jonathan said, not really wanting to hear the answer. He pointed at the guns and added, "This is no vacation home, and you're not here to write a novel. I mean, look at this shit. These guns. That military radio. Not to mention the plane you lost." He crossed his arms, shaking his head. "Fuck, you're just like Mariya—a danger to others."

"What? If it weren't for me, you'd be in a Panamanian police station getting the shit beaten out of you."

Like Mariya, Natasha didn't appear to be the kind who'd take criticism easily, if at all. Her feistiness reminded him of Mariya, too, and he wondered if Natasha also used her elegance and beauty to deceive. *If she's like Mariya, she's also a killer*, Jonathan warned himself.

"You should be damn happy I'm even letting you stay here."

"You're some kind of covert operative, which means you lie, cheat and steal. You've given up any moral high ground, and for what? Russia? A bankrupt former empire? And you think—"

"Shut up! You have no place judging me. Do you know what *your* country did to this place, and to this region?"

"You were barely out of your diapers at the time."

"So what? It doesn't make it any less real."

"Why are you here, on the other side of the planet from your homeland, fighting a war that already ended? It's wrong. It's not right."

"Right?" Natasha asked, leaning forward, her arms crossed. "What the hell was right about you Americans arming and supporting the Contras, who butchered women and children in countless villages across this country. I've met the broken families. I've met the orphans, the widows. Or when the CIA trained and armed death squads, like the infamous Battalion 3-16 in Honduras—a bunch of thugs who murdered, raped and tortured villagers; who ran drug-trafficking networks; who kidnapped and killed local politicians, doctors, lawyers, and even priests? Or when they supported corrupt military regimes in Guatemala and El Salvador that executed hundreds of civilians without trial? Is that the 'right' you're talking about? Is that the justice that you, as a lawyer, find defensible?"

"You can't be so naive," he said, his anger rising. "Both sides were bad." He had no interest in debating the CIA's anti-communist crusades in Latin America—a past that he, like most Americans, had never taken the time to understand. What mattered now was the present.

"Yes, we did the same thing in other parts of the world," Natasha said, her words slowing. "But not here. My conscience is clear. I cause no harm to Nicaragua. I only listen, see, analyze, and on very rare occasions jump to other parts of the region when things go wrong. I've been here three years, and I love it as if were home."

"It's not home, and I'm sure if the Nicaraguan government found out about you, they'd arrest you or throw you out."

She put her hands on her hips and snorted. "No, the Sandinistas still run the show in terms of security and intelligence, despite the current pro-American president. Russians are still welcomed with open arms."

"Tell me, how many people have you or Mariya spied on, bribed, extorted, wounded or killed? How many have you framed for things they didn't commit? How many lives have you ruined carrying out your duties? Don't bother answering. I don't expect you to be honest. Hell, you probably don't even know the full extent of your harm."

"Who the fuck—"

"The truth hurts, doesn't it?"

Natasha frowned deeply, biting her lip. "Enough."

"You may be young, but you're clearly as brainwashed as Mariya."

"Enough! Don't judge me or my mother, ever, and that's—" She suddenly fell silent, clamping her mouth shut.

Jonathan stared at her, not quite ready to believe what had slipped through her lips.

"Your mother?"

Natasha turned away, her hand now covering her mouth. She walked out in a hurry.

Jonathan ran after her and grabbed her arm. "Mariya's your mother?"

She turned, her eyes now watering.

"Is she?"

She looked away, violently freeing her arm from his grasp. "Yes."

"Why didn't you tell me?"

"Because it's none of your business. She should never have involved you."

"I'm sorry. I didn't mean to say what I said about her."

She shook her head and wiped the tears away as Jonathan followed her into the living room where she, opened a drawer under the coffee table, took a cigarette from a pack and lit up.

"How is she?" he asked.

"In serious condition, apparently. My government wants to transfer her to a hospital in Cuba, but Panama is refusing."

"How much do the Panamanians really know about the raid?"

"For sure that *she* was part of it, but your name or Boris' has not come up yet, as far as we know. But it's hard to get solid details on the ground."

"Did Oleg tell you this?"

She looked surprised. "No. I know he's useless."

"Boris felt Oleg could betray us."

"It's only a matter of time before they find something—they're searching surveillance videos at gas stations, restaurants, bars, bank teller machines, and intersections and everywhere along your escape route. They're sifting through credit card transactions, phone calls, hotel records, airline passenger manifests—everything to find out who was assisting her."

"I'm sorry about what I said earlier—about Mariya."

"It's okay. You've gone through a lot in the last few days. I'm angry because of many reasons, not just about Mariya's situation, or yours."

The battle was over, it seemed. Natasha sat down on the couch, where she smoked alone for a while longer and then stomped her cigarette hard into the ashtray, exhaling the last plume of smoke across the table.

As Jonathan watched her in silence, he realized that Natasha had revealed more about herself in this confrontation than in the prior eighteen hours since they'd met. Her convictions made her a believer—albeit a blind follower, like Mariya—who roamed this earth clinging to an idealized image of Mother Russia and the necessary fight against the enemy—apparently still the virulent America of Cold War years. She, like her mother, had drunk the Kool-Aid, and confronting her was a futile exercise for which Jonathan had no more patience. And now that her mother lay near death, it was not the time to further aggravate a woman who'd saved his life.

*   *   *

"Come see," Natasha said loudly from her work room. Jonathan checked his watch. It was nearly midnight. He'd left her alone in her office for over two hours. In the meantime, over several glasses of wine he'd perused the dried paper documents he'd taken from the captain's cabin.

When she called out again, he got up from the couch, feeling slow and numbed by the alcohol. She opened the door wide just as he was about to knock.

"I decrypted the SIM cards from the Palm and one of the cell phones," Natasha said, pointing to the devices on the workbench. It looked like she'd taken apart all the hardware; bits and pieces were strewn around her.

She returned to her chair facing the computer. "Each SIM card has its own unique serial number and mobile subscriber ID, as well as various authentication and ciphering features. The Palm also had a rather lengthy contacts list. I just sent the data for further analysis."

"To where?"

She smirked. "Moscow, where else?"

"How quickly can they sort through it?"

"Be patient. I've got hackers, financial analysts, military experts, mathematicians, engineers and others on standby." She then tilted her head and grinned. "I guess you guys caused enough of a stink in Panama to turn everyone at the Kremlin into insomniacs."

Jonathan tilted his head. "Mariya told me they were already fired up before the raid. So they should work fast, right?"

"They'll try. There are one and a half billion GSM phone subscribers worldwide, each with a SIM card, and my agency doesn't have all that data at its fingertips, unlike the NSA in your country. Anyway, the contacts are meaningless unless we get a match in our databases."

"What about the laptop?"

"Lots of porn."

"I thought skippers got enough action in every port," Jonathan joked.

"Clearly, this one had a higher sex drive." She clicked through the computer's directory. "There are two folders of scanned documents relating to the ship's maintenance, and several certificates, licenses and insurance documents."

She then clicked open five PDF files.

"That's an insurance notice," Jonathan said, reading over her shoulder.

"Yes, apparently the *Nixos-Dakar* was previously named M/V *Gladius*, and prior to that it was called the

Zhìhuì Hai in the Lloyd's Register. They reclassified the ship, from dry-bulk carrier to multi-purpose."

"When?"

"Looks like all the changes have taken place since 2003."

"In two years? Strange." Jonathan had worked on a wide range of matters involving registration and insurance of merchant ships, and it didn't make sense for an older dry-bulk vessel to change hands twice in two years, and then have sufficient conversion done to be reclassified. "Someone clearly wanted to conceal the identity of the original vessel."

"To hide the new and original owners," Natasha added.

Jonathan nodded.

"Here, look at this one." Natasha gestured at the screen. "It's a letter confirming the original transfer from a company called China International Sea Enterprise. Do you know this company?"

"Of course. CISE has one of the largest merchant fleets in the world based in Hong Kong, particularly oil tankers and container vessels. But they are not known for having dry-bulk or multipurpose ships. Why would they sell an old bulk carrier so recently, and in such a covert way?" Jonathan wanted to know more about the transfers of title, but there was nothing more on the laptop except a voluminous collection of videos and pictures of lesbian orgies.

Fortunately, and with promptness Jonathan hadn't expected of anything Russian, more information arrived swiftly into Natasha's inbox. In just under an hour,

Moscow had sent two coded emails, which she decrypted and translated for Jonathan. They described the history of the *Nixos-Dakar* and confirmed the prior names they'd read from the skipper's laptop. But more importantly they learned that its current owner, Echis Global, had a portfolio that included only the *Nixos-Dakar* and two other vessels: the Ghanaian-flagged M/S *Santora* and the Liberia-flagged M/V *Muzhestvo*—Russian for courage. The latter two had been 1980s vintage dry-bulk carriers waiting to be scrapped in Bangladesh before being purchased, reregistered, reclassified as multipurpose vessels, and given flags of convenience. Natasha explained that after CISE purchased the vessels, they were transferred to Singapore and sold to Echis Global, which had purchased the *Nixos-Dakar* only a month earlier.

Natasha paused before translating the last few paragraphs of the final email, her eyes skimming ahead.

"What is it?" Jonathan asked, wishing his Russian vocabulary was far more extensive.

"You won't believe this..." She shook her head and continued translating. "Six of the cell phone numbers in the SIM card are associated with Luis Rojas Muñoz— one of the most talented welders in Central America."

"I don't understand."

She spun around in her chair to face Jonathan. "He was arrested in June in Cartagena, and the Americans want him extradited. For years, drug traffickers have used this guy to refit cargo ships with hidden compartments to transport cocaine and marijuana across the seas. He's also worked in Malaysia, Venezuela, Vietnam, and

Thailand, among other places. He even built submarines for the Norte del Valle cartel. With his help Colombian drug lords have exported hundreds of tons of cocaine to your country, Europe and Russia."

"How do you know all this?"

"As much as you may dislike what I do here, part of my work is monitoring drug traffickers. Yes, I actually do good things."

"Don't get me started."

Jonathan tried to tie things together. Had Muñoz worked on the *Nixos-Dakar*? Had he converted the vessel somehow to carry radioactive materials in a hidden compartment? That would explain the Geiger counter readings, although they appeared to emanate from portable gear, and neither Boris or Jonathan had had the time to search other parts of the vessel for hidden compartments. And what of the other two ships? Who were the faces behind Echis Global? He wanted answers more than ever before, now that this investigation had nearly cost him his life on more than one occasion.

Information continued to trickle into Natasha's computer over the next few hours, and by 2:00 A.M. he and the Russian had constructed a fairly solid matrix of circumstantial and direct evidence pointing to something sinister, though the essential details still eluded them. But the name that kept appearing in countless emails and documents she'd received from Moscow was Ong & Carrington, a boutique law firm based in Singapore.

The *Nixos-Dakar* and *Muzhestvo* were purchased through brokers managed by the law firm's managing partner, Wesley Ong. He'd also negotiated the contracts for their two-month refitting in Lumut, Malaysia, a port the welder Muñoz had frequented at around the same time, according to an interrogation report from the Colombian police, which obviously had been stolen by Russian intelligence.

"His firm handles business transactions for some of Asia's richest men," Natasha said, reading from another message. "As well as for two Russian mafia bosses."

She clicked on the law firm's website.

Jonathan took the mouse from her hand and navigated the pages. "It's only an eight-lawyer firm." He scrolled down the page showing the names and head-shots of the firm's attorneys. "What does that tell you?"

"Discretion. Trusted middlemen. Easy to reward and buy silence, if needed."

"Exactly."

Jonathan looked at Natasha as if she already knew what to do next about Ong.

"What?" she asked.

"Here's the answer." He froze the page to the picture of Ong and then clicked the link to his bio. "Ong knows which clients purchased the ships. That is key."

"Of course."

"So, Natasha, any idea how to solve this?"

Another coded email arrived as they spoke. She cut and pasted the lines of characters into the program she'd used to decrypt the messages. She sighed and again spun in her chair to face him. "We're not the only ones to know this. My bosses are already on it. It's apparently quite urgent."

As if touched by a sense of professional courtesy—or perhaps just empathy—for a fellow attorney, Jonathan asked, "You're not going to hurt him, are you?" He saw Natasha's glare and added, "I mean, he's the lawyer, not necessarily the villain. The client is who we want."

"We'll be gentle," Natasha said with a rough grin.

"There's been enough bloodshed and destruction," he said, but he realized how ridiculous his concern must sound to her.

She patted his shoulder. "Very gentle."

"When you say that, I can't help but think of your mother. She shot an unarmed man in cold blood. She didn't have to. She could have arrested him instead."

Natasha's face turned angry. "What do you know about my mother?"

"She kills people."

Jonathan had again hit a nerve, and the distraught daughter jumped to her feet and swiped the workbench with her hand, flinging the stapler across the room.

"Just because she's done what every top operative does for their country, that doesn't make her evil or crazy! We all do what's necessary, or sometimes we simply obey orders even if we don't agree."

"I can't expect you to be objective, but—"

Natasha stood up, pushed her chair back and stepped up to Jonathan with the swagger resembling that of a man twice her size. "You really want to bring up my mother?" Her eyes narrowed, and she inhaled deeply. It could well have been fire coming out of her nostrils. "Do you know what it is to be a survivor in an unjust world? To be a Jew in the Soviet Union? Do you know what it's like to be told that you can't be who you want to become? That even if you're smart, charismatic, resourceful, talented, observant, compassionate...that you're stuck—with a ceiling imposed over you, just because you're Jewish and everything about your identity is branded a Jew—your passport, your civil records, your employment records, everything!"

Jonathan silently observed her.

"She had done very well in school—brilliantly, in fact—but getting into the two or three good high schools that accepted Jews was nearly impossible, and getting into university just about unheard of. She couldn't go far unless something happened, something that could change the rest of her life. By sheer luck she met someone who took her under his wing. A man who got her into the intelligence services and, by a miracle of sorts, managed to erase her past. He took away everything Jewish about her and her parents, and for the rest of her life she's lived with a sense of betrayal to her own soul."

"Is this person your father?"

"No. My mother is by no means a saint, but she has conviction and courage and has struggled more than you ever have or ever will. Now stop talking about her. It's upsetting enough that she's seriously injured and alone in a hospital very far from here."

This time Jonathan would not further fan the flames. It was pointless. And for all Mariya's flaws, he felt sorry for her, and for Natasha's anguish. He looked into her eyes and at that moment only saw a daughter aching for her mom.

Natasha's eyes had turned red and filled with tears. Her lips quivered as she gazed up at him. He held her shoulders and without an ounce of forethought saw her bridge the distance. "The last twenty-four hours have been very difficult for me...for both of us."

Jonathan nodded, studying the least brave face she'd shown him so far.

Natasha suddenly leaned up and kissed him. Not just a kiss among strangers, but the kind that fires electric bolts deep into the skull, and so hard it shut out the world around him. His lips didn't leave hers except for the briefest moment to grasp a sliver of air. He tasted salt and honey on her tongue. He caressed her silky hair, her perfumed neck, her slender shoulders, his angst and confusion evaporating as though her lips were laced with morphine. Their bodies intertwined, their lips warmed, and it all seemed right, even if he knew it was dead wrong. Her chest rubbed against his. His hands descended gently from her shoulders to her elbows, past her fingers, down to her hips and around to her back. *Twenty-something*, he thought; her skin was smooth, tight.

He felt her hands wrap around the back of his head and neck. She unbuttoned his shirt, her lips now roaming near his ear. Faint moans from her mouth told him this was real, that she was his that very instant, no matter what the after-thoughts would bring, no matter the questions that would follow, or the discomfort that could arise. This was dangerous, and he understood it, but he had already surrendered.

He sensed her heated, perspiring cheeks and jaw as

they continued to kiss. His hands explored her stomach, sliding under her shirt and upward to her bra-less breasts. He touched her hard nipples, all the while thinking of the silkiness of her skin. He momentarily questioned if his extreme arousal was only because it had been so long since he'd touched another woman. But it wasn't that. Her presence, the feeling of a strange, peaceful yet intense aura dazzled him well beyond anything he'd ever felt in years. Her scent and the way her body responded to his touch were so inviting. He pulled her shirt over her head and began easing down her pants, and she did the same with his. And when there were no more clothes to remove, she pulled him by his arm and led him down the hallway to her room, to her enormous bed, to feather pillows that cushioned their leap across the mattress. He grabbed and caressed her thighs as he entered her, gazing into her half-closed eyes. There was nothing else on this earth that mattered. Not a damn thing.

*   *   *

For a moment Jonathan thought it had just been a dream. His newly awakened mind sprinted through mental snapshots of Natasha's flawless, nude body as he gauged his surroundings.

He was alone in bed, the sunlight slicing through the blades of the closed blinds. He looked around, confused. Had it really happened? He was in her room for sure. He could still hear the moans of her orgasms. Two or three of them, it seemed. He could still feel her nails scraping his arms as he thrusted deep inside her. It was all still so tangible. Real. *We had sex,* he thought and then smiled. For the first time in more than two years. He sat up, shook his head and turned to the clock on the nightstand.

"Dammit." It was past ten in the morning. He'd overslept. "Natasha?" He got up and opened the bedroom door open wider. "Natasha?"

Hearing nothing, he got dressed and looked for her throughout the house, but she was gone. He went outside, walked partly around the isthmus to the dock and saw that the small motorboat wasn't there.

He sat down on the grass, under the shade of a large tree, and soon a feeling of guilt crept into him. Linda was back on his mind. He could hear her voice, her words from their last call. And then he sighed, images of Natasha flashing in front of him. He'd just had sex with her, and it disturbed him as much as it confused him that Linda still gripped so much of his heart. *An ex-wife isn't supposed to drown me in guilt.* He breathed the heavy air and stared at the still lake. "Forgive me," he whispered and shook his head.

At eleven he began to worry and decided to wait on the porch with the sliding glass door open to hear the phone in case she called. When noon came and went, his mind began racing with fear as to why she would have left without telling him.

It was at nearly one in the afternoon when the putt-putt sound of a worn engine filtered through the gentle breeze. It came from somewhere behind the distant trees of a neighboring *isleta*. A small motor boat with a canopy, like the one they'd used the day before, turned the corner and headed toward him. He spotted Natasha seated behind the helmsman. She waved, and Jonathan ran down to greet her, reaching for her hand to help her jump to the small concrete pier on her property.

"Why did you leave without telling me?"

"Because you would have insisted to come with me."

"Where did you go?"

She pushed him back toward the house. "I had to solve your problem."

"What problem?"

"That you have no passport."

Jonathan shrugged. "What do you mean?"

"Here," she said, pulling out a manila envelope from her bag. She tossed it on the kitchen counter. "We're leaving tonight for Venezuela.

"We?" Jonathan hadn't yet thought about whether or not he should go, but was surprised she'd already decided.

"Yes, you're coming with me."

"Why?" he asked. "Was I that good in bed?" He smiled, but the joke was his way of coping with a sudden rush of anxiety.

"You're not staying here, for sure. And frankly, you know a bit too much about me and this place for me to simply let you walk away."

"So, you're going to kill me in the end?"

"Don't be ridiculous. I want to trust you, like my mother has." She pointed to the envelope. "Those are your travel papers."

Jonathan quickly tore the edge of the envelope and let the contents drop. It was a red passport, with the gold-embossed word CANADA on top and the words "diplomatic passport" in both English and French printed under the coat of arms. Inside it had stamps from Morocco, Brazil, Finland, Hungary and Sudan, places Jonathan had never traveled to.

"You think I'm going to use this?"

"You have no choice."

Jonathan flipped to the picture page and was surprised to see his picture. "This is from my old firm's website years ago."

"We're good, aren't we?"

"How good is this forgery?" He held it in the air and tilted it to one side. "This thing could land me in jail for a long time."

"It's from one of the best in the business. I didn't have to go far. He's in Managua." She grinned.

"When did you have this made?"

"I asked for it last night, and I picked it up in Masaya, about thirty minutes from here."

Jonathan examined the passport's pages more closely, feeling unsure that it would pass scrutiny by an immigration officer. He returned to the picture page. "Reginald Piketon? Who chose this ridiculous name?"

"You don't like it?"

"Do I look like a Reginald?"

"Oh, Regi...I like the sound of it," she said, smiling.

"Maybe if I were a butler in an English manor."

"It doesn't matter. Venezuelan immigration doesn't have access to the most important databases that can cross-check this identity. You'll be just fine."

"And why Caracas?"

"The other ship, the *Muzhestvo*, just left Cuba and is believed to be headed to Venezuela for the second time this month, so headquarters is telling me to go there. They also said that Echis Global was apparently established by a man name Bo Huang, one of China's richest men. They want us to find Echis Global's warehouse in Caracas."

"Bo Huang, huh?"

"Yes, though he apparently also uses the aliases Lou Huang and Tao Zhou."

"How will you find the warehouse?"

"We'll track down the manager. We have his name and address. He'll also know more about the vessels, I'm sure."

"Where's the third ship?"

"The M/S *Santora* disappeared for now. No one knows. It was last seen three weeks ago going through the Canal to the Caribbean." She grabbed the Canadian passport from Jonathan's hand. "I'm telling you, you'll be fine using this. And as I said, you don't have a choice. A team is coming to this house tomorrow afternoon. They know you've been here. They may take the house away from me. They may burn it down. If they find you here, they may hurt you. I just don't know, now that so much has been compromised. They are the kind of Russians you don't want to meet. You're at least safer with me."

He took in a deep breath and thought about it from many angles. He'd gone through hell to reach this point, and he was anxious to learn what this mess was all about. He couldn't stay here and it would be hard to get out of the country without Natasha's help, especially if her compatriots had his name and photo. But he also didn't want to die for someone else's problem. He looked at Natasha, and suddenly another thought came to him. Mariya would not want her daughter to go alone, not when Jonathan was perfectly able to go with her, help her, maybe return the favor and protect her life. He felt a sudden obligation to protect Natasha as best he could. It now seemed inconceivable for him to run away. "When's the flight?"

"We'll leave for Managua in three hours." Natasha caressed his face but as he turned, she withdrew her hand. "Are you okay? I mean, about...you know...having sex."

Jonathan returned a muted smile. The ghost of Linda was hovering above him and he sensed Natasha had seen it in his eyes. "It was wonderful."

31

Singapore

CLACTON ROAD IS A TRANQUIL TREE-LINED, DEAD-END street with a half-dozen large homes in the posh historic area of Katong, about two miles east of Singapore's central business district. As Wesley Ong drove his ruby-red BMW 7-Series into the driveway of his two-story house, he had no way of knowing that this dead-end street might become just that—a dead end.

At that moment a few blocks west on Mountbatten Road, a van proceeded at half the maximum allowed speed, carrying four men with the simplest of instructions transmitted to them by coded short-wave: make him talk.

Ong walked into the foyer, entered his code on the alarm's keypad and strolled past the collection of antique European swords that adorned one entire wall of his spacious living room till he reached his leather chair by the bay windows that opened to the pool. He slipped on his sandals and reclined into the depths of the chair with a Cohiba in one hand, a glass of port in the other.

It was time to unwind from the lengthy conference calls that had consumed most of the work day at his 38th floor office downtown.

He gazed through the smoke rising from his cigar, at the other wall, dominated by an original Cézanne secured in an ornate gold-leafed frame—his single most prized possession. It represented the fruits of his diligent advocacy for some of Asia's most prominent business-men and companies. The forty-one year old *bon vivant* had only nineteen years of practice since his graduation from Cambridge Law School but had amassed a clien-tele that included seventeen of Asia's top-fifty richest men, and he'd often attributed his success to one key factor: discretion. That's what his clients demanded, and that's what they got.

The sound of car doors disturbed the stillness. He checked his watch. Seven-thirty was a bit late for the gardener. Ong was mildly curious, but he stayed seated, savoring the perfumed air.

A burst of noise bolted across the room. The front door tore open and smashed into the foyer's wall, and four armed men wearing balaclavas and black fatigues charged into the hallway, knocking down vases and a large plant as they raced toward him.

"What the—"

Ong's feet had barely reached the floor when the weight of the assailants crushed him back against his chair, knocking the breath from his lungs. A punch nailed his jaw, and another hit his stomach as two of the men lifted him up and dragged him across the living room in a chokehold. He tried to shout, but a gloved hand muffled his sounds. And then his kidney took another punch.

The assailants stayed silent. Ong frantically studied them, his eyes partially obscured. They didn't look like cops, nor were they simple robbers. They let go of him, and he fell hard onto his back, his head hitting the tiled floor. An immediate jolt of pain spiked through his skull. Suddenly he felt a wire loop around his neck, and a hand yanked his head back by the hair. His eyes shot upward, at the balcony of the study that overlooked the living room. One of the assailants went up and began tying the wire around the guard rail, just as another intruder lifted Ong to his feet and raised him to the top of a bar stool they'd dragged in from the open kitchen. They tied his hands with a plastic clasp.

"If it's money you want, take—"

A punch came into his thigh. Ong stood precariously on the stool, barefoot, his neck strained by the wire that tightly connected him to the railing fifteen feet above.

"Shut up or you will die," the closest man said in Mandarin through his black hood. He was not fluent but Ong couldn't decipher the accent. "All I have to do is kick this from under you."

"Don't, don't!" Ong squeaked as the wire gouged into his Adam's apple.

"We want something."

"Take anything you want—the jewelry, the artwork, whatever."

The man chuckled. "No, we want your client names and files."

Ong paused, confused. "I don't keep those here."

"You have remote access to them," the closest attacker said coolly.

One of his cohorts reentered the room with a laptop, which Ong recognized as his.

"You're going to help us log in."

"I don't have access, I swear."

"Let me show you right now what lies will get you."

The masked intruder next to the leader pressed a piece of duct tape over Ong's mouth as a third man walked in from the living room with an 18th Century French cavalry saber Ong had recently purchased from a collector in Rotterdam. The tip of the sword dragged across the tile floor as the man approached.

"No! Please, no!"

Ong saw the man swing the saber with what seemed like his entire weight. A thump sounded, followed by a jolt to his foot, and then the pain bolted up as if his lower leg were now on fire. "Ahh!" He yelled a full breath, the duct tape flying off his face.

Ong's eyes watered and pain focused on his foot, a deep, throbbing, electrifying ache like he'd never felt before. He glanced down, his tearing eyes blurring his vision, but not enough to obscure the obvious. His right foot's pinky toe and surrounding flesh were on the rug a short distance from the stool. Blood drained onto the large white tiles. His knees weakened. His legs shook, but he struggled to stay standing on the stool.

"You're fucking nuts!" he screamed.

The fourth man looked up from the laptop. "Tell me your access code."

Ong did not want to give up the information. His

firm had spent nearly two hundred thousand dollars customizing a secure, state-of-the-art program to encrypt client files, but he had no choice.

"Bamboo," he groaned. "That's the code."

The intruder typed it in and looked up. "Now, the ID and password for the program."

Ong knew that surrendering access would not only defeat the hefty investment in the software, but it would expose much of the firm's client records. Clients who demanded anonymity. Clients whose records could land them in jail and risk collapsing entire business empires. "For security reasons, we only have access during business hours," Ong lied, barely able to speak between his heaving and moaning.

"Give us the fucking code!"

"It will not work, I'm telling you."

"We're going to do more damage to you, Wesley."

Would dying now be worse than dying at the hands of vengeful clients? Ong's heart raced. The throbbing intensified. He could barely stay standing.

"The police will be here any minute, so why don't you leave now...just go."

The lead intruder laughed. "Do you think we're stupid? No one is coming for you, even if your alarm works. We hacked the dispatch's computers at Bedok and at the Marine Parade and Geyland stations."

Ong knew many policemen and investigators at the Bedok Police Divisional Headquarters, but if the assailants were right, none would come to his rescue.

"You're all mine for about thirty minutes, and it's your choice if you live or die."

"Just leave. Take that painting—it's worth more than you can imagine. Take my money too—there's some in my bedroom, the bottom drawer of the dresser. I have more in the wall safe, upstairs in the closet of the study. Just don't kill me, please. I beg you."

The leader grabbed the sword with both hands and brought the blade up to his shoulder.

Ong screamed. "Please, don't!"

"I have to make your feet look even, don't I?" He raised the weapon and swung.

A loud thud exploded into the air. The pain rocketed up Ong's body. He vomited and screamed at the same time, his body wobbling, almost falling from the stool. His knees bent and the cord tightened around his neck. Dizziness blurred the searing pain and Ong struggled to stay upright, knowing that if he collapsed, the cord would snap his neck. His soaked eyes could barely focus on the newly severed toes. His limbs trembled.

"The ID and password, you stupid man!"

"Napoleon zero one—all lower case."

The men laughed. The one at the laptop typed in the code and pumped a fist in the air.

Ong's head lightened as he watched the blood gushing from his feet. His breaths slowed. The vomit oozed down his chin and neck. *It is finished,* he said quietly to himself. He knew his fate, whether at the hands of these butchers or on the orders of the clients he'd just betrayed.

32

Havana, Cuba

SAL EXTINGUISHED HIS CIGARETTE, CHASED TWO PILLS down his mouth with the last of his Scotch whiskey and rose from the wicker chair in the U-shaped outdoor gallery of Havana's Hotel Nacional, where he was lodging that night. It was a luxury he could no longer indulge in anywhere else, but here he dared to bask in the relative anonymity that Cuba offered him, even in this opulent, tourist-filled hotel.

He gazed at the darkened sky and checked his watch. 7:50 P.M. It was time. With a large duffel bag hanging from his shoulder, he headed through the long, spacious lobby. He gazed down at the coded message that someone had left at the reception. "The four gifts have arrived." If the message was true, four hundred thousand dollars had been deposited in a bank in the Bahamas under his son's name. So far, Chermayeff had done his part. But he wanted more money, much more. And it was sitting in Caracas, as long as he could keep Ron's paws off it. And for that he'd already planned his move, so long as he could leave Cuba in the morning. He walked through the corridor, down the front steps, to a cab waiting out front.

"*Regla, por favor,*" he said, suddenly noticing that his words sounded a bit slurred. "*Calle Maceo, esquina La Piedra.*"

He cracked open the window, the balmy air filling the pristinely maintained '56 Chevy taxi as they drove past the high-rises along Avenida 23.

The Regla municipality occupies the east shores of the capital's strategic port and it was no coincidence Chermayeff had selected a warehouse there, a block from a disused dock. The cab stopped at the corner, under the lone streetlight. He handed the driver a large tip and asked to be picked up in a half-hour at Guaicanamar Park, a few blocks away.

Sal's shirt was drenched from the heat and muggy air, but also from the meds. The slight shaking of his hands hadn't subsided. His body's decline was well underway, but he consoled himself with Chermayeff's promise. Sal's son had a guardian angel of sorts, and that protection would be assured so long as Sal fulfilled the Russian scientist's instructions, and that's all that mattered.

As Sal stood in the intersection, he thought about his cardinal rule that brought him luck: the Bible placed face down with a virgin bullet resting in it. And his other rules...wearing black before each hunt; sleeping facing east. But he'd broken them all tonight. He was on the run, with no time to latch on to these superstitions, at least not until he could make it to Caracas, finish the job for Chermayeff and collect the money.

He studied the desolate intersection. The dilapidated single-story stucco and brick buildings around him, the stray dog poking through the garbage containers, a page of the newspaper dragged across the pavement by the ocean breeze. All seemed tranquil. He headed down the dead end of La Piedra Street, passing a bruised Lada parked in front of a warehouse. He touched the hood. It was cool.

Sal unzipped his duffel bag halfway and knocked four times on the corrugated metal door of the warehouse. He waited, glancing at both ends of the street.

"*¿Quien es?*" said a voice from behind the door.

Sal leaned in and said, "*La bala.*"

The door opened slowly and Sal was greeted by a sweaty, shirtless man with shifty eyes and a revolver tucked behind his belt. As the man quickly shut the door behind him, Sal detected the distinct smell of pot.

"*¿Dónde está Caldero?*" Sal asked, realizing again that he'd been in Eastern Europe so long that his Spanish accent seemed more Russian than English.

The man pointed to the adjacent room and ushered Sal into a shoddy office where the only light came through an internal window into the warehouse's main storage area, and the scent of weed grew stronger.

A tanned man sat facing the window with his bare feet propped up on a scarred desk. When Sal walked in, the man snapped to attention and quickly drew his legs down.

"Don't get up." Sal eyed Caldero and then glanced at the first man, who stood close behind.

"Why weren't you here two nights ago, when the

crates were taken to the ship?" Caldero said, choosing to speak in English.

"Crates?"

"Yes, you missed the party...very strange with those angry looking Chinese guys running around."

"They're North Korean, not Chinese."

Caldero rolled his eyes.

"Just the two of you here tonight?"

"Yes. I was told no one else could be here until Sunday."

"Good." Sal casually scanned the furniture for where Caldero might keep a gun. "Did you clean the floors?"

"*Si, claro*," Caldero said, chuckling and eyeing his colleague. "All fucking day with José scrubbing. Why was it so important?"

"And where did you put the cleaning materials?"

He pointed at the back of the storage space. "In the dumpster outside, behind that door, like we were told."

Sal sensed a hint of uneasiness in the man's voice. "Did anyone else come here since the shipment left?"

Caldero shook his head. "No, but why did—"

"You ask too many questions."

Caldero shrugged and got up. "So, tell me, why *la bala*, huh? That's a funny code name." He then smiled at his colleague standing behind Sal. "Is 'bullet' really what they call you?"

"No," Sal said loudly. He instantly spun around, grabbed the pistol grip protruding from José's waistband and pulled the trigger. José curled over his crotch, screaming, and fell as the deafening shot reverberated through the small room. Caldero dove for his desk, but Sal quickly slid his other hand into his duffel bag, pulled out his own SIG Sauer P239 with suppressor and swung at Caldero, hitting the top of his head with the butt of the gun and knocking him down before he could open a drawer. Sal stood over Caldero and aimed the weapon at his bloody face. "It's not a code word at all; It's simply what I'm delivering: a bullet." He fired the point blank shot. Blood splattered over the floor. He turned back to José, who lay wailing in pain. Sal emptied two more rounds and the noise ceased. He breathed in the scent of gunpowder that blended with the skunk smell.

Sal leaned to the window to make sure there was no one else in the place. He tossed the weapons into his bag and removed four cylindrical containers. He pulled a cap off the end of one, pressed a switch and left it on Caldero's laptop. He had six minutes—enough time to place two of the other incendiary explosives in the file cabinet just outside the office and in a large trash can in the hallway, where he dumped the dead men's cell phones. He raced through the warehouse to the back door and activated the last explosive device in the dumpster located in the walled-off courtyard.

He quickly returned to La Piedra Street through another door and then headed down Maceo Street, walking at a brisk pace. When he reached the next block south, he heard the first blast.

Seconds later, he heard screeching tires and spotted two trucks, their headlights off, turning onto Maceo Street several blocks south, and headed his way. A police car and two more trucks followed through the same turn about five seconds later, all of them racing north.

Sal crossed the street, walking quickly but not running.

The first pair of trucks passed. He glanced back at them. They were filled with soldiers, some wearing black fatigues, others green camouflage. None looked Cuban, but he couldn't be sure in the darkened street.

The squad car suddenly screeched to a halt twenty feet from him, cutting off the side street that Sal had just crossed. From the corner of his eye, Sal spotted three *Policía Nacional Revolucionaria* officers—one black and two mixed race, all three wearing grayish-blue uniforms with beige berets. They emerged accompanied by a pale-skinned man wearing all-black military fatigues and holding a radio. The men stayed near the car and surveyed the speeding convoy of trucks. They ignored Sal, who continued along the same sidewalk without making eye contact. Then Sal heard one of the men call for him to halt.

His heart racing, Sal ignored the demand.

"*Alto, señor!*" the uniformed officer shouted.

Sal turned, his chest tightening as the cop approached. The other officers stood a few feet away leaning onto the patrol car as the pale-skinned man shouted orders into his radio and gestured at the last passing truck, his body leaning onto the patrol car.

"*Identificación, ahora.*" Sal shifted his bag from his right hand to his left in order to access his back pocket, but as he did so, the sirens faded and Sal could hear the words being spoken into the radio by the pale-skinned man, Russian words.

Sal knew what this meant. The assault force in the trucks were Russian, not Cuban. Chermayeff's clandestine locale must have been discovered and was about to be raided, just like what had happened in Vladivostok. His master's cloak was withering, and at some point, Sal feared, he'd run out of places to hide.

As Sal slowly reached into his back pocket, he realized that his fake Russian passport might not get him out of this predicament. His head buzzed. There was but one option now. His quickness would either set him free or send him to his grave.

He stretched out his hand out, holding the passport, but then deliberately dropped it. As the cop's eyes followed the falling document, Sal whipped out his SIG from the bag and gunned down the officer nearest him. He clocked the second policeman next, and then shot the Russian. He then lunged forward, aiming at the last officer who'd barely reached his holster.

Tok, tok, tok. Sal emptied three rounds into the man, who fell like the others. There was no time to waste. His pistol's suppressor may have quieted the shots, but all hell was breaking loose three blocks north, and soon the forces would wonder why that Russian was no longer giving out orders on his radio.

Another device detonated in the warehouse as troops poured out of the trucks. Sal ran toward the park and heard another explosion. His heart raced as he pushed his legs for all the speed they could give him until he reached the waiting cab. As they drove away, Sal caught his breath, puzzling over how the Russian assault forces had found the secret warehouse. Perhaps they'd been tipped off by the Mossad, or by Ron and the CIA, or whoever else Sal had betrayed by joining Chermayeff's side. And having deserted both intelligence agencies, he couldn't be whisked away to a safe house, or to a boat or a waiting submersible. As the cab hurtled past the hilltop Castillo de Atarés along the Malecón, Sal tapped the driver on the shoulder and told him to turn around and head for Terminal 3 at José Marti International Airport. There were a few flights left at this hour, and his fake Russian passport was his only hope. If he didn't leave tonight, the chances were slim that he'd make it out of Cuba, let alone reach Caracas.

33

Moscow, Russia

SPEARHEADED BY TWO POLICE CARS, AN ARMORED LINCOLN Town Car trailed by a black Suburban filled with security and staff snaked through the heavy traffic that usually plagued the road from Sheremetyevo Airport to downtown Moscow. A heavy late afternoon downpour brought the endless stream of cars and trucks to a standstill, but the police cars cleared a corridor to allow the convoy to proceed, a perk reserved for Russia's richest oligarchs and the highest ranking Kremlin bureaucrats.

Glen Sanders glanced out the dark tinted windows of the sedan, silently recycling the tense discussions from the briefing he'd attended only fourteen hours earlier in the White House Situation Room. It had been a rushed gathering, with the Chairman of the Joint Chiefs of Staff, the Director of National Intelligence, the Director of the CIA, the National Security Advisor, the Secretary of State, and the White House Chief of Staff, all summoned at the President's behest. Other participants had joined via video and telephone conference. Satellite images were passed around the table, as were excerpted transcripts and redacted memos, all haphazardly assembled to show that Russia's intelligence apparatchik was frantically mobilizing in various parts of the world. The President had assembled the team ultimately to answer the festering questions: why were the Russians so paranoid and what were they up to?

Having barely started his second year as Director of Operations, Glen didn't like crises because that's when things can go terribly wrong. He also worried whether he was the right man for the task in lieu of the Director himself. But it was the President who'd made it clear he wanted the Agency's head to stay in D.C., and that sending Glen to Russia was more prudent.

"I'm still mystified," the man seated next to Glen said somberly. Chester Hines was nearly seven-feet tall, a stature that made him look uncomfortable in a seated position. But when standing, Hines made an impression like no prior U.S. Secretary of State, towering over his counterparts across the globe, which always looked great for the press.

"You're right, Mr. Secretary," Glen replied. "The whole situation is incredible and dangerous."

"I can't believe the Russians have gone this far without alerting us. What the fuck are they thinking?"

"But there's a lot we still don't know, and—"

"Are we certain—absolutely certain—that they are the source? I mean, the freighter is Chinese, the company is Singaporean, the crews are Chinese and North Korean, and the few questionable transactions we've identified ran through Swiss and Cayman Islands accounts, all with no connection whatsoever with Russia."

"It's the other evidence we've dug up."

"Yes, but it's mostly circumstantial and somewhat iffy."

Glen understood the Secretary's dilemma. The last thing the head of U.S. diplomacy wanted to do was confront the Russians based on anything less than compelling evidence. But they'd gone over the information while at the White House, and earlier at CIA headquarters and it had become clear that keys to the unfolding crisis lay somewhere in Russia, and time was of the essence.

"My folks stand by the initial findings. They sent me another message a short time ago, reconfirming the results—the radioactive signature appears to exclude North Korean origin."

"But not Chinese." Hines pointed out.

"Not yet." Glen shrugged. "But the two electronic intercepts we talked about can't be interpreted in any other way. It's a Russian problem for sure, and they are in panic mode."

"I want to be absolutely right, and not overstretch what we know."

"I'll stick to what we're certain of, for sure. But it's clear to me that they're going nuts."

Hines raised his brow and rubbed his cheeks. "A cornered bear is a dangerous animal."

"And an unpredictable, untrustworthy one at that."

Hines tilted his head. "It was Stalin himself who once said, 'Sincere diplomacy is no more possible than dry water or wooden iron.'"

Glen nodded. Prior to today, he had only met Hines once before, at a State Department reception, but he was familiar with the man's reputation. As a former Ambassador to the Soviet Union and having served three terms in Congress, including two on the House Permanent Select Committee on Intelligence, Hines had the gravitas to lead a tough tête-à-tête with the Russians, but he would not waste his credibility on poor intel and innuendo.

"We're almost there," the driver advised.

Glen checked his watch, noting it had taken a mere thirty-five minutes to reach the Ministry of Foreign Affairs headquarters on Smolenskiy Boulevard. He peeked out the window again as they turned the corner, spotting the Stalin-era skyscraper that resembled a shorter version of the Empire State Building. Glen grinned, his anxiety momentarily subdued by a hint of nostalgia. He'd been here before two decades ago as a junior "political officer" at the embassy—the typical title given to CIA operatives working under diplomatic cover.

"I would have liked to have had your boss with us today," Hines said, buttoning his jacket.

"They'll listen far more intently to you, Mr. Secretary."

The car pulled through an arched side entrance reserved for VIPs. Glen and Hines exited the Town Car and were joined by their interpreter and two Diplomatic Security Service officers, who'd ridden in the Suburban. Together, they walked into the building and were ushered to a waiting elevator.

When the elevator doors opened on the fifth floor,

Yuri Voltovsky, the pudgy, rosy-cheeked Minister of Foreign Affairs, quickly shook hands with Hines and then with Glen, and introduced them to his Deputy and the Russian President's National Security Advisor—a lanky, pale-faced former-KGB official by the name of Alexander Limov. They also greeted a uniformed man Glen knew to be a Major General in the GRU, the main intelligence directorate of the Russian Armed Forces.

Through their interpreters, Minister Voltovsky boisterously joked with Hines about Moscow's weather as he led everyone into a conference room featuring pristine wood floors, antique furnishings and early twentieth century paintings of rural Russia. After brief introductions with the other Russians on Voltovsky's team, and after being served tea and bottled water, the Americans took seats opposite their hosts at a long table in the center of the room.

"We don't understand why you haven't told us the exact reason for this sudden visit," Voltovsky said and waited for Hines' interpreter to finish. "And our President is surprised by the cryptic explanations from your government, and the refusal of your President to speak by phone."

"We apologize, but this is indeed a very critical and sensitive matter," Secretary Hines said in his deep voice, looking directly into the eyes of his counterpart. As the Russian interpreter finished, Voltovsky chuckled and shrugged.

"Then please tell us this great mystery."

"The urgency is as much yours as it is ours," Hines said.

"I don't understand." Voltovsky frowned, his heavy eyebrows furrowed.

Hines shook his head. "We need your immediate cooperation regarding a security issue...one that our President believes poses a direct threat to the United States." Glen listened intently, and it appeared to him that Hines was keen to not have anything lost in translation.

"With all due respect, what are you talking about?"

"We know you're looking for lost warheads, and we're holding you responsible if any of them target the United States, our allies or our interests."

"*Shto za yerunda!*" the minister growled, throwing his hands in the air.

Hines' interpreter skipped the comment and kept on translating as Voltovsky continued to talk. "You came all this way to tell us this?"

"The evidence is overwhelming." Hines said. He turned to Glen and raised his chin. "Tell 'em."

Glen cleared his throat and spoke without notes, though he had plenty of typed and handwritten pages of materials in his attaché case. "Your Excellency, we have learned that a few hours ago Russian special forces raided a warehouse in Havana with clear instructions to find certain radiological devices." He eyed Voltovsky's interpreter, who jotted shorthand and followed in Russian. "We also found two hidden compartments in a bulk cargo hold of the *Nixos-Daka*r, the ship now stranded in the Panama Canal, with significant traces of radioactivity consistent with—"

"*Ostanovites, pozhaluysta,*" Voltovsky interrupted in a raised voice and gestured for his interpreter to stop speaking. He then turned to his colleagues and whispered in Russian. His Deputy and the Major General both rose from their seats, shrugged at each other, and exited the room, leaving behind only the Minister, his interpreter and Limov, the Kremlin's National Security Advisor. Once the door had closed, Voltovsky let out a deep sigh and nodded for Glen to continue.

"We found equipment and tools associated with the transportation of the Russian-made 9M714V *Oka* missile warhead. The radioactive footprint in the vessel is consistent with the emissions known for this weapon. We've also intercepted instructions from your SVR leadership to track two other freighters apparently owned by the Singapore-based company that also owns the *Nixos-Dakar*. And during the past forty-eight hours your government has dispatched radiological weapons decontamination teams, along with assault forces, to Saint Petersburg and Vladivostok, where they've been raiding docks and warehouses in both ports. You've also sent recon teams to Singapore, Macau, Panama and Cartagena. Shall I go on?"

The interpreter spoke, giving Glen time to gauge the demeanor of both Russian officials. Voltovsky's eyes widened and did not blink as the interpreter finished reading from his notes. On the other hand, Limov simply observed, calmly, his face devoid of expression.

"I encourage you to be up front with us," Hines chimed in. "There is no time to waste. Our President requests full and immediate disclosure. We are mobilizing our Navy's Fourth Fleet and other military and law enforcement resources in the Caribbean in the coming hours and days, and your actions and statements right now, at this table, will determine whether or not we take an aggressive military posture towards your country. On the other hand, we are eager to support your efforts, and we stand ready and able to help find these deadly weapons."

The Russians listened. Judging from Voltovsky's rigid posture and stiffened shoulders, Glen suspected he was caught off guard and hadn't expected such straight talk. But it was the approach Hines had chosen when they had debated the strategy during their flight in.

Limov suddenly patted the Minister's arm and slowly scooted his elbows across the table, leaning in towards Glen and Hines. "Yes, there is a problem, but it's under control and not as serious as you have made it out to be." Limov's English was better than a native Londoner. Their interpreter whispered to Voltovsky.

"We can't simply take your word on this."

"A few unassembled low-yield tactical warhead components are unaccounted for, but we really don't think there is a serious issue here. We suspect a small group of traffickers have hidden some of the materials in Saint Petersburg, Murmansk, Vladivostok and perhaps Samara, but we have no reason to believe they've put together any usable weapon. We have also tracked possible shipments to Cuba and Venezuela, but we doubt they are connected to any impending threat, because the trafficker's network seems to be limited to Russia."

Glen knew this was not true. Everything he'd been shown in Langley pointed to a network that extended into the Caribbean. He made eye contact with Hines, attempting to relay a telepathic message that Limov and Voltovsky were full of shit.

"What about the *Nixos-Dakar*?" Hines asked.

"What you shared with us is interesting, but we—"

"This is not a game," Hines interrupted, raising his voice and slapping the tabletop with his palm. "Our government is taking action as we speak, and we need you to be more forthcoming."

"We have nothing to do with this. It is a law enforcement matter, and there is no evidence that the suspects are targeting your country. In fact, it is our cities that are in danger."

Glen jumped in. "Not targeting our country? For heaven's sake, the *Nixos-Dakar* docked in New Orleans and Houston prior to being attacked by your people in Panama. And it was scheduled to arrive in Los Angeles next week, possibly after more unknown stops along the way. And it appears that one of the sister ships may have docked in Miami in July."

Voltovsky frowned and squirmed in his seat, but Limov remained composed, removing his elbows from the table and sitting up straight. At that moment, Glen guessed that Voltovsky had been in the dark and Limov was the man in the know. He turned and spoke directly to the Kremlin advisor.

"We have a lot of resources to help find the weapons, but we can't do it unless you tell us everything you know. How were the warheads disassembled? What components have been found, and which are still missing? Where were they shipped from? What did you find in your raids? We need answers."

"May I remind you," Limov said, looking down his nose at Glen, "that mere components are not fully functional weapons, and without assembled weapons there cannot be the kind of imminent danger you're talking about."

Hines sighed. "Even one screw from that weapon is enough to make us all lose sleep. We want answers. If we walk out of here empty-handed, I assure you our President order the most aggressive response since the Cuban Missile Crisis. With all due respect, your denials are putting us on a collision course."

Limov stood up and paused, glancing at Voltovsky and then at Glen and Hines. "The Minister and I need to step out for a moment before we say anything more." He exited the room with Voltovsky in tow, lobbing a cold gaze at Glen before closing the door.

34

Caracas, Venezuela

AN EMPTY SAFE DEPOSIT BOX SHOULD HARDLY MAKE A man's heart skip beats, unless he expects something valuable to be inside, something so important that his life depends on it, that his future would likely end badly without it, and because the contents are missing, and not only in one box, but two.

"When was he here?" Ron Felder asked, containing his rage as best he could, though he was tempted to begin breaking some skulls.

"Yesterday...early morning, *señor*," the attendant replied, her voice shaking, from a few feet away and standing behind the bank manager. "Right when we opened."

"Did he come alone?"

"He brought his attorney," she said. "They gave me the notarized papers, and I went straight to Señor Rodriguez."

Ron could barely find the strength to rub his face. He stared at the empty metal boxes on the counter in the middle of the large vault, its walls filled with locked boxes. For a moment he recalled what his two briefcase-sized containers looked like with 1.8 million dollars' worth of diamonds and crisp, new, untraceable bills. All that purchasing power had vanished—a vital lifeline he'd intended to split fifty-fifty with Sal in case things went wrong. A financial escrow of sorts that tied them to some notion of fair dealing or mutual assured destruction. And they'd picked Caracas as an ideal venue because Hugo Chávez's antagonism toward the West made Venezuela less transparent to U.S. law enforcement and intelligence agencies. But now it was all gone.

The bank manager's face was as red as Chávez's beret in a framed poster hanging on the wall.

"Fucking idiots," Ron whispered to himself and then turned to the duo. "It didn't occur to you to verify the documents or at least call the phone numbers you have on file?"

The manager stepped forward. "Mr. Felder, obviously there's been a big misunderstanding—"

"Misunderstanding? It's a god-damn *fuck-up*. How the hell can someone walk in with a few letters and contravene the instructions we had clearly set out when our account was opened three years ago? How could this happen? We had specifically agreed that Mr. Brusca and I could not access the boxes individually, but rather only if we were both present, in person."

"But they provided the documents that you were deceased, and Mr. Brusca's lawyer is well known here in Caracas."

"The documents are fakes, obviously, and if you pay

a lawyer enough money, he'll do or say anything you want. I want to see the papers. Right now!"

"They are not here."

"I don't give a fuck! Go get them."

"Mr. Felder, please calm down. I called our company president, and he is sending a representative right away to resolve this—"

"There's nothing you can resolve. My possessions are gone. All fucking gone!" Ron knew there was nothing he or the bank could do. The diamonds and cash were not documented—and never could be. The treasure he and Sal had accumulated was the result of well-laundered funds, and they'd never told anyone what had been secreted into these boxes. Sal had found a way to defraud the bank managers, and Ron was screwed.

The bank manager shook his head, looking down at the floor.

Ron turned to the attendant. "Did you at least get an address?"

"No, but when he removed his identification from his wallet, his hotel card fell on my desk."

"Did you see a name on it?"

"Yes, I picked it up and gave it to him. He was staying at the Gran Meliá Hotel downtown."

Ron was certain this was no accident. Sal wasn't the kind to slip-up. He must have intended to let Ron know, most likely to kill him, Ron assumed. Ultimately, the only way to assure complete secrecy between two people is when one or both are dead.

Ron left the bank without saying another word. He got in a taxi at the curb. Confronting Sal required artillery, and he'd fetch it at his own hotel first and then proceed to the hunting grounds at the Gran Meliá. Today, one of them would die. He only hoped it would be the son-of-a-bitch who'd taken Ron's share of the escrow.

Like a storm hovering marooned,
its drenching grayness unending,
the norm I seek idles cocooned,
yearning to exit the madness, festering,
only to see myself stabbed, close and far
by visions you share of neither journey nor destiny.
This neglect remains my scar,
my love, into thin air stolen.

35

Caracas, Venezuela

JONATHAN'S HEART FELT LIKE IT WAS POUNDING OUT OF HIS chest. Just as Mariya had done a few days prior, it was now his turn to trick an immigration officer into letting him through with a fake passport. He walked to the booth reserved for diplomats and crew. Whatever confidence he'd gained listening to Natasha's reassurances during the flight had now evaporated.

He slid the Canadian diplomatic passport into the opening under the glass. When the Venezuelan officer grasped it, Jonathan's worries suddenly compounded. *Will he feel warmth or perspiration on it? Can he sense my nerves crackling? Is my shirt throbbing from my racing heartbeats?* He didn't dare look back at Natasha, who had gone to another line.

His back now drenched with sweat, Jonathan remained composed as best he could, his eyes glued to the document's reddish cover that seemed to glow in the officer's hand.

The man glanced up at Jonathan. "*¿Cuántos días se*

va a quedar?" he asked and then looked down at the photo before flipping through a few more pages. With his other hand he typed into the keyboard and gazed intently at the monitor.

"*Una semana, más o menos,*" Jonathan said, though he had no clue how long Natasha had intended to stay.

The officer stamped the passport. "*Disfrute de su visita.*" He handed it back. It was as simple as that.

Jonathan now understood how Mariya must have felt slipping through Panamanian immigration. His nerves were rattled, his heart was still pounding, but a strange sense of exhilaration caught him by surprise. *That wasn't as hard as I thought it would be*, he mused, breathing in deeply as if he'd been without air for minutes. He headed past customs with the carry-on bag he'd borrowed from Natasha and reunited with her in the terminal.

They arrived at the Embassy Suites hotel on Avenida Venezuela just past 11 P.M. after the long cab ride from the airport that passed through tunnels and skirted a mountain. Not wanting to give Natasha the wrong signals, Jonathan stayed somewhat standoffish, as he had throughout the day, from their drive to Managua, during the entire flight, and now. He was uncomfortable that they'd had sex, though he felt perplexed at how incredible the intimacy with her had felt. At the touch of her hair. Her perfumed skin. Her melodic moans. He was awestruck, though troubled at the same time. *It's guilt,* he told himself, delving further into his conflicting thoughts and feeling like he'd betrayed Linda—however irrational he knew this to be—though now he was also bothered by Natasha's nonchalance.

They'd barely walked into their ninth-floor room when she turned to him, her cell phone in hand. "I have to meet someone now. I won't be long."

"At this late hour? Who?"

"It doesn't matter, but...but I must go alone. Because I just can't explain *you*."

"Tell me who?"

Natasha sighed. "My contact at the embassy. I have no choice but to coordinate with him."

"I trust you know what you're doing."

"While I'm gone, don't call me from the landline. I'll try to get you your own cell phone." Before leaving the room, she added, "And don't go anywhere."

But shortly after, he did. For the next two hours, he surfed the Web in the hotel's business center and scraped up all he could on the Chinese businessman Bo Huang, reading as many English-language articles as he could find, and eventually a very strange picture emerged. That of a wealthy shipping mogul whose eccentricity ranged from amassing one of the largest collections of rare snakes in a private zoo to having his own fleet of hovercraft. But more intriguingly, he lost a daughter—his only child—to a stray American bomb that had hit the Chinese embassy, apparently by mistake, during NATO's bombardment of Serbia some six years earlier. He found two additional news articles corroborating the death of his daughter, who'd been in the Serbian capital as a journalist. Suddenly the elation that came from the discovery began racing through his veins. He'd figured it out, having fully recycled, retwisted, rehashed and finally, reordered the haphazard clues and trauma from the last seven days since he'd first set foot in the Orleans Parish morgue. *There's no logical alternative*, he told himself. *Bo Huang must be avenging his daughter's death.* Jonathan was excited to share his findings with Natasha, but when he arrived back at their room, he discovered it was empty. She hadn't returned, and it worried him.

Almost three hours after she'd left, the phone on the nightstand rang. Jonathan picked up, thinking it could only be her, and it was.

"Hey, I'm testing a cell phone I got for you." Her shaky voice gave away that she was walking fast, with the noise of cars in the background.

"Where are you?"

"A few blocks away. I'm going to...wait a second."

He heard ringing and guessed it was her own cell phone. "Natasha?"

"Wait." She sounded as if she was digging into her purse. He then heard her speak Russian, her words choppy and her tone harsh, and then only the noise of traffic.

"Natasha, you there?"

A deafening scream ripped through the phone and the line went dead.

"What's going on?" Jonathan jumped to his feet. He dug into his pocket for the paper on which she'd written her number and dialed, but she didn't answer. He redialed, but again, no answer.

He left the room, raced to the elevator and slammed the button to head down. He assumed that she was in a public place, but there was no telling what happened.

The second the doors opened at lobby-level, he
sprinted through the atrium, shoving his way past
bystanders to reach the front entrance, where he slid to a
stop at the bellman's desk.

"Did you see a young woman—long, dark brown
hair, blue blouse, black skirt—about three hours ago?"
he asked in Spanish. "Attractive, about your height."

The bellman shrugged and turned to a colleague.

"Please, think. It's urgent." Jonathan barely uttered
the words, his voice collapsing from his wide breaths.

"*Ah, si...fue por ahí,*" the other bellman said,
gesturing to the left end of the boulevard facing the
hotel.

Jonathan ran along the broken sidewalk—part cobbled, part asphalt, part concrete—of the heavily-trafficked tree-lined street crammed with cars and all the
human buzziness that consumed every square inch of
downtown Caracas at night. He ran, scanning ahead for
any hint of Natasha.

He heard his breaths, his shoes pounding the pavement. He weaved past pedestrians and crossed side
streets, determined to find her quickly, his mind now
obsessing over a promise he'd made to himself the night
he made love to her. He would protect her, at all costs.
He could not let Mariya down.

"Natasha," he cried out, still running, locking his
sights onto every tall, dark-haired woman. He glanced
down the alleys he passed on his left. He scanned the
other side of the street, too, and the storefronts, the
restaurants, the kiosks, alert to every single place where
she could be.

He continued, the street now angling leftward. Five blocks had passed and still no sign of her. Then, fifty yards ahead, he spotted a woman in a blue top kneeling down under the bright streetlamp. He raced her way.

"Natasha!" He now saw that she wasn't kneeling, but rather was seated on the sidewalk with one leg bent, the other straight out, leaning against a fence, her hands covering her face. She didn't move.

"Are you okay?" he shouted as he ran past the last cross street. Some passersby had slowed down to gawk but most just picked up their pace as Jonathan elbowed his way through to her on the sidewalk.

"What the hell happened?" he asked, kneeling at her side. Her cell phone lay on the ground. Her purse, too, by her farthest foot. "Are you hurt?"

She was sobbing, her cries muffled by her hands.

He slipped his hand between the back of her head and the jagged metal fence. "What's wrong?"

"No, no, no!" she voiced, her face still covered. She continued to weep.

Jonathan had no idea what had happened or what to do. "Did someone hurt you?" He glanced at her body but didn't see any signs of injury.

"No," she again said between her tearful breaths.

He straightened her, holding her wrists. "Tell me."

She lowered her hands to her chest. Her cheeks were awash with tears, and her eyes half-closed. "My mother," she uttered, her voice cracking. Her face cringed, and a wail exited her lungs as if it were taking every molecule of air with it. She reached her arms around his neck and pulled him down onto her. "She's dead."

Jonathan felt as if a snake had suddenly coiled around his heart and choked the blood from it. He gasped for air, as her cries filled his ears. He felt her legs kick. Her fingernails dug into his shoulders.

"I'm...I'm sorry." He held her tightly, staring at her cell phone that lay a few inches from the gutter. Mariya was gone. The quixotic, troubled and unbearably complex Russian vixen he'd come to fear, respect, admire, challenge, disdain and even cherish—in a wholly confusing way from the very first time he'd encountered her—was now gone. Murdered by a nameless tattooed crewman on the *Nixos-Dakar*.

As Jonathan pulled Natasha closer, a sudden vision of Mariya washed over his mind: The subtle wrinkles around her dark eyes. Her inviting smile, when she let herself give one. The way she'd commanded his attention with a piercing gaze, like no other woman had ever done so easily. The images continued in random fragments. The strange way she dog-eared the page of her poetry book by bending the bottom corner. Her serene gaze through the airplane window on their way to Panama. Her hair waving in the breeze as she perched forward, one hand gripping a sniper rifle over her shoulder, the other holding the safety line at the front of the RIB on their way to intercept the *Nixos-Dakar*.

Mariya. Jonathan's eyes felt heavy and tired as he thought of her sudden frailty—and Natasha's, too. *No matter how brave they are as spies, no matter the hair-raising schemes they perpetrate, or the causes they fight for—whether right or wrong—they're as vulnerable as the rest of us mortals.*

"You're not alone," he whispered into Natasha's ear. He brought her head to his chest and rested his chin on her silky hair as her weeping subsided.

"I'm so sorry," he said, softly caressing her hair and helping her get up off the ground.

Natasha's shoulders shook. "*Blyad, blyad!*" she said, cocking her head back, her eyes welling up again. "Alone! She was alone—when she needed me the most. Dammit!" She pounced on Jonathan's chest and then grabbed his arms, her nails clawing into his skin as she burst into tears again.

"I understand." He stared into her pitch black hair and kissed her head gently, holding her tightly. The wetness from her tears had gone through his shirt.

She wiped her eyes with her hand as her cries diminished to sniffles. "Let's get those fuckers," she said in a harsh whisper as she let go of Jonathan to stand upright.

*   *   *

Jonathan put his arm around her shoulders as they headed up the elevator to their room at the Embassy Suites.

"I know this is a difficult time for you," he said, looking into her puffy eyes.

She nodded. "My contact told me things about Bo Huang."

"I found out more, too, but we don't have to talk about it now."

"It's okay. Bo Huang is coming here or maybe has already arrived," she said. "He funded Echis Global's purchase of the first two freighters, and perhaps the third, but we think he had a partner in all this."

"How do you know?" Jonathan said, as he opened the door to their room.

"We looked at the Singapore law firm's files," she replied as she walked in behind him and plopped down on the bed. "Despite using multiple aliases, we found a link to a Russian man—a scientist—who we think is his partner."

He brought her a bottle of water from the refrigerator.

"No, bring me vodka."

He did, with a glass, but she twisted off the lid and downed the small bottle of liquor in one gulp—as if it were water.

"Give me another."

"Who's his Russian accomplice?"

"Yuri Chermayeff, a nuclear physicist the Americans have been complaining about for years, accusing him of trafficking in controlled products, but no one in Moscow ever believed them—until now, it seems."

"Then your people must raid the *Muzhestvo*. It's probably carrying contraband and might yield more answers."

"There's something more important." Natasha downed a second and then a third small vodka bottle. She looked up into Jonathan's eyes. "We must find the Echis Global warehouse—I have the address of the man we believe manages it. Something big may be happening, my contact told me. Big. But no one can figure it out."

"Or no one is telling you..." Jonathan leaned over to the nightstand and grabbed a news article he'd printed earlier. "Here, look...Bo Huang's daughter died six years ago."

Natasha skimmed the two pages.

"She was a journalist in the basement of the Chinese Embassy in Belgrade, Serbia," Jonathan added, "when a U.S. B-2 bomber mistook it for a legitimate target."

"Yeah, a map error," Natasha scoffed. "I was in training at the time. It was no accident, you know."

"So wouldn't that be motive enough to transport radioactive materials to and from the U.S.? And now that you tell me about Chermayeff, it seems like a perfect partnership: a Russian gets the nuclear material, and the shipping magnate finds the means to clandestinely transport them to New Orleans."

"Perhaps." Natasha fell back on the bed and turned to her side.

"Can I bring you anything? Something to eat?"

"No, I just want the vodka to knock me out," she mumbled, her face now buried in the pillow.

"Get some rest," Jonathan said, wrapping the comforter over her. "We'll look for the manager first thing tomorrow morning."

36

THE TAXI-DRIVER HUMMED ALONG TO A SHAKIRA TUNE ON the radio as they crossed the city eastward along the Autopista Francisco Fajardo, past a military airport, and across the vast urban expanse of the capital on their way to the *barrio* of Petare—one of Caracas' most dangerous shantytowns, Jonathan recalled Natasha saying.

Ten minutes into the ride, the cab exited and turned onto a narrow potholed street, heading toward a hill that Jonathan thought could only be a slum, judging from the ramshackle collage of ugly metal and brick structures. He leaned forward and scanned the narrowing alley that snaked up the foot of the hill under the dreary overcast sky. The mound of hundreds of cramped, unlicensed housing resembled an inverted hornet's nest. Jonathan imagined the dwellings were barely acceptable for animals, let alone humans.

The taxi-driver stopped when the eerily vacant alley became too narrow for a vehicle to squeeze through. He turned and held up the note Natasha had given him with the directions to their destination.

"I think," he said in Spanish, "it must be one of the higher alleys, probably on the right side of the hill?"

"Are you sure you're okay to do this?" Jonathan asked Natasha.

"We must."

"*Cuidado*," the cabby said as Natasha paid him. He was right to warn her. Being pale-white and well-dressed in this place was probably reason enough to be killed on the spot. And Natasha's tightly fitted designer jeans and body-hugging long-sleeved top were likely to draw even more unwanted attention.

"Keep your eyes open," she said, stepping out of the cab. "Shootings, stabbings, kidnappings and fights are completely normal here, day and night. Like most *barrios*, this place is ruled by *Malandros*—violent thugs and thieves who think of people like us as trophies."

"You have a gun?"

"Of course," she said, patting her purse. "Got it from my contact last night."

Jonathan walked alongside her on the cracked, uneven pavement that rose up the steep incline between the tightly compacted dwellings, past two barefoot children playing with a ragged wooden toy. He moved ahead of her and turned into another alleyway. Brownish sewer water oozed down the side of the decrepit structures, the stench unavoidable. They turned into yet another desolate path, this one only about shoulder-width, passing under makeshift balconies and ledges that appeared barely sturdy enough to handle the weight of a cat. They walked further, and the path leveled out. He guessed that they had reached a plateau on one side of the hill, about where the taxi-driver had said.

He stopped to catch his breath and turned back to Natasha. Behind her, in the distance, framed by the primitive housing on both sides, a formidable sight appeared: the mountain of El Ávila, which formed a giant, jungle-green wall on the north periphery of the city.

Natasha turned as well and gazed at it. "At least the poor have a beautiful view." She poked Jonathan's arm. "Let's go."

Turning into another alley, Jonathan spotted an elderly man seated on a wooden bench, his back resting on the uneven red-brick wall of a dilapidated two-story structure that probably housed several families. Natasha asked him for directions, glancing down at her note.

The man glared at Natasha, opened his mostly tooth-less mouth and grunted.

"*Por favor, señor. Es importante.*" She handed him a small wad of cash.

He hesitated but then reached for the money and slipped it into his shirt pocket. "*Ahí, a la izquierda,*" he said in a raspy voice, pointing at a narrow opening twenty feet away. "*La casa de enfrente a esa puerta azul.*"

"*Gracias.*" Jonathan walked into the shaded pathway ahead of Natasha, his eyes surveying the windows and balconies above them. He spotted the blue door the old man had mentioned. It was the house across from it. He pointed at the entrance—a narrow, doorless opening.

"The third floor," Natasha whispered.

Jonathan went in first. The entryway was littered with plastic bags, old newspapers and empty beer bottles. The graffitied brick walls were browned by neglect. A disheveled young man lay asleep or passed out near the wooden staircase. Jonathan quietly stepped around the man, as did Natasha, and was slowly making his way slowly up the first few steps, when suddenly Natasha gripped his elbow from behind.

"Let me go in front," she said, opening her purse to expose her black pistol. "We want to stay alive, right?"

Jonathan quickly slid his hand into her purse and snatched up the weapon. "And we will."

"Do you know how—"

"Shh," he said, signaling her to stay behind him.

The stairwell darkened as they climbed past the tight confines of the second floor, proceeding to the third— the top floor.

He held the Glock out in front of him, his aim at the only door, some ten feet ahead, which didn't have a peephole. The musty-scented corridor was illuminated only by the light coming through a small, half-shattered window. Faint sounds from a television crept into the hallway from the apartment.

"Hide your gun," she whispered, stepping to one side of the door frame. "I know what to say."

Jonathan moved to the other side and concealed his weapon behind his back.

Natasha knocked. The TV sounds muted.

"*¿Quien es?*" a male voice came from inside.

"*¿Mariano?*" Natasha said in a voice that was slightly breathier and higher-pitched than her usual tone. "*Soy del Servicio de Salud. ¿Podemos hablar?*"

There was no telling whether the man would fall for

her ploy, but her confident tone told Jonathan she knew what she was doing.

"*¿Por qué?*" The man's voice became louder, as if he might be standing right behind the door.

Jonathan listened, the gun growing heavy in his hand, as Natasha explained that some people in the building next door had been taken very ill, so the Health Services were asking to test everyone.

The man said nothing.

Jonathan heard footsteps moving away from and then coming back near the door. *Not good,* he thought as he eased his finger onto the trigger, his weapon clenched tightly and now resting up against the door.

Another twenty seconds passed without a sound coming from inside. Then, as Natasha was about to knock again, a deadbolt snapped loudly, and another, and a chain then loosened. The door cracked open.

A lanky, sweaty-faced man with an unshaven jaw and a greasy mop of curls appeared in the opening. "*¿De qué mierda está hablando?*" His droopy eyes flickered languidly over Natasha. But then his gaze slid sideways towards Jonathan and he stiffened.

Natasha shoved open the door, lunged at the man and punched him in the chin with such force that he collapsed backward, his head hitting the floor like a brick.

"Jesus," Jonathan blurted as Natasha jumped on top of Mariano, knocking over a stand by the door. She rolled him onto his stomach, kneed him in the ribs, put him in a headlock and twisted his right arm over his back.

Jonathan ran past her, into the living room, his gun

drawn, choking on stagnant cigar smoke. A holstered revolver lay on the TV stand. Jonathan snatched it up as he made his way into the bedroom. The room held only a mattress and empty cardboard boxes, the outside light blocked by filthy curtains. Jonathan emptied the revolver of bullets and threw the weapon under the bed.

Satisfied that there was no one else in the place, Jonathan returned to the entrance, where the man wailed in pain as Natasha, straddled over him, attempted to get answers the way Russians seemed to know best: with pain.

"*Dame la dirección del depósito,*" she shouted, yanking Mariano's contorted arm further up his back. She asked more questions, rapid-fire: What was the warehouse used for? Why was Bo Huang coming to town? What did he know of the Russian named Yuri Chermayeff? What contraband was coming in by ship?

Mariano responded only with cries of pain.

Her deep frown told Jonathan she wasn't about to let up. "*Responde, hijo de puta!*" She twisted the man's wrists to a breaking point.

Mariano glanced at Jonathan, his eyes wide open and sweat pouring down his face. "*Sáqueme esta puta de encima.*"

Jonathan tilted his head to one side. "She'll probably stop if you give her answers," he replied in Spanish and smirked. "But maybe not."

"*Gringo de mierda,*" Mariano shouted back, his head jerking up with drool running down his mouth onto Natasha's arm, which she had locked around his neck.

Natasha freed her arm to grab a pen from the floor.

She then jammed the tip into the man's right ear and shouted, "*¿Donde está el depósito? Responde!*"

Jonathan heard voices coming from the stairway. He rushed to the door and looked down.

"*¿Qué pasa?*" a woman's voice echoed from the stairwell, one floor down.

"*Nada. Todo está bien,*" Jonathan slammed the door shut and turned back to Natasha. "Keep making him scream, and the cops will be here in no time."

"Trust me, no cop will come."

"You can't keep torturing this—"

"I can do whatever the fuck I want." She shoved the pen further into Mariano's ear as he screamed in pain. "*Esto es por Mariya!*"

"This guy had nothing to do with that."

"I know, but he'll take us to the assholes who killed my mother." She twisted Mariano's head further to the right as she pushed the pen even deeper into his ear. His whole body jerked and swayed violently to shake her off, but she held on, planted astride him as if she were riding a wild bull. His deafening cries and curses ricocheted across the room as her steadfast grip kept the pen in place.

Jonathan cringed. The bloody instrument deepened into the man's skull. "Stop, you're going to kill him!"

She leaned forward, her hand pressed harder on his head. Blood began streaming from his ear, down his neck. She again barked the same questions at him.

"Natasha, stop." Jonathan kneeled next to them, trying to pull back Natasha's arm. But she jerked away from him, pressing into Mariano as his contorted face twisted against the floor.

"*Responde!*"

Mariano shrieked and then spat out, "*Hotel Gran Meliá...Bo Huang...y el europeo.*" He writhed under Natasha.

"Let him up," Jonathan said.

Instead, she shoved the pen in so deeply that Jonathan suspected it had gone halfway into the man's head.

Mariano's cries abruptly subsided as he mumbled the address of the warehouse, his voice tapering into a long slur, the blood pouring out of his ear as his upper body twitched.

Natasha pulled out the crimson-stained pen and threw it at Jonathan. "Write down the address."

Jonathan tore off a page from a magazine on the coffee table and jotted down the street name and number, the warm blood staining his fingers.

"It's by the port," she added, "near the airport, too."

Natasha slowly rose from Mariano's prone body as his lungs vented weak moans. Still holding his arm, she threw herself forward, twisting his elbow to a loud snap. Mariano wailed as Natasha let go of his arm, which flopped to the floor at a skewed angle.

"Shoot him," she told Jonathan.

"Are you mad?"

"He'll talk if you don't."

Jonathan stepped back. "We're not killing anybody."

Natasha lunged at Jonathan, grabbed the Glock from his hand and whipped back at Mariano. "We have to kill him!" Jonathan kept his grip and tried to pull her off, but she twisted his arm down and struggled to aim the gun. The shot went off.

Mariano's head jolted to one side and blood splattered in a straight line across the floor. The bullet had hit his temple.

Jonathan immediately let go of the weapon. The flashback of Mariya doing the same thing ten years earlier suddenly locked into Jonathan's brain. "Oh my god, you're completely nuts..." He shook his head.

"I'm just getting started." She held her gun tightly in her hand and headed for the door.

Jonathan stared dumbfounded at the bloodied corpse as he stumbled forward. As Natasha opened the door, Jonathan again heard voices coming from the floor below.

"They've heard the gunshot," Natasha said. "We better leave now."

37

JONATHAN AND NATASHA HEADED OUT OF THE HUGE shantytown by weaving through the narrow alleys on the other side of the hill, a distance that seemed like a mile. Unable to find a cab, Jonathan convinced her to take the *Linea 1* subway going westward toward the city's center.

"Killing him was completely wrong." he said as they huddled together on the train. "He could be completely innocent, working for Bo Huang without knowing anything."

"Don't be naive," she said gruffly. "Managing a secret warehouse from a slum makes him complicit— and they killed my mother."

"We don't yet know enough! Very little, in fact; but you're shooting first before we can piece things together."

She looked away, waving her hand dismissively.

Jonathan grabbed her arm, forcing her to look back at him. "What you did back there disgusts me."

Her eyes narrowed as she stood up. "It was necessary. Now, get up, we're at the Plaza Venezuela. It's our stop."

They emerged onto the plaza, where Jonathan flagged down the first taxi in sight. As they slid into the back seat and the driver took off towards the Gran Meliá Hotel, Natasha asked, "Do you think that the 'man from Europe' that Bo Huang's meeting is Chermayeff?"

"It has to be," Jonathan said.

A few minutes later, they drove into the grounds of the Gran Meliá, a towering hotel on Avenida Casanova. They headed into the bustling lobby, studying the faces of the guests passing by as they made their way towards the hotel bar.

"What does Chermayeff look like?" Jonathan asked.

"I don't know, but we should be able to recognize Bo Huang, right?" Natasha said. Her cell phone buzzed. "Stay here while I take this call outside."

Jonathan took a seat at the circular bar, eyeing the people coming in and out of the hotel. There were close to fifty people in the lobby, some seated in chairs at the center and far corners, others standing around, and several seated at or near the bar. Though a Chinese would be easy to spot, without a better description he had no way to distinguish the Russian scientist from the other foreigners.

Natasha returned hurriedly from outside and leaned into Jonathan. "We have a problem—a big problem—and you're not going to like it."

Jonathan was afraid to ask. "What now?"

"I've been told to stand down."

"Stand down?" he whispered loudly.

"Seems like you Americans are taking over, and they may be looking for a live nuclear device, perhaps on the *Muzhestvo*, perhaps elsewhere in Caracas. Not sure. But I can't do anything else at this point."

Jonathan jumped off his bar stool. "What the hell are you saying?"

"I just spoke with my liaison at the embassy. Hundreds of U.S. military personnel are landing at the airport as we speak, and the local *Brigada Acciones Especiales*—the city's SWAT team—are on their way here right now. We have to leave, or we're going to get caught up in the net."

The thought of the U.S. military landing in Venezuela seemed ludicrous to Jonathan, given Hugo Chávez's venomous attitude toward Washington, *unless*, Jonathan thought, the U.S. government had gone into a war footing.

"I'm warning you; they're about to raid this hotel, so we must leave."

"No. We're not—" Jonathan interrupted himself with a gasp. "Behind you...that's them, coming out of the elevators—those three men, right?"

Natasha turned discreetly. "Yes, I think so. That's probably Chermayeff with the white hair."

"And the third guy?"

"Protection, maybe."

The threesome headed through the marble-floored lobby toward the glass doors, with Bo Huang frowning, his eyes darting about the lobby.

"He's not going willingly," Jonathan added, whispering over Natasha's shoulder.

"You think?"

"Look at 'im. It's like he's being taken to the gallows." Jonathan grabbed her shoulder. "Let's follow them."

"I can't." Natasha peeled off his hand as Jonathan ignored the bar patrons glaring at him as though he were some jerk who'd just offended Natasha with a come-on. "I was told not to do anything more."

"We can't stop. You have to...think of Mariya." Jonathan left the bar and intercepted the men before they reached the doors. He shouted, "Mr. Bo Huang? It's me, Vince, remember?"

All three men stopped and turned. Moving to within a foot of the trio, Jonathan continued in the same boisterous tone, "How are you, my friend? It's me...remember, from the meeting last year in Singapore?" Jonathan reached for Bo Huang's limp hand as the Asian squinted awkwardly, his shoulders drawn in as his brows knitted together in confusion. As Jonathan shook Bo Huang's hand, he realized the Asian was trembling.

"We must go," the white-haired man accompanying Bo Huang said harshly, his accent as Russian as the odor of vodka that accompanied his words.

"But do you have a few minutes to chat?" Jonathan continued, glancing over at the hotel's lone security guard, dressed in a cheap, poorly sized suit, who was slowly turning to face the commotion.

"I said, we have to go," Chermayeff insisted, glancing irately at the third man, whom Jonathan noticed was sporting a bulge under his baggy, long-sleeve shirt at the waistband of his beige slacks. It had to be a weapon.

"Back off," the third man said in American English and shoved his hand into Jonathan's chest. He then turned and pushed Bo Huang toward the doors as the Russian yanked Bo Huang by the arm.

But before they had taken three steps, the hotel security guard stepped in and asked, "What is the trouble?"

Screams suddenly erupted from the back of the lobby. Jonathan whirled. A man brandishing a gun weaved rapidly through the crowded lobby toward them.

"Motherfucker!" The American next to Chermayeff pulled the weapon from under his shirt, knocked Jonathan to the side, and aimed past him.

Pop, pop.

Shots also rang out from behind Jonathan, who quickly crouched down to avoid the crossfire. The hotel guard began shouting, his gun raised in the air.

The American turned and shot him in the face.

Jonathan spun around, still crouching, and spotted Natasha taking cover at the end of the bar as patrons scattered, some scurrying to the back of the lobby, others jumping over the check-in counter, and others racing to hide behind a wall by the elevators.

The assailant who'd fired at them had taken shelter behind a couch. "You're a dead man, Sal," the man shouted. Jonathan couldn't see him, but he too sounded American. "You took our money, but you won't live to long enough to use it, you son-of-a-bitch." The man raised his weapon up over the top of the furniture and fired, three rounds hitting the wall near the entrance.

Chermayeff's man sprang up and advanced toward

the couch, firing several rounds as he walked deliberately ahead. "It's you who's dead, Ron. It's definitely you."

Pop, pop, pop.

Jonathan assumed that the Americans were rivals, but he hadn't heard of their names before.

Foam, wood splinters and fabric went flying as the bullets penetrated the couch. Sal reloaded his pistol and pumped more lead into the furniture until a loud thump echoed between the discharges of his weapon. He leaned over the couch and fired the *coup de grace* before racing back to Chermayeff, who'd huddled by a giant vase with Bo Huang still in his grasp. Sal stepped alongside the Russian, pointed his gun at Bo Huang and shot him point blank.

A second later two shots rang out from the area near the bar, and Sal's shoulder burst with blood. He stayed standing and returned fire toward the bar before darting out the front doors with Chermayeff.

Jonathan crawled along the floor and found Natasha huddled behind the bar, her gun still smoking. It was she who'd shot the American.

"You hit 'im, but he ran out." He reached to help her up, but she pushed his arm away and quickly stood up.

"I'm fine; I don't need your help," she said.

"Come on! We can't let them get away." He ran to the large windows as a few of the braver hotel guests began raising their heads and peering around the lobby.

Jonathan ran out the doors with Natasha close behind and scanned the driveway. "Over there!" he shouted as he spotted the duo jumping into a black Range Rover parked some fifty yards away. The vehicle took off, its tires squealing.

"Come with me," Jonathan said, pulling Natasha by her arm as he darted to a cab idling at the curb.

"What are you—"

"Shut up and get in." He open the driver's door and pulled the man out by his shirt. "*Lo siento, pero es una emergencia.*"

The driver wrestled with Jonathan but lost his balance. Jonathan threw the man down hard against a concrete plant holder. He then leaped into the driver's seat and pushed the passenger door wide open.

"Get in!"

Natasha jumped into the front seat. He grabbed the steering wheel and floored it.

38

"YOU DARE CALL *ME* CRAZY?" NATASHA SAID, GRIPPING the handle above her door with both hands as Jonathan swerved the car around a truck and made a sharp right turn onto Avenida Pichincha.

"Yeah, but I didn't kill anyone."

She pointed ahead. "They're taking the highway!"

"I see them."

The Range Rover sped onto a west-bound ramp some five hundred yards up the road.

"They may be going to the warehouse," she said.

"Why would they?"

"They have no clue that we know where it is."

"Do we *really* know? Mariano may have lied to us."

"Would you lie to a person sticking a pen in your head?"

Jonathan shook his head, recalling the ghastly scene. He sped through a red light, raced up the same ramp and merged into the westbound lanes of Autopista Caracas-La Guaira, the same airport expressway straddling the

El Ávila mountain that they'd taken the night before.

"Watch out," Natasha said, pointing at the opposite lanes, where two red and white Ford Broncos with flashing blue lights raced by, their sirens wailing.

"It's the *Brigada Acciones Especiales*," she added.

Jonathan checked the rearview mirror as the vehicles turned onto Avenida Casanova. "We're fine; they're going to the hotel," he reassured Natasha. "Do you think your Russian is headed for the airport instead of the warehouse?"

Natasha shook her head. "I doubt it. I hear there are U.S. Marines all over the airport."

"Who were the Americans shooting at each other in the lobby?" he asked.

"One is clearly on Chermayeff's payroll. The other, perhaps CIA. Your guess is as good as mine."

"I hope you're not hiding things from me, like your mother did," he said and then bit his tongue as he realized how insensitive it must have sounded to her. He reached over for her hand. "I'm sorry, I didn't mean—"

"You don't have to be hurtful," she said, disengaging her hand from his, "but you don't have to act like we're suddenly a couple, either."

Jonathan struggled to find the right words. "I didn't mean…I do care about you—"

"Look, I appreciate you helping me through this but what happened back at the lake house was, well…it was just sex, you know—simple, convenient, pleasant, uncomplicated sex, nothing more."

Jonathan shook his head. "Sometimes it's nice to give sex meaning."

She rolled her eyes at him. "I don't know why you Americans make such a big deal of it," she grumbled, pulling her cell phone out of her purse. "Now let me make this call and see what I can find out."

"Did you tell anyone the address of the warehouse?"

"No, not yet."

"Why not?"

"I don't trust everyone in Moscow, so it's often useful to withhold important facts."

"I just don't understand you Russians. Why on earth wouldn't it be better for a whole team of people with more than one gun between them to get to the warehouse before we do?"

"Can't you go faster? I don't see them anymore." The rickety taxi Jonathan had commandeered was simply no match for the Range Rover's speed.

Natasha spoke on the phone in Russian for several minutes, while Jonathan continued along the airport highway, passing through the first tunnel, and then the second. Finally, she hung up and turned to him, frowning, her eyes wide open. "There're four bombs, perhaps more."

Jonathan's heart leapt into his throat; causing his foot to slide off the accelerator. "You mean nukes?"

"Yes, four devices, possibly armed and ready, but no one is sure. One is probably on the *Muzhestvo*; two somewhere in Houston, Miami or New Orleans; and one possibly here, near the port."

"You mean the warehouse?" She nodded. "How come you're only finding out about this now?"

"Because Washington found out somehow, and they

alerted us, and then I'm told they gave Chávez an ulti-
matum—let them come in, or they'd turn the country
into a crater. So, I told you, they're here, at the airport,
with soldiers. And the U.S. fleet is offshore and may
already have intercepted the *Muzhestvo*. I didn't know
this before, but now I do."

"Does this mean that you can help me now?"

"Yes, but we can't count on Moscow."

"Good." Jonathan felt relieved that she'd changed
her mind and that at least one threat was about to be neu-
tralized by the U.S. Navy, but if she was right, that left
three weapons—one of them possibly at the warehouse
where they were headed. He glanced at Natasha, who
was staring intently out the window.

"Perhaps we should tell the Americans about the
warehouse," she said, brushing her hair back with her
hands. "Like you said, an armed militia can do a lot
more than we can."

"No, not if there's an armed warhead waiting to
explode," Jonathan said. "If they try to charge in with
helicopters and vehicle convoys, Chermayeff will realize what's happening and detonate the device before
they get anywhere near enough to stop him."

Natasha dug into her purse and checked her Glock.
"I only have six rounds left in here and just one spare
magazine. We can't do much with that."

"But we can penetrate with more stealth. Let's just
go to the warehouse now, scope things out from a safe
vantage point, and once we're certain that there actually
is a device in that warehouse, we can call in the cavalry."

Jonathan sped—as fast as the old cab allowed—

across the highway as it sloped down toward Simon Bolivar Airport and the coastal Maiquetia neighborhood, the deep blue sea coming into view under the patchwork of dark clouds. Several police and army vehicles raced past in the opposite direction with shrieking sirens. Jonathan spotted the airport terminal on the left. A large gray-colored cargo plane appeared to be on final approach to the runway.

"That's a C-17—a U.S. military plane," she said.

"There are two more in front of the far hangars." he slowed momentarily. "See them?"

"And helicopters, too." Natasha again pointed at the cluster of hangars about a half-mile away. Three helicopters near the cargo planes were taking off in sequence. They looked like the same Blackhawk helicopters Jonathan had seen flying over the besieged Wal-Mart back in New Orleans.

"Stay in this lane," Natasha said. "It will become Avenida Soublette."

They headed past the airport exit and merged onto a heavily-trafficked divided road. Just after passing a stadium on the left, Jonathan spotted two police cars moving perpendicular into the congested traffic from the right, with several officers walking along side and signaling vehicles to stop. He accelerated and maneuvered into the cluster of cars and buses that weaved into the last open lane near the median. He hoped to get through what looked like a police roadblock in the making.

"Keep going and stay calm," Natasha said. "And don't look at them."

The lead patrol car moved ahead of the walking patrolmen and turned sideways to block the two right lanes. But cars and buses kept going. Jonathan steered the cab behind the closest bus, his hands perspiring, his heart thumping hard. It was all he could do. He kept his held his breath as they inched along. Time was ticking; Chermayeff and his American thug had likely beaten the traffic snarl and were probably already at the warehouse by now.

The cops continued to signal, but most traffic still poured through. They finally squeezed by. Jonathan floored the accelerator and let out a long exhale.

A few blocks later, Natasha tapped the dashboard. "Turn right here on Calle Nava," she said, removing her firearm from her purse and holding it over her lap. "Look for number 23 but don't stop in front."

Jonathan turned and continued slowly, driving past the warehouses that lined both sides of the street.

"That one's 24," Natasha said, pointing at a modern cement-walled complex on the right. "So it must be the one on your side."

Jonathan drove past the block-long warehouse—a rundown, two-story red brick building. He noted three tall garage doors, all closed, and no windows on the street-facing side.

He turned at the next street and parked at the curb. "Let's take a look."

She eyed him back. "Yes, but if we're outgunned, we leave."

"We may not have time to be choosy."

Natasha got out. "Give me your passport."

"Why?" he said, pulling it out of his back pocket.

She took it from his hand, walked to a sewer grate by the curb and threw it down. "At this point, you're safer without this, especially if the Americans arrest us."

They headed to the south side of the warehouse, where Jonathan slipped through a narrow gangway that separated the structure from the building next to it as Natasha waited alongside the warehouse's wall.

He scanned the four-foot-wide alley, which was littered with fragments of shipping crates, metal lubricant drums, disused machinery and rusted parts that looked like marine engine components. Looking up, he noticed a row of barred windows about five feet above his head.

He scooted an empty drum close to the wall, climbed onto it, crept up to the corner of the window and peeked through the filthy glass. The interior was poorly illuminated, but he was able to see the left quarter-panel of a vehicle. He wiped the grime off the glass with his palm and then used his hand to block the daylight. Sure enough, it was the Range Rover, parked between pallets, boxes and wooden crates piled high.

He gave Natasha a thumbs-up.

"Then follow me," she whispered loudly, holding her Glock out in front as she tiptoed down the alley and moved in front of him.

Jonathan quickly trailed her until they reached an eight-foot high chain link fence topped with razor wire.

The fence circled a small square of asphalt that appeared to be a dumping ground for more engine parts, coils of wire and piping, and other equipment. As he peered through the fence at the warehouse, he spotted two partly-opened swivel doors some ten yards away that connected the fenced-in area to the warehouse.

He motioned to Natasha. She handed him her weapon, kneeled down and dug into her black purse. She pulled out a small tube that looked like a can of mace. She unscrewed the lid and replaced it with a small, tube-like applicator.

"Stand back," she whispered, holding the tube above her head. She tilted it toward the fence and began spraying. The aerosol made contact with the steel wire, which instantly let out a sizzling sound. White smoke began rising from the metal. She carefully continued to apply the spray in a downward motion. Within seconds, the steaming metal wire began snapping loose, and a slit opened wide enough for them to squeeze through.

"Wait a half-minute—it will burn if you touch it now." She then replaced the applicator with the original lid and threw the tube back in her purse.

"Practical," muttered Jonathan.

"Works on locks, chains, handcuffs...you name it."

Jonathan grinned in spite of himself. "I suppose Mariano should be thankful you killed him with a pen and a bullet."

She ignored the feeble joke and held out her hand. "My Glock."

Jonathan hesitated. He didn't want to be unarmed. He reminded himself of the obligation he felt to protect her. "Let me do this."

"Hand it over." She impatiently motioned with her hands. "I was the best pistol shooter in my class of over three hundred agents—and the third best with sniper rifles—so, I don't know why you're being difficult."

He let her have it and then followed her through the opening in the fence, scanning the ground for something else he could use. He picked up a two-foot-long metal pipe. *Better than nothing.*

Natasha aimed her weapon into the darkened doorway and quietly sneaked in. Jonathan followed, careful to make no sound. She momentarily ducked behind a tall stack of pallets, looked in both directions and kept going. He kept pace close behind her as they moved through a narrow space between two rows of stacked wooden crates. When they reached the end, near the far wall, he began hearing male voices.

Natasha ducked closer to the floor and glanced around the corner, both hands gripping her pistol at thigh level. Jonathan assumed a similar position and then stopped moving so as to hear the words more clearly.

One man spoke what sounded like Korean or Japanese, but Jonathan wasn't sure given the poor acoustics. But he then heard another man speak Russian, and it sounded like cursing.

Natasha signaled that she was moving one aisle over. He followed again, turned the corner and kept close behind. They huddled at the base of a 20-foot shipping container surrounded by stacks of other industrial crates and storage boxes, but in between them was a small opening about two inches wide and an inch high that offered the view toward where the voices were coming from. His head butted up against Natasha's as they both tried to peek through the opening.

Jonathan spotted four men standing near a large, olive-green metal chest about twenty yards away. The chest looked a like a coffin, only taller, and lay in an open space between wooden crates on one side and on the other what appeared to be farm equipment wrapped in clear plastic.

Chermayeff spoke in Russian to two Asian men facing him from the other side of the chest. He then peered down into the container, holding himself on the edge with both hands, as the Asian men, wearing green overalls and semi-automatic weapons—an Uzi and a stockless AK-47—strapped over their shoulders, pointed at something inside. One of them seemed to know Russian and appeared to translate for the other. Jonathan had spent enough years in the shipping industry to know the different sounds and intonations between Japanese and Korean—even without speaking the languages. He was sure they were Korean.

Next to them, seated shirtless on the floor, was Sal, the American who Natasha had wounded at the hotel. He held a bloodied bandage over his shoulder, cursing and in pain, and disengaged from the other men's conversation.

Natasha leaned into Jonathan and whispered, "Get ready, because I'm ending this shit right now."

Jonathan dug his fingers into her forearm and shook his head at her, frowning. They needed to sneak out and call for backup. A lawyer with a metal pipe and an armed Russian chick who was low on both ammo and patience was hardly what he'd call a fighting force.

She bent down, which he took as acquiescence. But as he let go of her arm, she slid her purse onto the floor, pulled out her only spare magazine and sped off soft-toed to the other end of the shipping container.

Fuck! Jonathan screamed inwardly. She looked determined. The only chance they had now was a two-pronged assault. He crept to the other end of the container.

Natasha suddenly darted out, turned the corner and began shooting.

Bang, bang, bang.

Jonathan turned the other corner, gripping the pipe tightly even as he knew it was useless against firearms.

Bang, bang, bang, bang...

The shots kept going. She'd taken down both Koreans in an instant. She continued to fire, then ducked, reloaded, and fired again, but Chermayeff had scurried behind another shipping container. Sal had run back, too, but then popped out from his cover and fired two rounds in Natasha's direction before disappearing again.

Natasha let out a cry and lost her footing, collapsing forward just as Jonathan dove to take shelter behind the large metal chest on the floor, ramming his back into it. She fired two more shots over the chest, jumped forward but banged her head on the container as her body came to a loud stop.

"You're bleeding," Jonathan said between his hard breaths.

"*Blyad!*" She turned her thigh inward. A three-inch gash in her jeans appeared above the knee, exposing blood and flesh. "It's only a scrape, I think," she said, her expression neutral as she inspected the wound with her shaky fingers.

Jonathan crawled forward and pried the Uzi from the hand of one of the dead Koreans, but doing so he noticed a dark object on the man's upper arm, partially exposed from under the man's T-shirt. He pulled the man's sleeve to the shoulder and saw what it was: the tattoo. The same snake and anchor design as on the corpse in New Orleans, and the same as on the man Boris had killed on the *Nixos-Dakar* the night they'd stormed it in the Panama Canal.

As Jonathan crawled back, Natasha raised her Glock and fired again until she was out of ammo. She threw it to the floor and reached for the AK-47 lying next to the other dead Korean, grabbing it tightly over her chest as her face cringed in pain. She slid toward Jonathan's side just as rounds began hitting the metal chest that was now their only cover. Jonathan raised his weapon above his head, let off a few rounds blindly, and then brought his weapon back down.

"What now, genius?" Jonathan said, terrified that being held up in the middle of the warehouse was the worst possible position to be in, with multiple vantages from which others could target them.

"I don't think Chermayeff is armed, and if he is, he's worthless. It's the American I'm worried about. He may be hurt, but he's still dangerous."

Jonathan took a deep breath to calm his racing heart and tapped the metal container with the Uzi's barrel. "Is this the device?" he whispered.

Natasha shrugged. "Could be." She then pulled her cell phone from her pants pocket, raised it above the container, snapped a picture and then viewed the image.

"Uh...it's definitely a warhead."

"How bad is the radiation, with us this close to it?"

She cracked a smile. "Less than if it explodes."

Fuck me, Jonathan thought as he glanced both ways, looking for any flash of movement. *If I make it through this, after every goddamned thing I've been through since New Orleans, I'll probably die of radiation poisoning.*

"Are you...are you American?" shouted a man in English with a heavy Russian accent. It was Chermayeff. He sounded about fifteen yards away and out of breath.

"Fuck off!" Jonathan said. "That answer your question?"

"That is 40-kiloton bomb," the Russian said loudly.

"Drop your weapons and come out, or he's going to blow us all up and incinerate a seven-mile radius," Sal added, his voice sounding closer, perhaps right behind the nearest stack of crates that Jonathan could see from the corner of his eye.

"He's bluffing," Jonathan whispered to Natasha. He quickly peeked over the nuke's container but didn't see anything and promptly ducked back down. "He would have blown it up by now, if it were armed."

"Don't know, but if we give up, we're dead for sure," she said, tilting her head back, her AK-47 still in her grip. "There must be a problem with it. That's probably why Chermayeff was arguing with them," she added, using her chin to point at the two corpses by her feet.

"We're gonna die here if we don't move."

"You heard me?" Chermayeff's voice boomed across the warehouse. "Americans must die, you must all pay."

"What's your problem, Yuri?" Jonathan shouted. "Killing innocent people in Caracas makes no sense."

"This bomb did not go to Chicago like I planned, but there are more. You will pay very soon."

"Pay for what?"

"You kill my son!" Chermayeff still sounded out of breath. "He was beautiful man and your government kill him. They murder everybody on *Kursk*."

Jonathan wasn't sure if he meant the submarine *Kursk* that had gone down some years ago.

"And you killed my mother, *mudak!*" Natasha broke her silence and lunged up, firing in full-auto in Chermayeff's direction. Jonathan leaped up behind her and fired in the direction of Sal's voice. Bullets ricocheted off of the warehouse's brick walls and metal surfaces, whistling by Jonathan's head as smoke rose from their assault rifles' barrels.

"Where are the other bombs?" Jonathan shouted as he and Natasha dodged back to their cover.

"Just follow the mushroom clouds, motherfucker," Sal said loudly.

"Cowards without a cause. That's what you are."

Suddenly, the rumbling of approaching vehicles echoed through the warehouse walls, loud clanking sounds accompanying the growling of engines. As Jonathan adjusted to the noise, he also heard the thump-thump-thump of a helicopter circling above.

"Keep your head down," Jonathan whispered, staring at the closest garage door about twenty feet behind

Natasha. He sensed what was coming. He tossed his Uzi across the floor. "Throw yours, too."

She clutched the AK-47 to her chest. "Have you lost your mind?"

"Throw it now."

"Why?"

"Do it." He kicked her good leg. "Or they're gonna kill you." He leaned forward, grabbed the AK-47 from her hand and threw it far.

Boom!

The garage door and part of the wall burst inward as a military-type truck rammed through it. Jonathan dove on Natasha and covered her head with his body as smoke and debris poured through the warehouse. An explosion, followed by another, ripped through the building, sending concrete and metal shrapnel flying past his face. The cavalry had arrived, and they weren't friendly.

"Nobody move!" a man barked.

Jonathan saw a dozen dark-clothed armed men racing towards him through the cloud of pungent smoke.

"We're Americans!" Jonathan shouted, turning flush against the floor, when suddenly the full weight of a person landed on top of him. Then another person crushed his legs. "For Christ's sake, we're Ameri—"

39

"ARE YOU JONATHAN BROOKS?"

The man's words filtered through Jonathan's ringing ears like a triple-echo. As he eased back into consciousness, an ambient light began to glow behind his closed lids. He opened his eyes but the bright lights on the ceiling made him squint at first. Glancing down at his feet, he realized that he was lying on a gurney, wearing the same clothes in which he'd started the day. He wiggled his fingers and toes, then flexed his shoulders and knees. Apparently, he was uninjured.

"Well?"

Jonathan looked up at the African American man standing a few feet away from him, wearing a large gold watch and matching cuff-links, a dress shirt and dark pants.

The man gazed at him, then dropped his leather portfolio onto a chair. "Are you Jon—"

"Yes," Jonathan replied, his voice raspy. He felt as if he'd swallowed sandpaper. "Where am I?"

"You're in a hangar, and there's a plane outside about to take you home—*if* you answer some questions to my satisfaction."

Jonathan heard the sound of a helicopter. "How do you know my name?"

"Looks like you have Russian friends willing to put in a good word for you."

Jonathan sighed. "Is she okay?"

"Who?"

"Natasha."

The man grinned. "She's on a plane to Moscow."

God knows what they'll do to her, Jonathan thought, suddenly feeling sad that he hadn't spoken to her before she left. "How long have I been—?"

"About four hours. Your ears are probably still ringing from the stun grenades, but you made it out alive. You should consider yourself lucky."

Jonathan sat up. "Who are you?"

"I'm George," he said casually, approaching Jonathan. "George Porter. CIA. Mind if I ask my questions now?"

"But the...the warhead? What did—?"

"Disarmed, and Chermayeff's dead."

"But there're more, in New Orleans, Houston, Miami...I think that's what he said."

"All taken care of." Porter spoke so calmly that Jonathan thought he might be talking about a stage performance.

"And the North Koreans, are there more of them?"

George tilted his head, chewing his gums. "How do you know about them?"

"By their tattoos. They're North Korean, aren't they? What were they doing for Chermayeff?"

His friendly tone vanished. "I'll ask the questions."

Jonathan's grogginess dissipated. He swung his legs off the side of the gurney and straightened his back.

Porter leaned in. "Why are you working with the Russians?"

"I'm not. I was investigating a dead body in New Orleans, and—after more grief than you can imagine—I ended up here in Caracas. We then tracked down the Russian scientist and his Chinese accomplice, along with two Americans—I'm guessing one of them was working for your folks. I've gone through a lot of shit, and now I'd appreciate a few answers myself."

"Mr. Brooks," Porter said, crossing his arms. "I'm not in the business of giving information."

"I can see why." Jonathan shook his head. "I'm probably right to think there's been a giant screw-up on your end—on a scale rivaling 9/11."

"We weren't entirely in the dark. It was a motley crew, but they're done for—all of them."

"Is the North Korean government involved?"

Porter raised his eyebrows. "No," he said. "The Koreans in the warehouse were defectors."

"My ass. They were divers—special forces of some kind—and they weren't defecting. They were working for the people transporting the warheads."

"Looks like you know more than what's best for you," Porter warned. "Tell me what you know, including names of everyone you encountered or spoke with in connection with this mess."

"And you'll let me go?"

"Yes, if you're truthful."

"And if I say no?"

"Let us do our business. I want to know what you know, and then we'll put this behind us. State secrets should stay secrets, don't you agree?

Jonathan shrugged. "That depends on whose best interests are at stake."

Porter nodded and smiled. "I'd say that right now, it's your best interests at stake. There are about ten FBI special agents outside this door who would like to chat with you about being an accessory to a murder; using a forged diplomatic passport to enter this country; assaulting a ship and killing and injuring police officers in Panama; collaborating with foreign agents on U.S. soil; unlawful possession of automatic weapons; and God knows what other serious violations—and they're not here to make deals."

Jonathan paused, stretched his back and crossed his arms. He wanted to go home more than anything. "It started in New Orleans. I'd gone to the morgue to identify a body, but it wasn't just any body." For almost an hour, he went on to explain everything that had happened in as much detail as he could recall—his arrival in Panama, the raid on the ship, the escape in Natasha's plane, and how they'd tracked Bo Huang and made it to Caracas, and finally the warehouse."

Porter listened and took notes. After hearing it all, he closed his notepad and coolly eyed Jonathan. "Anything else?"

"No. Can I leave now?"

Porter tilted his head. "New Orleans, huh?"

"Yes."

"I'd wait it out, if I were you."

"No, I need to get back. No matter what's waiting for me there, it can't be any worse than what I've gone through the past few days."

"My Agency and the FBI may have follow-up questions for you in the coming weeks, but for now I'll tell them to hold off until you're back home and settled in. I got close friends there, in Metairie, and I know they're struggling. So, I understand and wish you luck."

"Thank you."

"Well, all right, then." Porter pulled out a document from his portfolio and tossed it on the gurney. "Sign this and I'll make sure you're on a flight home within the hour."

Porter watched as Jonathan read through the three-page non-disclosure agreement.

"Disclose anything about what you've just told me and you can bet your law license that federal prosecutors will have your ass in jail before you can plead the Fifth."

Jonathan glared at Porter as he weighed the pros and cons of penning the document, its provisions filled with threats of prosecution if an iota of information were ever shared with anyone. The pros? He'd get to go home. The cons? Porter would feed him to the FBI team waiting behind the door. But even if he agreed, if any secrets came to light, he might have to prove that the leak didn't come from him. And that might be dangerous. But if he wanted to get out of this nightmare, he didn't have a choice. He uncrossed his arms, stepped off the gurney, and nodded at Porter. "You got a pen?"

*   *   *

"My God, I was so worried about you," Linda said the second Jonathan called out her name into the phone.

She sounded sober and this gave him hope.

"I'm sorry I didn't call you earlier," he said, holding the receiver of the pay phone so tightly he thought he might break it. "I can't begin to tell you what's happened, to me, to others, to New Orleans. It's been terrible...a nightmare...a horrific nightmare like never before."

"I've seen the news; I understand."

"No, there's so much more. I can't tell you on the phone. In fact, I only have another minute to talk."

"I'm coming to New Orleans."

Jonathan's heart skipped a beat and he almost dropped the phone. "When?"

"In two or three days. McSweeny's gave me a short term freelance gig for post-hurricane coverage on Katrina."

"Are you up for it?"

"I think so," she said. "I'm also waiting on a possible foreign assignment from AP. Things are moving."

"That's fantastic," Jonathan said. "You sound better."

"I've stopped drinking," she said. "And I think that when all the news broke about the hurricane and I couldn't get ahold of you, it knocked some sense into me. I realized how much I'd put you through, and I was terrified that I wouldn't have a chance to make it right."

"Linda," Jonathan said, "none of that was your fault. If I hadn't been dragged into the mess that happened ten years ago, we wouldn't have had to go through the things that we did. Please don't blame yourself. If it was anyone's fault, it was mine."

"No, you tried to help but I've been such a fool. I was so worried about you that I was tempted to pick up the bottle again—but I didn't. But I can't promise anything. I think I'm ready to face New Orleans again and maybe I can see you while I'm there."

"I want to see you, too, but I can't promise anything either. Things are going to be rough for me for a while. I have to earn some money fast, and I can't do that in New Orleans right now, so I'm likely heading to Europe for a few weeks for one of my clients, Cramer—remember him?"

"I do."

"I'm hoping his project is still on—I'll confirm as soon as I'm back in New Orleans. There's not much I can do for my other clients for the foreseeable future. But I want to talk, very seriously, about everything. I care about you."

"Me too," Linda said. "But no matter what happens with us, I need to get my life back in order. I think that returning to New Orleans—after running away—will help me with that. And it will help me to see you, too, but only when I feel ready."

"I understand," Jonathan said as a man in a flight suit approached, motioning at him to hurry. "Linda, I have to go. I'll call you when I'm back in New Orleans and get a working cell phone—might be a day or two from now, but I'll be in touch soon." He hung up.

A minute later, the Air Force officer ushered Jonathan into a C-17 cargo plane where he was led to a bucket seat in the main cargo hold.

The aircraft took off a short time later. He recycled Linda's words during the two-hour flight to Homestead AFB near Miami. There, he had a twenty minute lay-over, just enough time to call Cramer to let him know he'd be arriving in New Orleans. He boarded a Florida Air National Guard C-130 loaded with medicines, blankets, generators and sleeping bags to support rescue efforts in New Orleans.

40

New Orleans, Louisiana

As the National Guard plane's props wound down, Jonathan sprinted across the tarmac at New Orleans' Louis Armstrong Airport, where hundreds of military and rescue personnel rushed about, evacuating streams of wounded, disabled and elderly people from helicopters and onto waiting aircraft. More men in uniforms unloaded cargo from dozens of civilian and military aircraft as others sorted through supplies and equipment strewn across the apron. Jonathan inhaled the scent of jet fumes and hoped that help—real help—for this beleaguered city had finally arrived.

As he reached the terminal, he heard someone shout his name and turned to see Cramer leaning against the side of an enormous, gray-colored armored vehicle with a gun turret on top and a chassis that sat three feet off the ground thanks to huge tires.

"You okay?" Cramer said, smiling.

Jonathan waved back, briskly walking toward his client. "Thank—" he said, choking up. Not only was he finally back on his home turf, it was the first time in a week that he'd felt any sense of comfort.

He smiled and gave Cramer a hug. "Thank you, thank you, thank you."

"When lawyers get in trouble," Cramer said, chuckling, "they may need a client to help."

Jonathan laughed. "It's usually the other way round, right?"

"So, what do you think?" Cramer said, slapping the side of the armored vehicle. "It's on loan from the Dallas Police Department."

Jonathan scanned the vehicle and smiled, thinking about how different things would have been if this tactical vehicle had been at Wal-Mart when he and Boudreaux needed to clear looters.

"That reminds me," Jonathan said, "I need to get a cell phone and call Sergeant Boudreaux, my NOPD buddy—let him know I've made it back and tell him where to find his grandmother's truck that I borrowed to leave town."

"There's no cell service except in Metairie and Kenner," Cramer said, "but I'll have the SWAT boys here radio the message."

"How did you get this?" Jonathan asked.

"I've got connections; you know that," Cramer said. "And I've got good news for ya, too."

"Tell me. I could use some."

"Your neighborhood didn't get much flooding, so your house should be fine."

"That's good to hear. I'd pretty much figured it would be gone. To be honest, I'm more worried about the office. How's the Central Business District?"

"Well, Julia Street didn't fare so well. Hardly any flooding but lots of looting. We're headed downtown now, so hop in and we'll get you home."

"Could you drop me off at the office?" Jonathan said. I need to check on client files, the safe and the computers. I can find my way home from there."

"No such thing as a trolley, bus or taxi in this city, bud," Cramer said.

"That's okay," Jonathan said. "I feel like I could use the walk."

Jonathan followed Cramer through the back door of the vehicle, joining four SWAT team members in the cramped space as the beast's engine roared to life, shaking everyone as it lumbered forward.

"Drop him off near Julia Street," Cramer shouted to the driver over the loud gnashing of the clutch that accompanied the brusque changing of gears. "And radio Sergeant Boudreaux at police headquarters; tell him Brooks is back in town."

One of the SWAT officers reached up to the armor-plated ceiling and swung open the large hatch. "Enjoy the view," he said.

Jonathan and Cramer stood up and gazed out, the balmy wind hitting their faces as they sped down I-10, the vehicle's tires letting out a deep whining sound. Ten minutes later, Jonathan spotted the flooded streets. His heart sank, and images of his frantic escape from the morgue with Garceau and Latisha flashed through his mind.

As they neared Greenwood Cemetery, the vehicle made an abrupt turn off the Interstate, crossed over a grassy stretch with intermittent standing water, drove over a knocked-down fence and turned onto Canal Street, where the floodwaters were about a foot high—and no problem for the armored vehicle.

Jonathan stared in dismay down the side streets as they sloshed along Canal. As they approached downtown, the Superdome came into sight, and drawing nearer, he discovered that the level of destruction in the neighborhood was even more apparent than when he'd tread through the floodwaters on foot just days ago.

Abandoned cars were haphazardly parked everywhere. Litter and debris were piled high where waters had receded. Buildings had lost their roofs and walls. People had lost their lives—perhaps thousands. Jonathan felt his sadness rise.

"We're almost there," Cramer said.

Jonathan turned and caught his breath. He'd expected to encounter eeriness and desolation on Julia Street but not what lay before him. From his high vantage point atop the vehicle, the breadth of the destruction was astounding. Every storefront in sight was smashed, with glass and debris strewn across the pavement and sidewalks.

There was no flooding here, not even much wind damage, he guessed. Instead, the businesses were ruined by vandalism and looting. The few cars still parked along the street were battered beyond repair or simply burned, their charred shells echoing a reminder to Jonathan that bad people will do bad things no matter what kind of tragedy befalls a community.

Street lamps were down. Postal boxes and newspaper dispensers were scattered across intersections. The only sign of order was a stack of fallen traffic lights that appeared to have been piled neatly at the steps of a pizza restaurant.

Cramer called out for the driver to stop. The vehicle rumbled to a halt in front of Jonathan's office building.

"You sure you don't need a ride home?" Cramer asked. "I can swing by later and pick you up."

Jonathan ducked to exit the vehicle. "I'll be fine."

"Take these." Cramer handed him a set of keys. "I own a duplex in Kenner. It's small and unfurnished, but it's dry and has a generator in the back. If your generator at home isn't working and you need a place to stay, you're welcome to it. Just go to the nearest police station and have them drive you out there—the address is on the keychain. Or use a phone at the station to call me. I'll find a way to pick you up."

Jonathan's eyes filled up. "I don't know what to say."

"It's okay. I want you in good enough shape to get some work done for me in Ukraine next week."

"I really appreciate it," Jonathan said, shaking Cramer's hand. "I really do."

Jonathan approached his office, eyeing the shattered remains of the glass door that lay on the sidewalk about five feet from the frame, close to the charred skeleton of a pickup truck.

He took a deep breath and walked in.

The Vietnamese nail salon was hardly recognizable— tables, massage chairs, the receptionist's desk, even the HVAC vents destroyed and tossed about as though the hurricane had actually torn through the place.

He headed up the stairs to his law offices. The front door had been bashed down, dislodged from the frame. The glass with the names of the three lawyers was shattered into unrecognizable pieces, bringing Jonathan a strange moment of near-joy—for the first time, he was able to enter his firm without having to read his co-tenants' names.

As he walked in, a mold stench filled Jonathan's lungs. The soaked, cheap carpeting released a squishy sound as he stepped toward Amber's cubicle, which had been ransacked, with papers and supplies strewn everywhere. A huge hole in the ceiling gave him a direct view of the sky through the roof. Amber was right, he realized—the once-small leak had opened up like a showerhead as a result of the storm.

But as much as the storm damage chilled him, it was the looting that shook him the most—the sheer disregard of personal property. And at a law firm, of all places.

Jonathan glanced left. The door to his office was split in half, the wood slats protruding upwards, having been kicked open, he guessed. His desktop computer was gone, the monitor too.

Papers and file folders were scattered across the damp hardwood floor, along with glass from the windows—only one window pane had survived and even it was cracked at the top.

The TV and VCR he'd used to view video depositions were gone, and the cart that held them was knocked over onto its side, in the corner of the room. It was an old television, he reminded himself. How could anyone see any value in it, or the VCR that only worked every other time Amber smacked the crap out of it? He leaned into the damaged window frame, gazing emptily at the debris littering Julia Street.

Why?

He shook is head. As he turned back to his desk, he noticed something shiny sticking out from under some loose pages of transcripts near his feet. He reached down, cleared the papers aside, and then his heart skipped a beat.

It was the box of Russian chocolates, the one Mariya had given him—the gift that had launched an eleven-day storm within a storm.

Goosebumps crawled up his spine.

He kneeled down, sat on the floor and rested his back to the wall just below the windows, clutching the box with both hands. He closed his eyes, holding the gift to his chest and feeling a strange warmth flood into his veins.

Mariya's voice rang in his head as he thought of her stubbornness, and her unique, illogical blend of spitefulness, bossiness and occasional praise that only a Russian could manage to blend and that had so often left him beleaguered and confused. Her pensive face flashed by, her dark eyes deconstructing him.

Jonathan looked at his battered desk and took a long breath as he stared at the drawer where he'd found the money she'd left him so long ago. *Here I am again,* he thought. *Once again, I'm broke and my legal practice has been destroyed.*

He held out the box of chocolates, lifted the cover, and picked out one of the sweets, unwrapping the gold-colored foil. Cyanide? he mused, smiling for a minute before his thoughts quickly flashed to guilt that he hadn't been able to save her. He thought of the pain that now burdened Natasha, having lost her mother. *She and I both have to start over,* he realized, *and it's not going to be easy for either of us.*

His thoughts moved back to the storm that had passed with such destruction to all that was familiar to him—and the pain that surrounded him—in his neighborhood, in the city, in Louisiana, everywhere along the coast. He remembered the random bursts of gunfire shattering the blackout night as he hunkered down under siege at the ransacked Wal-Mart. He recalled the torment he'd gone through from the time he'd jumped into that boat with Mariya and Boris in their insane raid in the canal. He recalled Mariya's crimson-stained blouse—and her moans—and her body in a fetal position in the backseat of the SUV. More thoughts crashed through his mind in waves—the Panamanian police firing at him, the crash landing in the lake, the shots in the lobby of the hotel in Caracas, the countless near-death events.

He sighed, tossing the candy in his mouth, the bitter-sweet cocoa tingling his taste buds as it gently melted in his dry mouth. He swallowed it and reached for another.

But as he pulled it from the box, he noticed some-thing odd through the clear plastic tray that held the chocolates in place. There was a white paper tucked underneath the chocolates he'd just eaten. Ink appeared to bleed through it from the other side.

Jonathan quickly tilted the box until all the remain-ing candy and the transparent holder fell out onto the floor.

Another note?

It was folded once, like the first note he'd found in the box days before. His hand trembled lightly as he opened it, his heart racing.

The penmanship was unmistakably Mariya's—the words scribed with such exquisiteness, beautified by their precision—an art form of its own.

But it wasn't a letter. The words were broken into a structure that reminded him of...*a poem? She wrote me a poem?*

His hands continued to shake as he remembered her asking if he'd read everything in the box, and becoming upset with his answer and then sad. It hadn't made sense then, but it did now. His eyes began to tear.

Mariya.

Jonathan turned, leaning his head against the window ledge as he held the note up into the outside light.

He began to whisper her words. "The answers come my way like splashes of boiling water from fretful questions that only simmer the wounds..."

The Jonathan Brooks Series

TRANQUILITY DENIED

THE SERPENT'S GAME

THE PYONGYANG OPTION

LETTER FROM ISTANBUL

DIE BY NOON

Note to book clubs, bookstores and libraries:

A.C. Frieden gives readings across the country and overseas, including fascinating presentations about his globetrotting research that goes into writing his books. If your book club, bookstore or library would like to feature A.C. Frieden, please contact us. We would be delighted to co-sponsor such an event.

Please contact us at:
media@avendiapublishing.com

Printed and bound by PG in the USA

USA2019PGIL